NEW WORLD'S GEAR

Seb D Law

Matador
9 Priory Business Park,
Wistow Road, Kibworth Beauchamp,
Leicestershire. LE8 0RX
Tel: 0116 279 2299
Email: books@troubador.co.uk
Web: www.troubador.co.uk/matador
Twitter: @matadorbooks

ISBN 978 1838594 794

British Library Cataloguing in Publication Data.
A catalogue record for this book is available from the British Library.

Printed and bound in Great Britain by 4edge Limited
Typeset in 11pt Minion Pro by Troubador Publishing Ltd, Leicester, UK

This book is dedicated to the following people:

Viet Trinh
Mattias Evans
Ilyas Taoussi
Daniel Stefanofski
Oscar Niblett
Sanjay Sankaranarayanan
Benjamin Davey
Alex Wain
Bryce Garcia
Joe Wills
Sowmien Ratnasingam
Antony Lishak
Numair Tejani
Kazuki Usuki
Claudius Grabner
Fab Kozlowski
George, Erin and Vicky
Mum, Dad and Dom
And everyone reading this.

Enjoy it!

INTRODUCTION

The war was over.

After the twelve years that almost saw the fall of the planetary system known as Atlas, the war was over. Aeterno could not believe it. Never since he had entered a never-ending life as a god had he seen a war of such large-scale catastrophe. And for it to end now, so abruptly, from such an unexpected turn of events...

His mind drifted back to before the Stygir War – no, to even before that, to when the metal known as divinite had yet to be discovered and only mortals existed. Back then, on the planets Drakon and Primium, society had fallen into anarchy. Psychopaths and criminals terrorised civilisation faster than the few righteous warriors could deal with them, and insidious cults with malign motives spread like diseases. At the time, he was one of those warriors – and had been for most of his life – until the day he noticed an odd, glistening line next to the sun, like a strand of gold. It was on that day, having activated his air-scale, he proceeded to fly to investigate.

It was a foolish move, especially at a time when the two planets were in crisis. Foolish, until he touched the strand and discovered what it was: divinite. The metal from liskous myth that made whoever touched it an immortal deity.

Instinctively, he knew what to do. Gathering his warband and all the most righteous souls in Atlas, he formed a pantheon to restore order to the system. The effect was immediate. Warriors who could not be harmed quickly put an end to the injustice gripping Primium and Drakon. The cults were vanquished and the peoples of each planet unified, with a ruling body formed for each race. As for the shard of divinite, it was transformed into the citadel known to later generations as the Heavenspire, which became the symbol that all Atlas' four races rallied under.

The ever-swelling ranks of deities made sure peace was absolute. They thought themselves invincible. And they were, until twelve years ago when the stygir first appeared.

The stygir: those enigmatic beings who came from beyond Atlas. For reasons unknown, they attacked the system and, as they did, two terrifying truths about immortality were revealed. Just as a mortal could kill another mortal, so could the stygir cut down the deities. All those whose roles had no affinity to battle perished instantly. The second truth related to how others died in a different way. It was discovered during the events in the war that the immortal forms of the deities were sustained by mortal faith. Those with the most fervent followers had the most power, but those whom every mortal lost hope in crumbled away like eroding rock. Nothing made Aeterno shudder so much as that sight.

He had used his full power, as much as he could, until any more use would endanger the system; although he heavily crippled the advance of the stygir, it only slowed their daunting assault. He still could not believe that man had defeated them so easily with his invention.

"Aeterno!" called Galvok – who was the god of protection and a dwarf clad in thick plate armour – from a nearby asteroid. "Can you believe what those damn men are doing?"

The planet of Primium was home to the species of men, elves and dwarves. Whilst elves were dedicated to learning the art of magic and dwarves to perfecting runecraft, men were constantly finding new lifestyles that infuriated Galvok in rising order. With a grunt of anger, the dwarf god slammed his axe into the asteroid.

"What have they done?" asked Aeterno calmly. "Is it another combination of magic, runecraft and slate-scales? Actually, wait… first tell me how in Heavenspire the stygir have been forced into retreat by a single, mortal man?"

"He's not mortal anymore," corrected Galvok. "He's now the god of his invention: that metal junk the men call 'technology.'" He then pointed to a large device that orbited Primium, like a second moon. With the shape of a bevelled cuboid and the shining-silver colour of the finest dwarven armour, it was like nothing Aeterno had seen before. It was hollow, like a cavern, and the cavity pulsed with a bright glow.

"He calls that Industria," Galvok continued. "It's what defeated the stygir in the end, and the only good thing to come out of this technological mess."

"I have a hypothesis on how it works," Aeterno said. "Does it somehow generate energy in the form of heat, and fire it out at the enemy, like a cannon but more advanced?"

"Sorry, I speak Atlasian," Galvok remarked sarcastically. "It blasts stuff on a big scale. You can try asking the guy who made it, but he's more tight-lipped than a cavern clam when it comes to his secrets."

"The Void is on the move!" a disembodied voice echoed everywhere. "I repeat, the Void is on the move!" The voice came from the odd, handheld devices the human army had.

But now is not the time to wonder about that, Aeterno thought, flying towards the edge of the system as fast as he could, with Galvok following him using a rune of flight. *If Industria doesn't succeed, we're in grave danger.*

Where the stygir first began their attack, they left behind a small patch of unknown matter, which was darker than regular space. As they took over more and more of Atlas, destroying everything in their path, that patch grew and spread to encompass their territory; it had become known as the Void. It was where the stygir launched their attacks from, as well as where they spawned their various minions. The Void surrounded Atlas currently, like a ring of death, and any tightening of this ring would be disastrous. Sure enough, there it was – a tendril of obscurity stretching out like a ravenous tongue, with the stygir's minions in front of it.

Aeterno's vision was blinded suddenly by a bright beam of light erasing everything from view. When his vision returned, the attackers were nowhere to be seen. "They've used a diversion of some kind!" he exclaimed, "Galvok, go—"

"No. They've been completely destroyed," Galvok corrected him. "If the range of that weapon were any larger, the Void would be gone."

"But we aren't harmed..." Aeterno mused, stroking his chin thoughtfully. "Interesting... How do you think it works?"

"Who cares?" replied Galvok. "It works, but what doesn't work for me are those oversized imbeciles covering the planet's surface with metal junk! Just look at Primium; look at it from a distance!"

Aeterno's gaze met a world more silver than green or blue.

"How the hell can anyone live there?" queried Galvok.

"Nothing works!" two voices heavy with vexation spat in tandem. Eldrit, the god of magic, and Eitri, the god of runecraft, approached Aeterno and Galvok, with disgust scrawled across their faces.

"Well?" asked Galvok. "How many more seconds until the two of you fight? Who started the argument this time?"

"HUMANS!" yelled Eitri. "That technology stuff... whatever it is, as soon as they plated Primium with it, magic and runecraft would no longer work on it. No elf or dwarf can use either!"

"How can my people live on a world where they can't use my wondrous art?" cried Eldrit. "It's unspeakable!"

"We will come to a conclusion soon," Aeterno assured the distraught gods. This topic was becoming a breeding ground for conflict and he wanted to sterilise it as quickly as possible. "For the time being, have the elves and dwarves migrate to new planets. That's all I can say for now." Aeterno turned and began to fly away.

"Where are you going?" questioned Galvok.

"I'm going to the Heavenspire to think," replied Aeterno. "Atlas is in a fragile state, and if we are to keep our duty to protect the system, we need to adapt to this new world quickly. We need new deities, maybe ones of this era… but how are we to find out who is worthy?"

ONE

An exodus was in progress.

Ever since the incumbency of the technology god Mekanyon, the planet Primium was being gradually transformed into a world of steel, wires and gears. It would take Bob fathomless years to get used to all those new machines, and even more time to find living in a house – and not in a shelter where rations and fear of the stygir ruled his world – normal. Outside, he could see thousands of ships leaving for various destinations. After the orbital weapon known as Industria had decimated the enemy, technology was added to Atlas's accumulation of discoveries. Humanity had insisted on making Primium an industrialised world, much to the disdain of the elves and dwarves. Their two sacred arts – magic and runecraft – had been weakened to the point of non-existence on the planet they had once ruled supreme. The racket coming from the emigrants was so loud that, even with the soundproof technology wrapped around Bob's new settlement, the clamour of their conversations could clearly be heard.

"I understand that that new god's turret saved us, but those stupid machines that took away our magic aren't beneficial to our survival," grumbled an elf. "Who needs a metal contraption for heating when you can have enchanted flames instead? At least, on Arcanast, our skills will be as they were; no, better, thanks to the magic-empowering nebula around it."

"As for my people, we're leaving for the metal-rich planet of Ferraheim," said his companion, a dwarf. "It was thought to be uninhabitable until Hydrax gave it a sustainable water supply. This mechanical folly will stay on my grudge list forever!"

Their races were scattered around them in their entirety, along with various other species Bob had never seen before, except in the few colouring books his shelter had possessed. One of them, a dog if he recalled properly, bounded away from the humans guiding it, rushing towards his house's direction. Curiosity got the better of him, and he opened his door to have a closer look at it. Its fur felt soft and warm, and it was likely in the same state as Bob: going into a new world it had never experienced before and unsure how to feel.

"Boy!" came the voice of one of the handlers. "Drop the mutt and go back to your house, unless you want to go with it to Gaia."

"Why is the dog going to our moon? I thought you couldn't survive there?" Bob immediately wished he hadn't said that, as it made him feel naïve and childish, as if the twelve years he had spent in the shelter had never happened.

"Haven't you heard? The non-sapient species aren't needed in this world of tech. Aeterno and that lot have melted the moon's carbon dioxide ice caps and given it an atmosphere. Now it's full of nature and all the conditions for these guys to live."

Bob nodded absent-mindedly.

"I feel sorry for Sequia, though," rambled on the handler. "Deities get weaker as their believers disappear, and now the nature goddess has lost an entire race. Only the elves and the liskous worship her, and I doubt these beasts here give a toss."

At that moment, there were some angry outbursts from the elves and dwarves, many of whom were now trying to smash the nearby hologram adverts and other tech-related gizmos.

"If your magic and rune items can't make you leave this planet, use the ships we've provided you with," said one of the humans, trying to get their peer species to calm down.

Hurtling through the air, a hammer hit the man who had spoken to Bob in the chest. Spitting blood, he collapsed to the floor.

"By Heavenspire, I reject your ruddy offer!" spat a dwarf. "Give us back our runes!"

Others cheered him on and reached for their own weapons. The humans each drew an energy blaster from their belt.

"Hide behind your damn toys, why don't you?" taunted an elf, who then threw a spear.

A figure dashed into the fray, and the spear hit him directly in the chest. However, there was no spurt of blood and not a single sign of maiming. Like a glass bottle thrown at the ground, the spear shattered.

"Guys! What is this?" the figure addressed the crowd of emigrants and the humans. He picked up the man who had taken a hammer to the chest and ran his palm over the wound.

With a jerking start, the man sprung to his feet.

"You got lucky there," the figure said with a chuckle. He was diminutive in stature, yet not as much as a dwarf, and a golden goatee sprouted from his chin. Around his neck was a gaudy chain with a symbol Bob didn't recognise: a hollow hexagon with two stylised arrows inside it. His gilded coat studded with all manner of jewels flapped behind him and everyone kneeled. "Let's be civil!" he exclaimed. "We're all Heavenspirian citizens, aren't we?"

Surprisingly, nobody retorted.

The figure went on, "Think of all those millennia our species have lived together! I'm sure the thing with technology stopping magic and runecraft was an error nobody wanted, and humanity will work to fix that, right?"

The humans nodded in agreement.

"Remember," declared the figure, "our true enemy are the stygir. Nobody else. Let this never happen again. For those who wish to leave, I'm sorry to say you have to use the spaceships."

Grumbling and vowing to destroy the cursed crafts after they landed on new planets, the elves and dwarves headed to the hangar situated in the middle of the street.

Amazed at what had just happened, Bob stared at the figure, with wide eyes and mouth agape.

"Are you OK?" the figure asked, noticing Bob.

Bob nodded. "W-who are you?" he asked. "How could you survive that pointy stick? I'm Bob."

"Nice to meet you, Bob." The figure chuckled. "I'm Aurik. I'm a god and, along with others, I protect the system."

"I think you're on my family's shrine," Bob mumbled.

Aurik let out another chuckle.

"Well, thank your family for the support. They're lucky to be praying to the right god!" Aurik looked at his gold and crystal watch. "I've got some deity stuff to attend to. I can't say it won't be boring; it's like school on steroids with Aeterno. The protectors of the system do need to deal with great threats… Bye, Bob!" The god dashed away to a spaceship of his own.

After waving goodbye, Bob returned to his house and prayed to the deities for the tension between the different species to stop. Aeterno, the first god, sat in the centre of Bob's household shrine, whilst three other liskous gods – Lapideis of the earth, Nimbus of the sky and Hydrax of the sea – formed a circle around him. His family didn't have much space on their shrine, so only the human deities that had survived the Stygir War accompanied the original four on their piece of holy rock. In the corner, there was a statue of Aurik, who had a wide grin plastered across his face and rained money down on the poor; the writing underneath his feet labelled him as the half-human, half-dwarf god of money, luck and success. Opposite him, the goddess of the future, Kosma, held up a telescope with one hand and grasped a crystal ball in the other. Half of the shrine was empty, ready for a statue of Mekanyon to be glued on top of it.

Mekanyon. Bob had not yet seen the god, but had just heard his name and his great deeds. What was the true nature of this ultimate saviour, who indirectly gave Bob his new home and directly defeated an army not even the greatest could vanquish?

If he had saved the world once, could he save it again?

TWO

One year later

Technology was improving the world, making it into a utopia.

As Bob's alarm-bot injected him with waking fluid, he sprang up, ready to start the day. The nourisher in the corner of his bed activated by default as he awoke, producing his breakfast instantaneously. There was no machine to carry him around, though, or he would surely become obese like the caricatures in the elf and dwarf propaganda posters. He walked over to the food-making machine, and pulled out his toast and beans. Whilst a table-bot began rising from the floor, he started thinking of the time when he wished that magic, tech and metalworking could exist side by side. Laughing inside at the thought, he was mystified as to how anyone could survive without technology. This reminded him that a new piece of technology was being set up in the basement of every household in Primium, and his mum and dad were probably playing around with it right now. Dumping his breakfast in the bin, which converted it to energy, he rushed downstairs and into the basement.

"Bob, why didn't you finish your breakfast?" asked his mum as soon as she saw him in the basement. "It took Mekanyon ages to make that nourisher, you know!"

"How did you find out?" replied Bob, confused.

"This new machine told us so," said his dad, pointing towards a massive hologram with the words "BREAKFAST UNFINISHED" emblazoned in red, and a large picture of Bob underneath it. "It's called a holoceiver," he continued, swiping away the writing with a flick of his wrist. "It allows us to know exactly what's happening inside our house and allows us to message other households we are friendly with. Naturally, the Heavenspire is on that list by default."

"Now go back upstairs and eat some break—" His mum was cut off by the tumultuous sound of a gong coming from the holoceiver's speakers and a familiar symbol appearing on it. It was the Timeless Link, which was the emblem of the deities and the Heavenspire. It depicted two linked arrows within a hexagonal barrier. Bob knew all about the symbol and its significance; the arrows represented Primium and Drakon: two separate planets yet united as one. The barrier characterised the deities, who formed a shield around the two worlds, yet without oppression – this was depicted by the empty space between the barrier and the arrows. Of most significance were the shapes themselves. The arrows had a prominent point, which could lead to a destination; that is, a place where their journey would terminate. The hexagon had no such thing; it would stay as it was forever, defending the arrows and allowing them to reach their destination unharmed. Elves and dwarves had protested for a new symbol with four arrows, but the sigil was so widespread that it was hard to change in a matter of days.

Bob clicked a button that read "Receive" and, in a flash, the image of a god began speaking to them. He was humanoid, but the reptilian scales covering his body and similarities to the dragons of old human folklore marked him out as a liskous. He wore a gilded breastplate, with the Timeless Link on it, over a white toga, and he carried a heavily decorated shimmering staff. The bright light coalescing off his golden scales, visible even in the cyan hologram light, meant the family knew exactly who he was.

"Warmbloods of Primium, Arcanast and Ferraheim," boomed the deep, monotonous voice of Aeterno, his face an expressionless mask. "Some of the damage dealt during the Stygir War is irreversible. We began with about a hundred deities. Now, only twelve – me included – remain. Of course, technology is a marvel, and it has made the old ways of hunting and farming redundant, but it will not be enough. Each household must nominate one person to journey to the planet Drakon to be taught in an institution unlike no other, to attempt to pass a test that will result in immortality. And I cannot stress this enough, only one may be nominated. Too many deities and not enough mortals to sustain them could prove disastrous, and now is the worst possible time to test the boundaries of our symbiotic relationship."

"But, remember, being a deity is not a privilege but a burden. You never die, whilst everyone else around you does, and you must answer the pleas of an entire system. I am not at peace with many things and will never be for the rest of my immortal life." The god paused for a moment, as if lost in thought, before continuing. "My race has elected their nominees already, and they are waiting for you in the central plaza of Helother city. I will see you there." The image of Aeterno vanished.

Several minutes passed.

"This is… unheard of," Bob's dad managed to say. "Before, we had to prove our worth as a deity with a deed, not undergo a simple test!"

"This seems like a bad idea… Maybe we should just leave our faith in technology," suggested his mum.

Bob said nothing; outwards, he was motionless, but inside him was a swirling cloud of thoughts. He remembered Aurik and the effortless way the god broke up the street fight. Then he remembered the naïvetés that surrounded him like a thick cloak as he began to explore the new world. *Up until now I've just been another kid from the shelter, looked down upon and felt sorry for. This can all change… The world can… no,* will *remember me as something more. I can* be a deity, I *can* work alongside the system's heroes, and I can *save lives!*

"Allow me to go; let me, PLEASE!" The words sprang out of his mouth in a blur.

His mum and dad stared at him, as if they found his words inaudible but knew exactly what they meant. "I have to go," he continued, "this is my chance to become something!"

"It's too dangerous. I'm not having some stygir creature tear you apart!" replied his dad.

"YOU FOUGHT IN THE WAR AND SURVIVED! YOU SAW MEKANYON ACTIVATE INDUSTRIA AND SAVE US ALL!" yelled back Bob, unable to bear what he was hearing.

"Your father's right. And, as you said, the gods are doing just fine as they are with their orbital turret," stated his mum in a soft voice, trying to calm her son down. "Anyway, you have to go to school now, and we'll sort out this problem ourselves." She tried to switch off the holoceiver, but the gaping mouth of the portal remained.

Grudgingly, Bob grabbed his satchel and strutted out of the house.

THREE

The class was half-empty. Those who hadn't bunked off or gone to Drakon felt bored to death by the dry, wheezing voice of their teacher, Mr Tedium. Everyone waited for the bell with longing, whispering to each other as their professor trudged through his lecture.

"Who got nominated from your family?" Bob's friend Dirk asked him. The question was intended to be a conversation opener, but it felt like a blade through the back.

"Nobody," came the reply. "My family says that deities should not be chosen in that way, and technology is protecting us enough already."

"Bob Solis! Dirk Smith!" snapped Mr Tedium.

With a jolting start, the two boys turned to face their teacher, with their expressions blank but terror rampant inside. Whilst infamous for his dull lessons, the old teacher was feared around the school for another reason.

"We were discussing the... thing you were talking about!" spluttered Dirk.

"I'm guessing you know all about the parts of an atom, right? You two can stay behind and dust the bookshelves of the library for that. As a final parting before the holobook replacements arrive. Oh, and then clean the lost-property physical education kits, but not before washing my spaceship." Smirking, the teacher then turned on the smartboard, and he announced that the new government was being formed and that everyone should pay attention.

"Switch to the news!" commanded Mr Tedium.

The screen changed to show a distraught reporter surrounded by an angry crowd of people with signs.

"As we all know, the previous government died fighting in the Stygir War, protecting us to the last," the reporter explained, trying to be heard over the angry shouts of the sign-holders. "They were great heroes."

"UNLIKE THEIR REPLACEMENTS!" someone yelled.

"I am here at the election ceremony of the new human government," the reporter continued. "Unfortunately, many candidates have disappeared or resigned, leaving only just enough to form a ruling body."

"LEAVING ONLY THE VERY WORST, WHO ARE UNFIT TO RULE!" a protester howled.

A portly man wearing thick spectacles waddled onto a stage behind the scene. "I am Mick Nugnodge, the leader of your new government," he announced.

A clash between loud cheers and boos commenced.

Undaunted, he continued, "We will keep the golden age of technology and make humanity great; so great that the pointy-ears and midgets will regret their silly decision to turn their back on Mekanyon's wondrous creation. For Heavenspire!"

"FOR HEAVENSPIRE'S SAKE, GO ON A DIET!" someone bawled, and they threw a sign at Mick Nugnodge.

The government leader let out a squeal and called for the military. Arriving at the scene like a stampede of khaki wildebeests, armed soldiers began to suppress the protests. Not a single shot was fired; after one look at the battle-hardened military, the protesters dropped their signs and ran.

"This is it from the Primium News Network," the reporter called out, narrowly avoiding the crowd of running humans. "Will the new government be as good as the old? They've definitely handled repairing the damaged cities at a rate that only Aurik could beat and are looking good at the moment, but will they follow this up well? Stay tuned!"

"Switch off!" commanded Mr Tedium. "That reporter offered a good question. Discuss for it ten minutes, then go to break. Except you, Bob and Dirk, the bell's just rung, and it's dusting time!"

"Dusting those books and cleaning those kits would be a sojourn to the past." A figure strode into the classroom, with an ill-fitting, thick cloak obscuring all his features from view. Two bumps which could've been the tops of two sleeping bags or a weirdly shaped rucksack could be seen protruding from the back of the cloak, and Bob swore he could hear a faint whirring noise every time the figure took a step. "Technology is the medium through which the future inhabits the present, yet you choose to eschew it for old-fashioned and inefficient forced labour that overcompensates. Really, Tedium? And, for the discussion, I say the government is great."

"You can't tell me how to run my class!" snapped Tedium. "Who in Heavenspire are you? Get out, tramp!"

"I can and I will," the figure replied. "For once in your failed career as a teacher, how about you try giving a regular detention instead of some extra work?"

"I don't know who you are, but this is none of your business. Go away!"

"I don't take orders from someone sitting in the shallow end of their career, teaching children from the shelters the most basic of education. How many times did you fail teaching to get here, might I ask?"

"Why you..." snarled Tedium, and he drew an energy pistol from under his desk. As if possessed, the gun jerked out of his hand and exploded.

"You're fired, Mr Tedium. I am not your employer, yet I will ensure you will find work someplace else." The figure then turned to face Bob. "Bob Solis, you are coming with me."

How did they know his name?

Bob had been warned about strangers, but he seemed intrigued by the mysterious figure underneath the cloak and he decided to go with them.

The two of them left the classroom and walked out of the school. Once they got outside, the figure handed Bob a jetpack – one of the most expensive and hard to make pieces of technology – and a small package that expanded into a spacesuit at the push of a button. The boy took a moment to marvel at the items before donning them.

As if sensing his thoughts, the figure said, "You will have to give me the equipment back once we reach Drakon. To return the spacesuit to its compact form, press the button again."

"Wait, we're going there? Why?" enquired Bob.

"You know why. Anyway, that lesson was dull, but there were matters of importance in that news broadcast. What is your opinion on the new government?"

Bob couldn't think of an answer; he had only seen one of them briefly on the news.

"Follow politics, Bob Solis, to follow the minds that govern your planet. But be assured that they are the greatest humans for the task, proving themselves more than worthy with reparations and managing order. Any who hate them must love the damage and chaos the stygir brought with them."

"Who are you? How do you know my thoughts?"

"You like to ask questions, don't you?" chided the figure.

The two bumps on his back split open into propeller blades, shredding the cloak. Underneath the cloak was a suit of silver-coloured armour emblazoned with the Timeless Link, which could have belonged to a baroque-era knight were it not for the countless steam-valves, gears and gauges adorning it, which were whirring and clanking at a faster rate now that the propellers on its shoulders were spinning. Beneath his visor, the flicker of a green light was visible.

"Many have been held back by family members, just like in your case," stated Mekanyon, god of technology. "Your feelings of upset were a beacon on my emotional sensors. Now, let's go to Drakon."

FOUR

The journey between planets would likely have taken years were it not for a phenomenon known as divinite-radiated hyperspace (DRH). In a system with a large piece of divinite located in it, space travel becomes extremely fast due to the strange emissions given off by the element. It would still take a couple of months to traverse the entire system, but it only took around three hours to reach a neighbouring planet such as Drakon. Despite being held aloft by propellers, Mekanyon could still fly through space as if it was air. These were a new innovation of his, space-travel rotors, which he took great delight in telling Bob (for DRH also allowed for communication in space). However, when asked about Industria or his armour, the god refused to give a smidgeon of information.

"In the past, when humanity had magic users, there was a saying that went 'a magician never reveals their secrets'," Mekanyon told Bob, "and it applies to me if you replace magician with inventor. Simply put, I wish for my greatest inventions to remain unique, iconic creations, not reproduceable products."

Bob nodded awkwardly, unsure of what the god meant. "Do you think I can become something?" the boy mumbled.

"You are something," replied Mekanyon in a puzzled tone. "A physical being of flesh and blood."

"No, I didn't mean it that way. I mean, do you think I can become someone, you know... important?" Bob's voice shifted gears into a faster pace. "Someone who can save others, and be looked up to, and, like... this all happened really quickly, I-I just realised today that I don't just want to be another kid from the shelter, I want to do something, and not—"

"You're asking me to spoil the end of a story which I don't know about," Mekanyon interrupted him. "Even Kosma can only see a short distance into the future. Answer that question for yourself, Bob Solis." Once more, Bob nodded silently.

Soon they reached the planet of Drakon, a world of mountains, dunes and geometric rock formations. Several cities consisting of tall, stalagmite-like spires were dotted around this lithic landscape. Linking these settlements were winding roads of an odd, glowing rock. The two landed in a city built upon a raised plateau. Besides the spires Bob had spotted earlier, there were transparent, cuboid buildings containing rows of flat, fist-sized rocks in various colours, and large fields of blue plants which some of the townspeople were eating. On the edges of the city were small, arena-like structures where groups of muscular liskous practiced their skills with a staff. All of this was built around a colossal, cylindrical structure filled with books.

Bob could do little to hide his shock at his surroundings,

so different to the silver buildings and holographic signs he was used to.

"Mekanyon, this place is really weird," he told the god of technology. "There's no technology anywhere!"

"We do not need it," came a serene voice. A grey liskous walked up to Bob, with one of the flat rocks in his hand. "Slate-scales are what our society runs on."

"Slate-scales?" asked Bob. "What's that?"

"Why would you like to know?" the liskous retorted. "Isn't this too weird for you?"

"They're rocks that are found on Drakon, which respond to your mind and unleash a power," Mekanyon explained. "But the more advanced powers require a more advanced mind."

"Greetings, Mekanyon," the warrior said with a bow. "I am honoured for you to visit our city. Who is your blunt companion?"

"Bob Solis," Mekanyon introduced the nervous-looking boy. "His parents wouldn't let him be a nominee so I had to take him to Helother myself."

"But Helother lies below us," the warrior explained, gesturing to a settlement built at the foot of the plateau and surrounded by barren wastes. "This is its twin city, Jenyrilka-Nohbi."

"Apologies, Bob. My mistake," said Mekanyon.

"Not to worry, Mekanyon." The liskous gestured to the glowing bridge connecting the twin cities. "Our scale-bridge is made of the finest speed-scale and manned by experienced scale-wardens, so you'll be taken there in an instant. Go to the bridge and stand on it." Bob and Mekanyon did as they were told.

A liskous that Bob presumed to be the scale-warden was standing by the bridge, and tapped it with his staff. The scale-bridge glowed brighter and in a matter of minutes, Bob and Mekanyon found themselves in Helother.

After a brisk farewell, Mekanyon flew off in some unknown direction, leaving Bob with the crowd of nominees. A cable with a hand extended from the god's armour, removing and taking back the jetpack and spacesuit Bob had used.

"Is that Mekanyon?" asked a voice that came from behind Bob. A thickset dwarf who looked around the same age as Bob gazed up at the god, scratching the beginnings of a beard. In his hands were a hammer and pickaxe; not exactly looking like they were meant for farming and building, these tools seemed to emanate an aura of battle.

Remembering the dwarves and elves back on Primium, Bob cried out and staggered back.

"Are you OK?" the dwarf asked. "You look like you've seen a stygir."

"Y-yes, I'm fine," Bob told him. "And that was Mekanyon; he had to bring me here because my parents wouldn't let me come."

The dwarf burst out laughing. "That's the total opposite of my family!" he exclaimed. "They're all saying stuff like 'Caesium, make our clan proud,' and 'Caesium, how can you become a god? You've only prepared for two hours! Train up, boy!'"

"How's life on Ferraheim?" asked Bob.

"Like my old cavern on Primium, but it's the whole planet," replied Caesium. "There are perfect conditions for metalworking and runecraft, with someone building something every second. How's Primium? Also, what's your name?"

Bob thought about mentioning his views on the superiority of technology, but his encounter with the liskous in Jenyrilka-Nohbi made him opt not to. Instead, he simply introduced himself and began to talk about his planet. After the tension building up between men, elves and dwarves, both Bob and Caesium were relieved to find out that both races were approachable and seemingly friendly.

At that moment, silence was called for, and a figure approached the crowd, hunched over a staff similar to Bob's but with more pieces of stone attached to it. He was a deep-blue liskous, who addressed himself simply as an emissary of the deities, and the overseer of the nominees' training and education.

"What's your name?" someone asked.

"Cognitio," he replied. "I will now be taking you to the site of your education, the Below-Heavenspire. It is situated in this wild area of Drakon, the Free Dunes." Cognitio gestured to the wastes surrounding Helother. "Despite its looks, this sector of the planet is teeming with life and the keen eyes amongst you may be able to spot some extraordinary animals."

"Why are you so bloody robotic?" an irritatingly high-pitched voice whined. "The gods should be here, not some old fart like you! Are they too lazy or something?"

A gasp went through the crowd, and everyone stared at an extremely thin boy with a blond fringe that almost covered his eyes.

Caesium nudged him and told him to shut up, but he kept on talking. "And of all species, a lizard that thinks it can talk! Why not a human? We invented technology!"

"Oakley Jenkins, I've told you about this before," Cognitio said calmly, yet with a hint of tension. "Keep your behaviour disciplined—"

"Or what?" the boy scoffed. "Don't order me around, you filthy reptile! Pay me respect for technology!"

A colourless piece of slate on the emissary's staff began to glow, and he fired a powerful jet of water at Oakley, knocking him to the floor with a squeal.

"Rule one: deities aren't racist!" Cognitio snapped. "You speak of technology, yet Mekanyon isn't racist in the least. And, I think I *can* speak, filth! Without borrowing the voice box of a mouse, either!"

Caesium burst out laughing, as did many others, whilst Bob tried to suppress a smile. Yet at the same time, a part of the human boy felt sick. *Was what I said to the warrior earlier as rude as that?* he wondered, direly hoping that that was not the case.

Without bothering to say anything to the crowd of nominees, the emissary strode off and everyone else followed.

"Now that's one teacher I wouldn't want to get on the wrong side of," joked Caesium.

"Yeah," replied Bob, remembering his encounter with Tedium back on Primium. "But he did deserve it. How could Cognitio fire that water, though? Wouldn't that make Hydrax a pointless god?"

"It's a type of slate-scale," Caesium explained. "You know, those rocks the liskous have at the ends of their staffs. Don't you remember, humanity used to travel through space with air-scale and wind-scale?"

"Nope. Up until now, I've been stuck in a shelter. I thought all children were. Where were you?"

"I come from a warrior clan. It would ruin our pride if I didn't fight, so I was trained to battle and then sent to fight in the war."

Bob gasped in surprise.

"Yeah, I know. The stygir's armies were *tough*. For the love of Heavenspire, even their lowest underlings were hard to beat! Industria saved us all. Unfortunately, it also saved that Oakley guy from earlier."

Suddenly, roaring and growling filled the area. Everyone stopped talking and began looking around. Behind them, an ominous shadow skimmed across the ground.

"Calm down!" ordered Cognitio. "It's nothing much, just a wild basilous."

This statement only made the situation worse. Children were running everywhere and adults talked frantically about whether Cognitio was sane or not.

"What's a basilous?" asked Bob.

"You're stupid, aren't you?" remarked Oakley. "Look above!"

Beating its four pairs of wings, a behemoth of scaly, ultramarine flesh and overlapping armour plates circled in the sky above the group of nominees; its long, crooked beak opened to reveal hook-like teeth and three prehensile tongues. Whilst its body was best compared to that of a large dragon, its head and neck were akin to a vulture's, save for a large, pulsing crest that glowed with a cyan light. Each one of its ten legs ended in several miniature, scythe-like talons that writhed like swarms of bugs.

"Don't worry, they don't—" Cognitio was cut off as all of the basilous' talons shot towards him on tendrils at breathtaking speed. They wrapped around him, digging into his flesh, and then began to retract, reeling him in like a fish on the end of a rod. His staff clattered to the floor.

Chaos erupted.

The crowd was in hysterics, with countless individuals trying to escape yet blocked by swathes of others.

"*What do we do?*" cried out Bob, narrowly avoiding being trampled.

"WE STAND AND FIGHT!" yelled Caesium, raising his hammer at Cognitio. A rune on it glowed, and the unconscious emissary was soon being pulled down to the ground by a new-found force.

The basilous roared its disdain, pulling Cognitio with all its might. Despite its massive form, it was locked in stalemate with the invisible attraction.

"FOR HEAVENSPIRE!" another dwarf screamed, flying towards their trapped teacher on a platform of rock engraved with glowing runes. He drew from his belt a sword wreathed in a crimson aura and sliced through the tendrils holding Cognitio. Unconscious from shock, their teacher was about to plummet before the dwarf caught him and rested him on the platform.

Immediately, more talons grew from the basilous' legs, yet they were large ones akin to broadswords this time. It swiped these at the dwarf, who parried them with incredible skill. However, ten legs proved too much to counter at once, and a coordinated series of swipes saw the dwarf fall from his platform, his armour cracked and flecked with blood. The runes on the platform stopped glowing, and Cognitio was met with the same fate. Caesium changed the direction he was pointing his hammer, and both of their descents were slowed down to that of feathers.

"You fought well," he commended the other dwarf. "Someone, stem the blood flow!"

Bob did so instantly.

The basilous shed its claws, and they fell like bladed ordnance. Blasts of magic, both lightning and flame, incinerated them before they could deal any damage; a group of elves, calm in the midst of the chaotic sea of nominees, had destroyed them, yet besides this one act they did nothing more than observe. New claws grew: the miniature scythes from before. They shot out at Caesium this time, but he was ready. Grabbing a tendril, he began to climb up it whilst avoiding the others deftly. He raised his hammer, and the monster's head was drawn towards it. Jumping from the tendril he was on, he prepared to strike with both weapons. A wing struck him, and he began to fall.

Out of nowhere, a pillar of water began to rise.

Instead of hitting the ground, Caesium landed harmlessly on this pillar, which then began to shrink in height, taking him to the ground safely.

"*Nominees,*" a voice rang out in everyone's heads, seemingly coming from their own thoughts. This unnatural occurrence made everyone stop in their tracks and see an azure liskous walk towards them. His figure seemed to bear aspects of a calm elder and a powerful warrior in his prime at the same time. His featureless eyes were lambent, like sunlight bouncing off the surface of water, and he carried a rope studded with slate-scales.

Immediately, most of the nominees knelt and Bob felt obliged to do the same.

"I am Hydrax, god of water. How about we take down this rogue beast together?"

"Or how about you do it, lazy ass?" remarked Oakley. "You're the god here!"

Everyone gasped and stared at him incredulously.

"Very well," said Hydrax telepathically, with not a sign of contempt. *"All those who want to help, join me. If you don't have any weapons with you, think clearly that you don't and I shall aid you."*

A second later, a blaster and blade, seemingly made of water, appeared in Bob's hands and in those of many other nominees'. Despite their wet, runny feel and liquid appearance, they acted like a solid in every way. Cries of amazement sounded throughout the crowd, with many elves remarking how they had never seen water manipulated so well.

The basilous roared and shot out its tendrils.

"SOLID STREAM: WATER-ASCENSION CONSTRUCT!" Hydrax's voice shouted telepathically.

"What?" asked Bob, puzzled.

"The deities' most powerful moves require their names spoken," a nearby liskous explained. "Look!"

Like a swarm of sea serpents, pillars of the solid-like water erupted from the ground, lifting up those with weapons to the basilous' height. Stretching out towards the basilous, the pillars of water formed a path for some of the nominees to assault it at close range. Bob threw his blade to the ground, hung back and began to shoot it. Bullets of pressurised water made cracks in the basilous' armour, yet the recoil almost made Bob drop his gun. As the basilous lashed out in all directions, many were struck down. Whilst nobody was dead, the water beneath them began to become coloured deep red.

"You!" a voice called to Bob. A diminutive boy with thick spectacles and a laptop tucked under one arm thrust an odd, pulsing device into his hands. "Take a healing unit and help me treat the injured!"

Bob sped towards the nearest wounded, a human writhing in pain. He placed the device on his wounds; the smaller ones disappeared instantly, but, for the larger ones, Bob had to remain by his side for fifteen minutes. It was at that point that he noticed almost the entirety of the liskous and elf nominees were down on the ground, watching the fight with bemused expressions.

"HEY!" Bob hollered. "WHY AREN'T YOU HELPING? COWARDS!"

"And it shall end there," called out Cognitio, flying towards the basilous. He placed a hand on its forehead, and it ceased its attack. "Thank you for your help, cold sister. Although, didn't I tell you not to go too overboard?"

With something akin to a sigh, the great beast flew off. Everyone stared at Cognitio with a puzzled expression on their faces.

"Shall I explain?" asked Hydrax.

"As you wish, my god," replied Cognitio. He then flew to where Oakley was and struck the disrespectful boy across the face with his staff. "As for you, respect your deities!"

"It matters not, Cognitio," spoke Hydrax. "On the battlefield, in a crisis and in situations of danger, there will always be those in a greater position to help than others. Cognitio devised this scenario to test some of your mettle as heroes. I commend Caesium Ironwill and Baldaer Urbok for their immediate call to action. I am pleased to see so many turn into valiant warriors and even selfless medics, thanks to devices made by Gary Raptor!"

The boy with the laptop grinned at these words.

"But many of your thoughts think the elves and liskous cowards. They are not. The basilous, known as the cold brethren to our people, are a species that has lived alongside us for generations – no liskous would lift a finger against them! And the elves figured out that this was a test; I can tell from their thoughts. Nominees of these two species, I am sorry you couldn't prove yourself in this scenario, yet you have proved yourselves to liskous culture, and plenty more opportunities will arise as you undergo your education." The god then flew to Bob's side. "You think me a useless deity, for slate-scales can also shoot water, and I will admit they can do this, just as magic can and toy guns can. Yet only I have infinite and utter control over it. It is the same with Lapideis and Nimbus – we are the epitome of our elements. Oh! A new thought… Why do I communicate telepathically? Because I prefer it. Farewell!" Beating his wings, Hydrax flew off into the distance.

The pillars of water went down slowly; everyone was dumbfounded by what had happened.

"There's a rumour that he does it in order to suppress something," Caesium whispered to Bob. "My grandad says that there's a second aspect to him and others say there's a curse on him, but no one really knows. Deities can't read the thoughts of direct allies, so not even they know."

"Maybe he just prefers it?" wondered Bob. "It is a cool way to talk to people."

"Any questions?" asked Cognitio.

No one spoke.

"OK, let's continue walking," Cognitio suggested, and they all did just that.

After what seemed like an eternity, they reached a barren building that blended in with the rocky terrain of Drakon. The attempts at trying to recreate the image of the Heavenspire could be seen in its architecture: a skyscraper-like base led up to a sharp point, with two spikes flanking it that looked ready to collapse. Cracks could be seen scattered across its badly built structure.

"It doesn't look much on the outside, but it's a wonderful building on the inside, I promise," stated Cognitio, trying to control the crowd of now-agitated nominees.

After their encounter with the basilous, walking for several hours and seeing the disastrous-looking Below-Heavenspire, many were having second thoughts about whether learning to become a deity was a good idea.

Voices could be heard shouting and clamouring, howling complaints and yelling insults.

"ALL COLD BRETHREN, I HAVE SOME PREY!" shouted Cognitio.

The nominees sped into the building, smashing holes around the entrance in their frenzy.

FIVE

"There's nothing inside here!" gasped Bob, looking around at an empty room.

"Look down! There's a ladder in that corner," responded Caesium, pointing to a very thin, wiry ladder, made of an odd, neon-pink material, leading down a tunnel. Without bothering to check if there was an alternative to this precarious route, he began to climb down it. Suddenly, he disappeared in a burst of light. Before anyone could react, Cognitio entered the room with a massive grin on his reptilian face and began to speak excitedly.

"Excellent! Excellent!" he exclaimed. "The phasing ladder is a tool that can only be used by those with the mindset to control it. And that dwarf there has activated it skilfully like he's been switching realities for his entire life. A god in the making!" As everyone shared confused looks and wondered what was going on, he continued, "I was lying a bit when I said this was the site of your education. It is... but not in this reality. Plenty of alternate realities exist, and the tools used to traverse them are phasing ladders, like the one here. The deities have kept them secret, since it would cause chaos with the general public.

The way it works is that you must climb down the ladder, whilst thinking clearly of where you want to appear in the other reality. Any questions?"

"What are these realities like?" an elf asked. "Is the one we're in right now just a tiny section of a bigger picture?"

"No, we have pinpointed this as the base reality that all others stem from. Every other reality we've seen is like a pocket dimension, with no sign of life, although maybe that could change. The universe is a vast place, and there is no chance in Heavenspire that anyone knows everything about it." With those words, he then climbed down the ladder and phased to the alternate reality.

A tidal wave of nominees surged towards the phasing ladder, each individual member wanting to phase realities before the others. Due to the fact there was only one ladder, chaos soon erupted, and the subsequent fights left the Below-Heavenspire looking even more like a fault plane. Desperately, Bob and a few others tried to calm them down, but it was in vain. After a while, the non-injured had all phased, the unluckier members of the battles limped after them, and the ladder was free.

Take me where everyone else went, Bob thought, climbing down the ladder. An iridescent pink blast knocked him back, slamming him into the tunnel wall. Stunned by the blast, he tried again, thinking, *Take me to the place I can become a god.* There came another less intense blast.

"Hurry up!" came a voice from above, impatient and irritated.

Take me to the site of my education, Bob thought.

Blast.

Take me to the site of my education.

And with an exhilarating, new-found sensation, akin to flying the jetpack but greater, he was flung out of his reality.

*

Bob woke up in a large, towering, dark-green building, circled by an azure coil of a luminous material. A vast and complex network of lifts hung above his head, which was apparently the main method of transport in the building. Doors were omnipresent, but the only obvious way out was the phasing ladder he had used to get there and another one in the centre of this current room. Many of the other nominees were already using the latter to phase out, and Bob decided to follow. No sooner had he done that, he felt a scaly hand grab him by the shoulder.

"You do not know where that goes or why they are going there, yet you choose to follow. Why is that?" queried Cognitio.

Bob said nothing.

"An important lesson is to never follow unless you have a reason. The reason that others are doing so is invalid," continued Cognitio.

"So I shouldn't go?" asked Bob.

"You should, after I tell you why," came the reply. "The bitter truth about deities is that every one of them has to fight at some point in their never-ending lives. Whilst there have been completely peaceful deities in the past, who helped society flourish, Atlas needs fighters nowadays who will protect Heavenspirian society as we know it. The Stygir

War was the main catalyst in this shift, but there have always been rogues trying to get divinite for their own purposes, and there are sometimes still cults in hiding, practising their malign rituals. Besides, the ruling bodies of each race can handle politics in the absence of deities. In order to ascertain your fighting abilities, we shall have a battle that pits everyone against everyone. Teams are allowed, if you have friends, for you may be outnumbered in a real battle. If you don't have weapons, there is a wide variety in room 265, floor eleven, which will become your personal armaments."

"Wait, real weapons aren't—"

"Yes, but nobody will die; go on, pick some weapons."

"How will that—"

"Now!"

A part of Bob wanted to inquire further, yet faced with his intimidating teacher, he couldn't bring himself to do so. Until this moment, he had not realised how much he would shake with terror at the prospect of a real fight. Sure, thanks to technology, he had played some video games involving violence, but you could always come back to life in those. There was no button to come back from death and no chance of victory when you had spent most of your life in a shelter.

Bob got into one of the lifts, which was operated by voice recognition. Once he had said the name of the room, the lift moved off at an alarming speed. "*Ping!*" went the lift as it reached its destination. Bob exited the lift and stepped into a long, narrow passageway lined with seemingly endless doors. In front of him was one with the number 265 etched on in spidery scrawl.

Behind this door lay a vast room that belied the close space between each door. Weapons from each of the four species' cultures were strewn across its floor, along with a notice for each describing what the weapon was and what it did. Disregarding anything but technology, Bob went to find his weapons.

There were no jetpacks left but plenty of substitutes for one, and the optimum choice lay right before his very eyes. A futuristic-looking suit of the same green as the building with structures similar to jet engines scattered on its surface. The label read like this:

Turbine Suit (technology – human). A suit of armour with mind-activated, space-compatible turbines that can either cause the wearer to levitate off the ground; augment their jumping and movement capabilities; or, most importantly, blow away projectiles and opponents for better performance with a ranged weapon. It also has a spacesuit function, although you must remember to check its oxygen tanks regularly, since it does not have as large a capacity as a regular spacesuit.

Without hesitation, he grabbed the suit and put it on, only to be overwhelmed by its weight. *Foot turbines, switch on,* he thought. They did so, and the suit lifted off. The suit didn't weigh as much when Bob was airborne. No, it was truly weightless. Gripped with excitement, Bob began to fly around, forgetting the grave situation and laughing with joy.

Then one of the arm turbines activated, ploughing his arm into a series of weapon shelves. They fell like dominoes, smashing apart on the floor. *Turbines, switch off!* thought Bob hastily. This command only made more turn on, and soon Bob was crashing into every possible part of the room. When the turbines stopped finally, he decided to look for a weapon.

Amongst the rubble he had reduced the room to, he found an ancient model of energy blaster with this label:

Joule 1.0 (technology – human). This is the first energy blaster devised by Mekanyon during the Stygir War, and is a type of firearm that relies on a fossil fuel source, coal, in order to fire blasts of concentrated kinetic energy. This model is considered obsolete and not as effective as some of the later generations, mainly due to a poor firing speed and primitive fuel source).

There was no way he would choose that. Absolutely no way would he be seen with a Joule, especially not the first and worst of that outdated make. He began to dig through the rubble to find a good firearm, hopefully a Fusior 38 or a Catalys mark 9.

Before he had made much progress, an AI security system began to raise the alarm. "Floor eleven, room 265 has been heavily compromised! The suspect is still in the room! My sensors are blurry, but they have an outline of a male elf or human, garment colour dark green—"

Bob grabbed the Joule 1.0, dashed out of the room and made his way hurriedly back to the main room downstairs.

Back on the ground floor, the emissary was interrogating some male elves and humans, all of whom were wearing dark green. They were unsure what was going on, and he quickly gave up. For a split second, it looked like he was about to interrogate everyone, but he simply said, "Proceed to the new dimension and form alliances if you have friends."

Bob was approached quickly by Caesium, who was wearing a set of sturdy, dwarf-wrought armour, and carrying his rune-encrusted pickaxe and hammer.

"Caesium, what was going on whilst I was getting my weapons?" Bob asked.

"Somebody wearing dark green demolished the weapons room, and nobody can figure out who it is. However, I saw the surveillance footage and the outline of the culprit looked like they were holding a Joule 1.0 and wearing a turbine suit…"

"How did you know?" gasped Bob. "Don't tell the emissary, please!"

"If I wanted to, I would've done it already," Caesium responded with a chuckle. "Though I might if you don't ally with me!"

Bob felt a warmth in his heart as he knew with certainty that he had already made a new friend, or at least a companion. "Is blackmail really what a god-in-training should be doing?" Bob joked. "What would your family say? That's *very* disappointing, but I'll ally with you."

"OK, buddy!"

A cry of despair echoed around the Below-Heavenspire. Bob and Caesium turned around to find Oakley running after a group of people, who began sprinting towards the phasing ladder. Cognitio had to intervene after Oakley threatened to shoot the phasing ladder if they didn't let him join their group.

After the group had phased and the incandescent insult match that followed had died down, Bob asked Oakley if he wanted to join their alliance. The emissary turned his head around in disbelief before phasing. Caesium looked aghast at the idea.

"No, obviously not!" came the screeching response from Oakley. "I want to be with the other cool and popular humans, not with a dwarf-loving retard like you! Why do you have such an old blaster and a suit made for saddos?" he whined, showing them his Fusior 38 and jetpack. "Anyway, I could pin you down!" With a swish of his fringe, he then activated the phasing ladder only to be reprimanded by the emissary in the third dimension in a row.

"You're too kind," Caesium told a shocked and dismayed Bob. "Don't worry about him; nobody likes him because he's racist and arrogant." A smile began to tug at the dwarf's lips. "Anyway, he couldn't form an alliance from the start due to the rules we were given."

"Why?" enquired Bob.

"Didn't the emissary say you could only form an alliance if you had friends?"

They both chuckled with laughter at the joke.

Caesium then took off his armour and pulled out some coal from his pockets. "Here, you'll need this for your blaster."

"Thanks. Where did you get it?" asked Bob.

"It's 'good luck' coal from my family. I don't have much use for it though, and your gun could run out of energy. Now let's phase and let's win!"

The two went to the ladder and phased to a new reality, which they found they wanted to escape from immediately.

SIX

The new dimension was nearly indescribable and inscrutable.

Shifting and coalescing into new dangers by the second, it looked like a vision from a nightmare. All was dark coloured, and shadows obscured most things from sight. When the crowd of nominees moved, it was only to dodge wicked, barbed darts or to avoid pitfalls that opened and closed randomly.

Visibility was heavily crippled, but they could see a short distance in front of them. There were no phasing ladders in sight.

"I will explain what this place is for those too afraid to question me earlier," called Cognitio's voice from some unknown direction. "This is Inferd, the ever-shifting realm, and where we will be fighting. It is the closest thing we have to the Stygir Void that circles our system and where your future battles may commence. As you can see, it has no fixed shape, and you must also be wary."

"Why are you trying to kill us?" came another, more worried voice.

"Rest assured, I will never try to do that. Atlas needs warriors, not corpses. If you 'die' in this dimension, you will feel pain, but you will phase back to the previous dimension with your body whole. You will be able to spectate for the rest of the fight by thinking about it. If you or your alliance wins, a ladder will appear for you."

A moment of silence descended as everyone took this in slowly.

"Oh, and I'm fighting too," announced Cognitio. "Begin!"

The deep black was soon lacerated with crimson as the battle commenced. Bob saw a cave-like opening and shot towards it, his turbine suit allowing him to evade everyone.

"Hey, wait up!" yelled Caesium, trying to follow him.

A group of liskous tried to strike him with their staffs, but he took them all out with a decisive blow of his hammer. He then stopped, as if a barrier was blocking him. Knowing the landscape of Inferd, one very likely was.

"In here!" called out Bob. "Quick, before it shifts!"

Caesium sprinted in Bob's direction and jumped into the cave-like opening; the two were now shielded from view as the battle raged on. Many more had the same idea as Bob, yet they went deeper into the cave and, such was their haste to escape the battle, they ran straight past Bob and Caesium.

"That was close," breathed Bob, watching the brutal combat outside.

The fights were not determined wholly on fighting skill. At one point, Bob saw an elf knock a human to the floor with a rapid stream of punches amplified with lightning sparks, only for a chasm to open underneath the would-be-victor's feet, swallowing her whole. In the distance, the glowing slates on the emissary's staff lit up a hard-fought but one-sided fight. Although many nominees had teamed up against their teacher, none had succeeded in even landing a scratch on his scaly hide or escaping the blur of a staff that blocked their futile attacks.

"This is humiliating!" exclaimed Caesium. "We should be out there fighting, not cowering in here!"

Bob tried to shush him, but around five people had discovered their hiding place. Bob froze in fright; Caesium began hacking at the air with his pickaxe, in random, uncoordinated strokes, and then he disappeared somewhere.

So much for my new friend, thought Bob as he activated his turbine suit. Unfortunately, the wrong turbines fired, slamming him into the cave wall. His blaster flew out of his hands and clattered onto the floor. The five opened fire and charged at him, whooping in delight at such an easy kill. It looked as if his time on Inferd was at an end.

Suddenly, a hand holding a glowing hammer appeared on the floor and, in a swift motion, tripped over all five. Bob stared in surprise at what had happened, and he was even more nonplussed when the hammer glowed even brighter and his gun flew towards it, as if it were a strong magnet.

"See, I told you we should fight," came a muffled-but-familiar dwarfish voice.

"Where are you?" called out Bob, only to be answered by a fragment of the sky cracking open and the familiar face of Caesium grinning from behind it.

His five assailants tried to escape, but Caesium killed them with a single swing of his hammer.

"I've got a wormhole-rune pickaxe and attraction-rune hammer," explained Caesium. "I can make tunnels through space by digging through the air with my pick, but they disappear after a while, and I can't make new ones continuously. Come through this one, I have a plan to win." He then paused, as if realising something. "Wait... where are the others who were hiding here?"

"They're still here; they're either well-hidden or went further into the cave," confirmed Bob. But the cave ended where they stood.

"Maybe they ran out?" suggested Caesium, pointing his hammer in the direction of the exit. Yet he was pointing at solid rock. Whatever exit there had been before, it was now non-existent. Both ends of the cave were closed, and Caesium's portals had disappeared. He could not bring them back. And, from all directions, they could feel a cold, unearthly miasma getting more intense by the second.

"I've read about this feeling before," said Bob, terror creeping into his voice. "It's known as Stygiomiasma, the feeling one gets when one of the stygir or their servants are approaching."

"That's impossible," scoffed Caesium. "The stygir don't venture outside the Void, and there's no way that they would be here."

A split second later, he turned a dark shade of purple and ruptured. But that was not the worst part. When he burst, what came out was not his innards but creatures with no detail on their bodies, beings that could have been mistaken for silhouettes had they not moved of their own accord. Their icosahedron-shaped heads were attached to their multiple spindly legs by a thick stalk, and they were soundless when they moved. Bob knew about them from the time he was told to read the disclosable information on the basics of the stygir in case he would one day have to fight in the war.

They were the macrovirus: the deadliest to any form of life of the stygir's known creations.

SEVEN

Those who study diseases know how a virus reproduces. It injects its DNA into a cell and uses the cell to create more copies of itself, then the cell ruptures, and the new viruses infect other cells. The macrovirus acts in the same way, but with one vital difference: instead of infecting one cell at a time, it infects a whole living being in one go.

Millions of such creatures circled Bob by the minute, ready to inject their malign DNA into him. A desperate volley of shots from an outdated blaster could kill a few of them, but it would not cripple their victory in the slightest. Why the viruses had not killed him yet was part of their wicked design: they only attack when the victim is not suspecting them to, or when the victim is scared out of their wits by the aura of fear the macroviruses exert. Knowing this, Bob tried to act stoically, loading the blaster with the coal that Caesium had given him and firing another few rounds. Macroviruses fell to the floor by the thousands, but, however many died, there were multiple times more poised to kill him.

Bob was at the end of his wits.

Leaping towards him in one synchronised motion, the macroviruses prepared to infect their hapless victim. And, at that moment, Bob decided to let his last hope ride on his mercurial turbine suit. It didn't matter which turbine activated; it didn't matter if he was humiliatingly splattered against the walls. Much to his surprise and elation, the cave walls had melted into the floor, so when Bob flew (which could otherwise be described as being dragged across the floor at a high speed), he escaped his would-be murderers, who had the unfortunate luck to fall into a large pit that opened up beneath their feet.

Luck really is a key element in battles, thought Bob as he deactivated the turbines and staggered to his feet. As he looked around, the terrain of Inferd seemed to be completely devoid of life. Was he the victor? There was no ladder in sight.

Crack! Without warning, his turbine suit split in two and crumbled away, rendering him unarmoured.

"The water-scale: one of the strongest scale-slates we liskous use!" Descending from the sky, Cognitio prepared to fire another jet of highly pressurised water at Bob, but a shot from Bob's energy blaster shattered the colourless slate on his staff.

Everyone spectating was amazed at Bob's lucky shot, but Cognitio had more powered slates on his staff. A red one glowed, and a jet of fire shot out of his mouth, incinerating the area around Bob. With his enemy trapped in a circle of conflagration, Cognitio began to breathe a spiral of molten metal at the area where Bob was trapped. However, there was a way Bob could escape. A small pillar had formed by his feet and, by jumping off it, he could land on a nearby ledge and leap out of the fire from there. He would suffer some burns, but he would be alive. For the second time, it seemed the shifting of Inferd had aided him. Putting his plan into action, he jumped off the pillar, only just about managing to grasp the ledge. He began to pull himself up, but then fatigue struck him like a bullet. He fell directly into the flames, screaming as they scorched his flesh.

*

Bob awoke, this time back in the previous dimension. His turbine suit was intact and his blaster fully fuelled, with not a single scratch on either. Nobody seemed to be around, but there was a sign leading him to his dormitory.

After he had taken the lift to it, he was massively surprised at the state of it. The term 'dormitory' invoked the image of a plain, cramped room with a large number of beds, but what Bob was looking at seemed like the most upscale establishment in all of Atlas. Grand and detached, with its gargantuan door and superfluous amount of decoration, it looked almost as magnificent as the Heavenspire itself. Countless other similar buildings lined the 300th floor like a vein of gold. A notice on the side of the door read, "Floor 300, boys' dormitory 401: Caesium Ironwill, Jeff Johnson, Gary Raptor, Oakley Jenkins and Bob Solis." Next to that was a biometric lock, which was activated by any of Bob's fingerprints.

Beyond the door lay a room that overtook the door in grandness. An lift system in the centre of the room took Bob up to a carpeted floor with two bunk beds and one four-poster bed, where a fight had broken out.

"Bob, that was amazing!" exclaimed Caesium, defending himself against his two combatants. "Good shooting with that pistol! But how did those stygir creatures get there?"

"Hey Bob, do a pull-up!" jeered Oakley.

"Yes, show us an *amazing* pull-up!" repeated a human next to him.

Away from the fight scene, the bespectacled boy from the encounter with the basilous typed frantically on a laptop, paying no attention to anything else.

"You fought great too," Bob told Caesium, "I had no idea you could defeat five on your own! And you have a good point; we need to ask about those macroviruses." Bob's attention then turned to Oakley's sidekick. "Before I show you that, can you show me the *amazing* bribe money Oakley gave you to be his friend?"

Oakley shouted something so high-pitched it was inaudible; Caesium burst out laughing.

"I-I just copied Caesium's joke from earlier," stammered Bob, taken aback by how much noise his comment had made. "Maybe I shouldn't have said it—"

"You have no reason to laugh, dwarf; the four-poster bed is mine! YOU'RE TOO SMALL FOR IT!" roared Oakley at Caesium, swinging impotent punches and kicks at his more skilled opponent. "Jeff, you get Bob!"

The fight escalated to the point where the four-poster bed was heavily damaged as Oakley dodged a stream of Caesium's blows, and the grandiose carpet became a frayed, stringy mess. Nobody showed any intention of stopping. With a terrible aim, Jeff threw a piece of broken wood, which hit the laptop boy on the nose, causing the thick spectacles perched at the end of his nose to go flying.

"COULD YOU JUST DECIDE WHO GETS WHAT BED AND NOT MESS ANYTHING UP?" Gary shouted in a surprisingly rough voice.

"OK, Gary, who should get the four... I mean three-poster?" replied Caesium.

"Whoever tidies this mess up!" declared Gary.

The truth was that irreversible damage had been done. Once an amazing room, it had become a dishevelled mess. Bob, Caesium, Oakley and Jeff limped around and tried to restore the room to its former state, but to no avail. Frustrated, Gary typed some more on his computer before creating from it intact copies of all the broken items in the room, then he placed them by each of their wrecked counterparts. A blue glow flickered, and the damaged items vanished, seemingly replaced by the copies.

Awestruck, Jeff asked him what he did to make that happen.

"Can't you figure it out? This laptop's main function is an advanced 3-D printing system, which can print off most materials and combine small amounts of non-organic matter. I built it myself."

"Nerd!" sniffed Oakley.

Gary ignored him and began typing again.

"What's so interesting on that screen that you have to look at it twenty-four-seven?" asked Caesium, taking a look at Gary's laptop. "Wow!" he exclaimed with a laugh. "You... What do you call a person who breaks into other people's screen images?"

"A hacker," came the reply. "See, this is the list of all the challenges they're going to set us and what they expect… Oh no."

"What is it?" queried Bob.

Gary showed him what was written on the laptop:

The challenge of the roommates. For a ruling body, diplomacy and a compromising, clear mindset are some of the most important skills needed. The nominees have been given some normal beds and one overly grand one. If they possess these skills, they should find a peaceful way to decide on the sleeping arrangements, such as taking turns on the grand bed or simply giving it up in a civil manner. Those who don't possess these skills in any way will fight each other immediately.

"Crap," muttered Caesium.

"Don't worry, I can hack into their near-primitive security system and wipe the footage from their security cameras," said Gary. He then began to type frantically on his laptop.

"Let's get to know each other more," offered Caesium, trying to start a conversation. "Why do you guys want to become gods? And where are you from? Bob, you go first."

"I want to become a god so I can save people instead of just being helpless all the time," Bob said. "I come from Boltsdon. It's a tiny district on the edge of the capital, I think."

"That's so poor!" exclaimed Jeff. "Oakley and I live on the Isle of Sparks."

"Apparently, it's where Mekanyon thought of technology," boasted Oakley. "The mansions are massive, with so much more tech than your average house and everyone's rolling in cash! Beat that!"

"Sheesh, you like to brag," muttered Caesium. "Why do you want to become gods when nobody would worship jerks like you?"

"You can talk!" snapped Oakley. "And why wouldn't we want to become gods? You get your own set of powers and the respect of an entire system! Besides, aren't the current gods, except for Mekanyon, a bit old-fashioned? We can help them get more with the times."

"Yeah, that," agreed Jeff. "But, for me, that's a secondary reason. It's clear the stygir are going to try to get rid of their biggest threat sooner or later. If they succeed in destroying Industria and killing Mekanyon, the system's doomed. Plus, we're trapped by the Void and cornered in our own system! So I'm going to get so strong that I can wipe out the stygir completely."

"That's awesome!" Bob congratulated him. "But isn't that also a bit ambitious?"

"Mind your own business!" Oakley spat before Jeff could reply. "You can talk! How the hell can you not be helpless if you can't climb onto a flat ledge?"

"Helpless would best describe the first non-sacrifice to get killed in the battle royale," spoke up Gary. "Look at the records of Oakley's battle: 'He randomly fired and missed all his shots. His teammate Jeff selflessly sacrificed himself to keep him alive. This was in vain, though: Oakley just squealed for help in a corner until Gary Raptor printed out a sniper rifle and silenced him.'" The hacker grinned smugly at Oakley.

"Hey, besides the dwarf none of us have fought before!" protested Oakley. "What about you, huh? Tell us about yourself!"

"I come from a little-known town, New Baux. I just want to be known as something other than a hacker," stated Gary.

"As for me, I want to see the sights of Atlas," said Caesium. "I've only ever seen tiny bits of Primium and Ferraheim, but as a god I'll be questing all across the system." He then added with a chuckle, "Plus, I've got to make my family proud or they'll kill me!"

At that moment, the holoceiver in their room gonged, and a picture of Cognitio flashed up. From a small screen on the side of it, Bob could see that all the dormitories' holoceivers had opened communications as well.

"All nominees meet me at the ground floor," ordered Cognitio. "I have prepared your next lessons."

"Another battle?" a voice asked.

"No. Whilst combat has become the main duty of the deities, there is more to ruling a system than battle. In some cases, mind is greater than might, and I would hate to be protected and ruled by the uneducated. I have prepared an hour of each of the three sciences."

A chorus of gasps and surprised noises could be heard from the various dormitories.

"How will we get stronger from that?" asked Jeff. "If the stygir attack, are we going to solve their equations for them or something?"

Similar comments poured in like heavy rain until Cognitio called for silence. "All of you, listen up!" he snapped. "The next one to issue a single complaint, a single grumble or act annoyingly in any way can wave farewell to touching the Heavenspire!"

There was silence.

Cognitio went on, "To the 5.45% of you who didn't start moaning, you are on the path to becoming a deity; you will do what it takes to lose the mortal life without complaint! I must warn you that I have a very perceptive sense of hearing and have picked out those in the remaining 94.55%."

There came another period of silence.

"Aeterno himself, besides being Drakon's greatest warrior, was also a very successful scholar, and he carried that scholastic mind into battle. The ability to accurately predict the trajectory of projectiles, from energy blasts to fireballs, will help you aim them perfectly and avoid your enemies. Battles against the stygir will happen in space, and you need to know the various laws that govern it to fight at your best. The various divinite reactions, from being immortalised to using deity powers, should be studied in detail. The stygir themselves and their minions need to be learned about. And, of course, there is more to being a deity than war. Agriculture, construction and similar skills are necessary. See where this is coming from? Meet me on ground floor," commanded Cognitio.

"I guess there's no choice, if the next person to annoy him is going home," muttered Jeff, switching off the holoceiver.

"It's an empty threat," stated Oakley. "The system can't lose protectors at a time like this."

"We're not anything yet," Caesium reminded him. "The protectors will be those who work. Come on, Bob. Let's go."

Bob, Caesium, Gary and Jeff took the lift downstairs, hoping the next three hours would be more enjoyable than they sounded.

Upon catching sight of Cognitio, Bob and Caesium questioned him about the creatures they had encountered in Inferd.

"Oh... them. Such matters do not concern you," was the brief reply Cognitio gave. "However, we will learn about them in a couple of hours' time." Upon catching sight of Gary, he suddenly turned towards him with a glare likely to terrify the stygir's viruses. "Somebody hacked into the system. Do you know anything about this?"

Gary shook his head.

"Lies!" spat Cognitio. "I might not be Mekanyon, but I can use a basic security system! Give me your computer now!"

Sheepishly, Gary handed him the laptop.

"I CAN TELL A PRINTED FAKE APART FROM THE REAL THING!" his teacher roared. "The real one, please!"

Gary handed it over with a startled expression on his face.

Cognitio then regained his calm composure. "OK, nominees, enter the lab in the top-left corner of this floor. And, by the way, Oakley Jenkins, you will come out and show yourself!"

Oakley had no choice but to do as he was told, and, a wingbeat later, he and Cognitio were soaring up the Below-Heavenspire. The nominees would have looked up to see the scene unfold, but the feeling of Stygiomiasma turned their attention elsewhere.

A featureless, soundless, black creature skulked across the ground floor. It was anthropomorphic, but, instead of hands and feet, it had tapered extensions that were likely to be some form of blades. Bob recognised it as a karapo, which were the stygir's basic fighting troops. Everyone was petrified at the sight of it; the braver souls tried to attack it, but it knocked them all to the floor with a swipe of its arms. The rest seemed to be rooted to the ground, transfixed by an aura of fear it was producing that was similar to that of the macroviruses.

With one leg, it scratched out a message on the floor:

Invasion will happen soon. The death ray orbiting your machine world may have stopped my masters from taking the divinite, but their Void still circles the Atlas system, out of the orbiting machine's range. Remember that they can create beings like us. And then those beings adapt, forming new ones. We have a plan to stop the ray, and the Void will become all.

Nothing seemed to happen after that. Seconds seemed to prolong into hours. The creature could have killed them all, but, for some unknown reason given to it by the stygir, it didn't. Instead, it became formless – a whisper of dense gas traversing the air until sight could not find it.

Cognitio flew down to ground floor with Oakley just after it had disappeared fully.

"And guess what?" sniffed Oakley. "I was right! Wait, why have so many of you tripped?"

"Caesium, Jeff, Baldaer… why are most of you on the floor?" Cognitio asked.

"Sty… gir," spluttered a liskous, getting to her feet. "Look! They engraved a message on the floor!"

"What are you on about?" queried Cognitio. "Do you mean to say they used invisible ink?"

Everyone looked to the floor, only to find a clear surface and a growing feeling of dread in the pits of their stomachs.

The message was gone.

EIGHT

Back on Primium, Bob had been fascinated by the sciences, but all he could feel was unease as the two encounters with the stygir creatures played over and over again in his head. What shook him even more was Cognitio's lackadaisical attitude towards them.

Once again, all his teacher gave was a dismissive, "Such matters do not concern you," and a speech on how they would cover them in biology. After learning about the ominous creature that had overpowered them, the nominees were then given a history class in which they covered the devious threats in Atlas pre-Stygir war.

"The cults were as powerful as they were deranged, some being the size of entire nations," Cognitio droned on. "Among the deadliest were the Thinkers of Mordrev, a group who worshipped a silver idol and sacrificed thousands to it, claiming they were gaining 'forbidden knowledge'. But the cults weren't the only threats to Atlas. There was once a man called—"

"Nathan Paxton!" exclaimed Jeff.

"Good," grinned Cognitio. "Can you tell me more about him?"

"He was a pyromaniac who used to terrorise Primium," Jeff said energetically. "Eventually the dwarf and elf warriors called Aesik and Volundur imprisoned him, but then he escaped. There are so many conspiracy theories about him and when I find him, I'm going to kick his—"

"Thank you, Jeff," Cognitio interjected. "All of you, go research some battles the warriors of old fought and make notes on key turning points and strategies used."

"I can't believe the enemy is so close," Bob whispered to Caesium whilst looking at a holobook full of equations. "What did it mean by 'adapt'?"

"In the war, when we found a way to drive back the stygir, they would always create a new type of minion to counter it," Caesium explained. "They've tried that countless times with Industria but failed every time. Still, isn't it suspicious how Cognitio seems to know about the stygir creatures here but won't tell us? He could be on their side."

Everyone around them was whispering of the same thing, but that was far from the only mystery around: apparently, somebody had seen a grey, rotting army in Inferd and another had felt Stygiomiasma in their room.

"Silence, all of you!" commanded Cognitio. "Quit whispering. Talk all you want when we get to group work."

"I'm going to find out what's going on," wrote Caesium on his parchment, and he showed it to Bob.

Using his plastic stylus, Bob swiped in the air, switching between the pages of his holobook until he found an empty page. He then switched his stylus to writing mode and wrote a reply before swiping in the air to send the projected page to Caesium's table. His reply read, "So am I, but maybe after this lesson, just in case missing this would makes us less likely to become gods."

"Really?" sighed Cognitio. "Note passing is noticeable enough, but with a holobook? Bob, go to room one on floor 1,347 and get some parchment."

Bob hurried out of the room. He ran in the direction of the lift, before making a slight detour to where the phasing ladder to Inferd glowed. Failing to phase was not an option – the explosion would alert Cognitio. Steeling his nerves, he placed his hands on the ladder. A flash of pink later and he was in the nightmarish world.

Whilst it had been ominous before, now that Bob was alone, the realm was an even greater terror. *Deities don't fear,* he kept on telling himself as he walked through the capricious terrain. He looked around, but it was impossible to make out the forms of any stygir creatures against the obscure, black scene. The fact that they made no sound didn't help either.

The room he told me to go to was very high up, so I have some time before Cognitio realises something's wrong, Bob thought. *But I still have to do this quickly.*

Suddenly, a blaze of orange lit up the darkness. Bob activated his turbine suit and soared towards it. The light seemed to come from some sort of fire, and it illuminated a vast cavern as well as a series of pitfalls riddling the floor. It was at that moment that the turbine suit played up. Screaming as his suit flung him around like a paper hat in a storm, Bob had to use every muscle in his body to not land in one of the pitfalls. Eventually, he slammed into the floor, missing one of the deeper ones by a centimetre.

Then they came: macroviruses, crawling towards him by the thousand. Groaning with pain, Bob tried to get himself up, but he failed. The macroviruses began to crawl over him, their aura of fear greater at such a close distance. He told himself that he felt no fear, but his heart was pumping faster than ever before. Sweat poured down his face, and his body began to shake against his will. Any second now, they would attack.

"That's just pathetic!" Bob didn't recognise the owner of that voice. It was feminine and thick with disgust.

"HELP!" he howled. "HELP ME, PLEASE!"

"Why do you think they aren't attacking you?" the voice asked. "I'm not sure if humans know this much, but these stygir creatures attack those who are in total fear of them."

Bob could feel it now; amidst the Stygiomiasma, there was another cold force: a strong and bitter wind. The macroviruses covering his eyes were blown away and standing in front of him was an elf who he recognised from before, staring down at him with a look of contempt. She wore a white robe and a silver circlet with many intricate, glowing amulets around her neck. Her right hand was raised and from it came a potent wind that swept over Bob's body, pushing the macroviruses just out of reach of infection. With a simple flick of her wrist, the macroviruses were sent flying in all directions. Another flick, and they all ignited.

"You're the false second place, aren't you?" she asked Bob. "Shouldn't you be in class with the rest? Now that there are two here, I can't phase out of here."

"Shouldn't you be in class as well?" replied Bob.

"No, I know all of that stuff already. I'm part of the Sovereign Sect, and I have work I need to do. Cognitio knows that, and I'm excused."

"What's the Sovereign Sect?" asked Bob.

"What do you humans teach each other besides how to fiddle with wires?" she sighed. "It's the elven ruling body, and is like your government, but it's not filthy and corrupt."

Although Bob was insulted, he felt amazed as well; she looked and sounded around his age, and he couldn't imagine a young teenager being a politician.

"Anyway, I finished the work and now I'm trying to figure out why there are stygir creatures here," she told him. "What are you doing here? Did you get lost without your gadgets to tell you where you were? Or are you trying to get a victory again by doing nothing? It won't work."

Then Bob remembered who she was: the elf that had been taken out of the battle royale by the ground opening up beneath her feet.

"Actually, I'm trying to find out the same thing," Bob said. "Isn't Cognitio acting suspiciously? He could be with them." No sooner had he said this than he felt that his turbine suit weighed more than ever before. Looking down, he saw rocks had somehow attached themselves to his legs. He tried to activate his turbines, but they were immobilised.

"So, a Stygir War veteran is likely to be our enemy?" the elf spat. "What about a race that drove out two others and trashed their planet?"

After a second, he felt a spark of electricity against his skin, causing him to cry out in pain.

"Think about what you're saying, human," she snarled.

"OK! I'M SORRY!" yelled Bob. "GET ME OUT OF THIS PRISON!" The rock exploded, knocking him to the floor. "Don't you have to chant?" he asked. "I thought magic is controlled by chanting."

"Lesser magicians may have to," she stated. "I am a seculous, which is a magician of such calibre that I don't need to do so, and I can dispel other spells at will. And, once again, the limit of human intelligence shows itself – magic comes from the mind, obviously. No wonder your race could never use it properly, always mixing it with runes and slate-scales before ditching it completely."

"I get it! You hate humans!" Bob cried. "I understand why, but just think for a bit. Am I the government and did I change Primium? Just think!" He walked off in the opposite direction to the pitfalls. *There are bound to be some like her,* he told himself. *Most can't be as open-minded as Caesium.*

"Wait, human!" The elf flew behind him on a gust of wind. "Repeat those last few sentences."

"Ummm…" Bob hesitated. "Am I the government?"

"You actually seem to disassociate yourself from the fools. Is it that you wish to be elf or dwarf, or that you're against technology?"

"I'm not against it," stated Bob. "I just don't see why there has to be so much battling over it."

"Because our homes were destroyed for it. All the glades and forests that we had lived in throughout the ages were destroyed, and so were the dwarves' caverns. Even Eldrit and Eitri, two constantly bickering gods put their differences aside when Primium was trashed."

"Why don't you just live on Gaia?" Bob asked.

In response, she gestured and a gust of strong wind hit him. "*The moon?*" she exclaimed. "Not only is it too small but it's also close enough to Primium to interfere with our magic!"

"Sorry, I didn't realise," Bob apologised. "I see why you hate it, but I just can't imagine life without it." Taking a page out of Caesium's book, he hastily thought of a way to continue the conversation. "You're part of the elf government, right? Is it one government for the whole planet like we have? And what's happening in politics with technology?"

"The Sovereign Sect," she corrected him. "And yeah, it's a planetary ruling body. But it's chaos. Everyone hates technology, but everyone has their own response to it. Some are trying to come up with a technology-jamming spell, some are shouting at your government every day, and some are even thinking of war."

Bob gasped. He couldn't imagine another few years in the shelter, not when he'd barely had a year to experience the world. "What about you?" he questioned.

"Anything but war. We're still allies and the stygir are who we really should be attacking. Peace would be best for all of us, like it always has been. Say, you're reasonable, for a human. Open-minded. People like you should be in the government, not rich fools in gaudy houses."

"Bob Solis! Imryth of the Sovereign Sect! What are you doing here?" A robotic whirring heralded the arrival of Mekanyon. Even though his face was obscured by his helmet visor, it was clear he wasn't pleased.

Hurriedly, Bob began to explain; Imryth fixed the god with a death stare.

"I have telepathy, remember?" prompted Mekanyon. "It's OK, I'm not mad at you; I'm impressed you have a thirst for knowledge and answers. Those 'stygir creatures' were created by me; they're automatons with the same powers and abilities to give you something to train against. Cognitio knows about them, so that's why he's not alarmed. They were meant to be kept a secret, so that the more heroic amongst you would try to figure out why they're in the Below-Heavenspire. For we are trying to train your will, your ability to act in a way you believe to be just, and of your own accord. That is the greatest quality for any hero to have." Suddenly, a static sound similar to a gasp escaped Mekanyon's mouth.

"What is it?" asked Bob.

"That… that karapo from your mind… I programmed my automatons to stay within Inferd!"

"But our defences would've been alerted if—"

"The stygir can adapt! We don't know how quickly and they could've made creatures undetectable to any security system!"

*

Back in the original reality, alarms were sounding on four planets as an attack began.

NINE

Once out of Inferd, the three were greeted by all the nominees in ranks and files, led by Cognitio and the deities.

Aeterno began giving out orders in a stoic manner. "I know you've only had one fight and a few hours of science to prepare you for this, but you must try your hardest. At stake are your homes and possibly the whole system. I believe it logical for us to all defend our own homes, since we know the surrounding areas better. After we phase, those non-liskous should stay close to me, for I can use my powers to speed up the time it takes for you to reach your homes." He then caught sight of Mekanyon. "They've done it, haven't they? Made creatures immune to Industria."

"More than that: I can sense they're beginning to destroy it!" exclaimed Mekanyon. "I'll repair it!" With that, he left.

As the god of technology sped off, Bob checked his gun and coal supply. He'd need both to work perfectly if he was to survive. As the army of nominees advanced towards the phasing ladder, he heard Caesium's voice shout, "GOOD LUCK, BOB!" and Imryth's follow up with, "BE STRONG, HUMAN!"

Bob woke up on Drakon to a horrific sight. Brushing the rubble of the Below-Heavenspire off him, he could see the ground was littered with corpses: liskous and all manner of strange creatures. Above him, an aerial fight was commencing with units of staff-wielding liskous and their basilous allies battling against their shadowy foes but with no sign of the actual stygir themselves. Yet there was no time for taking in details.

A fleet of spaceships waited for those from other planets. Whilst Bob had never flown one before, there was no time for a tutorial. Warily, he entered the nearest one and began pushing random controls. Aeterno made a gesture similar to the one used by Imryth to perform the wind spell, and – in a blur of space, stars and planets – Bob had arrived on his home planet.

No sooner had he landed than his spaceship – now with a shredded cockpit – was under attack by legions of battle-thirsty karapo. Hurriedly, Bob got out of the spaceship. By firing his blaster, he managed to kill some of the ones around him, but they were replaced by twice as many in an instant. As if they were one being, they charged forwards with startling speed. In response, Bob activated his turbine suit, and the ones in front blew back into the blades behind them in a domino effect.

Not waiting to see if it had worked, he ran to the nearest populated area. It seemed strange how less powerful they were compared to the one in the Below-Heavenspire, but there was no time to think of that. If that many creatures had attacked a lone person, fathomless amounts would be ravaging the streets and cities.

No one was in sight, but everything had been razed to the ground. In the next street, there was nothing; nor in the street after that. Bob shuddered as he realised that his own street could be under attack and in dire need of help.

He soon arrived at his street, and saying his fears were true would be an understatement.

What resembled a hornet but was twice the size of a house flew after a crowd of the street's citizens, with the creature's total silence making the crowd's screams more audible. Its mandibles shot out on a tendril of shadow and grabbed a line of its prey before retracting. Unfazed by their screams, the two parts of its mouth closed down slowly, crushing them one by one. Surrounding it were vast swarms of macroviruses, scuttling into each house and returning with their ranks bolstered.

In order to get the hornet-like creature's attention, Bob loaded his blaster with coal and blew off its mandibles, taking care not to harm the survivors. Its attention transferred to him immediately, and the creature turned around and unsheathed a large stinger, dripping with some sort of viscous, dark liquid. Before Bob could react, the stinger extended, impaling him through his left shoulder. The liquid stuck to him like a powerful adhesive, leaving him glued to the wall. Pain seared through his body, but most of his turbine suit was still intact. Activating it proved useless, however, as the liquid seeped in between the propeller blades, rendering them useless. The hornet-like creature retracted its stinger and blood spurted from Bob's wound. Flowing at a fast rate from the massive hole made in his shoulder, the crimson downpour was a sign he was going to bleed to death. Leaving him for dead, the creature began to attack a nearby house.

His house.

Bob struggled and screamed, trying to get out of his sticky prison; all he did, however, was make his wound bleed more. Macroviruses scuttled towards him. Where were the other human deities and nominees? Where was Primium's army? He was alone and helpless. The shadowy macroviruses approached. With the last of his strength, he just about managed to pull the trigger on his blaster. A few died.

Just as the swarm pounced, blaster fire decimated it. From around the corner, a platoon of human soldiers bearing energy blasters rushed to Bob's aid.

Their leader began to speak to him. "I'm Sergeant Aigari of platoon 365. Who are you?"

As Aigari's men tended to Bob's wound and tried to free him from the liquid, Bob was able to muster a few details: his name, the deity training and what he knew about the creatures attacking his street.

Aigari continued, "We are sorry we couldn't come earlier, but the government didn't have enough supplies for us after three-quarters of the supplies were taken by the elves and dwarves. Don't blame them, though; it's not their fault the stygir attacked."

"Save… my… house… quick!" Bob groaned.

Aigari turned and fired several well-aimed shots at the hornet-like creature, severing its wings and abdomen. What remained of it slumped to the floor and was disposed of rapidly by more soldiers.

No sooner had it died than its corpse exploded, sending out a wave of umbral force.

Bob and the soldiers were knocked to the floor, but their armour managed to shield them from the brunt of the blast. Unfortunately, the wound in Bob's shoulder opened up again and started bleeding with more vigour.

That was the least of his worries, though. The remnants of many bodies littered the ground in front of him, like autumn leaves. Some were still stirring, yet some had fallen still. All had an expression of the gravest fear on their faces.

Nausea and horror gripped him, and also guilt. Before he knew it, tears were mixing with the blood pouring from his wounds. *If I had dodged the stinger, I could've saved them!* he thought melancholically.

The soldiers reached for their dropped medical kits and rushed to the sides of those who could be saved. Bob could only remain motionless. All manner of stygir creatures approached the scene slowly, drawn to the explosion like moths to a flame.

Bob couldn't keep his eyes open any longer. As he slumped to the floor, Aigari and many other soldiers rushed to help him, unaware of or deciding to ignore the approaching enemies. Reinforcements, led by someone typing frantically on a laptop, appeared, but it seemed they were too late.

The world for Bob darkened sluggishly to the shade of the stygir creatures and then vanished.

*

Coming back to his senses, Bob expected to be in the unknown place people go when they die or at least in a hospital, but he was in neither. Looking around, he saw a familiar street, Aigari and a crowd of soldiers, plus a liskous god fighting in the background. Wait, what?

"What did I miss?" he asked the sergeant.

"You were about to bleed to death, but, luckily, your friend with the laptop printed off some sort of healing device to save you," Aigari explained.

Gazing down at his left shoulder, he saw a healing unit taped to the wound, pulsing as it slowly regenerated him.

"He said it would regrow your flesh in about an hour. Then Lapideis here came along with an army of liskous; they've defeated the enemies on Drakon and have come to help. Now, we must hurry!" she declared.

The two rushed to the fight scene, only to find a one-sided fight had commenced. Lapideis, who was a mountain of earth-brown scale lacerated by endless scars, cleaved through foe after foe with his claws, instead of using the traditional staff, whilst manipulating the earth to swallow and impale more. The rest of the soldiers were supporting him with fire, along with Gary, who was printing off grenades.

The stygir creatures swarmed at them by the thousand, yet not a single human died. For crushing the enemy was a side task to Lapideis. Using his deity power, he created walls of rock to block the shadowy blades and bullets, then modified them to make fortresses for the soldiers to shoot safely from. Karapo hacked and slashed at him, carving more scars on his scaly hide, like red tally marks, yet he was unfazed and knocked his foes aside as if they were mannequins. Bob fired at a horde of macroviruses, whittling down their number, whilst Aigari trained her blaster on a creature resembling a large, spiked ball. It seemed like victory was assured.

That was until what seemed like a thousand times more than the unit they had just faced charged at them from countless directions. Macroviruses and karapo burst from the floor in their thousands, jumped off buildings and appeared from behind houses, led by a six-armed humanoid riding a creature of the same hornet-resembling species Bob had faced before. Even with the unit of soldiers, the amazing properties of Gary's laptop and Lapideis' deity power, it seemed like the tables had fully turned. Bob activated his turbine suit, but it was in vain; these creatures seemed to be impervious to the gales created.

"WE'VE DEFEATED THEM ONCE," roared Lapideis, wreathing himself in jagged rock and slamming into the stygir creatures' leader.

Almost unaffected, the six-armed humanoid outstretched his hands and hammers formed in them.

"WE CAN DO IT AGAIN!" the god of earth yelled, even as his layer of rock was shattered.

The fragments of stone grew into jagged stakes and flew towards the hammer wielder's mount. Soldiers gave him supporting fire, yet most had lost morale.

Three questions burned in each of their heads: *Where is Mekanyon? What is he doing with Industria? Have the stygir's new creations succeeded?*

Lapideis' fortresses buckled under the horde. He paused in his fight to try to repair them, but a swing from a hammer knocked him to the floor. Stone crumbled and a swarm of black surged forwards. A few minutes later, nearly all of Aigari's men had been ripped apart or had supplemented the macroviruses' numbers. The survivors, including Lapideis, were barely staying alive.

Suddenly, a large beam of some sort of energy lit up the entire planet in an inferno of unearthly light, which engulfed Primium for several minutes. When it subsided, the surviving fighters were still in one piece, somehow not blinded, and their surroundings were also unscathed. Only their enemies had perished. Looking up, they could see two beams of the same energy starting from a metallic turret near Gaia and travelling far into space.

Everyone let out a large cheer as they realised what had happened. Everyone except Bob, who slumped to the floor, seeing the deaths of those he had failed to save playing over and over again in his head. Nobody else seemed to notice, though, and they continued to revel.

Mekanyon descended to the scene, his armour dented and the light behind his visor flickering like a candle in the wind. Upon noticing Bob, Mekanyon limped towards him, with every step an ordeal. "It is… good that… you use one of… my first… inventions," he spluttered. "Yet just remember that technology… is about the future… not the past…"

Bob continued to stare at the ground, still melancholic.

"Oh! I'm—" Racked by a coughing fit, the god fell to the floor. "Sorry. It was not your fault… but that of the enemy. It happens… sometimes there are those even a god can't save. Don't worry… Industria avenged them…"

Everyone turned to look at Mekanyon, as the usually majestic god was sprawled on the floor.

Mekanyon continued, "The reason I'm in a weakened state is that... well, you need to know Industria's mechanics first. It's powered by a legendary engine... that converts the kinetic energy gained from orbit. An army of adapted stygir creatures had destroyed... not only the control panel but also said engine. With my deity powers of technology, I could act as the engine, but at the cost of a large amount of my energy."

"Energy?" asked Bob.

"Deity powers are like an exercise routine," explained Lapideis. "Once you've mastered certain capabilities of them, they can be used without expending energy, but to use more powerful and ambitious capabilities risks not being able to use the power or having a fatigued soul. Both side effects can sometimes last months... You prove yourself as one of our greatest protectors again, Mekanyon."

"Thank you, Lapideis. Unfortunately, both side effects have affected me. Industria has no power source... if it is to repel future inventions, we need to get a new one quick. I have a quest... for all available deities."

The light turned to a sickly green that died out every other second; Mekanyon passed out, and Lapideis held him up before he could hit the floor.

"If so, then you should not join that quest, my lord, until you regain your health completely," said Aigari. "How do we power it?"

The god of technology was able to regain his consciousness for a sparse amount of time, and managed to say, "Find... a shifter core... to power Industria."

Everyone gasped at the mention of the legendary artefact referred to in liskous myth; described as a potato-sized glowing rock, it was said to be able to affect certain lifeforms in a variety of ways, depending what kind it was.

"A shifter core!" breathed Lapideis. "Like the one from the fable *The Catacombs of Knowledge*? That does explain why we don't feel its fire yet the stygir do. I always thought those rocks were myths, but maybe he knew something we didn't. I'll take Mekanyon to the nearest hospital before going on this quest. Nominees, head back towards the spaceships!" he ordered before flying away.

"You fought great, Bob," praised Gary. "I thought we were dead though… Industria is something else."

"You fought well too," replied Bob.

He and Gary set off for their spaceships, which they reached eventually, accompanied by Aigari, who had some questions to ask the nominees. Besides a few mechanics, who had arrived to patch up the damaged crafts, the only other one there was Oakley.

"I have a question for all nominees who fought in this area," said Aigari in a soft, compassionate tone. "The military need help identifying the fallen, so they can be remembered. Do any of you know anyone who passed away?"

"Of course not!" snapped Oakley. "I don't come from this dump; I just came here because things finished up pretty quickly in my area and Mekanyon's meant to be here. And what do you mean 'the fallen'? Nobody died at all in my area; if anyone died, they deserve a medal for dying from such a—"

Bob's gun made an audible crack as it connected with Oakley's jaw. Enraged, he prepared to strike again, but Aigari and Gary held him back.

"THESE PEOPLE WERE JUST LIKE YOU AND ME!" he roared, trying in vain to break free of those holding him. "And if they were too weak, isn't a god meant to protect them, not mock them? Huh?"

There was no reply, just a whimper of pain.

*

The journey back to Drakon was completely silent.

TEN

Back in the alternate reality, Bob watched the news from a TV outside Cognitio's office. After they had arrived in the Below-Heavenspire, Oakley had told the emissary about the unprovoked beating he'd received, with Jeff as his key witness; naturally, the result was that he had been sent to sit outside Cognitio's office as he awaited his punishment. For the most part, the news had been about the stygirs' attack, but only Primium was mentioned. The footage of the scene showed the god Aurik and the goddess Kosma defeating wave after wave of creatures, their powers of seeing the future and increasing success working in excellent tandem. There was nothing about the shifter core or the fight on Bob's street, but, then again, that was on the outskirts of the places attacked, unlike the central cities the two deities named were protecting.

"Tension between our race, elves and dwarves has been increasing," droned the news reporter. He was surrounded by a large amount of soldiers, and Bob could make out Aigari in the uniformed crowd. The reporter went on, "This is mainly due to the fact that our army didn't have enough supplies, since the elves and dwarves took most of them. People predict a war will happen soon—"

The reporter was cut off as a surge of noise erupted from the army. Bob expected it to be a protest, but it wasn't. It was a cheer. The soldiers, with the exception of Aigari, were jubilant at this statement. The sergeant who had helped defend Boltsdon tried to make her voice heard, but a single cry had no impact on such a massive crowd.

Where are the others? Bob thought frantically. Normally, when something like this happened, there was more than one supporter of peace present, but they were nowhere in sight at that moment. His stomach lurched at the thought of even more destruction, especially against his allies.

"Come in!" demanded Cognitio.

Bob switched off the TV and headed into the office. It was very frugal accommodation, more of a small cave with furniture than anything else. At a desk, by which his teacher was watching a hologram of Oakley explaining the attack from the infirmary, he noticed there were documents piled up like paper skyscrapers. They were stacked everywhere possible other than the floor. Although they were in liskous glyphs rather than the human, elf and dwarf alphabet, he could tell by the pictures that they were all about different types of shifter core. On looking closer, Bob could see that Cognitio wasn't paying any attention to the hologram, maybe except for by hearing, and focusing on a pile of such documents.

"So Industria generates power through energy attained by planetary orbit, and projects it via one of these..." Cognitio muttered under his breath, before turning to look at Bob.

Oakley had finished talking and the hologram switched off.

"Bob, why did you attack Oakley unprovoked? I did so, but on a much lesser scale and with reason. Yet I cannot make assumptions without your side of the story. What happened?" enquired Cognitio.

"There were people who died," Bob forced the words out, "Lots of them. And he was mocking them, saying they deserved a medal for dying. I don't know what came over me, I just got really angry and—"

"Filth!" spat Cognitio. "Does that boy have no respect?" He slammed a fist on his table, sending papers flying everywhere in a white maelstrom. "I'll have to move the lesson on discipline to way earlier in the training than I expected. And, Bob, I know you've probably heard this before, but those deaths weren't your fault. In fact, this stygir attack resulted in the fewest deaths out of all our encounters with them, proving that your efforts were brilliant."

At that moment, heavy footsteps could be heard as thunderous noises echoing throughout the office. Cognitio dismissed this with his usual aware-but-bored look. Suddenly, a figure appeared behind Bob, his chest a massive bulk, his arms muscular, and his facial features squashed in the middle of his small head and flanked by large ears. Realising what the creature was, Bob screamed and raised his blaster.

He had heard theories that, supposedly, when humans, elves and dwarves had just evolved from a monkey-like creature, they had fought bitter wars for supremacy against another, more feral group of semi-sentient species – ogres, orcs and trolls to name a few. Although their foes were hulking brutes, the gap in intelligence eventually drove them to their extinction. Or so it was thought.

For some reason, the troll in front of him carried no club or boulder, but, then again, the claws on the end of each muscular arm looked like they could shred Bob's turbine suit as if it were paper. Just before Bob could pull the trigger, Cognitio swung his staff and a gust of wind knocked the Joule 1.0 from Bob's grasp.

"And you think you're better than Oakley?" Cognitio scolded. "Just because Antony is a troll, it does not mean he is going to hurt you!"

Looking into Antony's eyes, Bob saw no killing intent, just a docile and puzzled gaze.

"The little-known truth," Cognitio began to explain, "is that, way before divinite was discovered, the trolls and their kindred species fled to the region of space now swallowed up by the Void in order to escape the prejudice against them."

"Oh no, don't worry; it's fine!" responded the troll with a chuckle, and he gave Bob a clawed hand to shake.

Bob shook it gingerly, still a bit taken aback at meeting this supposedly hostile and cannibalistic being. However, whatever views the scientists on Primium held about trolls, Antony was the opposite: approachable and docile, albeit a bit eccentric and weird. At one point, he began cracking a seemingly endless series of jokes, which Cognitio laughed at no matter how unfunny they were, and Bob felt obliged to do the same.

Then, Antony looked startled, as if remembering something, and pulled out a board that projected a series of holograms. "Mekanyon is still in hospital, and the others are all happy and healthy on their quest!" he reported to Cognitio, who nodded in response. "Eldrit and Eitri are fighting again, though."

"What a surprise," Cognitio sighed. "When don't they?" Seeing Bob looking somewhat puzzled, the emissary began to explain, "Antony is in charge of monitoring the conditions and whereabouts of each deity, and he does so with the help of this board device. It can tell us whether they're safe or not, what condition they're in, and what they're doing."

"Don't worry, I won't get 'board'!" added the troll.

Bob tried his best not to wince.

On closer inspection, each of the device's holograms was in the shape of one of the gods, and all of them were represented, with the health status, name and powers underneath each one. Most of them were grey and in a sleeping position, and Bob didn't recognise these. When he asked about them, he was told that these pallid figures represented the deities who had died at the hands of the stygir, and were kept on the board so that they wouldn't be forgotten when new ones were elected.

"Wait…" Bob began to ask as a suspicious thought crossed his mind. "How long have you been doing this?"

"Since the war began," replied Antony.

That's very strange, thought Bob. *If Mekanyon invented technology near the end of the war, how could this device exist? There has to be an explanation.*

Before Bob could pry further, all the living deities' holograms began to flicker, with the light sustaining their forms slowly fading. A moment later, red warning signs lit up the board like ominous flames.

Cognitio switched from his calm demeanour to his furious state, letting out a storm of shouts of disbelief. "NO WAY!" he gasped. "ALL THE DEITIES ARE IN GRAVE DANGER? WHO WILL FETCH THE SHIFTER CORE NOW?"

"Can't you send us out?" asked Bob.

"I was forced to send you out once, accompanied by deities. Are you asking me to send you out without them? You have little to no experience, and you want to do something even immortals have failed at?" questioned Cognitio.

"Cognitio, your meeting is now!" an automaton alarm began to call. "Cognitio, your meeting is—"

"*Already?*" exclaimed Cognitio. "I have to try to stop war from breaking out at this conference. Farewell!" Grabbing a handful of documents, he then dashed out of the office, looking like a deep-blue blur, and headed towards the nearest phasing ladder.

Antony began checking his machine instinctively to see if it had malfunctioned. Bob just walked out of the office, unsure what to do. His head was a swirling storm of thoughts, with the problems of the war and the shifter core burning in his head like embers. A subconscious thought awoke, which was about the shelter: when the adults began to decline in number, kids as young as six were given training and information on the stygir, knowing that it would be their turn to face them and their spectral minions. What if the deities all died on this mission? What if they were the ones who needed saving this time? He would have to train and to hone his skills to a fine point that was capable of defeating anything the stygir flung at him.

At that moment, he saw Caesium waiting outside the room, wearing his armour and carrying his weapons.

"Hey Bob," the dwarf greeted him. "Cognitio just gave everyone permission to train in Inferd before rushing off somewhere. Jeff's already there, and I can't let him get stronger than me! Want to join me?"

"Yeah," replied Bob. "Do you think war will happen?"

"Nope," said Caesium. "There have been many meetings on it, but, every time, nothing happens besides arguing. This is the eleventh one, so what's going to change?"

ELEVEN

Imryth couldn't believe her ears. From her thorough training, she knew that one false move could ruin everything, and this meeting comprised a hundred of these moves. Around her, her fellow Sovereign Sect members were bickering with the human government, or rather with the holoceivers carried by drones that they had decided to send. The dwarf clan leaders were supporting them, and the liskous high scholars each played the part of a responsible parent, trying to calm both sides down. As the youngest member in the meeting, nobody paid Imryth much attention or gave her many chances to speak.

"Of course we won't attack your planet; it holds the key to stopping those shadowy half-wits, but I warn you, if any robo-cyber-techno-device comes near our quarter of space, magic bolts will take it down!" cried Volundur, the Sovereign Sect's leader, his embroidered, phoenix-feather cloak flapping behind him. His haughty pride had long been the cause of many arguments, and this was no exception. When one government member had suggested a raiding party to Arcanast and Ferraheim for supplies, the debate tower on Drakon had become a war zone.

"The chances of our victory are as large as those ears, elf," mocked one of the humans. "You won't attack our home, but we can attack yours. Besides, who has the energy blasters, and who has the swords and bows?"

"REMEMBER THE CAPTURE OF NATHAN PAXTON!" another elf hollered. "Before the deities came, a pyromaniac terrorised the crap out of Primium, and who stopped him? Volundur and Aesik. Who let him escape? Incompetent human prison guards."

"Sorry, we aren't as ancient as you geriatric fools," another human spat. "Shouldn't your carer be with you?"

"No, because we elves do not wither after a mere eighty years like you!" the same elf declared.

"This is all pride and foolishness," came the voice of Cognitio, like a calm breeze in the gale around it. "Our common enemy is the stygir, and we should team up on them before we start bickering. The fact that the deities have disappeared reinforces this – we should wait to see what they think. Anyway, those three-quarters of supplies probably belonged to the elves and dwarves to begin with. We can learn from mistakes—"

"You liskous are meant to choose your leaders based on intelligence, aren't you?" interrupted the dwarf leader Aesik Ironwill. "Well, that's clearly not the case. We should team up on these techie fools, and of course we should attack their planet, Volundur! They won't use Industria anyway, and that blasted tech god is there in a hospital. They're defenceless; defenceless, I tell you! We outnumber them, and we use two legendary arts that have helped grow and protect society for eternity. Sorry, humanity, but silver tarnishes and iron rusts if not cared for properly! The tech age is *over!*"

The elves and dwarves cheered this comment.

Imryth was about to object, but she was interrupted by a voice from a holoceiver. "Very well. The war will start in two weeks, which is unfortunate for the elves and dwarves, those disgraces to Heavenspirian society! High scholars, try to stop this war if you want, but it will not work!"

"WAIT!" shouted Imryth.

"If it's a petty insult, don't say it," sighed a high scholar.

"Where are your parents? Shouldn't it be your bedtime?" mocked one of the government.

"Give those metal pieces of crap a roasting!" egged on a member of the sect.

"I understand why some want war. Technology ruined our homes and negated the arts we spent ages practising. But this war is foolish. I know the elves are happy on Arcanast, and the dwarves are probably happy on Ferraheim. A few supplies wouldn't have changed the outcome of the stygir's assault. If anything, the previous fight should make us want to band together, to join our forces once again and push back the Void to non-existence! Not all humans are technology fanatics, not all elves are magic fanatics and not all dwarves are metalworking fanatics. This war must not go on," declared Imryth.

Everybody looked dumbfounded; they did not expect this view or the sophisticated speech that came with it.

"Well, scholars, you have one supporter. Good luck!" came the snide remark of a dwarf.

There was silence.

Volundur bristled; he raised his fist as if he were about to strike someone. "HOW... HOW COULD YOU THINK LIKE THIS?" he managed to yell. "THESE COWARDS

STEAL OUR HOMES AND APPEAR AS HOLOGRAMS!
WE HAVE DONE NOTHING WRONG!"

"But have any threatened to kill all of us or circle our system in the Void?" Imryth replied.

Volundur began a low, sonorous chant and flames began to swirl around him, but, before he could cast his spell, his cloak was set ablaze and he was knocked to the floor by a gust of air. Laughter echoed all around from the government.

"That was hilarious!" cackled one hologram face. "Because of that, we'll arrange a scenario for you to at least have one chance at ending this war. Cognitio, you run some sort of school, don't you? Send out your students to find that shifter core Mekanyon told us about. Fix Industria, and we'll allow for a few negotiations."

"But some are just kids!" protested Cognitio. "None have experience—"

"And yet they're your only chance at ending this war. Take it or leave it," offered the same hologram speaker.

"Very well," accepted Cognitio with gritted teeth. "But I and one other will join them as well!"

"Fine. Goodbye elves and dwarves; I hope you're ready for war," the hologram signed off.

The holoceivers then switched off almost in unison. The high scholars seemed a little pleased by this result, though not much, but the elves and dwarves, especially Volundur, were seething with rage.

"Out!" he roared at Imryth. "Get out! You are not a member of this ruling body anymore!"

To this, Imryth said nothing. She walked out of the debate tower with the high scholars, seemingly unfazed but crumbling on the inside. Already, she could hear the sound of weapons being sharpened from the room the debate took place in.

"It doesn't matter," reassured Cognitio, though he seemed downcast as well. "I will arrange you in teams to go and look for that core."

"That could work, but will the human government listen to us?" questioned Imryth.

However, it seemed Cognitio had a solution for that, too. "I believe they likely won't, but there is something we should do before getting the core. The deities are still in trouble, aren't they? We need to rescue them and then have them end the conflict. I believe that those warmongering fools will listen to those with authority above them. And anyone who rescues them has a right to join their ranks."

"Why aren't you a god?" asked Imryth.

"I refused," came the reply. "It's the same with Volundur and Aesik. It may seem foolish, but we are the mortal leaders of our species, so we would like to keep a mindset that doesn't take things such as not dying for granted, to better relate to our people. Liskous, elf and dwarf lifespans are centuries long anyway. More importantly, why are you a politician at your age?"

"I have always been adept in matters of the mind," Imryth told the emissary, "even for an elf. I just thought someone like me should be putting my talent to good use and helping my people."

"That is a very noble thing to do," Cognitio commended her. "But remember, you are still a child by elf standards. Should you wish to quit the Sect, feel free."

"I will quit it if I become a deity. But otherwise, I will not run from the duty I chose. Speaking of duty, we have one to fulfil right now. Let us gather those who wish to rescue the deities and find the shifter core."

Without any more conversation, the two rushed to tell the other nominees of their plan.

TWELVE

Gary typed on his laptop back in the room. He had that heard Bob, Caesium and Jeff were training in Inferd, but there were more important things to do. A few more lines of code, and he would almost be finished.

There was a knock on the door. He thought it was probably more visitors who had heard about the shifter core and wanted to ask him why he didn't just print it off. The answer would always be the same: he could only print off basic things made of basic materials, such as wood and steel, but that never satisfied the endless horde of deity wannabes. Well, he could print off two complicated substances, but they would have to wait until later. The Below-Heavenspire's security system appeared on the screen, fully accessible. Even so, something bothered him: a certain file called Document 3+1. He could not hack into it, no matter what he tried. It was not related to the plan in any way, but it irritated him that, even when the security system fell, the document remained protected. What was it? Anyway, there were more important things to do.

He could understand why some would see his actions as wrong, but he had to carry out the plan. He thought back to the plagues, the Grey Triptych and the barren world, and he knew the plan was right.

I wish I was known as something other than a hacker, he reflected.

He chuckled to himself at how easily the other four had bought his excuse.

A blue liskous entered the room. He was the one who had stolen Gary's laptop earlier on, so Gary instinctively hid it. But all the liskous did was drone on and on about some sort of crazy mission to rescue the deities, in addition to finding the core, and how they didn't have to join because it was dangerous, many had quit, blah, blah, blah.

Who would want to rescue them? *Good on the quitters!* thought Gary, but he couldn't quit. Not yet.

The blue liskous gave him a map of some sort and began droning on again. These were apparently based on his estimates. Out of the corner of his eye, Gary saw some of the locations marked as places to look and was startled to see that one was exactly where the plan was being carried out. How was he so accurate?

Gary told the blue liskous that he would not quit and would like to see that location first, his excuse being that Aurik, who had disappeared there, had helped him a lot before. The liskous acknowledged him briefly before moving on to the next dorm. Gary was jovial.

Soon, nobody would be suffering ever again.

THIRTEEN

Aigari sprinted down the alleys of Primium where soldiers weren't on lookout duty. By order of the government, deserters were shot on sight, as well as any army members that disagreed with the new war. She would not become another corpse on that heap.

Mekanyon was still hospitalised and likely didn't know about the foolish declaration. Thinking fast, Aigari had decided to alert him to the situation; if there was one voice the government would listen to, it was the god's. Of course, the location of his hospital was kept a secret by the government, but, after a quick scan through their files, she knew exactly where to go.

Abruptly, a soldier jumped out from behind a corner, his guns blazing. However, he was an amateur, and Aigari could easily dodge his fire before she delivered a headshot. As with all non-stygir kills, she regretted it immediately afterwards, but, in situations as dire as this, guilt would not prevent her from achieving her goal.

In front of her stood an old, dilapidated pharmacy. Rust streaked across it like some form of tinsel, and the windows had no panes but jagged shards across their edges.

There was no door, and she sprinted into it, hoping that some soldiers weren't using it as cover. Inside, the building looked even worse, like a slaughterhouse. Blood lined the walls in a similar manner to the rust outside, splayed across the ceiling and floor. A bookshelf held a macabre display of mutilated organs, including the skin of a liskous. Besides the gore, she could see a scrapheap of metal parts, including what appeared to be an unfinished jetpack.

"Who are you, human?" came a raspy whisper from behind her.

Against all survival instincts, she shrieked before turning around to be greeted by an odd figure. She supposed he worked there, but, instead of wearing a chemist's attire, he wore a set of thick armour that covered his entire body, with two slits for eyeholes. It was immaculate and had been shined to the point it could act as a mirror. A name was engraved on the helmet: "Alex".

"I… I have come to see Mekanyon… you're looking after him… right?" she stammered. *What race was he?* she wondered.

The armour made to suit the figure was humanoid, but there seemed to be the stub of a tail protruding from the leggings.

"Indeed. Mekanyon. The one who made technology. I'm his assistant – his best assistant," Alex gasped in the most reverent way he could. "He is downstairs in the basement of my lab. Yes, he chose my lab; my lab! Take the stairs."

Unsure what to think of him, Aigari walked down the stairs. The steps were another reminder of the building being derelict, as they moaned and splintered as her feet went down them. An unnatural chill became more prominent the further she got down the staircase. *If the stygir or their minions are down there, I must be ready,* she thought as her training kicked in automatically.

"Alex… have they got the core?" spluttered the weak voice of Mekanyon from further down.

Aigari reached a door eventually and, upon opening it, came to the weakened god. The green light in his eyes was gone completely. Whether he was still alive was unclear, although it was likely life had left him; he wouldn't move or make any noise at all, not even his telltale whirring. Out of the corner of her eye, she saw another Mekanyon. But how? Her mind had to be playing up.

The other Mekanyon still had light beneath his visor, even if it was like a dying ember. He was trying to move, but even the smallest of movements was too big a strain. "S-s-s-t-y-g-g-i-r," he spluttered. "N-n-o-t sure what it's planning… g-g-g-et… help…" Then his light disappeared completely.

At this point, a crucial detail stabbed Aigari's mind like a knife. She had fought against every type of stygir creature. She had defeated every type of stygir creature. But she had never even seen one of their creators.

The first Mekanyon stood up, his body and life force fully functional.

"*Why are you attacking? Why are you here?*" asked Aigari in a demanding tone.

There was no answer. Fake Mekanyon moved soundlessly, just like its minions. A blaster extended from its armour. Thinking fast, Aigari shot multiple times at the ceiling, and it crashed down on the stygir, immobilising it. Although it tried to escape the trap, she blasted off its hands and feet. A second later, the appendages reattached themselves. Even so,

Fake Mekanyon was having trouble escaping, buying Aigari enough time to get upstairs and tell Alex.

"*Stygir defiling the technology?*" he snarled, grabbing a scalpel and storming towards the stairs.

"Wait! That thing can regenerate very fast. Do you know where any of the deities are?" queried Aigari.

"Lost, lost, lost. Public does not know? Ah, all lost, but yesterday, I, Alex, became a god of deception. Come with me, technological one."

The two hurried downstairs, where the two Mekanyons lay unchanged. Upon seeing the stygir trapped underneath the ceiling, Alex pulled an experimental-looking blaster from his armour, pointed it at the debris and fired. The debris turned to dust, freeing the stygir.

"*What?*" Aigari exclaimed.

"I told you, I'm the god of deception," replied Alex in a smug tone. The soundless god advanced towards the fear-stricken Aigari, and he was now bearing a serrated blade.

I will not be afraid, she told herself. *I will show resistance and keep fighting.* She did just that, and a blur of useless bullets, the last she had, bounced off the armour of the Fake Mekanyon.

The last words she heard were Alex's fervent, eerie pleas of, "May I dissect her, master?"

FOURTEEN

The Below-Heavenspire's canteen, typically a bustling, raucous place, was surprisingly empty, as if half the nominees had disappeared.

Strange, mused Bob as he sped down the long, narrow path that was meant to house a lengthy queue. *Maybe they're all in Inferd? No... I can't see anyone here but Caesium, besides me.*

"No weapons in the cafeteria!" snapped one of the canteen staff, a dwarf who was brandishing a ladle menacingly.

Looking down, Bob saw that he still had his Joule 1.0 tied to his waist with a makeshift holster. Despite being coated with the remains of the automatons while he was in Inferd, it was pristine in this reality.

"Hello, can you hear me?" asked the dwarf.

Reluctantly, Bob ran to his room to leave it there, where he noticed Oakley and Gary scrutinising various maps with locations marked on them.

"What are these?" Bob asked.

"Ah, our third team member!" called Gary. "Let's go and rescue some deities! Do you know where Caesium and Jeff are?" The enthusiasm in his voice seemed too exaggerated to be real, but Bob had other things on his mind.

"Jeff refuses to stop training, Caesium's having lunch and I'm just about to have mine. So, are you going to go train in Inferd?" questioned Bob.

"Nah, there's no point in having lunch or doing that," remarked Oakley. "The most important thing is that if we rescue anyone or find this core thingy, we become gods!"

At this point, the holoceiver in the room began to gong. Bob answered it and a hologram of Cognitio flashed up.

"Attention to all dormitory groups! Your groups of four will be given an extra one or two members. Unfortunately, a large number of nominees have quit and the only ones left are in their dormitories. They are coming round with some important documents about the shifter core, a translation-scale and staff for groups without liskous and crucial details about the Human-Elf-Dwarf War," explained Cognitio.

Bob gasped in horror, shaken to the core upon hearing those words. *No... that can't be!* he thought.

That had to be a lie. The war would not happen.

"Bob, are you OK?" asked Gary.

But Bob was oblivious to the rest of the world. *This war is pointless... pointless... I can't go to the shelter again!* Tremulous thoughts ran through his head until, unable to withstand it, he collapsed to the floor.

"Bob? Bob?" The voice calling now was gruffer than before and unmistakably Caesium's.

Mustering all his mental strength, Bob stood up. "The war... can't happen..." he gasped. "The war... won't happen..."

There was a knock on the door. Bob decided he could not let anyone else see him in such a weak state and went to a bunk bed, pretending to be asleep. He could hear fragments of a conversation with the newcomer and realised that the rescue mission was almost about to start.

All the training will not go to nothing at the mention of a war, Bob decided, and he staggered out of bed.

"Greetings, Bob," said Imryth. "The mission's starting early, so get everything ready."

"Did you hear about the war?" Bob asked, his voice coming out weaker than he had expected.

"Duh! It was broadcasted on the news and on the holoceiver," sighed Oakley.

"Yes, but if we find the shifter core, the government will allow us to negotiate with them and, hopefully, make peace," Imryth told them. "All of my dormitory quit, so I'm with yours now."

These words quenched Bob's dismay and all signs of weakness were washed away. "Well, then, we'd better start thinking of a good speech," he said in a more confident voice. "Let's head down to the ground floor."

They all followed Bob's suggestion, got into the lift and headed downstairs. Eventually, the lift reached the ground floor, which was filled with the buzz of nominees discussing subjects such as the mission and the war. The team got out of the lift and approached the others. The only one silent was Cognitio, who stood in the centre of the room, holding a bag of small, metal rods with a glowing, pink stripe down the middle. Bob noticed a figure he hadn't seen before, a pale elf in a dark cloak, standing next to Cognitio.

"Where is Jeff?" Bob asked them.

"I'm here," Jeff said in between large pants, as he limped slowly towards them, his body slick with sweat.

"For Heavenspire's sake, what have you been doing?" exclaimed Cognitio. "We're about to embark on a mission!"

"I've been training," wheezed Jeff. "Do you have water?"

Cognitio tossed him a hip flask. "Don't drink with your lips touching the flask. You have determination I can admire, but try not to overdo it."

After everyone had arrived, Cognitio called for silence and began to speak, "You already know why you were called here. You're the ones who didn't run back home, and are going to find the deities and the core. But there's more to it. As clichéd as it sounds, we must all work together. This is no petty competition, but a dilemma that the strongest beings in this system couldn't avoid. The next generation of deities will display teamwork, maturity, intelligence and martial prowess. Now, come and collect your new mode of transport."

Everyone looked around the area, but could not see anything that could carry them through space. Cognitio held up his bag of metal rods, provoking a wave of shocked and confused muttering.

"This isn't like the stygir raid where each race goes back to their home in the craft that suits their culture," he continued, using a sound-scale to amplify his voice. "Instead of arguing whether to use an air-scale, spaceship or some other form of transport, I have collaborated with Mekanyon and Aeterno to make these phasecrafts." Cognitio held up a handful of rods. "They work like an improved, compact phasing ladder." He then began distributing its contents to all the different groups, ignoring the storm of questions he was being bombarded with.

Jeff grabbed a phasecraft and, immediately, his team's surroundings changed to a glowing, metal plinth floating in the middle of a seemingly endless, white space. At their feet lay a bundle of documents which they presumed to be the instructions for using the vehicle. A projection similar to that of a holoceiver lit up above them. It read, "Reality 582, the Below-Heavenspire."

"A pocket dimension," mused Gary. "This is a great way to travel, but how do we get out?"

Imryth began reading through the documents. "It says here that we should just think in unison of getting out," she said. "We can re-enter the base reality at any place in Atlas, if all of us have that place in mind. But before we go anywhere, we need to think of a plan."

"Easy!" exclaimed Oakley. "You fools get out of this group and—"

"Oakley, maybe we can save the beef for after this mission," Jeff told his friend. "We need to work together and save the system."

"I guess you're right," replied Oakley.

"I think I have an idea," spoke up Caesium. "How about we head for the place the four liskous gods were last seen? They're the most powerful, so it would make rescuing the others and finding the core a lot easier if we found them first."

"I like that plan," said Jeff. "But they're only estimates, so I think we should split into different groups: one to go directly to where they were last seen, and about two more to check the area around that point, maybe fifty and a hundred metres from it? If other groups have the same idea as us, we should—"

"Me and Jeff in one group, nerd and dwarf in another group, and Bob and elf in another group!" butted in Oakley.

"After that, can we try to rescue Aurik?" asked Gary. "He's helped me in the past, and I have to help him back."

"Of course," said Caesium.

Bob tried to think of something to say, but couldn't. He realised he had to try to make more contributions to the mission, as he was already looking like a useless member. Underneath the impression of a pointless sidekick, Jeff had shown both a tactical mind and a dedication to battle, and Oakley had said something at least.

"Um…" he mustered eventually. "I'll check the area closest to the estimate."

"OK. I guess we'll check the fifty-metre point," decided Caesium, to which Gary responded with a nod.

Imryth handed out maps of where the gods had last been seen; upon looking at the maps, everyone gasped in astonishment.

"You're kidding me… they were last seen in the Void!" exclaimed Oakley.

"No. They were last seen on its borders," replied Imryth bluntly. "Any cowards can look for another group."

There was silence within the phasecraft.

Imryth clarified, "If we don't take risks, we can't stop risks."

"She's starting to sound like Cognitio," Gary whispered to Bob.

Imryth's head turned in their direction, and Gary pretended to be using his laptop.

Everyone thought of going to the edge of the Void, but nothing happened. On the second try, the platform shook around violently, almost tipping everyone standing on it into the white chasm below.

"What's happening? We all thought of phasing, didn't we?" asked Jeff, bewildered.

"Maybe our trains of thought are interrupted by some of us being too scared," said Imryth. "Just think of becoming a deity or whatever motivates you, whoever the coward is."

Instantly, they saw the words on the projection begin to disappear and, ten minutes later, they were replaced by the words, "Main reality (reality zero), outer area of system Atlas." Bob activated the turbine suit's spacesuit function, Caesium put on a talisman with a rune of breathing and Imryth cast a sphere of air around herself, whilst Gary printed off space suits for himself, Oakley and Jeff. The phasecraft reverted to being a small rod in Jeff's hand, leaving everyone on a small, uninhabited planetoid.

They could see the Void and the way it really did encircle the system like a layer of wrapping. Despite the blackness of space, it was still distinguishable, being a shade so dark it seemed to drain away everything else.

Imryth raised her hand again and moved it in a complex, swirling motion. "I have created a large sphere of glowing rock at each of the locations we should explore," she stated. "Let's go!"

Bob activated his turbine suit, but he was propelled off the planetoid instantly due to it having a weaker gravitational pull. Before he could do anything about it, he found his breathing becoming more and more difficult by the second. Holographic text flashed in front of him: "OXYGEN TANK LOW". A sickening feeling stirred in his stomach as he thought back to its description in the weapons room. The irony of the situation almost made him laugh. He wasn't going to die from whatever made all the deities disappear; he was going to die from his own stupidity! His consciousness was passing away, and the world was so blurry…

*

Bob woke up, breathing fresh air. Looking around, he could not see anything, just the same umbral shade that made up everything around him. Could he have gone too far into the Void? He could not see the orbs Imryth had mentioned. A horrible realisation came to him that the stygir and their minions weren't the worst part of the Void. Everything looked the same, and he was already lost.

Panicking, he began to run frantically, calling out the names of everyone he knew. There was no reply, just the same silence that accompanied everything to do with the blasted stygir.

Why are they attacking? What is the point of all this? Everything is just so stupid and so stupidly meaningless. Well, all that remains is to die here, alone in a place of no escape, thought Bob.

"*Wow. So dramatic,*" said a voice telepathically. It seemed to exert an aura of dominance and every syllable dripped with power.

Bob snapped out of his delirious state and looked around. Was it another mind reader? Could it be one of the deities?

"Who are you?" Bob called out. "Where are you?"

"Are you blind? I'm right in front of you," the voice smirked.

But all Bob could see was the same old Void. Who could it be?

"All right, you don't seem to get it. Maybe if I turn on my aura you will."

Cold filled the Void; it was too cold to be regular Stygiomiasma.

Instantly, Bob whipped out his blaster and activated his turbine suit, soaring upwards. *If there was air in here to breathe, there should be air to power my suit,* he figured.

"WHO ARE YOU?" Bob yelled, firing random shots everywhere. All the energy blasts seemed to travel like they didn't hit anything, but he could hear the voice laughing at him hysterically, stopping occasionally to make sarcastic pain noises.

"You're so funny! All I did was try to say hi and you— Owww! What an advanced weapon you have there. So much pain! We haven't attacked your system in ages!"

"Then answer this, stygir! Who launched an attack on all inhabited planets a few days ago? Who killed innocent people for no reason?"

"Sure wasn't us! You've got the wrong guys. We could never attack your system, not with your big death ray thingy and security satellites. We're lucky it's too heavy to be moved around by rocket thrusters, or we'd all be dead. So, how's life in Atlas?"

Bob couldn't believe his ears. *Mekanyon said there were gaps in the security system and the creatures that attacked Primium were definitely the same ones that fought in the Stygir War! Why should I believe the obvious lies I'm being told?*

"They're not lies. Ask anyone; we haven't been making troops in ages. And the tech guy can activate machines with his mind. How could he let us do so much harm when he could vaporise us all in a shot of that ray from anywhere in your system?"

"Because more powerful deity powers require more energy!" Bob explained, remembering Lapideis' words. "And you caught him off guard when he was far away from it! Activating something as powerful as Industria is probably too much energy even for Mekanyon!"

"Look, neither of us know what's going on and want to find out that, so we have a similar goal," the stygir said chidingly. "And those deities you're looking for are all over the system. I want to explore the system, but I'd get killed by your death ray. I need a human host. Maybe we should team up?"

"No way!" Bob snapped. "I can't trust you! I can't even see you!"

All of a sudden, a section of the Void became the grey of wispy smoke. In front of Bob was a very large cloud of gas, which was the same colour as the rest of the Void. A hand formed out of the swirling mass, waved, then disintegrated back into it.

"What, were you expecting a tall, demonic figure with glowing red eyes?" the stygir asked sarcastically. "Sorry to disappoint, but this is how my race looks. Oh yeah, I didn't introduce myself. I'm Morehk, kerphan of the first husk Thaumir."

Why Morehk wasn't making a move to kill him and what all the information he was being showered with meant remained a mystery to Bob. He just thanked his luck he wasn't dead yet and began thinking of the best way to escape.

"Say your name, human. Go on! And don't try to escape – by now, you should've guessed that I'm telepathic!"

"Why did you attack my system the first time? And why did you attack it the second time?" Bob repeated, his voice low and threatening.

"Are you deaf?" Morehk sighed. *"Those second attacks weren't from us. But the first time? I don't know. My salty twin Catarehk tried to explain it to me, but it was too boring, so I didn't listen. It said something about you being allied with the true enemy or some rubbish. I didn't just follow it blindly, though. My reason was that I was bored and killing stuff is very satisfying."*

Bob had heard enough. He activated all his turbines at full power and charged straight at Morehk. *Since it is a gas cloud, it should be blown in lots of different directions and die,* Bob thought.

Sure enough, Morehk let out a scream as its particles were scattered. Undeterred by its cry of pain, Bob continued the attack until all that was left of Morehk were a few miniscule, black wisps floating in the Void.

The suddenness of it all was a surprise to Bob. He couldn't seem to move out of a mixture of astonishment and triumph as thoughts rushed through his head: *Did I just... kill a stygir, on my own, with no help from anyone? And in literally no time at all? Did I really think I was a useless member of the team not so long ago?*

Finally, Bob let out a cry of victory and began trying to find an exit out of the Void, not with a sense of despair but one of determination. He thought, *I will escape this place, I will achieve more victories in combat, and I will become a god—*

"*You would first have to find someone with perfect Void-vision. There's the second-strongest stygir in existence, but, hey, who needs my help?*"

Bob spun around, but there was no sign of Morehk. But that was definitely the voice of that annoying gas cloud, so where was it?

"*Nice trick you did there. If you'd actually tried to incinerate my particles instead of scattering them, you could've damaged me. Just when I thought you were a reasonable person who wasn't going to attack me...*" Morehk went on.

Bob felt like a sharp blade was being pushed into his head. He fell to the floor in agony whilst the torment became worse and worse. "OK... you're somehow in my head... I'm sorry," he mustered, but he was ignored.

"*I'm so bored; I haven't killed anything in ages. Catarehk won't let me attack the other stygir, and you seem like you would give good screams of agony,*" Morehk slurred. It spoke patronisingly, as if it were scolding a child. "*But what a shame, Bob Solis. You and I could've been friends, solving the mystery of what's going on, but instead you chose to try to attack me. And just when I was about to ask you for a contract...*"

"I'll agree to the contract, whatever that is! *Just stop the pain!*" Bob squealed. He hated how pathetic his voice sounded; if anyone was watching, they would probably think of him as useless and weak, and not a god by a long mile.

"Oh, so the fun begins," said Morehk excitedly.

Slowly but gradually, the pain subsided.

"Just think about it – with your human looks and my powers, Atlas would be our slaughterhouse!"

"No. I don't know what this contract is, but if anything, you're going to help me kill whatever made the deities disappear," Bob stated, his voice showing a bit of strength.

"Fine. I'll explain the full terms and conditions, so don't whine at me later if this contract doesn't go your way. I take up residence inside your mind and give you my various powers, whilst you give me protection from the death ray with your human body, and you will carry out a simple task, which I shall decide on, at some point in the duration of this contract. This task is for you to kill something in an entertaining fashion. If you fail to do this or refuse continuously, your mind will be erased and you will become controlled by Catarehk. So, I will help you on the mission, and you will kill stuff or become possessed by your system's greatest enemy. Oh, and I have mind shielding to stop deity telepathy. Sound good?"

Bob had known that Morehk would probably offer up a malicious deal, but nothing as risky and dire as this. He couldn't lie to himself; he wasn't strong or clever enough for the mission. The others each had a brilliant skill set or top-of-the-range weapons, but he was stuck with a relic from the start of the age of technology and a suit that he didn't fully understand how to control. But would becoming Morehk's hitman be too much of a cost? No, the real question was whether he could get out of the Void without the help of a stygir. Besides, so many deities would not have disappear due to a simple coincidence. There was an enemy out there, and he could not afford to be the weak link again.

After a long moment of thought, he stated, "Fine. I'll form this contract with you. I'll kill stuff, and you'll help me on my mission."

No sooner had he said those words than the Void became bright green as Morehk went into his body. Looking down at his hands, he saw he was the same colour. The whole thing was like a large, oddly coloured infrared image. More importantly, he now knew the way out of the Void like it was second nature. As he flew towards the exit, he tried turning into a gas cloud and back again. Only a part of him did, but it felt like he was completely weightless.

More than that, he could see Caesium and Gary somewhere outside the large, green mass that made up his surroundings; for some reason, Caesium and the space outside the Void was red, and Gary was yellow. Bob wondered how he could get to them.

"You don't need to breathe and you are unaffected by the strength of your surroundings' gravity. Also, you can fly freely in a vacuum so speed up!" called Morehk from inside his head.

Bob thought of flying fast, and soared immediately towards Gary and Caesium.

"Hi guys," Bob said, in a voice that was half his and half Morehk's. "Any sign of the deities— *Aaargh!*" Again, pain burned through Bob's head, but so did something else: information, memories, laws and all about the stygir. Like an enormous wave, it flooded every inch of his intellect until it was too much to take in.

There were ten empty shells, stygir black and each the size of Primium, left abandoned in some unknown fragment of space. They were the husks. Out of one, two clouds poured, one howling and crying out in anguish, and the other simply flying off in some unknown direction. What the first was grieving for, Bob was not shown. He then noticed that a trail of pure darkness had formed behind it – the Void. It floated around the other husks, its particles rapidly moving, like the stygir equivalent of shivering in terror. A book of some sort was stuck in orbit of one of the clouds, so it materialised a hand to grab it and read. After a while, it began to tap each shell in a rhythmic pattern, and then it became still.

There was a flash of light, and Bob hoped he would regain his consciousness; however, he then saw the same place, in what appeared to be the same vision, flashback or whatever it was.

The first stygir was still waiting at the exact same spot, reading the same book. For how long it had been there was unknown. Eventually, nine other stygir emerged, one from each husk, and the second stygir from before had joined them. Immediately, as if waking up excited from a long sleep, the first stygir began to show them what it was reading, gave them names and told them how to use their powers. They were the kerphans. They all accepted the teachings of the one before them, calling it Catarehk, which meant "honoured light" in the language transcribed in the book.

There came another flash of light.

Catarehk caught sight of something – a faraway system – and became incandescent. Behind it stood countless hordes of the creatures used in the recent attack. It yelled at all the other kerphans and at some other stygir that must have been created in the time skipped by the second flash of light. They gathered their armies and all of them headed towards Atlas. Where they moved, the Void followed and war was imminent.

"Bob, are you all right?" asked Caesium frantically. "Wake up!" He and Gary had landed on a nearby planetoid, and they had laid Bob down whilst he regained his consciousness.

"What happened? Did you end up in the Void or something?" asked Gary.

Bob shook his head.

"Good. Regular humans are supposed to go mad in there after a few days. We haven't found any of the deities. What about you?" Gary queried.

Bob was afraid to speak in case his voice wasn't entirely his anymore.

"After knowing the history of the stygir from my point of view, we should be synchronised completely. Go on. Speak," said Morehk. *"You haven't found a deity but you've found something better, haven't you?"*

"No," sighed Bob. "Maybe the other three are having better luck than us."

Caesium began to dig a wormhole with his pickaxe, but was interrupted by the sound of gunfire. A platoon of human soldiers emerged from behind a rock, firing at a group of dwarves in a defensive position. Each blast carved out a massive hole in the dwarves shield wall until it was reduced to nothing.

To Bob, the dwarves appeared as the same red as Caesium, but the humans appeared as a new colour: an odd shade of metallic grey.

One of the dwarves pulled out a hammer with a rune on it and slammed it into the ground. The ground underneath the soldiers' feet collapsed into a deep pit, but then they flew up using jetpacks. More dwarves joined the fight, and so did a tank on the human side. Suddenly, the tank began to rust and crumble, until it was reduced to a pile of scrap and a startled crew. From behind the dwarves, an elf wizard finished his chant, grinning triumphantly.

"The war can't be this widespread already!" Bob exclaimed as the battle continued to rage on.

"As much as I hate to admit it, that's not our problem at the moment," said Caesium. "Let's go through the wormhole, and see if Imryth, Oakley and Jeff have found anyone."

The three jumped through the wormhole and found it was no more than a regular tunnel. Caesium hacked relentlessly through the fabric of space in front of them, until the wormhole came to a glowing orb. Strangely enough, despite being in open space, they could walk as if on solid ground. Caesium tried to use his wormhole pickaxe again, but for some reason it wasn't working.

"Weird," mused Caesium. "I had no idea you could find space like this. Is this normal?"

Bob and Gary shook their heads.

But, for Bob, there was something odder than that. Instead of being red, this particular area was coloured with the same pallor as the human soldiers. It unnerved him more than stygir black did before he had seen that dark hue as green. *Morehk,* he thought, *what does the grey mean?*

"I don't know myself. Usually, this side of space is red, meaning against me, but then all of a sudden this grey keeps on spreading. Anyway, focus on killing something, I'm bored," complained Morehk.

So, red was anti-stygir and green was probably the opposite.

What is yellow? thought Bob.

"Ah! The yellow one's your first target. Try to make him scream a bit," Morehk requested.

I'm being serious here! What does yellow mean?

"I'll tell you when you keep your part of the contract."

"Bob, is something wrong?" asked Caesium. "You look like something's really ticked you off."

Suddenly, the three felt like they had hit a brick wall; however, it just appeared to be empty space in front of them.

"It seems like this is some sort of building painted to blend in with space," said Gary, and he printed off a torch.

When he turned it on, they could see the outlines of two walls, with a gap in between them. On shining it through the gap, three passages were made visible. At that point, it became clear that what they were looking at was a maze; how large it was, they did not know, but it was likely that it led to where the deities had disappeared.

"This looks tough," Gary muttered. "How can we get through it successfully?"

"Easy," replied Caesium, and he began to dig a wormhole.

No sooner had he made one swing than everything glowed a bright pink – the same shade as a phasing ladder – and Bob found himself alone in the same maze, but he didn't know where. He tried calling Gary's and Caesium's names, but there was no reply. Sonorous footsteps echoed throughout the maze, each one accompanied by a low, mechanical groan and a dripping noise similar to a tap. Instinctively, he loaded his blaster with coal and prepared to activate his turbines.

"Don't activate those!" commanded Morehk. *"You saw what happened when your midget friend tried to cheat his way through the maze. Do you want to be taken somewhere worse?"*

What Bob saw next made him wonder if there *was* anything worse.

*

Imryth prepared another fusillade of fireballs, making sure she kept the protective dome she had raised from the ground intact; if she didn't, then the unconscious Oakley would fall prey to whatever was wielding the blades that appeared out of the fog to attack and then disappear. They had been separated from Jeff and found themselves stuck in dense fog no wind magic could blow away. Twenty-five swords melted, but thirty more appeared to the side of her. Nothing seemed to be working effectively: the fog didn't seem to be affected by wind magic and it was too high for Jeff to fly over it.

Then a knife soared through the air, hitting her in the head.

FIFTEEN

Caesium swung his hammer against a nearby wall, hoping it would break. The same thing happened: there was no effect on the wall, then pink light and a new location. This was not stupidity on his part, but rather part of a plan he had devised to find his way around the maze. Before each swing, he would carve a small, inoffensive rune of glowing on the floor. When two such runes are in the same area, a bright beam of light forms that connects them. That way, he could easily navigate his way through all the paths in the maze and, hopefully, find the deities, if any were trapped in the maze.

Just before he was about to carve another rune and repeat the process, he heard the sound of blades clashing. Following the sound, he came to a large, open space. Unlike the rest of the maze, it was made out of regular materials and strongly resembled a laboratory. Tables with countless pieces of scientific equipment, mainly scalpels and circuitry, took up most of the space. The clashing stopped abruptly. Then Caesium heard another sound: voices wailing in agony. He looked around, but saw no people.

When he walked past one of the tables, the top of it lifted suddenly with a hiss of steam. Inside it were countless mangled bodies. Humans, elves and dwarves all tried to move, to escape, but failed and collapsed into the pit of countless others. The stench of decaying flesh wafted through the air.

Caesium staggered back, petrified. There were so many lives, all rotting away there. Who had done it?

Rips and gashes opened up on their macabre forms, as if they were being hacked apart, but nobody else was in the room. Looking closer, he saw their eyes were closed, as if they were sleeping. Whatever they were doing or thinking, they were doing it subconsciously.

Mustering all his strength, he tried to stay calm. From a very young age, he had always had a perpetual fear of gore. Fighting, he was fine with and enjoyed it; during the first fight in Inferd, he knew no one was really going to die. But the pool of blood and critical wounds that heralded a gory death petrified him. Quickly, he began lifting the bodies out of the table with shaking hands, one by one, hoping that some were still living. An alarm sounded, but his own thoughts and the direness of the situation blotted out the noise.

He moved on to the next table.

It was more of the same, with dying victims. A tube of some sort lowered from the ceiling, but once again, he was oblivious. It seemed nothing could stop him – except the sight of three familiar faces. Oakley didn't move at all, Jeff was clutching his left arm in pain and writhed around, and Imryth had a gaping hole on the side of her head, with blood streaming from it like a waterfall.

Caesium screamed and dropped his group members, gasping and trembling. Unable to help himself, he vomited, then did it again and again, until there was nothing to throw up. A loud hiss echoed around the room. The air started to have a taste to it, with an odd, pungent odour. Immediately after Caesium noticed this, a mist began to swirl around him, covering everything from view. He could see blades glinting maliciously, getting closer and closer. He tried to lift his weapons, but was too weak.

Just before the first blade came soaring towards him, the mist blew away from him, as if a strong wind was moving it. A liskous stared at him with a look of disgust on his face, spinning his staff casually. From his pale-blue scales with streaks of white and dark grey, Caesium recognised him as Nimbus, the liskous god of sky.

"Don't vomit everywhere; it's disgusting," Nimbus muttered. The odd smell in the air came back, and with it the mist began to form again, but he lifted up his hand and both disappeared swiftly. "You don't look like you were brought here with the rest. Why are you here, dwarf?"

Caesium explained everything: the mission, the shifter core and the disappearance of all the deities.

Nimbus scoffed, "And who said we needed saving? The shifter core is in here, and we're going to get it. We've been battling a high-class stygir in here for ages; now what have you done?"

"So, what's this maze?" Caesium asked, trying his best to ignore Nimbus's comments. "And what are those… bodies doing here?"

"The maze is a secret we were trying to keep; it's a galactic phenomenon that was here before even the liskous and was probably used as a secret test facility. It's in use now, though, because some gas cloud's taken it over, and is using it as a base to guard a shifter core and to use these poor souls for its filthy designs. That gas you were about to stupidly breathe in creates an illusion. If you get hurt in the illusion and think its real pain, your real-life body suffers the wound. It's pathetic, really, how many have fallen for it."

Anger replaced Caesium's nausea at the god's lack of caring. "WELL, MAYBE NONE OF US HAVE WIND POWERS LIKE YOU!" he bawled. "These are your people; they're dying, and all you can do is scold them for not figuring out an illusion?" He put his hand to Imryth's forehead, stemming the blood flow. "Can't you heal them or something?" he asked in a calmer tone.

Nimbus opened his mouth and Caesium felt like a breeze had started blowing. "There," the god said, "I've added more oxygen into their systems to make up for the lost blood, and a wall of wind should be blocking any more blood loss," he explained proudly. Then he pointed his staff at Oakley. "Unfortunately, your friend here died in the illusion."

Caesium couldn't believe his ears. Oakley was rude to everyone and racist, but he didn't deserve to die. At least not this early; surely Nimbus was wrong?

"You're lying," Caesium said, trembling. "There's no way that he could've died like this."

"And what splits him from the other corpses in these piles? Ask any of their friends and family, and they would be saying the same nonsense as you." Nimbus then flicked his wrist and gusts of wind shattered all the tables. Several bodies fell to the floor. "Everyone who's still alive! You're safe now! I'll transport you to the Kumosphere!"

"What's that?" asked Caesium.

"Do you know anything about the deities, fool?" replied Nimbus. "It's a realm inside my soul, like an alternate reality but way more brilliant. I've always transported victims of conflict there during dangerous situations, where they will be safe and also restored by the healing energies it possesses. It only works on unarmed civilians and the like, though. Awesome, huh?"

"Quit bragging and do it," sighed Caesium.

After a long-winded response that the dwarf couldn't be bothered to listen to, Nimbus yelled "Kumosphere open!" and, underneath his skin, his heart became visible as it glowed with an extremely bright light.

The survivors mustered a series of thank yous to Nimbus as they disappeared in a flash of a similar light and a gust of wind. Imryth, having regained consciousness, refused to be transported, saying she would fight on.

"You can try," remarked Nimbus. "But if you end up injured and out of my reach, don't blame me."

At that moment, a slate-scale on Nimbus' staff glowed and a voice called out, "Nimbus! We've tracked it down to sector fifty, passage one!"

"Well, Aeterno has found our prey," Nimbus muttered to himself. "I'd better join him before it runs away again." He then gave Caesium a stern glance. "*No,* you're not joining me, I don't need you weighing me down. You fight with a hammer and pickaxe, but vomit at the sight of a little blood? Go to the nearest comedy theatre."

*

The majority of it was metal; it was a mechanical, anthropomorphic exoskeleton that was at least three times the size of Bob. It was badly put together, a mockery of Mekanyon's designs, and frayed wires and battered scrap metal covered most of it. Despite this, it moved in a way that signified it was robust and a powerful foe. But the rest of the foul monstrosity was even worse than the fact that another force had access to technology. Flayed flesh and blood vessels poked out of the metal, held in place by stakes. A hand moved around, as if trying to escape. Where the head would have been – if it were human, elf, dwarf or liskous – was a large, mechanical mouth with saw blades for teeth, which were drenched in even more blood. Bob staggered back, wishing he had never seen the gruesome sight.

"Now that's what I'm talking about!" exclaimed Morehk triumphantly. *"Let's kill this thing; look, it's already spilling blood for us!"*

"WILL YOU SHUT UP FOR A SECOND?" screamed Bob. He had grown to hate the stygir even more since the recent attack on Primium.

"Nope; the stygir never attacked your world."

"And stop reading my mind!"

"You can do it too, remember. Go and find out what's going on by reading that thing's mind, if it has one. Then kill it."

Bob read its mind and found that one of his worst suspicions about it was true.

"The flesh and blood shall power our creations. This is the start of a new era of life," a voice said, though its origins were unknown.

All Bob could read inside its mind were sounds.

"Are you pleased with my work?" Another voice began to speak, though it was drowned out by a loud beep.

"CRAP! SOMEONE'S PUT A MIND-SHIELD ON THIS THING!" he heard Morehk shout.

The beeping noise increased in volume until Bob had to stop trying to read its mind.

One of the exoskeleton's hands swept down and grabbed Bob; it moved with uncanny swiftness, and there was no time for Bob to fly away using his turbine suit. Thinking fast, Bob aimed his blaster at its shoulder, but the other arm knocked it out of his hands before he could pull the trigger.

Then the mouth closed over him.

Bob cried out in fright and prepared himself for the pain of being shredded alive by countless saws. However, he felt nothing. Was he already dead? He could hear the whirring of the saw teeth and see them piercing his body, but nothing was happening. Looking closer, he saw most of his body was now a wispy gas.

Of course, he realised, *I now have the powers of the stygir. Morehk, what else do you have?*

"Well, I can summon minions, but I wouldn't recommend it outside the Void; I can materialise in different shapes; and I have my husk power, kerphan nameright and kerphan avatar. But your body can't handle them yet. I'll tell you when it can," Morehk confirmed. *"And when I tell you about my nameright, don't overuse it or there'll be hell to pay."*

Bob remembered the havoc that one of the large wasp-like creatures had caused on Primium, and he thought one of those would help against his enemy. Turning all his body to gas, he floated out of the exoskeleton's mouth and thought of summoning the creature he had remembered. However, all that happened was that he reverted automatically to a flesh-and-blood state and began retching black smoke, though it appeared green to him.

"You idiot, I said I wouldn't recommend it outside the Void! You don't even know the name of what you're trying to summon!" ranted Morehk.

The exoskeleton was in a mad rage, swiping furiously at the first creature that survived its jaws. Discarding his flesh and blood for the gas of the stygir, Bob didn't feel any of the countless blows. After a while, though, he found that holding his gas form was a strain, both mentally and physically. His movements became slow and sluggish, and he began to flicker between solid and gas. Soon, he was knocked to the floor in a pool of blood, comprising both his and the exoskeleton's.

"Vesp! You can't fight now, so you might as well summon it. It's called a vesp!" Morehk offered.

Just as the exoskeleton brought two fists down, Bob thought of summoning the vesp again. Instantly, a cloud of black shot out of Bob's right hand, but, despite its appearance, it had a solidity made visible by the way it stopped and dented the exoskeleton's fists. Like clay shaped by an invisible potter, it began to take the desired form. Unfortunately, this made Bob feel like a large chunk of his body was being ripped out. He fell to the floor in pain, gasping for breath.

It feels ridiculous and pathetic, he thought, *that something else is fighting this battle for me.*

His blaster lay several metres away from the fight and he crawled off to get it.

The vesp shot out its mandibles and latched on to its opponent's torso. Blood and shreds of metal flew everywhere as the vesp shook it left and right, trying to sever the metal body. However, the exoskeleton grabbed hold of the tendril that connected the mandibles to the head, and pulled and twisted it until it ripped. Even so, it still dealt some damage, and the crackling of broken machinery could be heard. The vesp launched itself at the enemy, its legs outstretched. Each leg had extended three long talons. Bob shot at the legs of the exoskeleton, blowing off the feet. From that point on, the battle was short-lived and one-sided. Soon, Bob was looking at a pile of scrap metal, and a pool of blood and shredded flesh.

"*Yeah!*" Morehk exclaimed. "*That was great!*"

Bob didn't talk back. The direness of the situation was worse than he could imagine. Were there other beings like this here? How many of his people had been cut apart to give them life? Plus, he could not get up after the side effects of summoning the vesp. He tried desperately to stand, but failed after every attempt.

"Morehk..." he eventually wheezed. "How do I... get out of this state?"

"*Go to the Void; it'll replenish your energy instantly. Or we'll have to find another stygir and eat them,*" Morehk clarified.

"Just to let you know beforehand, we're going to the Void."

Suddenly, chains of fire wrapped themselves around the vesp. It tried to cut them with its claws, but then those were trapped as well. Bob then saw Cognitio emerge from behind a wall; the chains were coming off one of his slate-scales. Antony was with him.

"Wait!" Bob exclaimed. "Don't—" Pain rushed through his head, and he fell to the floor. *What are you doing, Morehk? We have to let him know the vesp's on our side!*

"And how are you going to do that?" Morehk asked. *"Only we stygir can make those things, and does it look like this guy's good friends with us? If you tell him that, he'll get suspicious and, eventually, find out about the contract."*

"Don't what?" asked Cognitio.

"Don't… hold back," stated Bob.

Cognitio activated another slate-scale, and the chains of fire exploded, immolating the vesp. It didn't detonate upon death, likely due to being summoned when Bob was weakened.

"Bob, is there any sign of the deities?" Antony asked.

Bob shook his head.

"We're also looking for an elf who was supposed to be with us," added Cognitio. "He wears a dark cloak and has very pale skin; have you seen him?"

Bob shook his head again.

Cognitio stared at him with a suspicious look. "Bob, you seemed like you wanted to stop me killing the vesp earlier," Cognitio stated. "Only the stygir would be able to create and make use of those. We don't know everything about them, but I know you are somehow allied with them. It's the truth, right?"

"Are you sure you're not just jumping to conclusions?" asked Antony.

The only response he received was the glow of countless scale-slates and a staff pointed at Bob.

"WAIT, STOP!" Bob yelled. "I'LL TELL YOU EVERYTHING!"

He couldn't believe that his teacher was trying to kill him or that he was so astute. Hurriedly, Bob explained everything: the Void, Morehk and the contract. This only made Cognitio press him for more information, and soon all Bob knew about the stygir was shared. Antony was speechless; Cognitio lowered his staff.

"The way you shared that information makes me certain you're on our side. Unless you've been telling us fake information. Either way, one thing's for certain: Aeterno won't admit it, and I hate to do so, but the stygir are stronger than the deities. We might need your powers if we are to succeed. I'll keep your secret and trust that you'll help us, but step out of line and you're finished, Bob and Morehk. So, your leader was mourning something we did and attacked us for retribution… It seems like that part was made up by you or implanted by your leader into your memories to give you a noble cause. How can I trust you?"

"Because no one would betray their own species and system for their attackers," replied Bob. "When you first met me at the Below-Heavenspire, you could trust me. Now, I'm the same person, just with the powers of our enemies. Anyway, I'm offering to help you, so why don't you accept?"

"Why don't you just shut up?" grumbled Morehk. *"Who gave you permission to tell them my life story? I'll send pain through your head until you drop to the floor again if you*

wish for it! And what's stopping him from getting his mind read by your deities?"

"You're probably wondering what's stopping you being found out if the deities read my mind or Antony's," remarked Cognitio. "The telepathy they wield doesn't work on their close friends or direct allies. If Mekanyon could use it on you when you two first met, it was because you hadn't actively done anything to show your alignment."

Antony began to sniff the air. Eventually, he pointed to his right. "I can smell four gods, one dwarf and a stygir that way!" he told them, and then he dashed off.

"Excellent work, Antony," commended Cognitio, who ran after him. "Perhaps we can use our old foes to our advantage in this new world," he muttered to himself.

Despite not being able to move very well, Bob could still activate his turbine suit and began to hover after them. He had no idea whether he had made the right move telling Cognitio that he was allied with a stygir, but he assured himself it was better than being blasted apart by the majority of the slate-scales' powers.

SIXTEEN

"GET OFF ME, DWARF!" roared Nimbus, trying to shake off Caesium. "QUIT FOLLOWING ME, ELF!"

The dwarf managed to grab on to his arm before he took flight and refused to be kept back from fighting alongside the gods. Nimbus began to spin his staff until it became a blur. Imryth followed after them using her wind magic.

"If being smashed against a wall or being deprived of oxygen doesn't scare you, get off before your skull gets cracked by my staff!" threatened Nimbus.

"Fine. Do it. You're a jerk, but you stay loyal to the rules of the deities. And one of those is to protect me," retaliated Caesium.

Eventually, Nimbus gave up, and the three flew above the maze up until they caught sight of three figures in front of them. Caesium jumped onto the top of a nearby maze wall.

"Aeterno! Lapideis! Hydrax!" Nimbus called out. "Where's the gasbag?"

"It disappeared soon after Hydrax found it," said Aeterno. "We're trying to track it down again."

"Aeterno, use your powers to help!" ordered Nimbus.

Aeterno let out a long sigh. "Nimbus, I've told you before. They are only to be used when in desperate need, as they could rearrange the fabric of the universe for the worse," he stated without a change in his voice. "What helps us now could curse the system for generations or ruin another part of the multiverse."

"Well, desperate need is now! We've been tracking down that thing and the shifter core for ages, and there's no way the other ones are just going to leave our system alone!" Nimbus grumbled.

"*We don't need another fight,*" interjected Hydrax, "*unless it's with the stygir.*"

Caesium noticed that the gods of sea and earth were being very quiet as the argument continued between Aeterno and Nimbus. "Does this happen often?" he whispered to Lapideis.

"Yeah, and always at the wrong moments. But they usually end after a while," Lapideis replied.

"Nimbus, as mortals, we studied together and fought alongside each other, but you are beginning to test my patience. The small possibility of a system being conquered is nothing compared to the large chance of the whole universe being torn apart," reiterated Aeterno.

Nimbus then waved his staff and a slate-scale flashed a shade of black. "Something's nearby," he said. "It's the stygir, yet I sense at the same time it's not."

Nimbus spun his staff with such force that a miniature tornado appeared, then he threw it like a shuriken. It spun in a large arc around them, before landing on its owner's outstretched palm. A dark cloud of gas had formed in front of them.

"I see it now," mused Nimbus. "Bits of you are all over the maze, watching us and sending those demented machines to try to kill us. Is this the whole you or are you cowering somewhere else?"

"Do not insult my venerable creations," the stygir snarled telepathically, and, like flocks of sparrows, vast masses of gas flew through the air and combined to form a gestalt cloud. Soon it was five times the size of Lapideis. *"I am Ghogiehk, the god of this world, and the upstart powers must be eradicated."*

"So you keep on telling us," muttered Nimbus, and he outstretched both hands, causing a massive wind to start up and split the stygir into many small clouds, each the size of Caesium's thumb.

The clouds tried to escape, but each try only made it worse, splitting every one of them into several smaller ones. Aeterno activated a slate-scale, which made his staff glow, and he hit all the clouds with a single swing. They disappeared in an instant.

"I swear that damage-scale's the only one you use," Nimbus said to Aeterno. "Don't you have anything more badass or flashy?"

"I don't need anything more 'badass' or 'flashy'. All I need is to be able to deal damage to all types of foes and that's what that scale does."

"Aw, you're no fun."

Suddenly, more clouds rose up from the floor and merged into one. Ghogiehk was back, albeit twice the size and likely stronger. *"I am the god of the world,"* it repeated. *"I cannot die."*

Thousands of exoskeletons joined the fight, each one able to fly due to rocket boosters made of stygir gas attached to their feet. Caesium tried not to let his fear get the better of him and raised his hammer and pickaxe. Suddenly, a large wave of water swept away all of them, the sound of their circuits fizzling audible.

"*I see they are not waterproof,*" a voice echoed in everyone's minds. "*Solid stream: water-ascension construct!*" Hydrax grinned and tapped the tip of a maze wall.

Instantly, a large section of the maze began to fill with water. The god tapped the maze again, and Bob, Cognitio and Antony were elevated to the scene of the battle on columns of water. Jeff floated upwards, unconscious; Nimbus transported him to the Kumosphere immediately. No sooner had they reached the top of the maze than all the water vanished immediately. Hydrax tapped the maze again, but nothing happened. Cognitio charged at him, ripping a large hole in one of his wings. Hydrax's face contorted in pain, but not even telepathic sound could be heard.

"COGNITIO! WHAT ARE YOU DOING?" shouted Lapideis, and he slammed a fist into the maze. Spears of jagged rock rose from the ground, but they snapped in half before they could do any damage. The god of earth charged at Cognitio, his claws outstretched. Lapideis slashed him across the chest and threw him, slamming him into a wall. However, instead of blood coming out, only a dark gas did.

"No way!" exclaimed Lapideis. "That thing can make minions that look like us!"

"*Because I am god,*" declared Ghogiehk, "*I can make any image I wish. I can negate the effects of the blasphemous powers you call deity powers. Do you see it now? You have been sent here, to the world, by god's will to aid me in my cause. You existed to power god's forms of life, but demons breathed life into you. There is still time to repent your sins, to be used for your original purpose—"*

"Oh, shut up!" said Nimbus. "The world's more than just this maze! There's a system out there and definitely even more than that! Jaws of vacuum!" The god breathed in audibly and a cyclone began to sprout from his jaws, dragging Ghogiehk in.

"Lies! Lies! Lies!" screeched Ghogiehk, struggling in the vortex. *"This system is an illusion that was probably instilled into you by demons! And what solid proof do you have to counter it?"*

The cyclone became a gale, then a breeze and then subsided. Nimbus clutched his chest, gasping for breath, whilst Ghogiehk's negation of his power didn't seem to cost it any energy.

"Very well… Call off the storm!" demanded Nimbus. Lightning blazed in his eyes and storm clouds materialised around him like armour. A roiling maelstrom charged up in his mouth, like a gathering of many storms. "Aerial bombard: caelum tormentis!"

Ghogiehk activated its power, and the storm clouds began to turn white, but not before Nimbus roared and fired a barrage of lightning projectiles from his mouth, which, although depleted, were many in number. This power drained Nimbus' final scraps of energy, and he plummeted downwards, but, luckily, he was caught by Hydrax. Ghogiehk split itself into smaller clouds and dodged the majority of the attack, but still took some damage. The real Cognitio saw this as an opportunity and struck fast, shooting a stream of fire at the stygir. It reformed, but was again slightly damaged in the attack. Aeterno dive-bombed it, landing strikes so fast that it could not react. This time, Ghogiehk's form was beginning to weaken and fizzle away. However, Aeterno's damage-scale was soon on cool-down, and his staff passed through Ghogiehk harmlessly.

Millions of winged karapo were being summoned, with a steady stream appearing all around Ghogiehk. Lapideis materialised a large stone tablet, and he, Caesium and Antony jumped on it as it flew towards the amassing foes. They were heavily outnumbered, but Lapideis slammed both hands into the tablet and sharp spears of flint flew out of it in all directions, killing thousands. About twenty-five had closed in on Caesium, bringing their bladed arms down on him at once. He responded by parrying most of them with his pickaxe and swinging his hammer in a wide arc, using the attraction rune to drag more foes towards its head. However, some still managed to hit him, drawing blood on the sides of his arms and nicking him in the leg.

Antony and Lapideis slashed at their opponents with their claws, using their strength to overpower them.

It was at that moment that the tablet began to crumble away, and the three descended through the air, pursued by the stygir creatures. Lapideis took flight shortly after and returned to the fight, whilst Caesium began to dig a wormhole for him and Antony. Due to the injuries on his arms, he took longer to form one and just about managed to avoid hitting the maze's floor.

Bob fired at Ghogiehk's minions, hitting one with each shot. Again, he was facing a being of metallic grey, but he didn't know what significance that had. Unfortunately, due to their large numbers, his attacks were like erosion on a large cliff-edge: there was no immediately visible effect and it would be a long time before it showed. *Morehk,* he thought, *who is that stygir?*

"*It's the kerphan of the second husk. It was always obsessed with having total power and control over everything. Not so long after the war ended, it went crazy and disappeared, but not after eating all the other stygir from its husk,*" Morehk responded.

What? How could it—

"*I don't know why it did that; maybe it was bored, like me. But it means we're facing the equivalent of a whole husk.*"

At that point, Bob realised that, despite Ghogiehk having no apparent weakness whatsoever, maybe its weakness was stored in its mind. Flying away from the fray, he began to read.

Ghogiehk was finishing its last meal: the remnants of another stygir. At this point, it appeared green to Bob. Bob looked up and saw that it was at least the size of a planet.

"*Ghogiehk, meaning honoured supremacy, of the husk Chaigidir,*" came a voice. "*You carry the ability to negate deity powers. You could be useful.*" A figure obscured by a grey pixel mosaic approached Ghogiehk, offering promises of the entire universe. It accepted and began to listen further, turning greyer with every passing second.

And then Bob's mind reading abruptly stopped. He tried asking Morehk what had happened, but he received no response. Ghogiehk laughed raucously.

"See, Morehk? See? *My powers transcend even that of the first husk! All fake deities are nothing, their powers crumbling before the true ruler of the world!*"

"Another stygir is here!" Aeterno told everyone. "Everyone, be wary! And don't try to use any more deity powers; we need to use other weapons and skills to defeat Ghogiehk!"

"This crazy fool... can't defeat me!" repeated Nimbus. With a lethargy similar to getting out of bed, he rose up and charged towards Ghogiehk's minions. Unsurprisingly, they overwhelmed him in an instant.

Hydrax pulled out from behind his back a long strand of rope studded with slate-scales, and he activated his own damage-scale. Using it as a whip, he managed to clear the area around Nimbus from afar.

"*Get back, Nimbus!*" he ordered. "*And consume this! River of energy!*" A trail of water began to extend from Hydrax's outstretched palm.

Before it was negated, Nimbus swooped towards it and managed to drink a single drop; the effect on his body was immediate. Whatever energy he had lost during the battle, he had regained it in an instant.

"*I can only make one of these per battle, so make the most of it,*" confirmed Hydrax.

"Thanks, Hydrax; I will!" Nimbus assured his fellow god. "Now it's time for this battle to turn in our favour!"

With his deity powers gone and no way to speak telepathically, the god of sea gave Nimbus a brief nod before swinging his rope in a wide arc; this hit most of the stygir creatures and was done with such force that they were cleaved apart.

Nimbus flew up to engage the remaining foes in close combat. He spun his staff but, at the last minute, flew up and threw it at Ghogiehk.

The stygir did nothing, expecting the weapon to pass through it harmlessly, but it was cut in half. One half then disappeared, completely eliminated. *"Mere wood shouldn't harm my divine gaseous form!"* it roared in surprise.

"No, it shouldn't," agreed Nimbus, augmenting his flying with a gust of wind in order to speed past Ghogiehk and catch his staff. "But I modified the DNA of this wood so that it deals massive damage to whatever it determines to be the biggest threat, with only fifteen minutes needed to charge up! Awesome, huh? It's such a shame you stygir aren't clever enough to—"

"ENOUGH GLOATING, NIMBUS!" bellowed Cognitio, who was fighting a fake Aeterno along with Lapideis. The fake, although a mockery of the true god, was still a formidable foe, and the two struggled against it. "There'll be celebrations after the battle!"

Hydrax swung the rope again and it wrapped around the fake's neck, cracking it.

"You only win in numbers, heretics!" Ghogiehk summoned an entire army of the Aeterno fakes, which depleted it to a few stray particles. Everyone with a weapon that could harm it saw this as an opening and launched an attack on it. However, even more black gas appeared, and before, the attacks hit, Ghogiehk was at least four times its previous size, if not bigger, and thus didn't take much damage. *"God never dies! Never!"*

A wormhole opened in the midst of all the fakes,

and inside were Antony and Caesium, wounded but still fighting.

"*What are you doing?*" exclaimed Cognitio. "You'll be killed! Retreat and fight from a more tactical position."

Ignoring him, Caesium began to dig another wormhole in front of him and many fakes fell in. He then tapped his pickaxe rhythmically, and the wormhole began to collapse, trapping the fakes. This wasn't permanent – the wormhole would reopen eventually – but it would keep them trapped there for several hours. "Don't worry. I know what I'm doing, and it's better than running due to a few scratches on me!" he said to his teacher.

"Yeah, I have to agree with him on this one!" added Antony, punching and kicking at the fakes near him. However, they dodged the blows easily and struck back with uncanny speed. If they hadn't fully inherited all of the original's strengths, they had definitely inherited a large portion of them. The troll staggered back, but he mustered the strength to not collapse as the horde closed in on him.

Caesium, seeing Antony was in trouble, used his attraction rune to drag most of them towards him and struck them with his two weapons in a spinning attack.

"*Even more heresy! To think they can make holes in the world's fabric as they wish! All troops, attack the dwarf, then get the troll once you're done,*" commanded Ghogiehk.

Every single fake turned their heads towards Caesium and charged. Struck with fear, he scurried further into the wormhole. No sooner had he done this than a fake flew inside, grabbed his pickaxe from his grip, and then flew out. He knew what it was about to do and began to run towards the wormhole's exit. The fake tapped the pickaxe, and Caesium could see the world at the exit disappearing with every passing second. Desperately, he began to sprint towards the exit, opening up a leg wound he had received earlier on. Caesium collapsed.

The exit was now just a tiny hole, not big enough to use. He gave up hope and didn't attempt to get up, just stared at the crevice in the wormhole that showed a tiny fraction of the base reality.

And then it widened.

Surprised, Caesium's eyes widened, and he got to his feet. Limping towards the exit, he saw that the fakes were all attacking something and ignoring the attacks of the deities. Did Ghogiehk want him properly dead, not just trapped? No, it was delusional but not stupid. The exit widened, and he saw Imryth was protected by a dome of floating rock, her palms outstretched and all her amulets glowing. She made a motion with her hands as if digging a tunnel and the wormhole widened enough for Caesium to escape.

Somehow she was standing, rescuing and fighting, even though there was a massive wound on her head, and she bore countless others as well. Not to mention ignoring the army that was after her. A crack appeared in the rock.

"What are you doing here?" asked Caesium, bewildered. "You're wounded and bleeding, there's a whole army that's only attacking you, and—"

"And there's a teammate who needed saving. There's an elven saying that states to watch your company die is to watch a part of you die. We've lost Oakley on my watch, and I'm making sure we don't lose anyone else."

The top of the dome cracked., and the fakes charged in a blur of gold. Imryth summoned flames all around her, forming a shield that whittled away at the enemies closest to her and Caesium. A wormhole opened up inside the shield of flames and out stepped more. Imryth summoned a gust of wind, which blew the pickaxe out of the hands of one of them and into Caesium's.

"Now it's time for revenge!" He grinned and tapped his pickaxe.

Imryth stopped casting the shield of flames and began to burn the fakes that had managed to escape the wormhole. All around them, their allies were defeating the other fakes whilst they were distracted. A thunderbolt formed in Imryth's hand, and she hurled it at Ghogiehk, ripping a hole in the stygir's gaseous form.

"*You blasphemous elf!*" howled Ghogiehk.

"Magic isn't a deity power, is it?" Imryth taunted, and she flew on a gale to face it.

SEVENTEEN

Bob had thought of a plan to defeat Ghogiehk. Whilst it was still reduced to a few particles, Morehk was able to speak to him again and decided to tell him what a husk power was.

The stygir from each husk share a common power; Ghogiehk was from the husk of Chaigidir, and therefore had the ability to negate deity powers. Because Morehk was from the husk of Thaumir, Bob had the ability to assume control of other stygir, as long as they weren't focused on attacking him, or if their mind and strength were inferior to his.

All the time whilst the battle raged on, he still launched hit-and-run attacks with his Joule 1.0, but he was busy charging up his husk power to control more of Ghogiehk. Despite Morehk warning him it would put a large strain on his body, one he probably couldn't take, he decided to take the risk; winning the fight was more important than staying conscious at that moment. Morehk agreed, but only because a stygir host's body takes the strain of the attacks it uses. Eventually, Bob released his charged power and felt as if he was crumbling apart. He passed out and fell, but, luckily, he landed on a cushion of water made by Hydrax.

Imryth created a large ball of fire and hurled it at Ghogiehk, who created more minions to take the blast for it. *It keeps on summoning troops to do its fighting for it,* she observed. *This probably means it's not too strong itself.* She summoned a large wind, which blew its particles in all directions, and blasted all of them with fire. However, one still remained and more appeared to join it.

"This is pathetic," sighed Imryth. "Why don't you just fight us with all your particles?"

"Why should a god need to use his full power against the lowly?" Ghogiehk responded.

It was at that moment that half of Ghogiehk materialised in the shape of a propeller fan, and blew the other half away. Several more particles were drawn out of their hiding places to join the dispersed half.

Not sure of what was going on, but ready to seize this opportunity, Imryth fired a rain of bullet-sized fireballs at the blown-away half, incinerating every single particle. The other half then imploded and disappeared. A glowing rock the size of a heart dropped from it: the shifter core. She used wind magic to direct it to her hands.

"So this is it," she breathed, staring at the object from myth. "It actually exists."

"Did you just... defeat him?" asked Antony in disbelief.

"YEAH!" cheered Caesium. "The shifter core is ours! The system's saved!"

Everyone else began to celebrate.

"Did we win?" asked Jeff, who had got to his feet. "What happened after we got separated and... where's Oakley?"

Nimbus, Caesium and Imryth fell silent.

"*He should be somewhere here with you,*" said Hydrax, who tried to fly over to him, but couldn't lift himself off the ground due to the large hole in his wing. "*What does he look like?*" the god asked, creating a wave beneath his feet to reach Jeff.

"I'm sorry to say this, but... Oakley's dead," said Caesium.

"*What?*" Jeff exclaimed. Tears began to form in his eyes. "No... this can't be happening... He was my first and best friend," he cried.

Everyone stopped celebrating immediately. There was no denying that Oakley was annoying, but he definitely meant a lot to Jeff and certainly didn't deserve to die so early.

"I've failed... in my goal," Jeff mumbled. "I couldn't save everyone..."

Hydrax put a supportive arm around Jeff's shoulder. "*He will be remembered. By you and everyone else he was friends with. And you can still meet him; the most important memories never fade away. Now all you can do is try to avenge him by rescuing the other deities and completing your quest. Every deity has suffered a moment in their life when they couldn't save someone. Even an ultimate weapon would have that problem.*"

Jeff's tears stopped to an extent at Hydrax's speech. "Y-you're right," he stammered. "Oakley's death will not be in vain. Which other deities are left to rescue? My family's shrine only had space for the human and liskous ones, so I'm not familiar with the elf and dwarf ones."

"There's Aurik and Kosma left; as well as Eldrit, elf god of magic; Sequia, elf goddess of nature; Shekina, elf goddess

136

of empowerment; Eitri, dwarf god of metalworking; and Galvok, dwarf god of protection," stated Aeterno. "Also, where's the human with the laptop? I didn't see him during the fight."

Bob got up to his feet. "What happened? All I remember is—"

"Don't get complacent, heretics!" a voice echoed all around. Ghogiehk reformed and a dark cloud emerged, twice the size of all the previous clouds combined. *"Your attempt at victory lay on the shoulders of a lesser being, the same species as me, except it wasn't god. This lesser being who was once classed as superior to me tried to take control of me, yet my divinity proved it futile! Now watch, foul demons! Kerphan avatar of supremacy!"*

Ghogiehk's whole form began to materialise as a towering being. It was quadrupedal, with the head of a dragon and cuboid-shaped structures covering its entire body. It roared, causing a swarm of gigantic projectiles of some kind to launch from the structures. Imryth began to raise a wall of rock to block them, but it crumbled away immediately.

"What?" she exclaimed in disbelief.

"All powers are futile now!" laughed Ghogiehk. "This is my avatar form; my soul given true form and true dominion over all! Do you see it now? I'm god. *I am god!* This is my universe and..." It noticed that the projectiles weren't hitting anyone. They all stopped in mid-air.

"It's true you've become much, much stronger," said Aeterno, flying towards where Ghogiehk stood.

Enraged, it fired another barrage of projectiles.

Aeterno lifted up his hand, and the blades stopped.

"But think shallow thoughts and that strength will be thinned across the narrow path you have cast."

"No... This can't be happening..." cried Ghogiehk. "I was promised the universe... my universe, to create life in and rule over..."

"A universe is not for one being," stated Aeterno. "Even we immortals choose to share it."

He was responded to by a roar and another volley of projectiles from Ghogiehk.

Aeterno simply lifted his hand again and they stopped.

"Why can't I negate this power?" howled Ghogiehk. "Why, why, WHY?"

It was met with no reply, only another raised hand. And then it moved no more.

"About time!" said Nimbus.

"I keep on telling you that my powers damage the universe and should only be used as a last resort—" chided Aeterno.

"Oh, spare me the lecture! We would've won way earlier if you had done this at the start!" grumbled Nimbus.

Suddenly, a projectile that had been fired separate from the main group struck Nimbus in the back. The god barely had time to look surprised before it detonated.

"MOVE NOW!" yelled Aeterno, hurriedly circling his wrist.

Nimbus turned around and saw that, whilst it had detonated, it was exploding at an extremely slow speed, so lethargic that it gave Nimbus time to fly away as the beginnings of shadowy flares sprouted from the projectile like growing shoots. Aeterno then clenched his fist, and it stopped exploding completely.

"What just happened?" asked Jeff, gazing with disbelief at the immobile stygir and explosion. "Why have they—"

"They're frozen in time," Aeterno explained. "Although I am more known for being the first deity, I bear the power to alter time and space completely. However, I cannot reverse the alterations I make and that is why I cannot use it on a whim. Stopping time here could alter its flow in some other part of the universe, and altering space could create a black hole big enough to disrupt orbit." He flew back, but found he couldn't move his left arm. "It seems that in my rush to stop the projectile, I altered time a bit too much," he stated. "Lapideis, can you make me a sharp piece of rock and pass it over?"

Lapideis carried out the request. No sooner had Aeterno caught the rock than he casually cut off his left arm. Everyone stood still, horrified. A spray of blood stayed in suspended animation, resembling a macabre crimson staircase. "Nimbus, can you stem the blood flow with an air current?"

"T-thanks for saving me," mumbled the sky god, still in shock from being hit by the projectile, "Yes, I will."

"Thanks need not be given," replied Aeterno, "just do not harry me about destroying the universe when there could be another way to defeat our enemies."

"Those powers he has... They're the ones Catarehk was talking about! They're real!" exclaimed Morehk.

What are they? asked Bob.

"He'd always mention that his true enemies had powers that could shift the fabric of the universe, and that Chaigidir, the second husk could not negate them! Besides, look at him

– does he look normal?" On Void-vision, Aeterno showed up red, like everyone else did. But he was a glowing, shiny red – like a sun – and it hurt Bob to look at him for too long.

"Aeterno, what is that power?" he asked incredulously.

"Truth be told, I do not know," Aeterno replied. "It was bestowed upon me by the divinite, yet I know it's not a deity power. If there was time to look into it, I would study it and try to find out. For now, let's look for the missing human."

EIGHTEEN

Another macabre metal-and-flesh monstrosity attacked Gary. He evaded it swiftly and plugged an all-purpose cable he had designed into an exposed blood vessel and his laptop. Quickly, the power was drained from his attacker, and it slumped to the floor, joining the others that came before it. Panting and dripping with sweat, Gary printed off a glass of water and drank it, but not before checking all around him to see if something else was coming. No sooner had he defeated one of them than another threat was already attacking from a different angle. Finally, after he had confirmed nothing else was coming, he began to walk to a different part of the maze. Had the others found the deities, if they really were trapped here?

"I've found him!" a voice came from above.

Immediately, Gary printed off an energy blaster and prepared himself for combat. Above him was the god Lapideis, whom he remembered from the fight on Primium. He was then joined by his teacher, some troll, other liskous gods and the rest of his team all except Oakley.

"Where were you, Gary?" asked Caesium.

"I was stuck fighting lots of creatures. You might not believe me, but they were technology powered by flesh," explained Gary.

"We fought their creator and got the shifter core."

Gary's laptop then began to beep. "Oh no! Not another one!" he exclaimed. It was a voice call from a member of another group. He answered it, and the sounds of battle blasted from his laptop's speakers.

"HELP!" a voice screamed. "I'm the last member of my group. Another has escaped with Galvok, but we are stuck on Atham battling—" The voice was cut off by the sound of an explosion.

"This is bad. From the five groups I had contact with, all five have called me saying something similar." Gary went to his call history and played some of his previous ones: "Gary! It's me, John. Please go to Atham and help defeat—"; "Longinus! Stop the Longinus Republic!"; and "Even Shekina can't stand up to them. Help us! HELP—"

"Wait." A look of concern crossed Aeterno's face for a brief second. "Did they say Longinus? I've heard that name before... but I can't remember where from."

"I've done a search on it, and, apparently, it's a group of rogues Nimbus defeated ages ago. They were a group of three, so I'm not sure if it's the same one; they can't be a republic and, from the sound of things, they had an army."

"The only way to find out is to go there," said Imryth. "Magic users were nearly wiped out by the stygir, but Volundur alone made sure all living elves at the time could use magic. These Longinus rogues could've amassed followers and formed an army."

Jeff pulled the phasecraft from his pocket and activated it. Immediately, their surroundings changed to a plinth floating in white space. This time, everyone thought as one, and, a few seconds later, the projection read, "Base reality, planet Atham." When the phasecraft deactivated, everyone was standing on a barren planet that looked uninhabitable, resembling Ferraheim before it got its water supply, but less metal-rich.

"Look, there's another group!" Jeff exclaimed, pointing to five beings about forty metres from them. He activated his jetpack and flew to where they were.

Everyone else followed him, hoping to get some information on what was happening on Atham.

When they reached the group, they could see that some were dead. Amongst the survivors, three still lived: two humans and an elf. They were trying to dig graves for the two casualties, but were in such a terrible state that they couldn't.

"Are you OK?" Jeff asked. "Don't worry, we have Nimbus with us, and he can help your injuries a bit. What happened?"

One of the humans tried to speak but could only groan and spit blood. He began to paint crimson letters on the ground with his fingers: "L O N G I N U S H A V E T H E D E I T I E S T H E Y A R E".

"Don't stress yourself, John; I can speak," groaned the elf. "We… failed Aurik. A group of rogues have the deities. They say they're working for the good of the system. Their city is…"

Nimbus began to use his powers to give them more oxygen, and Hydrax made a stream of water for them to drink, but the remaining survivors all slumped to the floor, lifeless.

"Damn it!" cursed Nimbus. "Longinus, huh? I should've killed them when I had the chance. I thought they wouldn't survive on such a wasteland with only three broken scale-staffs."

"HEY YOU!" roared a voice. A large platoon of human soldiers marched towards them, with jetpacks and ten tanks. "Why aren't you fighting in the war?" asked their commander. "And why are you in cahoots with the enemy races and the cowardly neutrals?"

"Your government gave you orders not to attack us. We have the shifter core to repair Industria," spoke Bob. "We're going to rescue the other deities and then—"

"Aha!" the commander exclaimed with a grin of triumph. "If we get that thing, we can easily win the war AND be remembered as heroes for ever! Attack them!"

"No, stop!" cried Bob. "I don't want to hurt you!"

"*YES, YOU DO!*" yelled Morehk. "*YOU COULDN'T EAT GHOGIEHK, SO YOU CAN AT LEAST DO THIS!*"

All of a sudden, the commander gasped and began breathing frantically. Then he fell to the floor. The entire army stopped their charge and screamed in fear.

"A little more and his head would explode," Nimbus spoke casually. "Thanks for needing to breathe, so I could use my favourite power on you. Pretty *breathtaking*, huh?"

"Enough gloating, Nimbus," said Aeterno and Cognitio in unison.

"WE SURRENDER! WE WERE ONLY FOLLOWING ORDERS!" bawled a soldier.

One of the tanks exploded in a shower of metal and flames.

"Didn't you hear us?" cried another soldier. "Show some mercy!"

"This isn't our doing," replied Aeterno. Look behind you!"

A man in a white hooded cloak stood behind them. The back and front of his cloak were emblazoned with a dark-blue spear shattering a block of a glowing golden material, which was likely meant to be divinite. He stood on a tank half the size of himself with the same design on it. On his hands were chunky gauntlets of the same colour as the lance on his cloak.

"What asylum did you spring out of?" asked a heavily decorated soldier, who was likely the second-in-command.

"Mortal fortis, deus mortis," the man chanted. "I am a Longinist. The path I take is a path for a better system, with no problems and no deities. There is still time to meet the Ruling Trinity and join us."

"No problems?" guffawed the soldier. "Well, there's definitely one in your mind. Boys, let's show him why we're the military!"

The man flicked his wrist, and another miniature tank materialised from his gauntlet. Its cannon locked on to the soldier and blasted him to pieces. The other one began to fire at a tank.

"A poor leadership results in downfall. Just like the deities will lead to the downfall of the system," declared the man.

The remaining military tanks all fired at him, blowing him apart. A cheer rose up from the victorious soldiers.

"Is killing a simple foot soldier really such an achievement for you incompetent fools?" came a voice.

Five more men with the same cloaks walked towards the soldiers. They materialised more tanks, and the military tried to surrender immediately. However, they were eradicated instead.

"Mortal fortis, deus mortis," the cloaked men said in unison.

"You have seen what happens to those who oppose Longinus, travellers. Join us and hand over the deities, or else!" threatened the one who had spoken first.

NINETEEN

"How many have you killed?" asked Lapideis. "Why are you doing this? And where are my fellow deities being held?"

"We have only killed those who oppose us. That is all. And why do you assume they're still alive?" responded the leader of the Longinist group.

"They're deities! If you mortals try to stab them, the blade will break. Unless you have a stygir or someone else who's had contact with divinite, you can't kill them!" The god of earth made the ground rise up and wrap around the arms and legs of the Longinists, trapping them.

The tanks immediately began trying to destroy the bindings that held their creators, but the ground below them swallowed them up. More of the ground rose up, this time becoming iron arms holding a gargantuan hammer. Lapideis made a swinging motion with his hands and the arms swung their hammer at the trapped Longinists.

Immediately, the hammer was reduced to barren dirt and fell to the floor, along with the bindings.

"*What just happened?*" asked Lapideis in a shocked tone.

"It took us an eternity, but we've managed to create a metal that can negate the effects of your powers, immobilise you or even kill you!" a Longinist explained triumphantly. "This is the silver to your werewolf; this is longinite!"

"AND THIS IS A VACUUM!" shouted Nimbus, and he made a gesture with his hand. "It *sucks* to be you!"

"Nimbus, stop," pleaded Cognitio.

The Longinists reacted by printing off helmets of longinite from their gauntlets and putting them on. They stayed alive. Cognitio flew into the sky, to which they responded by creating more tanks to shoot him. This caused the perfect distraction for Imryth to bombard the Longinists with fireballs. Cognitio then swooped to their tanks and burned them all with a slate-scale.

"Wait, Imryth. Let's keep them alive so we can interrogate them," said Jeff. "They seem to think they're doing the right thing, so maybe we can find out why."

"I like your thinking," Caesium told him.

Imryth made the fire burning them subside, and the heavily charred Longinists tried immediately to make more tanks. Aeterno flew to them quickly and smashed their gauntlets off their hands with his staff. Cognitio picked up the wreckage and began to scrutinise it.

"Where is your city?" he asked them.

"Longinus does not give information to its enemies," one hissed.

Another whispered to him and then said, "Actually, as of now, it does. I'll show you the way to it."

"That's suspicious," Aeterno stated. "Do you have a map or anything?"

"Look! One must've fallen out of his cloak pocket earlier!" said Gary, picking up a piece of parchment.

"Will you kill these ones, Bob?" asked Morehk threateningly, sending pain into Bob's head. *"They're your enemies; there's no reason for you not to. Do it now!"*

"NO, I WON'T!" hollered Bob out loud.

Everyone looked at him.

"I… won't have a detention after the quest is over, Cognitio," Bob added rapidly.

"If you say so. Try not to make it too obvious… that I'm a strict teacher." Cognitio then turned to Gary. "These Longinists use a heavily advanced 3-D printing system powered by their longinite. How does your laptop work?" he asked.

"It's a bit complicated," Gary muttered.

"I'm fine with complicated."

"Well, there's a processor that can generate matter—"

"Made of what?" Cognitio sliced the laptop open with his claws, revealing a large, dark-blue cuboid amidst a mass of wires.

As soon as he had done this, Gary printed off a large cloud of dark-blue smoke and began to run, along with the other Longinists. Everyone began to chase after him, but was soon lost in the smoke. When those who could fly flew, they found the cloud was extremely tall; it seemed there was no clear path in sight.

"Nimbus! Why aren't you summoning a wind to blow this away?" asked Cognitio.

"I can't! It's like this stuff's laced with longinite!" came the reply.

Bob activated his turbine suit, and Imryth used her

wind magic, causing the smoke to clear. Bob noticed that he could now see again as he did before the contract, probably as an effect of the longinite. After all, the stygir and the deities had some things in common. He cursed himself for not being concerned about how Gary showed up yellow on Void-vision. It was a strange feeling to have everything in so much detail after having only seen in basic colours with outlines.

"I've got his scent; he went that way!" declared Antony, and he pointed to their left.

Everyone began to run or fly swiftly in that direction. Soon, streaks of yellow began to flash in front of Bob.

"What… was that?" he heard Morehk ask very quietly.

Some strange new material our enemies have, thought Bob in response.

Eventually, they escaped the cloud, and Bob's vision returned to normal. In the distance, he could see a massive army of yellow figures and some red ones hanging limp, as if tied to a post. Above them all, a mist of a new colour coalesced into a person and back again repeatedly. It was blue.

Morehk, have you seen yellow and blue before? queried Bob.

"Yellow's an enemy of both red and green. I've not seen blue before, though," confirmed Morehk.

"Where is the enemy?" asked Lapideis, looking around, puzzled.

Of course, Bob realised, *Void-vision gives an x-ray-like effect.*

"Something's getting closer!" Aeterno alerted everyone.

Bob saw the blue figure had turned into a mist and was approaching them. Bob activated his turbine suit and flew up to intercept it. Instantly, the top half of a man clad in heavy armour materialised out of the mist. To everyone else, the armour was white and had the Longinus symbol on the breastplate.

"A stygir host!" exclaimed the man. At the height they were at, nobody else could hear him. "You must be the most powerful of the enemies. Face me!"

The mist then surrounded Bob, taking him above the clouds in the sky.

"BOB! AFTER HIM!" yelled Lapideis.

"Not so fast," came a chorus of voices in unison.

It seemed as if the entire forces of Longinus had gathered; there were masses upon masses of white cloaks with various longinite devices. Three figures with dark-blue hoods stood at the front of the army.

"What should we do?" asked Caesium.

"Bob's got much stronger now, and I'm sure he can win against half a floating man," said Cognitio. "Let's defeat these ones and rescue the deities!"

TWENTY

The man carried Bob to a large structure floating in the sky. It was completely transparent and shaped like a cuboid with cut off vertices.

"Welcome to the Sky Arena of Longinus," the man told Bob. "Who is your stygir?"

"Why do you want to know?" asked Bob.

"You're right. It would seem a bit dishonourable to know your strategy. I apologise."

The man then opened up a door in the structure and went inside with Bob. He materialised fully into a human form and went over to a transparent cabinet, producing a large glass bottle of a green substance. "I can tell your stygir is in a weakened state. Here's some gas from my last stygir-host opponent. Consume this until it gets better," he suggested.

"Isn't that still alive?" asked Bob.

"Only Catarehk and the kerphans can stay alive as long as a single molecule does," the man replied. "It's common for stygir to die when over 75% of their gas is destroyed. Now heal up."

"You do realise we're enemies, right?"

"Yes, but I joined Longinus to face powerful opponents, such as deities. There would be no honour in a fight where my opponent's weakened."

Gingerly, Bob opened the stopper and swallowed some of the gas. It was tasteless, but it made him feel less drowsy and in a better state overall.

After Bob had taken his fill, his opponent decided to introduce himself. "I am Lance, champion of Longinus. I fight for a good challenge, to get stronger and for personal honour. Who are you and why do you fight?"

"I'm Bob. I've just taken up the fight to rescue the deities, repower Industria and save the system."

"Ah, you're after a *noble* cause," Lance pronounced the word with irony. "The system doesn't need saving; you know yourself that we can all be allies, even the stygir. The ones who cause problems are the ones in charge now – the deities and Catarehk – who are trashing their system in their honourless war where the one with the most troops wins. Every side is pretty much the same. I'm with Longinus to try to take down the most powerful opponents, since they are usually on the other sides. Longinus offers honour; they built me this arena out of levitating, indestructible glass. With Longinus, I can defeat those steering the system in the dishonourable, wrong direction whilst achieving my personal goals of honour and strength."

"OK," said Bob, unsure what to think of Lance.

"Oh, I almost forgot to say. In this fight, I will use non-longinite armour, and I am a host for stygir, so my attacks will hit you despite your gas form. Is it fine with you that if all my stygir get displaced, I shall use longinite blades in order to land a hit?"

"I guess so. I'll be using a turbine suit and blaster, and I also host a stygir," said Bob.

"Good. Then may the strongest win. COMMENCE!"

On this word of command, the cabinet retracted into the wall and the door melted into its surroundings.

"Now your opponent isn't all human! Will you kill him?" asked Morehk excitedly.

If I say so, will you explain kerphan namerights to me? Bob asked Morehk.

"A kerphan!" Behind his helmet, Lance's eyes blazed with excitement. "This is the challenge I've been looking for."

Bob fired his blaster at Lance, hitting him three times in the chest. The armour dented a bit, but stayed intact. Bob fired again, but Lance dodged this time, moving with incredible speed despite wearing such a heavy suit of armour. Stygir gas materialised on his gauntlets in the form of knuckledusters. He moved so fast that Bob didn't notice him, and he landed a flurry of punches, breaking every single turbine on Bob's suit. Bob tried making a high-tech energy blaster out of stygir energy and a cannon in his other hand. No sooner had he done that than Lance punched both until they broke.

"HEY BOB!" Morehk roared. *"IN CASE YOU HAVEN'T NOTICED, WE'RE TRYING TO FIGHT HIM!"*

Bob materialised a set of armour all around him, covered in spikes, just as Lance threw a punch. His hand was speared, but he didn't halt or even seem to show any signs of feeling pain. In fact, his punch hit Bob's suit under the armour, shattering a bit of it.

"Dammit, Bob! Use my husk power!" ordered Morehk.

Bob did so and, instantly, found himself fully in control

of the stygir in Lance; it must've been a low-class one. He made it materialise blades and stab its host through the chest. However, a shield materialised over the place the blades were about to hit.

As they shattered, Lance threw back his head and laughed. "Not only a kerphan, but the kerphan of Thaumir, Morehk! How are you so weak then?"

"Why can you still use those powers?" snarled Bob.

"I said I was a host for *stygir*. The lack of an 'a' before the word, as well as the use of the word 'all' in a previous sentence indicate plural. Meet Pollux and Castor, twin stygir of the tenth husk Nehemir."

"*Stop controlling Castor, scum!*" a voice rang in Bob's head. It sounded noble and commanding, probably like how an upper-class knight from long ago spoke.

"Pollux! Right side!" commanded Lance.

Shortly after the command was issued, he split his body in two lengthwise. Bob tried to make both halves fall to the floor, but he could only control the left one. Lance responded by having his right side turn into gas and fly towards Bob, then become a fist and land an uppercut. Immediately, Bob lost control of the left side, and it soared up to meet with the right.

"And I really had my hopes up," sighed Lance.

Suddenly, the fist became gas again and was drawn towards Bob.

"*What's going on?*" asked Lance in bewilderment.

"*Don't call me or my host weak ever again, low-class peasants!*" Morehk cried. "*Your abysmal lack of power made it easy for me to control both of you at once. Bob, eat them!*"

Bob hesitated. It was fine consuming the dead gas

particles, but it seemed wrong to eat two immobilised living beings.

"*Well, most edible things were once alive! EAT THEM!*" Morehk loosened his control of Pollux and Castor a bit, and their frantic screams and pleas for help echoed around the arena. "*Do you listen to the enemy? Do the opposite of what they beg for!*"

"I can't take this…" spluttered Lance. Using the tiny bit of control he was given by Morehk, he coalesced his human form out of the gas and stared at it with disgust.

"*Sneaky,*" chided Morehk.

"I could take the fact that there are two of you. I could take the fact that you are weak enough for me to wrestle control of our contract with you. I helped you escape the Void, for honour's sake. But crying for help is dishonourable and cowardly!" Lance snapped. "I won't have it!"

"*We'll stop; we'll stop!*" whimpered Pollux. "*But… we need help in this fight!*"

"You ran away from the Void because you were unhappy with Catarehk's rule. Now I'm running away from you because I'm unhappy with your mentality," confirmed Lance.

"*Lance! You took us in because we had similar agendas to Longinus!*" Castor cried. "*Rescue us; the Ruling Trinity could still have uses for us!*"

"What, as jesters?" queried Lance with a smirk. "Those were obsolete many, many years ago."

"THERE'S NO HONOUR IN WHAT YOU'RE DOING!" screamed Bob.

He turned one of his hands into a long, sharp tendril of shadow. He sliced Lance across the chest, carving a deep wound. Blood gashed everywhere, but Lance didn't show a single sign of pain. He didn't even bother to seal it up. In fact, he seemed more invigorated than ever.

"Finally," he gasped and blades of longinite slid out of his gauntlets, "this is the challenge I need!"

Bob tried to fly away, but all his turbines were destroyed from Lance's previous punches. Swinging both blades in a series of rapid strikes, Lance incapacitated Bob within three seconds; all his limbs were cleaved off.

"Morehk, what should I do?" asked Bob frantically. He knew it was futile due to the properties of longinite, but he was panicking and losing his sense of reason.

Pollux and Castor, free from the control of Morehk, sped as quickly as they could to Lance. Bob half-expected Lance to slice them up or reject the contract in some way, but all that happened was that they re-entered his mind, and he sheathed his blades.

"Very well, I will give you one chance," stated Lance, "for that would be the honourable thing to do. But one chance only!"

Morehk, can you hear me? asked Bob, to which there was no reply.

Lance materialised a shadowy lance and charged towards Bob. Bob tried to wriggle away but couldn't move. Lance's lance pierced his side, but was stopped halfway, as if it had hit a shield. Bob materialised limbs out of stygir gas and stood up. He pulled out the lance and snapped it with his hands. And in that moment, a new feeling overcame him. It was exhiliarating and empowering. It was the feeling of strength. He could stand up to Lance. He could win this.

"Am I really so weak?" he asked sarcastically.

TWENTY-ONE

"There, it should work again," a Longinist mechanic told Gary, handing him his now fixed laptop. "Congratulations on the undercover mission."

"Thank you. Where's that idiot Lance?" asked Gary.

"Probably up in that arena of his, fighting someone," the mechanic told him.

Gary sighed in frustration. "Why? He'd be much more effective on the front lines!"

"Belial thinks so as well, but Jonas and Hestrus think it's fine."

Suddenly, a series of scalding geysers erupted from the ground, and Gary barely had enough time to print off a barrier to block the boiling water.

"They're here! I'll handle this," he told the mechanic and ran outside the building. He printed off a signal flare and fired a golden light into the sky, signalling a deity attack. Along with the golden light, a cloud of scented particles was shot into the sky to signal the same thing. In an instant, all the buildings had their outer layers flipped over to reveal longinite.

"Gary! My son, how did the mission go?" wheezed a

cheerful, hoarse voice. An old man with a bald head but a long, grey beard was standing next to Gary. He wore a hoodless version of the Longinus cloak but purple instead of white, which marked him as one of the Ruling Trinity: the founders and leaders of Longinus.

"Don't call me that, Jonas," Gary sighed. "It's patronising, and we're not even blood relatives."

"Yes, but Longinus is one family, as I keep telling you," Jonas told him. "Who's attacking us now?"

"The deities; are you getting too old to even smell the signal flares, you useless coot?" snarled another of the Ruling Trinity, stamping towards them. Over his cloak, he wore countless straps holding serrated longinite blades, and his face was charred and skinless, with pupil-less white eyes.

"A good day to you too, Belial," said Jonas, provoking another snarl. "It's always a pleasure to talk to you, isn't it? Have you seen Hestrus?"

"He claims he's preparing a stealth attack, but we all know he's doing nothing. I'll attack from the front. I can smell your computer boy. What's he going to do this time?" queried Belial.

"I'll attack from the front as well," said Gary, and he printed off a gun that fired longinite bullets.

"Wait. I've forgotten my weapons," declared Jonas with a chuckle. "Silly me! I'll go get them now."

"TO HELL WITH YOU, YOU FILTHY OLD MAN!" yelled Belial, and he threw a dagger at Jonas.

It purposefully missed his neck by an inch and shaved off most of his beard.

"THIS IS WHY I SHOULD BE IN CHARGE!" added Belial.

"You are. We both are, along with Hestrus," Jonas calmly replied, and he ran off to find his weapons.

"Then why isn't Lance beaten until he wishes to fight outside his arena? Why aren't you sent off to a retirement home? Yes, because you and that idiot Hestrus always gang up on my better judgement with your—" ranted Belial.

"Belial, calm down," Gary interrupted. "They're here! All troops, attack!"

Out of nowhere, a large amount of Longinist soldiers charged at the deities' side, only to be knocked to the floor by wind magic. They were kept alive by the Heavenspirians and were allowed to flee, likely for the same reason as before.

"I can sense our troops aren't faring so well," hissed Belial. "Luckily, I've formed a battle plan for this. Broadcast the deity room, laptop boy!"

Gary did as he was told, and everyone stared up at a large projection coming off Gary's laptop. It showed all the remaining deities besides Eldrit, Eitri, Sequia and Galvok, who were tied to the wall with spiked longinite chains. Stakes of the same material were pushed through their arms, legs and torso. Beneath their feet, a slab of longinite was set alight and burned them with eerie blue flames. This caused uproar amongst the Heavenspirians, who fought with even more rage and vigour at the sight.

"All you've done is make them angry," said Gary. "Was that your plan?"

But Belial was gone. Looking up at the projection, Gary saw that he was somehow in the deity room, sharpening two of his longest knives.

"Deities! Longinists! Temporary ceasefire, if you will?" he requested in an unusually calm voice for himself.

The Longinists obeyed immediately, but that didn't stop the other side from battling on.

Belial stabbed both of his knives, one into Aurik's shoulder and another into Kosma's. "A temporary ceasefire, if you will?" he repeated more slowly, dragging the knives downwards, grinning at the deities' screams of pain.

The fighting stopped completely.

He continued, "You know why this is happening. Your hidden crimes can't stay hidden for long. The secrets you have kept from Atlas—"

"Belial!" came an old man's voice from the projection. "We'll get to the torture part once we've gathered all of them. Have you seen my all-purpose longinite gauntlets?"

"SHUT UP, BEFORE I CUT OFF MORE THAN YOUR BEARD!" Belial roared, throwing knives everywhere in frustration.

"WHAT ARE YOU TRYING TO ACHIEVE BY THIS?" yelled Jeff.

"What do you think?" replied Belial. "A peaceful system, with no more trouble; by definition, a system with no deities." He then drew another knife and held it to Aurik's throat. "You especially. You owe me a face, sight and a family!"

The god whimpered pitifully.

"Longinus is one whole family," Jonas said off-screen.

"STOP!" bawled Antony. "How do we get you to stop?"

"Here's how. A portion of my troops will lead two of you to my position, for I wish to partake in the battle myself. Four of you will remain here and fight the main body of my army, whilst the remaining three will be led to an area by another group of Longinists," dictated Belial.

The Longinist troops then printed off miniature holoceivers, each one projecting the same image of the captive deities at the mercy of Belial.

"See? There's no escape, except if you're fine with Aurik leaving this world," Belial added.

"Aeterno?" said Nimbus. "Now would be a good time to use those time powers of yours."

"Where's the proof we cannot beat them yet?" Aeterno asked. "There's none. The enemy might be tough, but that alone is no reason to scramble the universe." He then turned to Belial and stated, "You've forced our hand, Longinus. We'll play by your rules. Hydrax, Lapideis, Jeff and Imryth, you stay. Caesium, Antony and Nimbus, you will be led to this area he mentioned; be very aware of your surroundings. Cognitio, you and I will face the leader."

Everyone nodded in agreement.

"Don't act like you're the heroes here, deities!" snapped Belial. "You know what you did and why Longinus was formed."

On the projection, Aurik trembled uncontrollably, his face pallid and streaked with sweat.

"Does anyone have a beard wig?" asked Jonas.

No one paid him any attention, not even Belial.

Everyone split into their groups and prepared to rescue the majority of the missing deities from what seemed like the most strategic and advanced group of rogues Atlas had ever known.

TWENTY-TWO

Turning his arms into machine guns, Bob fired a bombardment of bullets at Lance. Many of the bullets hit him in the wound, but he seemed unfazed as he sliced the majority of the projectiles in half with a pair of gaseous blades.

"Pollux! Castor! Prepare for the lure manoeuvre!" he commanded his two stygir.

Morehk, what's a nameright? Bob asked, panicked. *Nothing else seems to work on him!*

Lance turned into gas and charged at Bob. Bob fired, but Lance entered his body through his mouth as he breathed. All of a sudden, Bob felt like he was slowly being choked to death.

"Other races have more advanced respiratory systems, and deities don't need to breathe at all, but if any gas displaces oxygen in large amounts, it could prove fatal to the human body," he heard Lance explain triumphantly. "Currently, a human-sized mass of foreign stygir gas is residing in your lungs. What will you do?"

Battle them, Morehk! commanded Bob. *No... control them!*

Immediately, Bob felt oxygen rush into his body. He gasped and wheezed, taking in big breaths as he began to think of a way to escape the arena.

Then his legs broke apart. Bob tried to materialise a new pair, but his effort just made him feel nauseous. Next to disappear were his arms, which dispersed into the air. The form of Lance began to appear in front of him, but he was nearly as tall as the arena, with undamaged armour and no wounds.

"You can try to use your husk power, but I can use mine!" stated Lance. "Husk Nehemir has the ability to override the very weakest of minds and use their powers against them. Your already weak mind, deprived of oxygen as well, proved the perfect opportunity. If you had fought me instead of trying that cheap trick, maybe I wouldn't be stealing your stygir's particles by the second!"

Bob could see flickers of colour across his vision, but not green, red or yellow, nor blue, and not even the metallic grey; with Morehk disappearing by the second, so were his powers and Void-vision. Soon, Bob would be just as he was at the start of the quest: an ordinary human boy with a weak energy blaster.

"Don't just stand there watching those three kill me! Here, this is what a nameright is!" the last shreds of Morehk that weren't controlled whispered.

It was taking a long time to absorb Morehk because of the power difference between it and Pollux and Castor, and it could explain everything about the enigmatic power to Bob. After hearing what a nameright was, he realised how risky it was and why Morehk wouldn't tell him unless it saw proof of his martial prowess. But there was no larger risk than accepting defeat when there was still a possibility of victory.

"**Morehk; honoured destruction; kerphan of Thaumir, the first husk; witness to the defeat of Chaigidir, the second husk; enemy of deities and stygir alike; spawn of the Void, second only to Catarehk, honoured light, and no other stygir; and holder of Bob Solis' contract**," Bob chanted, like he was casting a spell or participating in a ritual. The words came out distinctively bold, and were said in a unique way which is impossible to describe with words. To truly know the tone and rhythm of Bob's speech, you would have to hear it firsthand.

Lance screamed in pain as the particles of Morehk were forcefully pulled out of his body and returned to Bob, reducing Lance to his original size. The wound on his stomach reopened, gushing out a fresh stream of blood. This time, he sealed it up quickly, panting as the dents on his armour reformed by the second.

"Namerights. I see," wheezed Lance. "Now I've got you right where I want you, **Morehk; honoured destruction; kerphan of—**"

His chant was cut off as a large, shadowy wave, similar to a vesp's death explosion but even larger, swept across the entire arena. In Bob's vision, Lance now appeared yellow, with Pollux and Castor drawn out of his body. His armour crumbled away, revealing a muscular man in a Longinus cloak. Undeterred, Lance stood up and launched a flurry of punches at Bob; however, without the armour, the most he could do was dent Bob's turbine suit.

"Your ren is mine!" Lance told Morehk. "And so is victory!"

The explosion Bob triggered did not come without a price; to be activated, the nameright needs one of the most vital parts of the soul to be exposed. The ren, as it is called, is a secret name all beings have that sums up their very existence, which has to be spoken in a particular way to be valid; as such, if one speaks the ren of another, they would have total control of that other. How the Stygir knew this vital secret of existence was unknown, yet one thing was clear: to let another being know your ren could spell certain doom.

"**Morehk; honoured—**" began Lance.

Bob materialised a tendril of shadow and wrapped it around Lance's mouth. "This fight is over, Lance," Bob told him.

"*Finally!*" sighed Morehk. "*Kill the two stygir first, then him!*"

There's no need to, Morehk. The fight's over, Bob replied.

"*Don't give me that crap! I saved your life. And remember the contract? Isn't being yourself better than being Catarehk's pawn?*" Morehk partially leaped out of Bob and took control of Pollux and Castor, then dragged them in front of Bob's mouth.

"*Well, eat them!*" it commanded.

But Bob still didn't want to. All food was once living, but did all food scream for mercy on the plate?

"*Show your inner warrior! Go on!*"

Bob wondered if he could sign contracts with them.

"*Or get me some underlings. But that won't fulfil your part of the contract.*"

Opting to save Pollux and Castor from being eaten alive, Bob made contracts with them. Unfortunately, no sooner had he done so than Morehk devoured them both.

What? Why did you do that? Bob exclaimed in shock and anger.

"There's only room for one stygir here. Now, let's deal with their human."

Unsure what to think of Morehk anymore, Bob approached Lance. The Longinist was scrambling around on the floor, albeit in a dignified manner, looking for shards of his longinite swords. He picked up a ridiculously small fragment and waved it around. "The fight's still on!" he told Bob. "I will defeat you, for my honour and for Longinus!" He threw the shard with extreme force and precision, embedding it in Bob's chest.

Bob spluttered blood and fell to the floor, his stygir gas arms and legs no longer functional.

Lance ran to Bob and pulled the shard out of his chest, then began stabbing him rapidly with it in the wound. "It's my victory! You've shattered my armour but I can still harm you!"

Bob remembered he still had one more weapon up his sleeve or, rather, on his belt. With all his remaining strength, he grabbed the Joule 1.0 strapped to his side with his teeth. Seeing the weapon, Lance prepared to stab it, but the shard, which was only a small sliver, crumbled from the strain of its previous stabs.

Panicking, Lance returned to the debris of his armour and began searching for another shard. Bob wrapped his tongue around the trigger and pulled it; it fired, hitting Lance in the shoulder. Bob's head was knocked back and hit the floor of the arena painfully. The gun clattered across the floor. Bleeding heavily from his shoulder wound, Lance began to stumble towards the blaster.

Bob tried to activate his turbine suit and fly away, but to no avail. However, the turbines still spluttered, and, somehow, he felt a bit better. He tried it again, and he could feel the tips of his arms and legs returning. The small gusts, although not powerful enough to lift him, were probably enough to blow away the small amounts of longinite embedded in his body, if they were pointing in the right direction.

Lance reached the blaster and fired at Bob. However, Bob materialised a shield and blocked the blast. Now with complete arms and legs, he materialised a tendril from one of his arms, pulled the gun out of Lance's hand and then shot him in the chest. Lance fell to the floor, clutching his stomach.

"And now, the finishing blow!" said Morehk excitedly.

No, I can't kill another human being, Bob told it.

"Remember the contract!"

Ignoring it, Bob walked over to Lance.

"That was a good fight," Lance spluttered. "Finish me."

"No, there's no point," said Bob. "You could join us. Are there any medical supplies in your cabinet?"

"To be dishonoured by the enemy like this..." Lance growled.

Bob stepped back and readied his blaster.

"NO!" Lance yelled. "I'll show you how a man of honour dies! Arena, open!" The door appeared again, and Lance pulled himself towards it.

"Wait! You're not planning to—"

Before Bob could finish his sentence, Lance jumped out of the arena. Bob tried to use Morehk's powers to fly, but they didn't work.

"A side effect of longinite," Morehk grumbled. "You'll have to wait if you want to fly. And this death doesn't count to your contract; I didn't get to see anything!"

The Longinist soldier's descent picked up speed.

"And, anyway, why do you want to save him?" queried Morehk.

He said the system was being trashed by honourless war, so he's probably seen horrible things that made him want to join Longinus. There was still hope for him; he could've been one of us, confirmed Bob.

"If you say so. I don't see any point."

Lance went past the clouds and disappeared from sight.

TWENTY-THREE

"Gary, what were your motives for coming to the Below-Heavenspire?" asked Lapideis.

Imryth prepared fireballs in her hands, Jeff reloaded his blaster and Hydrax pulled out his rope.

"What Below-Heavenspire? It's been destroyed by a virus in the security system that spreads nanobots everywhere. And guess what that building's linked to?" queried Gary with a laugh.

"No! You don't mean—" began Lapideis.

"The Heavenspire itself, by a hidden phasing ladder," Gary cut off Lapideis. He typed furiously on his computer and pressed enter, then laughed with joy. "And I'm just sending an order for them to phase and destroy it! Your fortress will be no more, and divinite will rain down on Atham!"

Lapideis made the ground below him turn into a spike and pierce the computer, but the longinite inside the computer nullified the attack.

"All troops, hold them off whilst I continue the programming!" commanded Gary.

The Longinists printed off countless tanks, which fired in unison at the deities' side. Imryth summoned a wind, which blasted some of the bullets back at them, but more tanks were printed off to shield the first ones. Hydrax threw his rope and activated a slate-scale that caused a violent series of explosions, carving wide gaps in the Longinists' ranks.

"*Imryth and I will hold them off!*" Hydrax said telepathically. "*Take care of Gary!*"

Jeff flew above the troops whilst they were focused on Hydrax and Imryth, and shot at Gary. He dodged expertly, then printed off his own energy blaster. He fired with uncanny accuracy, destroying Jeff's jetpack with three shots. However, Jeff had come prepared, and a second jetpack emerged from the remains of the first one.

"A regenerating jetpack?" exclaimed Gary.

"You'll regret betraying us!" replied Jeff, and he fired at the laptop.

Gary printed off a shield just before the blast hit, then fired at Jeff, who turned around, had his jetpack take the blast, and then had it grow back.

"Gary, why are you doing this?" Jeff asked. "We need your help! Oakley's died and—"

"So what?" asked Gary. "He was a pointless being, unfit for even Longinus to take him in. And you know exactly why I'm doing this, just ask the Grey Triptych—"

Before Gary could finish his sentence, Jeff fired rapidly at him, then dive-bombed and cracked his blaster across Gary's face. "Take that back!" he snapped.

Blood, teeth and shards of glass flew everywhere. Quickly, Gary printed off a glowing, blue chain and flung it at Jeff. There were a few blaster shots, and the chain was split in three places and fell to the floor.

"I never thought you would be this quick-witted," mused Gary, printing off another chain as well as a sniper rifle.

Jeff fired at the laptop again, but the shot missed as Gary tactically rolled away. Setting the sniper's sights on the regenerating jetpack, Gary pulled the trigger. For some reason, out shot a solid bullet instead of an energy blast. It struck the jetpack perfectly, and the resulting explosion sent Jeff plummeting to the floor. He hit the ground with a thud.

"You said you want to become the system's ultimate weapon," spoke Gary, printing off another chain. "The Void would've consumed the whole system if you were." He flung the chain, only for Jeff to get up and dodge it with no sign of injury.

"You like to talk," muttered Jeff, thanking his luck that he'd picked the latest shock-absorbing combat wear from the Below-Heavenspire's arsenal. He waited for his jetpack to regenerate, but nothing happened. "*WHAT?*" he exclaimed.

Gary threw the chain, and it began to automatically wrap around Jeff.

"The nanobots in the bullet should've eaten it away by now," smirked Gary. "Only a pitiful ultimate weapon would rely on a gadget."

"LIKE YOU CAN TALK!" shouted Jeff. He tried to shoot the chains off himself, but his arm was pressed by his side by the tight restraint. Sweating from the effort, he began to try to escape the chain with his own strength. All was in vain. "I'LL DEFEAT YOU!" he roared. "I'LL SHATTER YOUR ORGANISATION WITH MY OWN—"

Gary printed off a gag and silenced him.

"That's enough out of you!" growled Gary. He then opened up a call on his laptop and spoke into it. "Ruling Trinity, I've obtained a power source for Tabris."

*

"Awesome, Gary! Well done, my son!" Jonas congratulated with a grin. "Oops, I mean affirmative, Gary. Good work, agent of Longinus. What? Too cheesy? Fine. Affirmative, Gary." He then turned to Lapideis, who'd fallen into his trap.

"What just happened?" Lapideis wondered out loud, trying to break the longinite cage he was in. "I was flying, and then—"

"Oh. You must've fallen into the portal I made with my all-purpose gauntlets. I made the exit portal inside this cage to trap any gods or goddesses if they fell in. Are you a god or goddess, my good sir?"

Lapideis was confused at the man's behaviour. "No, but I've come here because I'm thinking of joining your group. Give me a few reasons why I should."

"There's so many!" Jonas exclaimed and shook his hands in excitement. "For starters, we're all one big family! The members of Longinus look out for each other and work together to accomplish their goals. Then, we have access to more-awesome technology than the new god can make. I met a guy like you once. He was very arrogant and span his staff a lot. He didn't like my idea of the Angel System. I think he was a god! He was sky blue. Do you know him?"

"Wait, what's the Angel System?" Lapideis asked. "How

are you still alive after all this time? What are you trying to achieve by being rogues? And what did Aurik do?"

"An elixir distilled from longinite has increased my lifespan, though it's only temporary, and we only have enough for three droplets a decade. The Angel System? That's my idea. For ages, a bunch of others and I have been riddled with plagues, famines and other nasties. We tried to contact the gods and goddesses, but they never answered our calls. It turns out that they were the ones who caused it and tried to cover it up with their relocation plan! So, eventually, I formed Longinus with two others – Belial and Hestrus – to try to take divinite for ourselves and our peoples so as to heal them. Everyone should have access to divinite, not just those chosen by gods and goddesses."

Lapideis was unsure what to do. His opponent didn't seem to care about defeating him, and he was rendered immobile and weak in the longinite cage.

Jonas pulled a book out of his cloak and began to look through it. Lapideis noticed that he wore gauntlets similar to the ones the regular Longinists had but more compact and with silver runes of some sort on them. The index finger on his right glove turned into a pencil and he began crossing off pages.

"Hmmm," Jonas muttered to himself. "So, those left are Eitri, Galvok, Eldrit, Lapideis... Wait, Lapideis..." He fixed his captive with a stare. "It's you!"

His gauntlets turned into longinite-firing machine guns, and he shot Lapideis multiple times in the chest. Lapideis fell down, with crimson coating the bottom of the cage.

"That will teach you to hoard the cure for most fatal

diseases and the key to eternal life!" Jonas exclaimed triumphantly.

The world in front of Lapideis was blurring. He gritted his teeth, pulled out the bullets and got to his knees whilst Jonas reloaded his gauntlets from a pouch in his robe.

"DIE, ENEMY OF FREEDOM!" howled Jonas. He fired, but Lapideis disappeared. "Oh, I forgot to close the portal," Jonas realised.

He opened up another portal, jumped through it, and came out of the one Lapideis flew into originally. The god was surprised when Jonas landed on him, but he could react quick enough to shake Jonas off before the Longinist could fire at point-blank range. Jonas opened up another portal and reappeared behind him, but Lapideis was ready. Having calculated the amount of bullets the gauntlets could store from when they were fired earlier, he created a floating rock wall for each bullet and arranged them in a line in front of him. Jonas fired, but, even with the negating power of longinite, his foe was unscathed. He printed off a platform of longinite held aloft by rocket boosters, which he placed beneath him, and flew towards Lapideis, reloading as he sped towards the god. Lapideis coated himself in stone armour to stem the blood flow and began to throw stone javelins at the speeding Longinist. Almost instantaneously, Jonas created a portal in front of himself and sidestepped hurriedly to avoid going through it; the javelins were sent through it and then sent back at Lapideis through another portal that he opened.

Realising the dangerousness of his enemy, Lapideis opted to use one of his more powerful moves. Shedding his stone coating, both his hands slammed into the ground as he yelled, "EARTH'S SHAPING: TERRA FIRMA!" Immediately, he collapsed to the floor from using up a large amount of energy in such a weakened state.

Seeing an opening, Jonas' gauntlets changed into harpoons on chains, and he fired them, attempting to spear Lapideis through the heart.

And then the very earth began to move.

The area around them was quaking at a rapid speed, and the ground split and cracked, with large shards of rock flying everywhere. Lapideis jerked upwards, his eyes aglow with golden energy. With new-found vigour, he dodged the harpoons and javelins with ease. Any wounds he had closed over, leaving only a few scars to add to his tally. He punched the air, and a shockwave struck Jonas square in the chest, knocking him off his platform. Reacting quickly, the Longinist opened a portal underneath himself and reappeared behind Lapideis. He began to print off a cage around the god of earth, but Lapideis moved so fast that he was far away by the time the longinite prison had formed. He slammed the ground, and a vast shockwave knocked Jonas off his feet. Even though the longinite could nullify the effect of deity powers, the shockwave had hit Jonas feet-first and sent the gauntlets flying from his hands.

The earth stopped shaking.

"You fought well," Lapideis commended his enemy, trapping him in restraints made of thick stone. "If you had managed to hit me with that longinite, the effects of terra firma would've stopped completely."

"You should meet Lance, one of my sons," Jonas told him. "Beat up and begging for mercy. Even if you stop me, the rest of Longinus will make you pay for what you've done! Plague-spreader! Human-experimenting filth! False protector of the system!"

"Wait, what—" Lapideis began, but he was cut off by blaster fire.

He formed a protective dome around Jonas before the bullets could hit him, then made it disappear. Troops in Longinist cloaks aimed their guns at their elderly leader from the top of a nearby mountain. One pulled out a device that resembled a projector and fired a beam at Jonas' gauntlets, drawing them to their position.

"I don't remember Hestrus making a tractor-beam," stated Jonas. "What's going on?"

One of the Longinist troops put the gauntlets on, and then they each pressed a button hidden on the inside of their own cloak. The garments changed colour to grey, and the symbol of Longinus disappeared.

"THE DEITIES' SECRET ORGANISATION!" roared Jonas. "TRAITORS!"

"We have never formed a grey-cloaked group," Lapideis told him. "State your business, defectors."

There was no reply, just a hail of longinite bullets.

Lapideis created the series of walls again to block them, then freed Jonas. "Who are these people?" he asked the Longinist.

"They are your secret group," came the reply. "Don't you know? Come on, you've spoken to Aurik once in your career, haven't you?"

"I believe I am yet to be acquainted with his friends then." Lapideis flew up to face them. "Grey-cloaked ones, what is your allegiance?"

The only reply was the whipping out of pistols loaded with longinite bullets.

Lapideis brought his hands together in a move that would shatter the mountain; however, a single shot was fired into its peak, protecting it from the move. Many more shots were fired at Lapideis, who began to block them with walls. Suddenly, one of the grey-cloaked pistoliers appeared behind him and shot him in the chest. Lapideis retched blood and began to fall to the floor.

"It's true," remarked the pistolier, who had reappeared on the mountain. "These gauntlets are amongst the finest of Hestrus' work, and these gods are powerless against longinite."

Another appeared in front of Jonas.

"BACK, BACK!" Jonas yelled, throwing nearby stones at his attacker, who laughed at those futile attacks.

"It seems that keeping you alive wasn't necessary for the plan, but I will make your death a slow one, you crazy, old man," drawled his attacker, who thrust his pistol into Jonas' chest. "This pistol has space for ten bullets. One is inside. How long do you think you'll last?"

The others laughed as Jonas began to howl and beg for mercy.

"No, no, let me do it!" requested the one with the gauntlets. He appeared in front of Jonas and readied the Longinist's former weapon for use against him.

Lapideis got to his knees, struggling and panting from the effort. *I... must... save... him,* he told himself, trying to stand on his feet. All the time whilst he was doing this, the words Jonas had spoken echoed in his head, demanding answers. Did the deities have allegiance with their enigmatic attackers? There was no time to think of that now, as it was clear that they would soon get tired of tormenting Jonas. But there was no way he could reach them or do anything about longinite in an even weaker state than before. Unless...

Lapideis cleared his throat and uttered the word deities would only speak when they knew there was no other option, the word equivalent to discarding all belief mortals had for you, the word that he hoped would reverse the order of weakness when it came to the new-found blue metal.

"DEUSNOVA!" shouted Lapideis, and a golden glow began to radiate off him. Titanic stalagmites erupted from the floor and shattered the pistols of Jonas' would-be executioners.

The one with the gauntlets turned to face Lapideis. "YOU SHOULD BE DEAD!" he screamed, and he began to fire at Lapideis. "You will be now, thanks to longinite!"

Lapideis lifted an arm. The bullets crumbled away, and then the gauntlets did. Cries of surprise echoed all around the area.

"You have weapons made of longinite – a type of *metal*," Lapideis explained. "If I force myself to exert all my power at once, I can control everything found in the earth for a limited time!"

"But exerting such a large amount of power would crumble away the body or at least make your power useless for centuries, millennia even!" exclaimed a man in a grey cloak.

"I'm a god. Neither of those matter," Lapideis stated.

He closed one of his fists, and the earth below the attackers' feet became thick quicksand. They sunk immediately and struggled, with no way to escape.

"Now, you will tell me who you are!" the god commanded.

"YOU KNOW WHAT TO DO!" one shouted.

All of them issued a mental command to a hidden bomb implanted in their bodies. Lapideis jumped in front of Jonas, wreathing his body in a type of blast-proof concrete, just before the bombs exploded.

"Why did you save me?" Jonas asked Lapideis, who had fallen to his knees.

The god's golden aura had disappeared, and he was writhing in pain. For it was just as the grey-cloaked man had said: this was the price paid for using the deusnova and exerting all of his power at once.

"Whose side are you on anyway?" questioned Jonas.

"The Heavenspire's," muttered Lapideis through the pain. "The side that protects the mortals of Atlas. What you said earlier, about the plagues… if we inflicted them and brought you here to cover it up, Longinus has every right to want revenge. But I am adamant that we didn't, and the grey-cloaked ones are hints of an enemy both our sides must face. By the way, your Angel System misses out one crucial detail: with no mortals to believe in them, the deities die. Faith sustains our immortality. Other than that, it would've been a great idea."

"Very well. This is sudden!" remarked Jonas. "Peace with the deities! Any sign of villainy and I will defeat you, though, mark my word!"

"Understood," confirmed Lapideis. "How will we spread the ceasefire, though?"

"If anything, we should try to find Belial first, before he gets out of control. But try to avoid fighting him," replied Jonas.

With that, both god and Longinist ran to the torture room, where a fierce battle was raging.

TWENTY-FOUR

"COME BACK HERE!" yelled Gary, shooting at Jeff.

A few seconds after being captured, Jeff had realised he could use his jetpack to burn through the power chain, and the fight had begun anew.

Quickly, Gary called the units who were fighting Hydrax and Imryth, "Troops, I require backup!"

"Negative, we've got our hands full at the moment!" a soldier answered. "Besides, you need to learn to fight something more than the military's machines; not every foe's cybernetic." The call ended.

Cursing, Gary printed off a horde of tanks that fired at Jeff, who responded by beginning to blast and destroy them. Despite their overwhelming number, he executed a series of strafing attacks swiftly – a manoeuvre he had spent hours refining – which used speed to pick them off rapidly. Whilst he still could, Gary crouched behind the tanks, printed off a blaster and shot, hitting Jeff on the side of his hip and breaking his combat wear.

How long until the nanobots destroy the Heavenspire? thought Jeff, and he had an idea. "I surrender!" he told Gary. "Call off your tanks!"

"As useless as Oakley to the end," smirked Gary, and he sent a program to the tanks to make them stop firing. Jeff took off his jetpack and walked towards Gary, with his hands above his head. Then, at the last minute, he pointed his jetpack at Gary's laptop and turned it on, melting the laptop. Gary shot at Jeff's wrist, and Jeff let go of the jetpack, which flew off.

"YOU'VE CAUSED IRREPARABLE DAMAGE!" hollered Gary, and he kicked Jeff in the stomach.

"Which you haven't caused to the Heavenspire!" Jeff laughed.

Gary pulled a spare power chain from a compartment in his blaster and threw it at Jeff. It wrapped around him, and Gary took his blaster just to be sure. Then, Gary violently kicked Jeff to the floor.

"You're lucky you have to be a power source for Tabris, or I would injure you more," snarled Gary.

"You can power Tabris – whatever that is – as much as you want, but you can never defeat the deities," replied Jeff.

*

Cognitio and Aeterno arrived at the torture room. It was an old, dilapidated building, with a faded Longinus symbol struggling to stay above the entrance. Around it was an abandoned slum, making it blend in to its surroundings. The Longinist troops who had led them there ran off quickly, likely to join some other battle.

"I don't like the look of this," Cognitio murmured. "It looks like a trap. I'll check around to see if there are any other ways in."

"Then I'll go through the entrance to confirm your theory," said Aeterno.

Cognitio moved ahead, whilst the god of space and time pushed open the door and walked in slowly, his eyes alert for any traps. A pressure-activated switch on the floor and two levers holding up glowing, blue chains were spotted instantly. He destroyed them with swift swings of his staff. An alarm began to wail, followed by familiar voices telling him to run away.

"Don't be foolish," Aeterno told them. "I'm not leaving my fellow deities behind!"

He flew further on, until he came to a large hallway. On either side, deities were chained to the walls like slaves, and their pleas for his retreat became more frantic. Only one deity was silent – Aurik – who stared at the floor with a look of shame, his eyes glazed and devoid of life. Quickly, Aeterno freed all the trapped deities by breaking their chains, causing the alarm to wail louder. Everyone ran, except for Aurik, who didn't move at all.

"What are you waiting for?" asked Kosma. "I foresee a bad future if we stay here. We should regroup our forces! Belial is too strong to face one-on-one."

A thought struck Aeterno, and he gasped. "Have you seen Cognitio?" he asked frantically.

"No, I haven't. Was he with you?"

Aeterno sped to the end of the corridor, where he was greeted by a brick wall. However, despite it feeling real, it was a projected illusion, and behind it lay a phasing ladder. A hole in the roof and its respective debris on the floor confirmed Cognitio had gone through it. For some reason, instead of being bright pink, this one was longinite blue. Aeterno tried to phase, but there was no reaction, not even a slight kick-back. There were blueprints next to it, which described Longinus' new phasing ladder, which deities could not use. It seemed there was nothing he could do to assist Cognitio.

"Dammit!" he said to himself. If he couldn't make himself useful in battle, he had to make himself useful somewhere else. But, wait, Longinus' motives seemed to lie heavily in Aurik. He flew back to the god of money and success, who was on his own now.

"Where's Kosma?" asked Aeterno.

"All... the others... left to find their... their weapons and... help... the other members of... your group," stammered Aurik.

"It seems you know a lot about Longinus' motives. Will you explain them?"

"NO!" Aurik yelled, and he fell to the floor as if pushed over. "I take back the relocation plan! It wasn't me! IT WASN'T ME!"

Aeterno decided to stay silent for a while. Usually, Aurik was a cheerful and calm god, the one who would crack amusing jokes at parties, and was liked by everyone. The broken shell in front of him was probably born during Belial's torture.

After a while, Aurik spoke again. "Fine. I'll tell you what you want to hear."

*

The dimension inside the phasing ladder was a small, white room, making close combat imminent. Cognitio activated a slate-scale that turned his staff into a hard metal and blocked the two knives in Belial's hands. However, a third knife held between his toes came up into Cognitio's stomach. Thinking fast, Cognitio activated a water-scale and a powerboosting-scale, shattering Belial's leg with a high-pressure jet of water. Instantly, the Longinist stacked the knives on top of each other and attached them to his hip; they fitted perfectly, as if made for that purpose, even stopping the blood flow somehow. Cognitio turned his staff to metal again and swiped at the leg, but Belial dodged expertly before throwing more knives. Cognitio couldn't dodge them this time, but, even for a skilled individual such as Belial, it was hard to throw knives whilst dodging, and they only scraped his foe's arms. Cognitio activated another slate-scale, causing a blade to pop out of the end of his staff. He cut off one of Belial's knife holsters, and Belial responded by grabbing it and swinging it like a whip. Knives flew everywhere, but Cognitio deflected with his staff the ones that would have hit him.

"Where are the deities?" asked Cognitio. "Release them!"

"I can't believe you fell for the illusion of a wall. They were right next to you!" Belial gloated.

Belial grabbed handfuls of knives and threw them at Cognitio, who responded by melting them with a jet of molten metal. Whilst Belial reached for more knives, Cognitio cracked his staff across Belial's head, knocking him to the floor.

"You put up more of a fight than some deities," said Belial, getting up and blocking the staff's next strike with his hand. "Join Longinus; we could use you in our quest for vengeance."

"I'M NOT JOINING YOUR GROUP OF ROGUES!" bellowed Cognitio, and he fired flaming chains at Belial. "Besides, what do you have against the deities?"

Belial dodged the chains expertly and threw more knives at Cognitio's wings, arms and legs, pinning him to the wall. "Everything! I can tell by your scent and voice you're a liskous. You probably grew up by a bookshelf, learning things peacefully and eating up Heavenspirian propaganda. If you lived with the community that became Longinus, you would know why all the system's so-called protectors must die!"

Cognitio activated a magnetic slate-scale, hoping to drag all the knives out of his own limbs, but nothing happened.

"Not all metals are magnetic, just like your precious divinite, which will soon be ours. But I'll pull them out if you want," offered Belial. As slowly as possible, he dragged out the knives, with their serrated edges claiming more of Cognitio's flesh.

Cognitio tried not to scream, but, in the end, the pain was too unbearable and he let out a cry. Belial grinned at this, continuing to pull out more knives. Once all of them were out, Cognitio slumped to the floor. Belial brought out a blue chain and wrapped it around Cognitio.

With that, Belial declared, "Unfortunately, I can't let you die. Once Tabris is complete, you will though."

TWENTY-FIVE

"Are we there yet?" Caesium asked the Longinists escorting him.

Wherever they were going, it seemed it was in the most desolate and remote part of the planet, as far away from the Longinus settlement as possible. The only thing stopping his desire to fight them was the ever-present threat of the captive deities being killed. Behind him, Antony was being interrogated by a few of the Longinists about why he was still alive, and more were debating whether they should attempt to capture Nimbus now or carry out their orders.

Suddenly, the Longinist observing the projection of the torture room began cursing loudly; everyone looked at it and saw that the deities had been freed. There was no sign of Kosma or Shekina, but, for some reason, Aeterno and Aurik stood in the middle of the room talking to each other.

"THEY'VE GOT NO HOSTAGES!" yelled Nimbus triumphantly. "ATTACK!"

Immediately, all the Longinists who didn't wear helmets fainted as Nimbus activated his vacuum power.

The remainder began printing off tanks as quick as possible, but Caesium and Antony were in close range of them and defeated them before they could do any real damage.

"Cowards! Attacking whilst our backs were turned!" cursed one of the remaining Longinists. "Well, mortal fortis, deus mortis! Our main force should be making quick work of your allies."

Immediately, countless Longinists appeared out of thin air, along with someone else. He wore the purple cloak of a Ruling Trinity member and his face was obscured by the blank visor of a bucket-like longinite helmet covered in runes.

"Enemies of Longinus," he said in a voice heavily amplified and deepened by his helmet. "Prepare to face me – Hestrus – Longinus' partisan expert!"

Nimbus summoned a gale, but Hestrus and the other Longinists vanished before it hit them. Then, Hestrus appeared behind Caesium and threw a glowing blue chain at him. Before Nimbus or Antony could respond, the partisan expert and his target were gone.

*

"*What?*" gasped Aeterno in surprise. "You didn't—"

"Yes," mumbled Aurik. "That was the relocation plan."

"Tell me more. Explain it in full detail."

"Fine, but I will not reveal the other two members of the Grey Triptych. The Longinists – these people on Atham – they were brought here by me when I promised them a better planet and a cure to the Great Plague.

The Great Plague was a disease wracking Primium, and not even the liskous could come up with a cure for the superbug causing it. It caused every symptom you could think of, literally everything – rotting of the flesh, loss of senses, uncontrollable spasms and the list goes on – but the worst thing was that the victim would never die. They would just sit there as their condition became worse. My entire family committed suicide to relieve themselves of the pain. And then the pathogens would just move on to another victim." Tears began to well in Aurik's eyes. "I just wanted to save them, and make a better world... a better world..."

"Continue," Aeterno told him. "I am sorry for your family's deaths. However, I remember you were credited with curing this disease; what happened?"

"Something had to be done. I spread the idea of a better planet across Primium, and a large number of the humans bought it. My work with charities and helping the poor had made me a god of... well, you think it's of success, but, actually, I am a god of transference. I can alter the position of small physical objects and, of course, spiritual quantities such as luck. The pathogens were airborne and could fit between molecules, and if their host died, they would find the nearest being and infect them. I stranded the humans on Atham and then transferred the planet's pathogens to them. I told them it was to help the deities, and they bought this at first.

"I thought it was foolproof, but three people turned rogue against the deities and formed Longinus. They found air-scale and wind-scale in the lowest layer of Atham's crust, and they rebelled, trying to take the divinite for themselves. Of course, they were crushed instantly by Nimbus, and, when no one was looking, I had a secret punishment prepared. I transferred half the planet's pathogens to the ringleader's face – they ate away his skin and made him lose his sight. But you can see where I'm coming from; I stopped the time of strife, saving a planet by sacrificing a few towns' worth of people."

"No," said Aeterno, "extremes only need to be taken as a last resort. To think you'd mistreat those you had to protect like this! If you'd allowed time to take its toll, you'd have given these liskous you mentioned the key ingredient they needed to find a cure. But what is the Grey Triptych you mentioned?"

"It started at around the time technology had just been developed; not when Industria was complete, but when energy blasters were available to regular humans and hospitals were given anaesthetics. We formed a secret society, hoping to achieve our goal of upgrading life to a perfect state of being. I was the only god, and my influence gave them the cover for their work. At one point, they said they wanted sapient beings to experiment on. We took some of the Atham dwellers who had been struck down by the Great Plague and performed experiments on them. It was to make them stronger, and to make them a master race better than humans, elves, dwarves or liskous. One of our members could create beings who took on the form of the deities. We used these fakes to convince the Atham dwellers that this whole thing was ordered by the Heavenspire. The humans we experimented on were pacified by the idea that it was all part of the deities' plan. This continued until the member who made the fake deities went mad, took our failed experiments and fled to the furthest reaches of the system. Then Atham was abandoned.

"When Mekanyon asked us to find a shifter core, I remembered that, at one point, a Grey Triptych member had an obsession with them, so I came here. I thought it would be threat free, with Longinus having been crushed and all.

"However, Longinus hadn't been crushed; it had grown. The whole community was in on it; somehow, the disease wasn't affecting them as much, and they'd made some stone that cancelled out my power, as well as their own form of technology. Our use of the fake deities had sparked their uncontrollable hatred of the real ones. I was captured and tortured, along with many others." Aurik buried his head in his hands. "I don't know what I've unleashed on the world. It's come back to haunt me."

Suddenly, a titanic blue hand the size of the torture room burst out of the ground, grabbing Aurik. Aeterno struck its joints multiple times with his staff, but nothing happened. It was followed by an arm so large that it blotted out the sun. Another one tried to grab Aeterno, but he flew out of its reach.

"TABRIS OPERATIONAL," a robotic voice boomed.

Aeterno activated a powerdraining-scale, and the hands' movements slowed down. Shortly after, they ground to a halt.

"TABRIS POWER DOWN. TWO OF THREE SOURCES ACTIVE," the robotic voice concluded.

*

Caesium burst out of his chains, cleaving them in half with his pickaxe. He appeared to be in another reality; he was in a plain, white room with no phasing ladder in sight. It bore a surprising resemblance to the phasecraft's pocket dimension. Surrounding him were Hestrus and the other Longinists, who began to attack. Caesium swung his hammer in a wide arc, knocking out some of the Longinists, but the rest disappeared.

The regular Longinists never returned to the plain, white reality, but Hestrus did, and he struck Caesium from behind with an esoteric tool. It was almost identical to a rune-carver, but made of longinite. Three runes of destruction blazed white on the dwarf's back, and then a series of violent explosions shattered his armour. Caesium began carving a complex rune, but then Hestrus struck him over the head. The dwarf fell to the floor as his opponent wrapped him in another blue chain.

TWENTY-SIX

"So, besides the Angel System and killing off the deities, Hestrus is after some upgraded form of longinite, and you're all after the dissolution of Heavenspirian society as it is?" Lapideis asked Jonas. The two were running to the torture room, where, according to Jonas, Longinus' ultimate weapon lay.

"Yeah, pretty much, but we all found a common goal in overthrowing the deities after your friend's relocation plan. And, to help us, we built an extremely powerful technological weapon, which is supposed to hold off an army of deities: Tabris, the angel of free will," explained Jonas.

"What's it going to do?"

"I don't know myself. Hestrus built it, and Belial designed it." The two reached the torture room; the roof had been torn apart, and the torso of a giant, humanoid being towered over them, with its head above cloud level. One arm was at its side, holding Aurik, and the other was trying to swat Aeterno, who attacked it from afar with a metalbreath-scale, causing a spiral of molten iron to sizzle against its longinite body. Much to Lapideis' surprise, any damage caused by Aeterno's attacks was cancelled out by regeneration.

"DO IT!" screeched Aurik. "FREEZE THIS THING IN TIME!"

Aeterno raised his arm, but then a cloud of stygir black gas enveloped Tabris. Hidden longinite printers pumped out the gas with an audible hiss until the robot was invisible. Aeterno gritted his teeth and froze the whole area covered by the gas, his concentration absolute. Not a molecule outside the smokescreen would lose the flow of time. It should've worked, but why was the smoke still billowing in the air?

Tabris stepped out, unaffected.

"*WHAT?*" exclaimed Lapideis, his entire body shuddering from surprise.

"Lapideis!" Aeterno called. "Although this robot is trying to attack us, Longinus does not have to be our enemy!"

"I know! Jonas here is trying to call a ceasefire," Lapideis replied. "The true enemy's some organisation Aurik's part of!"

At these words, Aurik hung his head in shame and sobbed. Vast, angelic wings spread from Tabris' sides, completely destroying the surroundings.

Jonas landed a punch on Tabris' side, then recoiled in pain. "AARGH!" he howled, clutching his bloodied hand. "Where are my gauntlets?"

"THE PARTICLES OF YOUR GAUNTLETS ARE AT THE SITE OF YOUR PREVIOUS BATTLE WITH LAPIDEIS," a loud, automated voice droned. Tabris pointed one of its hands in the said direction, still not letting go of the captive god.

"Hang on! The Ruling Trinity can control this thing!" exclaimed Jonas, and he gave Tabris another order.

"Release the two gods in your hands then repeat what I'm about to say!"

"MAJORITY VOTE: NEGATIVE," Tabris replied.

Belial stepped out of the building, dragging Cognitio across the floor behind him. He threw countless knives at Jonas, slicing through his throat, chest, arms and legs. Jonas fell to the floor, lifeless. Belial's face twisted into a grin at the sight.

"Finally," he declared with a laugh, "I've finally got the majority vote, killed the old fool and ended the reign of deities! But don't worry, Jonas, I'll carry out your last wish. Tabris, release Aurik. Throw him from as high as you can whilst still on Atham, then test out the longinite hand cannon!"

Tabris beat its wings, causing gales to level the entire slum. It flew until its torso was fully out of the ground and then stopped. Amidst the sound of the furious wind, Aurik's fervent cries for help couldn't be heard. A moment later, he was plummeting through the sky, still wailing as he approached the earth at an extremely fast rate. Before he hit the ground, a bright-blue beam fell from the sky, enveloping him. When the beam subsided, all that was left of him were a few wisps of smoke drifting carelessly through the sky. The hand that used to hold Aurik had transformed into a gigantic cannon, and its barrel was still smoking.

Belial sniffed the air and began to cheer, "It works! It works! YES!"

Lapideis couldn't believe his eyes. A moment ago, Aurik had been there, and then he just wasn't. Fatigue gripped the god of earth like a vice. It seemed the effects of deusnova were taking their toll.

Belial noticed him and reached for his knife belt. Lapideis ran towards Cognitio, dodging the knives he could and ignoring the pain from the ones that hit. The longinite, as it slashed his shoulders and arms, made him feel mortal again, and he knew that he would die as a result of losing his deity powers and now his immortality. Beating his wings, he took flight and, with his feet, grabbed the chains binding Cognitio. More knives came towards them, and Tabris' cannon began to charge up. Even with his strength virtually gone, Lapideis was a skilled flier, and he dodged the knives expertly in such a way that they cut off Cognitio's chains. Cognitio took flight immediately, and the blue glow in the cannon began to die down.

Then Lapideis felt it. His body was slowly crumbling away, like the deities whom everyone had stopped believing in. Why, he did not know. Maybe it was like his previous opponent said, and the deusnova would be his undoing. Or that everyone believed in Lapideis, the strong and resolute god of earth, not the dwindling mortal he was now. His legs were completely gone. Cognitio cried out something, but Lapideis couldn't hear it. The knives kept on flying, as if Belial had an infinite supply. Tabris stood motionless, unmoving, useless. Just like Lapideis was right now. Crumbling away more, the last thing he saw was Cognitio and Aeterno fighting on, continuing the quest for him. The god of earth closed his eyes and smiled as the remnants of him glided down to Atham's soil.

*

"The true longinite?" Caesium scoffed. "That's the biggest load of crap I've heard in my life!"

"BE QUIET!" yelled Hestrus. "You've been brainwashed by the deities! They beguile you with promises of power, but I offer something better: the path to the negation of all power. By adding runes and magic to longinite, and evolving it, I will make a metal that can stop anything: the immortality of deities, the power sources of war machines, even life and death itself! That is true science: to be the master of your creations, to have absolute command over them and to choose what happens at will. And the deities, obsessed with that inferior divinite crap of theirs, are hindering true science!"

Hestrus had given Caesium countless speeches like this; Hestrus was devoted to his work and, naturally, would fly into a rage if anyone insulted it. However, in the red heat of his rant, he had ignored the fact that Caesium was getting closer to finishing a rune by the second. It was a complex one, which was unknown to most of dwarfkind due to the nature of its ability. Yet Cognitio had taught it to the dwarf nominees, and it seemed it would come in handy right now. Hestrus' troops had gone, since Nimbus and Antony had joined Imryth and Hydrax in battle. There was no one to report Caesium's actions to Hestrus. With one more stroke of his rune-carver, he was done.

"Yes!" he exclaimed happily, looking at his rune. "My rune of viewing tells me the deities are beating your army!"

Hestrus disappeared, and, as he did, the rune began to glow bright pink. The plain, white reality disappeared, and Caesium found himself on Atham again. Hestrus writhed in agony next to him, with pink lightning crackling on his body.

"WHAT HAPPENED?" Hestrus shouted.

"That wasn't a rune of viewing," Caesium told Hestrus. The dwarf swung his hammer, but the lightning had subsided and his opponent vanished. "It was a rune of phase feedback!" Caesium turned around and knocked Hestrus' rune-carver out of his hands with his pickaxe, then smashed it with his hammer. "Cognitio taught me that rune. When someone tries to phase out of a small reality, it damages them and moves all beings from that reality to the base one. *But how do you have access to other realities?*"

"So, you figured out my secret," said Hestrus, and he lifted off his helmet. Underneath it was a bald head with crystals of a familiar, glowing pink embedded in it. "I managed to construct my own reality that I can phase into and then reappear anywhere on Atham."

"Th-that's phasing ladder material!" exclaimed Caesium, as Hestrus disappeared again.

Hestrus then appeared behind Caesium, holding a sword of longinite. Instantly, the rune's power activated and Caesium turned around to parry the new blade expertly with his pickaxe. Caesium struck with his hammer, but Hestrus was gone before the blow hit.

"But—" began Caesium.

"But only the deities have that technology?" Hestrus sneered, grabbing Caesium by the arm. "They didn't make it; they found it under this planet's surface, like we eventually did. And they took credit for it, hindering the world's knowledge and the path to the true longinite!"

Caesium found himself in Hestrus' reality again, but, without the chain wrapped around him, he could fight back. The small, enclosed room gave him the advantage he needed, and he knocked Hestrus to the floor in a few seconds. Blood flew from the Longinist's mouth in a cough, causing Caesium to flinch.

"Ah, it seems I've found your weakness," wheezed Hestrus, and he coughed up more blood. He then squeezed his wounds and grinned at Caesium's screams. "Then you'll love this," he gloated with a laugh, and he pressed his fingers against all the phasing ladder crystals in his head. They glowed in a rhythmic pattern, and, all of a sudden, the room changed to a macabre and morbid display of blood and gore.

Caesium screamed and fell to the floor, his hands over his eyes.

"I made this reality, so I can decide what's in it within reason!" Hestrus laughed again, and rotting entrails appeared in mid-air, wrapping themselves around Caesium's face.

The dwarf passed out from shock.

Hestrus made a rune of communication appear. "Belial, Jonas, I've got back the power for Tabris!"

"Though I predict you won't have it for long," came a mysterious female voice.

Hestrus spun around, and longinite swords formed in his hands. A human woman wearing a grey shroud had somehow appeared in his reality, holding a crystal ball and a telescope. Behind her steel-rimmed glasses, her featureless eyes glowed the colour of divinite, and her hair was covered by a shawl.

"*Kosma?*" exclaimed Hestrus. "This defies logic! DEFIES IT! You're trapped in the torture room, so this is probably a side effect of altering my reality, conjured by my subconscious—"

"It's a side effect of threatening the system, Longinist," Kosma told him sternly, and her crystal ball began to glow with a blinding, eldritch light.

TWENTY-SEVEN

Jeff felt his power drain from him again. The glowing, blue chain binding him was somehow sapping his energy, and his will to stay awake and alive. Gary had gone off somewhere, to help fight Hydrax, Imryth, Nimbus and Antony. He tried to break the chains again, but to no avail. If he had possessed his jetpack, he would burn through it, but that had been stolen by Gary. Hopping a few steps at a time was possible at one point, before the chains had begun to drain his strength.

In the distance, a large, blue being had risen from the ground, which seemed to be Longinus' ultimate weapon. Jeff rolled towards it, stopping after a few inches when it became too difficult. What could he do to help? Suddenly, the chains fell apart, and a slicing sound rang through the air. Jeff turned around and saw Bob standing behind him, panting. Despite his turbine suit being wrecked, he had survived his battle with whatever had taken him into the sky and returned to the ground.

Strange, Jeff thought, *he has no blade on him, but somehow managed to slice the chain.* But that was the least of the system's problems at the moment. "Thanks, Bob," he said. "I have a plan. One of us can help take on Longinus' main forces and the other can try to fight the big blue thing in the distance. Either is fine for me."

"You idiot! The guy you freed noticed something odd immediately!" Morehk hissed. *"You're lucky he didn't investigate further! Don't use my power so recklessly for trivial matters!"*

"I'll go take on the blue thing," Bob told Jeff, ignoring his stygir companion.

"Are you sure?" replied Jeff. "Well, good luck. Do you have any way of getting there quickly?"

"My turbine suit still works a bit. What about your jetpack?"

"Gary took it. We'll just have to sprint."

"REBELS ON ATHAM!" a computerised voice boomed down from above. "THIS IS THE MILITARY OF PRIMIUM. RETURN CONTACT, AND JOIN OUR FIGHT AGAINST THE POINTY-EARS AND MIDGETS! IF YOU DO NOT, WE WILL USE THIS WORLD TO TEST OUR PLANET-DESTROYING BOMB. YOU HAVE ONE HOUR."

"What should we do?" asked Bob, panicked.

"Rescue the deities and get out of here in an hour," replied Jeff, his expression unchanged. "We can do it. Good luck in your fight." Jeff then ran off into the fray, whipping out an energy pistol.

Bob used Morehk's flight and soared into the air. However, they were both exhausted after their previous fight and their speed soon began to decrease drastically. Out of the corner of his eye, Bob saw a dwarf on an iron dais covered in runes to make it fly. Judging by the length of his slate-coloured beard – which trailed down to his feet – and by his heavily decorated armour, he was probably one of the clan leaders.

"Clan leader, sir!" Bob called out. "I'm a nominee for deity education. Some deities are somewhere here on this planet and rogues have captured them. Also, the humans have a bomb ready to—"

The dwarf raised his giant hammer at Bob, and a blast of runic energy hit him in the chest.

"Ha!" the dwarf scoffed. "Nice try, double agent. As if that hasn't been tried by you techie fools!" He fired again.

Bob was forced to split his body with the stygir power to save himself.

"You have the powers of a stygir!" the dwarf exclaimed. "*How far are those filthy humans going to go?*" A rune of communication on the dais glowed. "Volundur! Carry on trying to disarm their bomb, but lend me a few of your troops; the humans have a stygir on their side!"

"Filthy, no-good, metal fools!" cursed a voice from the rune. "Fine. I'm sending five Sovereign Sect magicians your way. Give the gas cloud a beating, Aesik, will you?"

"I'm on your side!" Bob told the dwarf.

"Yes, you are for five minutes before you take me to where the tanks are waiting, gas cloud," came the scoffed reply in between more blasts from the dwarf's hammer.

The dwarf was a skilled marksman, and Bob soon began to plummet, with the voice of Morehk also half-dead inside him. He began to chant his nameright in mid-air, but stopped when the dwarf gave him a hand.

"Don't worry, I'm on your side," Aesik told Bob. He

then lifted Bob onto the dais. "I think we should start with stopping the bomb; no, the rogues; no… the double agent!" he cried, hitting Bob in the chest with his hammer as all the runes on it activated. Bob began to descend to the ground of Atham. "Payback! A taste of your own medicine! Bye, double agent! No spy like you can stop Aesik Ironwill!"

So, Caesium's dad has killed me in the same way as Lance, who begged not to die, Bob thought, with a grim smile on his face from the pointless irony. The ground drew ever-nearer; it was a barren bringer of death. Bob closed his eyes and braced for the impact, but was saved by falling on a pillar of soft sand that had sprouted from the ground.

"Are you fine, Bob?" Lapideis, god of earth, asked him.

*

"What have you to keep fighting for?" goaded Belial. The blood-lustful Longinist had refused instantly any talks of peace with the common enemy and had instead flung his knives at the two liskous. Cognitio pulled the serrated knives out of his body, ignoring the pain and flow of blood; they were nothing compared to Lapideis' slow death. He then faked a throw adeptly, making Belial duck, and then shot flaming chains at his former captor. "Two gods are dead, and the whole point was for you to rescue them!"

"But there is no point in your fight either," Aeterno told Belial as he struck him from behind. "The bomb won't kill us, but it will kill you."

Belial doubled over, his spilled blood sizzling from the heat of the chains. However, he let out a laugh as he cut the chains with more knives. "As if!" he cried, taking off his cloak to reveal a glowing, thin, pink suit. "You deities aren't the only ones with powerful named moves!" He then bellowed, "DEATHSWIND SHREDDER!"

A countless amount of knives flew out of the suit in every single direction. Aeterno began to stop time, but then a grenade emerged from Belial's suit and exploded, releasing the same gas that Tabris had used earlier. Suddenly, Aeterno found he could stop time no longer.

"Unlike you, when we found the vault underneath our planet, we deciphered all the instructions and didn't hide them from the general public, you one-armed fool," Belial sneered as Aeterno and Cognitio were stabbed all over their bodies and pinned to the floor. "The unraveller gas Hestrus pieced together really does stop those who shape the universe!" He then stopped in his victory rant for a bit and scratched his chin. "Hmmm, maybe I should've kept them alive to snuff out the remaining members of the Grey Triptych."

*

Aeterno felt like he was falling into an endless chasm, but without any plummeting sensation. Just drifting, drifting through nothing and everything at the same time. He found it to his liking, like freedom from the pain of immortality. Was it death? He wondered what the meaning of his existence was or if the fights he had won throughout his life meant nothing. He wondered about what had happened in his mortal life and whether the quests with his original warband trio were still secure in a vault in his mind. When there was a warband trio, before one became dust on the ground.

"Stand up, once again," came a familiar voice.

The blackness around him was pierced by streaks of gold, intersecting in the centre of his vision to form the Heavenspire. The deities appeared around it, all of them, the ones who had died in the war, the ones who people stopped having faith in and even the ones fighting now.

"Your heart and brain still have a spark. Ignite it further," added the same voice.

Aeterno knew his purpose in existence; it was to ensure that peace in Atlas could exist. The deities faded away, and Aurik reminded him of the Grey Triptych that had to be dealt with. But not before Longinus, and definitely not before the war had also been addressed. The darkness faded, and the god of space and time's eyes flickered open, if only barely. Tabris wasn't moving, but Belial was jumping in happiness.

"THAT'S THEIR HEAD KILLED!" he yelled gleefully. "Payback! Now that's payback! You and your Grey Triptych will be punished more, though. But don't worry, I did you a favour; aren't deities meant to be in heavenly realms?" A manic cackle erupted from his mouth, and he thumped the ground ecstatically. "If you're still somehow alive, albeit immobilised and heavily bleeding, know this: Longinus will continue on its path of justice and it will succeed! Mortal fortis, deus mortis! Time to truly send you off with a longinite pyre; I'll get the flint and steel!" He ran to the slums to search for the fire-making rocks.

Aeterno looked at Cognitio, who didn't seem to be moving. "Get up, Cognitio," he whispered, pulling out a knife when Belial wasn't looking. The serrated, blue blades littered the floor in multitudes, so it would be impossible for anyone to notice something had gone awry.

"You get up yourself!" commanded a voice behind him. "He's clearly distracted, so now's your chance."

Aeterno tilted his head back and saw an elf. Her hair was silvery-white, but not from age, and it trailed to the floor. Similar to Imryth, she wore a robe, which shone in the hue of divinite, but no armour.

"You were made a goddess during the Stygir War, weren't you?" asked Aeterno. "I know your figure, but not your name. Who are you?"

"Shekina, goddess of empowerment," she replied.

She chanted an incantation quietly, and, instantly, Aeterno felt more battle-ready.

"You were very injured, so this is the most I can strengthen you and repair your wounded organs. The cool-down time is a century," Shekina explained.

"What about Cognitio?" asked Aeterno, indicating the fallen emissary. More knives had hit him in the head than Aeterno and, similar to Lapideis, he had lost an eye. Or rather, both of them.

"My power works on refining the divinite in the body. Unfortunately, there is nothing I can do," Shekina said mournfully.

Damn you, Cognitio, thought Aeterno. *You said being mortal opens up more paths of knowledge, but what's cleverer than wanting to stay alive?*

"Wait…" An idea sprang into his head. His remaining

arm reached for another knife and pulled it out. "Take me to Cognitio!" he commanded Shekina.

Belial was growling about equipment that wasn't scented for his benefit.

"I'll go and take care of him," she told Aeterno, drawing a familiar mage's stave from the folds of her robe. She waved it, and amulets materialised around her neck.

"Eldrit gave you his callstaff?" he asked, surprised. He didn't remember a day when the elf god didn't boast about his greatest artefact, and to have it being wielded by a fairly novice goddess was a shock to him. "Even so, I need you to stay here for just a tiny bit more," he requested. Raising up the knife, he slashed himself across the chest with it. Blood spurted everywhere.

"What are you trying to do?" she queried, horrified.

Her deity powers were beyond that of regular healing mages, but the self-injury Aeterno had caused was beyond even that. His blood, rising like a fountain, sprayed everywhere, covering Cognitio.

"Divinite reacts with a being's particles, giving them the same atomic mass as itself, whilst still retaining their original elements and properties," he uttered. "Your power can work on him now."

Belial ran his hands across various rocks.

"I thought you liskous gods were meant to be clever!" sighed Shekina.

"Standing around here isn't clever," Aeterno replied. "Do it, and it might be a B-grade answer to the situation."

Belial turned around and, on smelling the goddess, he roared in anger.

Shekina was already chanting, and, inside Cognitio's body, the most vital organs were repairing; this network would now allow him to stand back up and fight. His eyes were still gone, but the rest of him was not.

"*Why have all our prisoners escaped?*" Belial raged and knives flew in all directions once again. However, they did not travel far, as a gale of extreme force blew them all back at him, summoned by another of Shekina's chants. They were all dodged expertly, with the scent of longinite catching their wielder's sensitive nose. Cursing, Belial invoked an unspoken command, and the suit he was wearing glowed, causing the knives to pass into it harmlessly.

"*How do you have phasing ladder technology?*" Shekina asked. From her fingertips, flaming chains similar to Cognitio's erupted, but longer and faster. They wrapped around Belial, but disappeared into his suit like the knives.

"Because maybe the deities aren't all that special!" exclaimed Belial triumphantly. "This phase suit is beyond anything your minds could come up with." The chains flew out of the phase suit, but this time aimed at Aeterno.

"Any mage can negate their own spells," stated Shekina as the chains disappeared in mid-air.

Suddenly, Cognitio appeared behind Belial and began punching him furiously. The Longinist doubled over in agony and spun around, launching his knives at his new attacker. However, Cognitio seemed to know the attack was coming and flew behind the ruins of a building, only getting a few cuts.

"Come back here!" roared Belial, and he ran behind the building.

Cognitio flew to the other side of the building. "*What witchcraft is this?*" he exclaimed.

Shekina summoned a lightning bolt to come down on to the furious Longinist, but it had no effect.

"That suit he's wearing leads to a reality that living matter can't pass through!" Cognitio told her. "Use physical attacks to damage him!"

More knives flew at Cognitio, but he had already ducked before they flew out of the suit.

"You've only recently been blinded!" exclaimed Belial. "Why the hell do you act like you can see?"

"Sight is not the only sense. Over my centuries-long lifespan I have honed the other four as well. Besides, I've found the time pattern to your shots," confirmed Cognitio.

Pain seared through Belial's back as Cognitio carved red trails in his back. Shekina flew up on a gust of wind and delivered a kick to Belial's face. The Longinist fell to the floor, coughing blood.

"Why... wasn't the suit working? Hestrus told me it was flawless!" Belial cried out in fury.

"Why did you do all this?" Shekina asked him. "What did the deities ever do to you?"

"Everything!" snarled Belial, getting to his feet. "But especially hiding the Grey Triptych from us. I know you're helping them, as there's no way a mortal, god and stygir could conduct hideous experiments on a whole planet unnoticed. And then the stygir went crazy and took half our population with it. Did the oh-so-great deities do something then? *Did they?*"

"Yes, they did," came a voice. Lapideis walked up to the fallen Longinist, his presence carving disbelief on

Aeterno's face. "The stygir Ghogiehk has been defeated, and the souls of your people rest. I understand you must be upset by the torture you've been put through, but vengeance leads to madness, and madness leads to more torture. How about we take on the Grey Triptych together?"

Belial stiffened at these words. And then he wept.

TWENTY-EIGHT

"How big is this terrorist group?" groaned Nimbus as yet another wave of Longinists emerged from the slums. He activated his vacuum power, making those who weren't quick enough to negate it collapse. He spun his staff and drew a large number of Longinists into a whirlwind for Imryth to stun with low-level lightning magic. "In case you haven't noticed, there's a bomb that's going to kill us all soon!" he chided.

"Even if I die, Longinus will live on and defeat you all!" replied an enemy soldier. "Mortal fortis, deus mortis!"

"*This is bad,*" stated Hydrax, crippling the soldier with his rope. "*At least three of us will have to fight the military force to remove the bomb threat, but then we would be defeated instantly by the Longinists!*"

In the middle of the ranks, Gary could be seen, now bearing a pair of longinite gauntlets in place of his laptop. Imryth noticed him and fired a jolt of lightning at him. He tried to print something off, albeit struggling severely, and was only spared the blast because another soldier stepped in front of it. The soldier fell to the floor twitching.

Immediately, shouts of, "Good for nothing laptop boy," and "We're only protecting you for Jonas!" rang out through the ranks of Longinus.

Gary stared at the floor glumly, as if the battle were an online game and he had disconnected.

"I CAN HELP HOLD LONGINUS BACK!" a familiar voice hollered. Jeff dashed towards the battle, shooting at the Longinists whilst running. "Some of you go to deal with the bomb!"

Upon catching sight of him, Gary charged forwards, pushing his way through the ranks to enter close combat. Antony delivered a punch to his stomach, but, out of anger and determination Gary still stood, his body damaged but not his mind. He whipped one of Belial's serrated knives out of his pocket and plunged it into the troll's arm.

Antony screamed in pain and Hydrax summoned a titanic wave that he sent at Gary, but he activated the jetpack he had stolen from Jeff and flew above it. The wave went upwards, but Gary simply sped to the side and dodged it. However, the wave moved after him, and he was soon caught in it. Hydrax slammed his hand down on the floor, and it crashed down on to the Longinus' ranks, swamping them all. Nimbus created another whirlwind that swept up the water and Longinists, trapping them in a whirlpool. Imryth then added lightning to the mix, causing electricity to surge through it.

"Do you think we've done enough?" asked Antony sarcastically.

Their enemy now lay sprawled across the battlefield, unmoving except for a few twitches. There was no apparent sign of Gary.

"Right, moving on to the bomb threat—" began Antony.

The Longinists got to their feet slowly, staggering but still ready to fight.

"When will you get it?" a voice rang out. "Your powers don't work on us!"

"Yes, but magic did," replied Imryth, gesturing to the lightning-struck casualties surrounding them.

"They were just too slow to print off a non-conductive shield around them," confirmed the voice.

"*Now they're weakened!*" Hydrax exclaimed. "*Imryth, Jeff, go sort out that bomb threat!*"

"But your powers can't—" began Jeff, but Hydrax's telepathic voice cut him off.

"*There are other ways to fight,*" the god told him, brandishing his rope menacingly. "*Now go!*"

Imryth cast levitation and air-bubble spells around Jeff and herself, and they flew up, in search of the ship that was ready to detonate the planet.

"We have half an hour before the bomb detonates. I hope they make it," muttered Nimbus.

Suddenly, a grey symbol flashed from a few of the Longinists' gauntlets: three gears forming a triangular shape surrounding a brain. They tried to cover it, but the entire Longinus forces saw them.

"HEY!" yelled a Longinist pointing at the symbol projected from a nearby gauntlet. "IT'S THEM!"

Those who didn't have the symbol were gripped with an unnatural rage, and they fell upon their former comrades, roaring. Most of them disappeared in an instant, but a few slumped to the floor, with the head and limbs of each twisted at odd angles by the sheer force of the mobs.

"What's going on?" asked Antony.

"What do you mean?" asked a Longinist, holding up the head of an unfortunate casualty. "These are your troops!"

"The Grey Triptych has been with us the whole time!" another exclaimed.

"But their double agents are actually useful," added a third with a smirk.

*

"We're ready for the mission," a Grey Triptych member said into her communication device. "What do you need us for, master?"

"Just wait," a voice replied. "It seems Belial can't complain about me doing nothing anymore. I've got an irritating goddess on my hands."

TWENTY-NINE

"You're so easy to foresee," taunted Kosma as she dodged effortlessly the blasts from the massive energy cannons that Hestrus summoned.

Her crystal ball fired out a beam of light at them, and she placed her telescope in front of it, magnifying it into an all-consuming burst. The cannons disappeared.

"And now you're going to summon a longinite cage to where I am," she stated dismissively, jumping away before the contraption had formed.

A pair of guns that fired longinite bullets appeared in Hestrus' hands, and he opened fire. "Did you see this coming?" he asked gleefully. The rain of bullets was incinerated in another burst of light.

"As a matter of fact, yes, I did."

Hestrus teleported behind Kosma, but the goddess had already turned around. However, he then teleported behind her and fired at her head. The goddess slumped to the floor, with a smoking bullet wound through her skull. A golden disc of some sort fell out of her clothes and clattered to the floor. It was probably a weapon – one she would never get to use again.

"Sure, you can predict it, but can you prevent it?" he replied with a cackled.

Now it was time to move on to a more important matter: the activation of Tabris. The help he'd called for had confirmed they were ready, and Longinus' ultimate weapon would soon be fully operational. The dwarf was still unconscious and couldn't leave the dimension, so he was an easy kill for later. But not before Hestrus educated him on the glories of true longinite.

His phone rang in his pocket and he saw it was from Flavius, the leader of the group he had summoned. "Greetings, Flavius," he said. "I presume the Grey Triptych infiltration division is with you."

"Yes, they are," came the reply. "The plan you made is foolproof; Tabris will be a fantastic addition to our forces, and then I can finally stop acting like a test subject."

Once, Hestrus would have tensed at such words. But now he paid them no heed; he was someone else now, and part of something greater. "Indeed it is. Where are you?"

"We've teleported to the outskirts of the slum, using up our last phasing bomb. Tabris isn't moving, and Belial isn't fighting the deities for some reason."

Hestrus exited his dimension and appeared beside Flavius. The scene around him was exactly how his subordinate had described it.

"Here, have these," Flavius said, giving Hestrus unraveller grenades, an energy blaster and a longinite-bulleted sniper rifle.

The latter observed that everyone else was carrying the same equipment. He almost shouted out a complaint that someone like him shouldn't have the same as regular, inferior troops, but he managed to stifle it; he could punish them infinitely better with Tabris in his hands. Hestrus aimed at the one-armed god with the unnatural, time-shifting powers. His target was on the floor, immobile and probably dead, but with an enemy like this he had to be absolutely certain.

The crosshairs intersected at the god's head.

However, before he could pull the trigger, his target vanished. The scope was now looking at a tear in reality itself for some reason. Holding back a cry of frustration, he looked left and right, then up and down, trying to relocate his prey. Then he heard screams next to him, and the god was there, knocking out his forces with his bare hands. A similar rip had opened up near them, drawing in dust particles like a weaker black hole.

"*What?*" exclaimed Flavius. "How could you—"

The god lifted him up by the throat, and he knew any attempts to escape were futile.

"If you must know, I used the space aspect of my power. And now you'll talk for me. What is your organisation about? What are your motives? I've vanquished your stygir leader, so I'll have no trouble with the likes of you," said Aeterno.

"Hestrus, help!" Flavius croaked.

However, there was no way Hestrus would help such an incompetent underling, especially not one who'd given him away. The god aimed a kick at Flavius, but he dodged the brunt of the blast and then activated his dimension, phasing himself, his foe and Flavius, then he phased himself out quickly, trapping the other two.

"Hestrus!" Belial called to him. "As much as I hate to say it, we've been wasting our time on the quest for vengeance. The deities aren't the cause of the Grey Triptych, and I know it won't make amends for anything, but we could ally with them to stop the war, and end the famines and plagues—"

"And who would want that?" came Hestrus' curt reply. "It was *your* quest for vengeance, and it was a pointless means to an end. What would we have done after Tabris retrieved the divinite from the broken Heavenspire, to heal your people, and defeated all the deity-followers? Nothing! We would just have been left with ordinary, stupid people living their ordinary, stupid lives. I now know what the true longinite is. It's not a metal that can rule over all. It's life! Upgraded life that will—"

"What are you on about?" asked Belial, aghast. "They're your people as well! You were there from the beginning when we were brought here as kids, my best friend, and then we met Jonas, and I came up with Longinus! You invented the elixir that prolonged our lifespans, you invented our weapons—"

"Not anymore. Belial, this is pointless! This community of unlearned people and diseases is nothing! I realised that, and the Grey Triptych took me in. In return, I let some of them infiltrate Longinus to learn more about your sort. They have the same quest as me, the true quest: to have knowledge of everything; to be fully in charge of the system, and operate it like a machine; and to become a master race befitting of such knowledge!"

"So you let them experiment on your own people; you let them—"

"Once my people, but not anymore. Humans and rodents both came from the same ancient mammal, but do you see scientists going berserk when a few lab rats suffer side effects from an experiment?"

Belial staggered back, not sure whether to believe what he was hearing or not. Anguish coursed across his face and through his mind as Hestrus – the brains behind Longinus, the first one to join him and the one who once hated the Grey Triptych as much as he did – teleported behind him and snared him in a power chain. The other deities began to attack Hestrus, but more Grey Triptych members in Longinist guise appeared and began to attack them, cutting them off.

"I knew that, out of the three founders, one was that mad gas cloud and one was the man-dwarf," Belial spat. "I never expected the last to be you!"

"And I can always expect you to be growling or raging! Shut up and let me explain what's going to happen," Hestrus retorted. "Tell me, what is a gastrobot?"

Belial responded by sending a deathswind shredder flying in Hestrus' direction. The traitor went into his dimension and came out again when the knives subsided, giving Belial time to cut the chain.

"I'll tell you what will happen: whatever you've got planned with your new friends will fail!" declared Belial.

One of the deities had defeated the Longinists around her – an elf in a golden robe – and, with a single chanted word, she set Hestrus on fire. Screaming, Hestrus dived into a flooded part of the slum.

"As much as it feels wrong to say this, let's form a temporary alliance, Longinist," the goddess offered, summoning a lightning bolt and sending it at Hestrus.

"Fine," Belial replied, and he fired more knives at Hestrus.

"FOOLS! OAFS! YOU CANNOT DEFEAT KNOWLEDGE!" the former Longinist roared. He disappeared into his dimension again, dodging all the attacks effortlessly, and reappeared behind Belial.

"You call yourself knowledge?" Belial queried scornfully, turning around and throwing more knives.

Hestrus dodged them again.

"Then why did you try to trap a god whose powers involve manipulating space in a pocket dimension?"

Suddenly, a small crack began to appear in the air near them, like it was an eggshell. The crack expanded outwards, shattering more of their surroundings until out stepped Aeterno, carrying an unconscious Flavius. Despite facing off against Hestrus' troops and suffering a massive injury, Aeterno was still acting like he was unscathed. Drops of blood still fell from the wound that had saved Cognitio, like the start of a crimson downpour, but he either didn't notice or didn't care.

Upon seeing him, Hestrus threw all his unraveller grenades, but they were incinerated by someone: *Kosma?* The goddess appeared behind Aeterno, with no bullet wound or any sign of her previous fight.

"Thanks for getting me out, Aeterno," she told her fellow god. "Hestrus, we meet again."

Furious due to the fact that she was not dead when he had clearly killed her, Hestrus screamed a battle cry and charged at her, with two of Belial's knives in each of her hands. She dodged effortlessly and fired a beam, which Hestrus evaded by teleporting away.

"The disc that fell to the floor is my true power," Kosma told her would-be killer. "It's my timewarp checkpoint. Once activated, I will resurrect at its location, as long as it stays intact. No matter what happens in the present, the future shall always exist."

"Stand back, everyone! I'm going to freeze time," Aeterno announced.

Rapidly, Shekina called upon one of her deity powers, quickening the speed of all the deities, and Lapideis raised parts of the ground into the air to carry to safety the mortals who were on their side.

"And this is why I say the world needs more knowledge!" Hestrus exclaimed. "Thanks for telling me your plans."

Aeterno simply gestured, and the ground around Hestrus' feet began to cave in, as if it was water in a bath and the plug had been pulled. Hestrus tried to go to his dimension, but then the area around him warped in the same way the ground did. By manipulating the fabric of space, Aeterno had turned him into a sitting duck.

"Blasted screwing with the universe!" cursed Hestrus. "If you carry on like this and Atlas will be uninhabitable or – even worse – the universe will be destroyed! I don't know the origin of your power, but the master race the Grey Triptych wants will soon equal it, minus the risk of destroying the world."

A look of guilt and sorrow crossed the god's face. "I don't know its origin either," Aeterno admitted. "But, rarely, do I use it. Furthermore, any race that conducts experiments on sapient beings, and gains knowledge through dark and illicit means aren't masters. They're weaklings who have to go to extremes instantly rather than act civilised to achieve what they want." He raised his hand to freeze time.

"TABRIS, SWITCH TO ERADICATION MODE!" Hestrus screamed. "FLAVIUS, GO TO THE GASTROBOT POWER SOURCE!"

Instantly, Lapideis made the ground rise up and gag Hestrus before he could issue any more commands.

Staggering to his feet, Flavius used a Longinus gauntlet to print off a grappling hook. Aeterno turned around and saw Flavius fire the hook into the tip of one of Tabris' wings and zoom off. He began to freeze time, but Flavius cracked open an unraveller grenade. Thinking fast, Aeterno sped up his time and appeared in front of the unsuspecting Grey Triptych member. He opted not to freeze time in the air above him, since it could be disastrous for the planet's atmosphere and anyone who inhaled that air, especially if he did it over too large an area. He cut the line to Flavius' grappling hook with his claw, but that gave his adversary the perfect moment to throw an unraveller grenade in his face.

"And that's why you don't fight with only one arm, you idiot god!" declared Flavius with a laugh. He climbed quickly onto Aeterno's shoulder on the side that had an arm and vaulted off, landing expertly on the tip of one of Tabris' wings.

Quickly, Aeterno warped the ground beneath his feet, but Flavius was ready with another unraveller grenade.

"Glory to the Grey Triptych! The master race of all knowledge! The three great leaders!" Flavius chanted, running towards the back of Tabris' head.

This was now above cloud level, and Aeterno would have to fly up if he were to manipulate space accurately again. However, as soon as he reached Flavius, the Longinist had jumped into a hole at the back of Tabris' cubic head. No sooner had he done that than he emitted a painful, nerve-wracking scream. Aeterno looked closer and saw that the hole he had jumped into was closing and opening rapidly, mangling Flavius' body.

"HELP ME, GOD!" he cried out to Aeterno. "HESTRUS SAID IT WOULDN'T HURT! AARRGGHH!"

Aeterno altered space around the opening-and-closing walls to make them stop, and he pulled out what was left of Flavius. "What wouldn't hurt?" he asked.

"All I wanted was to be part of the new epoch…" Flavius began, gasping from the pain. "The master race…"

"Get to the point. It's the least you can do in return for me saving your life."

"Usually Tabris requires three mortals to be bound by energy chains, sapping their energy, but stops just before they die, so they can be reused. But Hestrus… Hestrus was the cleverest great leader, and better than the man-dwarf and gas cloud combined. He built a gastrobot secretly on Longinus' ultimate weapon, which is a device that converts power from meat; one or two humans should be enough to last a lifetime. He planned to shove the two Ruling Trinity members in it and use his influence as the remaining one to command it. Then… then anyone who stood in the way of our master race would be destroyed. Anyone who stood against… the New World's Gear."

"The what?" asked Aeterno. "*What are you on about? What's the New World's Gear?*"

But Flavius had breathed his last breath. The blood gushing from his legless torso ended him. It sprayed everywhere like a scarlet waterfall, even into the gastrobot.

Machinery hummed, and, for the second time, Tabris rose.

THIRTY

Upon the azure cube of Tabris' head, twin lights blazed vivid yellow, signalling the machine's activation. It turned its head to Aeterno and droned in a low, robotic voice, "NOT LONGINIST."

The god had barely any time to fly out of the way as beams of heat shot out of Tabris' lamp-like eyes. Tabris took to the skies, and, with every beat of its wings, a gale devastated its surroundings. Like a paper hat in a hurricane, Aeterno couldn't move and was pounded continuously by the strong winds; he couldn't even lift his hands to manipulate space and time. Part of his mind said to do it without, but he knew it left the system at risk. His surroundings were becoming even fainter, and he knew he'd be at death's doorstep again soon.

"ENEMY OF LONGINUS," Tabris stated, gazing downwards.

The winds did not subside, and Aeterno felt his bones now being crushed from the strength of the high speed winds. But whatever Tabris was looking at, it was more important than its first prey.

"Cognitio, no!" Shekina told the emissary, holding him down. "You're blind! You can't save Aeterno by flying up there. I'm a wizard; I control the elements, so leave it to me!"

"Heavenspire, no!" Cognitio cursed. "I'm saving him no matter what, you useless newbie!"

"Listen to her, Cognitio," Lapideis told Cognitio. "Even if no wizard can match Nimbus' control over air, she's the best choice we have now."

Kosma said nothing, but kept looking through her telescope.

Shekina began to chant, and the winds began to subside, from gales to breezes. Aeterno began to plummet, and Lapideis prepared a pillar of sand to cushion his fall. However, it was not enough, and the effects of the spell ceased thirty seconds later. Once again, Aeterno was caught in the deadly vortex.

"Tabris, switch to default mode!" Belial commanded.

"USE OF THE GASTROBOT ISSUES A COMMAND STATING HESTRUS' FINAL ORDER CANNOT BE OVERRIDDEN," Tabris replied. "ERADICATION OF ALL NON-LONGINUS SHALL PROCEED."

"Dammit!" Belial cursed. "Earth god, remove Hestrus' gag!"

Lapideis obeyed, and, immediately, Hestrus began screaming for his release.

"What has happened, Hestrus?" Belial asked his former friend forlornly.

The once-proud member of Longinus began to rant about the master race, the true longinite and the Grey

Triptych's supremacy. "And no community of weak, brainless fools will accomplish either!" he cried. "You're lucky you're part of Longinus, but your new-found deity chums won't be so free of Tabris."

"WHAT'S HAPPENED, HESTRUS? YOU USED TO BE ONE OF US!" Belial howled. "But it doesn't matter. Your ridiculous scheme missed out one fine detail."

The earth shook as Tabris stopped flying and took a step forwards, positioning itself directly above Hestrus. Aeterno, knocked out and over his limits, plummeted towards the ground, but he was caught by Cognitio. Lapideis managed to stifle the tremor before it did any real harm.

"Longinists aren't targets when it's in this mode, but I'm not too sure about the amazing human-experimenting master race," Belial said. "In your arrogance, you've dug your own grave."

Hestrus stifled a scream as Tabris aimed its cannon at him.

"Tabris, what's rule one of the Longinus statute? Hestrus can tell you; he helped make it," continued Belial.

"SHOW NO MERCY TO THE ENEMIES OF LONGINUS," Tabris recited.

"TABRIS, SWITCH TO DEFAULT MODE!" Hestrus yelled.

"NEGATIVE. YOU HAVE ISSUED YOUR FINAL ORDER, HESTRUS," came the reply. "TABRIS IS OPERATED BY THE RULING TRINITY OF LONGINUS, NOT ANY TRAITOR."

Part of Belial wanted to save his former best friend – a very large part of him. As the energy blast descended towards the co-leader of Longinus – the reason they had such advanced tech, and the one who'd saved Belial countless times – Belial had to look away. Hestrus spluttered and screamed, begging for someone to save him.

Going against his instincts, Belial covered his ears and tried to remove the situation from his mind. "Goodbye, Hestrus," he mumbled to himself.

"You young ruffians!" someone huffed. "Show some respect for your elders!" An old man with the remnants of a beard and the cloak of a Ruling Trinity member walked towards the fight scene, waving his fist.

"Jonas?" exclaimed Lapideis. "But—"

"Oh, Belial hates to admit it, but he could never kill another Longinus member! Those knives were just trick blades with collapsibility, anaesthetic and fake blood – he plays that joke on me all the time!"

"SEVERAL HOSTILES SIGHTED," Tabris announced before making a swipe at the group of deities.

Lapideis summoned a pillar of stone to block the blades, but they simply passed through it like it was thin air. It was too late for anyone to move out of the way, but Shekina shattered them in a hail of large, sharp pieces of flint. At the same time, she summoned a firestorm and sent it flying at Tabris.

"Deity powers don't work on that thing!" Cognitio told her, scrabbling on the floor for something that could be classed as a weapon.

"And magic isn't a deity power," she replied, as one of Tabris' arms began to smoulder and melt from the heat.

She readied another, but then Tabris' arm formed into a cannon and launched a massive blast of energy at her. However, its course changed suddenly as it passed through Kosma's crystal ball and was sent flying back at Tabris. The blast ripped a massive hole in its body and it staggered back, one wing clipped off.

"It seems size is all this thing has," muttered Kosma, looking through her telescope. Then, all of a sudden, she screamed. "LOOK OUT! IT'S NOT OVER! *AIM FOR THE CORE!*"

"What core?" asked Lapideis.

As they spoke, the melted and incinerated pieces of Tabris began to piece themselves back together. Within seconds, it was fully restored, without so much as a scratch on it.

"DISPEL MODE ACTIVATED," it announced, and its arms formed into what looked like the nozzles of two vacuum cleaners. It then beat its wings, causing tempests to strike everyone.

Whatever weapons they each had fell out of their grasp immediately, and they were knocked to the floor. Aeterno, who'd been the most damaged before the winds started up again, spat blood as he was ravaged by the wind once again. Noticing this, Shekina cast magic to calm the winds temporarily, but it didn't work.

"STATUS OF AETERNO: DECEASED," Tabris informed them.

Cries of surprise and dismay were all that could be heard at that point. Nobody had expected the greatest fighter to be the first to die. Everyone felt a new-found fear sparked in them; they pushed it to the back of their minds, but had become somewhat anxious at having to face Tabris.

"It's my fault," Shekina told herself solemnly. "Why didn't my magic work?"

"I think it's those two hoover ends sucking all the magic away," Jonas commented. "Hestrus said Tabris needed them for getting closer to the true longinite, but, to me, they just made him look like he was made to be a butler! Where is he, anyway?"

The grisly remnants of Tabris' first victim had likely been blown away by the winds, but, even so, no one wanted to discuss the matter.

"If these winds don't stop soon, we'll all end up like your golden friend over there." Belial grimaced as a large piece of rubble from the slum missed his head by centimetres.

One of Tabris' hands turned into a cannon and fired at Shekina. Lapideis tried to save her with a barrier, but it was crumbled away by the force of the winds. Then the callstaff materialised in her hands. The tip of it glowed, the blast fizzled away, and then a bolt of lightning was fired from the staff's tip.

"Converting heat energy to magical energy?" Lapideis exclaimed. "I didn't know that was possible."

"ARTEFACT MADE BY A DEITY," said Tabris, stopping its flight and turning its cannon into a hand to grab Lapideis. "THEREFORE, IT WILL HAVE NO EFFECT ON LONGINITE. OUT OF THE HOSTILES, LAPIDEIS IS IDENTIFIED AS THE MAIN THREAT."

Lapideis struggled in its grasp, but there was nothing he could do when surrounded by longinite. Belial threw knives, which hit all of Tabris' finger joints but failed to cause any damage. Kosma picked up an energy blaster that had been discarded by Flavius, and she fired it through the large end of her telescope. The energy blast came out of the small end as a focused beam, which hit all the areas that Belial had struck first, severing Tabris' fingers. Tabris responded by firing its heat vision at her, but she foresaw it and dodged. Letting out a mechanised roar, Tabris brought its foot down on Kosma, squashing her like a bug. Everyone who could fight carried on the attack, waiting for her to come back to life with her power.

"Judging by the fact that she is revived by being part of Hestrus' dimension, I predict she's inside of it," Cognitio told everyone, slashing at Tabris with a jagged piece of metal from the remnants of the slums. He hit countless seams and cracks that were unnoticeable to the rest, but it seemed that regular blades could not harm Longinus' ultimate weapon. "Who has the phasecrafts?"

"Antony and Jeff," replied Lapideis, as he built a barrier to stop an energy blast in its wake. "But they're off fighting their own battles. Wait, when are we going to call a ceasefire now that Longinus is our ally?"

"That's temporary," added Belial, parrying Tabris' knife-fingers with his blades.

"I have no weapons. I'll try to find them and tell them to stop," volunteered Jonas. "The guy wearing the funny, blood-coloured sleeping mask over his eyes can help me."

"Fine, since blades have no effect on him, I will," said Cognitio. "Longinist, do you have any phasing equipment that leads to Hestrus' dimension? I know the algorithm to force-phase everyone out of a dimension and—"

"Nope. Where is Hestrus anyway? Is he working on his plans or something?"

Nobody answered. Cognitio and Jonas sped off to find the others. Tabris' cannon fired a blue gas, and, all of a sudden, Lapideis and Shekina felt powerless. Shekina tried to use one of the callstaff's many abilities, but there was no effect.

"Longinite gas," Lapideis muttered. "All our defences are gone now."

Tabris beat its wings, knocking everyone to the floor, and fired its heat vision and energy blast at them simultaneously. It would have immolated them instantly, were it not for the intervention of a dwarf on a floating, stone dais. The runes on his armour, hammer and platform glowed as one, and the blasts began to dissipate. All three items began to crack, but he did not move from his position and held out against the attack.

"YOUR FUNNY, BLUE METAL ISN'T THE ONLY FORM OF NEGOTIATION AROUND!" he screamed at Tabris. "DWARFISH RUNES ARE WAY BETTER THAN ANY METAL CRAP MADE BY HUMANS!"

Unfortunately, even as he spoke, his equipment crumbled away, shielding the blast but leaving him plummeting through the air. Before the dwarf could fall, an elf with wings of fire sprouting from his back flew and caught the dwarf, then cast a spell to keep him flying. Tabris fired another blast, but the two flew away before it hit. Its hands morphed into the anti-magic devices, but they were destroyed before they could take effect by streams of fire shot from the elf's wings.

"Don't do that ever again, Volundur!" the dwarf snapped at the elf. "My personal honour's just taken a massive hit."

"Your honour or your body, Aesik?" replied the elf. "Focus on what new horror the humans have made this time!"

"Clan and sect leaders!" Shekina called to them. "Stay back; let us handle it!"

Tabris beat its wings and dived at them, with blades outstretched. With ease, it cut Volundur and Aesik into many pieces, and the two fell to the floor in a shower of blood. Before anyone had time to react, it brought its foot down, crushing Lapideis.

"No!" Shekina cried.

Despite all three of them being seasoned warriors, they had died so quickly at the hands of this abomination.

"We must avenge them, Longinist!" declared Shekina.

"Tell me something I don't know!" replied Belial, who launched a deathswind shredder from his suit at Tabris.

"BLADES HAVE NO EFFECT ON THAT THING!" yelled Shekina, and she backed up Belial's knives with a firestorm.

The combined attack ripped a hole in Tabris' chest, revealing a pulsing, glowing, yellow rock of some sort, about as large as a human.

"Kosma said something about destroying a core!" exclaimed Shekina, and she used the same magic again. "Longinist, aim where you did before."

Belial did what she asked, and the combined attacks hit Tabris' core. However, they had no effect whatsoever.

"CORE CONSISTS OF HESTRUS' BEST ATTEMPT AT MAKING THE TRUE LONGINITE," Tabris informed them. "IT DEFINITELY NEGATES SIMPLE FLAME MAGIC AND CERTAINLY NEGATES BASIC BLADES."

Its right hand morphed into a Longinus gauntlet that

printed a cage around Shekina, trapping her. It was made of longinite and covered in anti-magic runes to prevent any means of escape. The bars were wide enough for blades to pass through. Tabris' hands became scalpels glistening with malice.

"RULE TEN OF THE LONGINUS STATUTE: THOSE WHO OFFER THE MOST RESISTANCE DESERVE THE MOST PAIN."

*

"EVERYONE, WE MUST ALLY WITH EACH OTHER!" Gary shouted over the raging battle. "Our former brothers and sisters have revealed themselves to be the group that trapped us here. We once thought the deities to be behind them, but we were wrong all along. They're unrelated to the human experiments that happened!"

"Shut it, laptop boy!" retorted a Longinist. "You may be Jonas' pet, but we don't follow you!"

"YEAH, IT'S THE DEITIES WHO'RE THE REASON WHY WE'RE HERE, NERD!" shrieked another. "SO FIGHT THEM, WIMP!"

"He's right! Guys, stop fighting," added Antony. "We have a common enemy here; this can be sorted out later."

"That's the guy who stabbed your arm, Antony!" Nimbus said, slicing a row of tanks in half with his staff. "In case you've forgotten."

"It's hopeless. Even in Longinus, I'm an outcast," Gary muttered.

The battle still continued, but to what avail? In the distance, Tabris was beginning an all-out attack on something, likely having been made to do so by the Grey Triptych. Once, when Gary was bored, he'd learned how to hack its core, but he couldn't get near it without an army.

"STOP THIS FIGHTING AT ONCE!" bawled a voice.

Everyone turned to look at two new arrivals to the battlefield: Cognitio and Jonas.

"The gods and goddesses aren't our real enemies; take a look at Tabris, who's gone mad and is destroying everything," Jonas told his army in the voice of a parent telling off a child.

"It won't harm Longinists, but—" Cognitio was cut off by a loud clamour of voices.

"So why does it matter to us?" asked a Longinist.

"This is Longinus' world, and it'll remain pure. Tabris is doing this planet a favour!" declared another.

"*LISTEN TO HIM!*" Gary hadn't shouted that loud before in his life; it left his throat sore and him panting, but at least everyone was looking at him. "I infiltrated their facilities," he croaked. "They have everything we need, such as medicine to stop the illnesses and food to stop the famines, and, what's more, they will give it to us for free. We've confused them with our true foes: the real threat we should be fighting against. I might be the laptop boy or Jonas' pet, but I can stop Tabris by hacking its core. But I can't do it alone: I have plans for a sneak attack, but I need an army to assist in it. Will you join me?"

"Random applause, everyone!" Jonas chuckled and began to clap.

Longinus followed their master, and the Heavenspirians joined in eventually.

"Here's the plan," said Gary, and he began to explain.

THIRTY-ONE

Shekina cried out in pain as Tabris flayed the skin from her left arm expertly. Her torturer's hands then turned into braziers of blazing longinite, and it pressed them against her skinless limb. It was all she could do to not pass out from the pain. Outside the cage, Belial was trying desperately to saw through a cage bar with some of his knives, but he was making little progress. She wished she could use her deity power, but she knew the longinite made it futile. Then Tabris unsheathed its blade-fingers and, slowly, began to work on the right arm. Still not fully over the pain of the first arm, Shekina's surroundings seemed to her to begin to grow blurry and faint, unlike the pain, which seemed to grow more prominent with every second.

"KNOW THIS, ENEMY OF LONGINUS," Tabris said, readying the braziers. "WE WILL ACCOMPLISH OUR GOALS, AND THE RULE OF DEITIES WILL VANISH. IN YOUR LAST MOMENTS, DO YOU SEE THE ERROR OF YOUR WAYS?"

Shekina couldn't muster the strength to reply.

"STOIC, I SEE. STOIC BUT NOT INVINCIBLE."

The braziers descended. Suddenly, a blast of magical energy lopped off one of Tabris' arms. The other was removed by a punch augmented by multiple runes of strength. Volundur and Aesik, their bodies somehow intact again, continued their assault, chipping away at Tabris before it could regenerate. Soon, they had exposed the core, but they had to retreat to avoid beams from Tabris' eyes.

"How are you still alive?" asked Shekina in disbelief. It was then she noticed that the two leaders had glowing white stitches all over their bodies, somehow keeping them alive.

An elf appeared from behind a broken piece of a slum house, his hands aglow with white energy. He wore a simple, russet cloak and had a ragged, dwarf-like beard that was the colour of steel.

"Dwarf cohort of the first-fallen stronghold; human troops from the war: crypt," he whispered.

Upon these words, specks of white energy flew from the reservoirs in his hands and grew into an army of dwarves wearing archaic armour and humans from the present-day military. Only something wasn't right about the soldiers. The dwarves' flesh was green and decomposed, with chunks missing, exposing mouldy bones underneath. The humans, although not in such a state of decay, were covered in wounds and gashes, with tooth-marks being a prominent sight on their skin. Each wore a look of constant, unchanging fear. These two forces charged at Tabris with either uncanny bravery or a lack of control of their own minds. Behind them, the elf stood and watched, a smile crawling across his face as they hacked and slashed at

Tabris' feet. It came as no surprise that, a few seconds later, they were squashed, blasted and slashed out of existence. However, this distracted it from Volundur and Aesik, who attacked Tabris' wings, clipping them off.

"Whoever said something and reeks of rotting flesh," Belial called out, "a bit of help destroying this cage! Also, even though my community is run-down, we've recently made a washing pit. Please use it!"

"Crypt bolster," said the elf, paying no attention to Belial.

Immediately, more specks of white energy flew and became more soldiers, this time bearing the emblem of Longinus amongst myriad wounds. They printed off miniature tanks, which fired at Tabris' knee joints, rendering it immobile. Volundur and Aesik then broke a hole through its chest, exposing the core. They then struck it with all their force.

The core should have broken from the impact. It should have crumbled away and stopped powering Tabris. However, as soon as it was hit, it immediately reformed, without so much as a scratch on it. Its two assailants' bodies ruptured immediately. The remaining dwarves and humans began to attack the core, but they could not harm it either, and, a few seconds after, the same thing happened.

By this point, Tabris' legs and wings had regenerated, and it stood up, causing the ground to shake violently as it did so. It readied its hand cannon and fired, only for the blast to hit a barrier of magical energy. Around a dozen elf magicians, combining their forces, had flown in and negated it. Dwarves, but without rotting flesh and wearing modern dwarf armour charged at Tabris, their weapons at the ready. One of them freed Shekina by hammering apart the cage bars, before sprinting off to join the fray. Once out, the goddess summoned a swathe of fire and sent it at Tabris' head, burning it off before it could fire its deadly beams. She then used her power on herself, regenerating her flesh.

"Goddess, where are Volundur and Aesik?" asked an elf.

"They died facing it, but somehow came back as soon as an elf who used white-coloured magic appeared," Shekina replied. "Then they died again."

"DODSFALD!" the elf yelled. "Cognitio saw something in you, didn't he? Come out and help!"

There was no reply.

The elf wizards and Shekina had to move swiftly to avoid all manner of weaponry that Tabris used against them, but the dwarves below were less lucky. Their runes of protection shielded them for a long time, enough for them to do significant damage, but then they were always thwarted, either being trampled or blasted whilst the damage they did was washed away by the tide of regeneration.

Suddenly, Tabris sliced up five of the elves with its scalpel and burned a sixth one to death with its brazier. It occurred to Shekina at that point that their superiors had lasted barely half a minute against Tabris, and, even though they were a much larger force, each warrior was going to fall eventually.

"Fall back everyone!" Shekina commanded. "It's too dangerous!"

None obeyed, insisting they had to avenge their fallen leaders. Shekina fired every single piece of magic she knew at Tabris, but no magic could dent the core. Even if it could, she was unsure whether there was a way to destroy it without exploding. She burned off Tabris' blade-fingered hand before it could do any more harm, but many dwarves and two more elves had fallen to its brazier by this time.

In the distance, a combined force of deities and Longinists sprinted towards the battle as fast as possible. Tabris was distracted, so this would be the perfect time to enact Gary's plan.

"Are you sure this will work?" Cognitio asked Jonas, who had put on a spare pair of his all-purpose longinite gauntlets.

"Gary's got it under control," Jonas replied, though his voice suggested a part of him thought otherwise.

"From what I know of Hestrus, he's not one to build an undefended core."

"Yeah, but Gary can probably hack his defences."

Eventually, they reached Tabris, but the battle was nearly over by this time. Shekina fought it with a handful of dwarves and one other elf, and all were striving to stay alive and dodge the devastating attacks and cages of Tabris. Upon noticing the host, Shekina signalled frantically for everyone to get back, but the plan had to be enacted if they were to take down Tabris.

"Now," whispered Gary to everyone else.

Nimbus used his powers to negate the gales from Tabris' wings, and Hydrax used his to lift Gary up on a pillar of water. The Longinists printed off bazookas and fired at

Tabris' back, blowing it apart, and the glow of the core filled the area. Before it could regenerate, Hydrax made the pillar rise extremely fast, and soon Gary was next to the core.

Up close and active, it was like a miniature sun, and looking at it was painful. But, even so, Gary knew he had to persevere or any chances of Longinus being saved by the deities were gone. As he ran his fingers across the surface of the core, he found the part that moved: the part that flipped over into a keyboard. Hestrus would have used it to program Tabris, but now it would be Tabris' undoing. His fingers a blur, he began to write out the code to undo all other code.

*

Aeterno woke up, his surroundings hazy. He could make out Tabris fighting Shekina, along with a combined force of Longinus, elves, dwarves and deities. Despite their combined efforts, they were losing badly and would all be wiped out if he didn't freeze time. With every movement requiring a great effort, he flew towards the fight, giving the order to get back as he prepared to freeze Tabris in time once and for all.

"YOU SHOULD BE DECEASED!" Tabris exclaimed, catching sight of the god.

"If that was a deathblow, then I've been killed 1,000 times over." Aeterno was about to freeze time, before Tabris enveloped itself in a black gas.

"RECOGNISE THIS, DEITY?" Tabris taunted. "MEET YOUR OLD FRIEND UNRAVELLER GAS. CONSIDER YOURSELF USELESS."

"Does anyone have a spare weapon?" Aeterno asked.

"*Here,*" a voice rang in his head, and a staff seemingly made of water floated up to his hands. It felt solid, despite having the same texture and feel as a liquid.

"Thanks, Hydrax," Aeterno said before bringing it down on Tabris' arm with such strength that it broke off. He then swung the weapon at Tabris' chest, which it cracked a massive hole in.

"What are you doing?" came a voice from inside said chest. "I'm trying to hack this thing!"

Inside the chest, typing away furiously at a hidden keyboard on the core, was a boy Aeterno remembered to be Longinus' undercover agent.

"Sorry," Aeterno told him, destroying Tabris' other arm before it could hit them. "What's the current situation?"

"Longinus and your side have formed an alliance. I know a code that will remove Tabris' programming, and I am typing it in right now!" confirmed Gary.

"GARY… IT SEEMS HESTRUS ISN'T THE ONLY TRAITOR!" Tabris declared. "I MUST WARN YOU, THOUGH, HE DID KNOW YOU COULD HACK ME AND THAT KEYBOARD CAN DETECT DNA. ANYONE BESIDES HESTRUS WILL BE—"

Tabris' speech was cut off by a blast of static. It began jerking backwards and forwards, occasionally clawing at its chest. Everyone backed away from it, so as to avoid its sweeping arms and wings. Eventually, the lights that were its eyes powered off, and it crashed to the ground, with Gary only surviving due to Aeterno flying him away. It seemed the menace of the old Longinus was at an end.

"Now, deities, it's time for your side of the deal," Belial

said as soon as Aeterno and Gary had descended. "We need medicine and housing."

"Housing wasn't part of the deal," Aeterno pointed out, "but it is now. After we rescue the remaining deities and find a way to end the war, we will take you to Primium and give you everything you need. Now it's time to shake hands on the alliance."

Belial shook Aeterno's hand vigorously, and, for the first time, his scowl was replaced by a grin. "I know my side has caused irreversible damage. There is no way we... no, I... can bring back all those I've killed. So let me travel with you, to at least be able to have an attempt at redeeming myself."

"Well said," agreed Cognitio. "But I'll soon be able to see again, that new goddess can regenerate my eyes—"

"Actually, it only works on deities and has a cool-down of a century," Shekina told him.

"And this is why I don't want to become a god. To avoid having useless powers like that," Cognitio scoffed.

"*Excuse me?* It saved your life!"

All of a sudden, Gary let out a bloodcurdling scream. He thrashed around on the floor as his flesh began to melt.

"Well, well, Gary, trying to reset Longinus' work?" Hestrus' voice boomed out from Tabris' core. "You really are the selfish, spineless hacker everyone says you are."

"DON'T LISTEN TO HIM, GARY!" Jonas shouted. "YOU SAVED US ALL! YOU HELPED LONGINUS!"

"No, it's true," Gary managed to reply before his mouth fully melted.

"Spineless you are, and spineless you shall always be," Hestrus' recorded voice taunted. "How are you finding the slow-activation heat waves that react to foreign DNA? You will exist only as a liquid, for you have not helped Longinus in any solid way."

Those were the last words Gary heard before his ears were added to the growing red puddle around him.

THIRTY-TWO

If anyone had been on Atham at the time of the fight between the deities and Longinus, they would still have been wondering about the human military's bomb and when it would hit. Back when Bob had been saved from death by Lapideis and resurrected for some as-yet-unknown reason, he and the god had taken separate paths, with him deciding to stop the planet-destroying explosive before it hit.

At the time, Morehk had been fully restored from eating Pollux and Castor, and Bob could fly into space without needing to worry about air or his broken suit. Leaving Atham's atmosphere, he noticed that it was surrounded by an entire fleet of spacecraft, with practically every competent fighting model patrolling the planet. An extremely large one – shaped like a zeppelin but with a gigantic array of guns and cannons attached to it, like an extra layer of protection – sat in the centre and was likely the flagship.

Morehk, I think that's the one with the bomb! Bob told the stygir he was hosting.

"You really don't say!" Morehk replied sarcastically. *"No,*

the bomb's in one of the escort-class ships; they're the right size to hold explosives that could destroy an entire planet."

What should we do?

"*We should cower by the planet's surface, ignoring the fleet of easy kills. Bob, stop acting stupid, materialise stuff and kill them all!*"

Whilst the stygir's simple, predatory desire was acceptable in smaller-scale fights, Bob knew he couldn't win against what looked like half the army of Primium alone. He stayed by the planet's edge and tried to think up a strategy.

"*I was being sarcastic, Bob,*" Morehk sighed. "*Don't really cower by the planet's surface.*"

All of a sudden, one of the smaller ships shone a massive light on Bob and gave some sort of signal to the others. Noticing him, the entire fleet circled him in a pincer movement and closed in.

"*State your business!*" a voice rang in Bob's head. "*Have you come to join the army? If so, you made the right choice. Come and watch us blow up this planet!*"

"*Hell no!*" Morehk replied to the voice telepathically. "*Like your crappy technology could ever defeat the amazingness of magic! Runes and metalworking are what you're meant to do with metals!*"

"*ENEMY!*" yelled the voice. "*FLEET, GET HIM!*"

"WHAT HAVE YOU JUST DONE?" Bob shrieked out loud.

"*There's only one option left, Bob. Fight them!*" Morehk materialised a suit of black armour around Bob as well as two anti-spacecraft cannons on the gauntlets. Rows of even more missiles rested on each of his shoulders.

Bob fired in all directions, destroying ten ships at once. The others fired energy blasts at him, and he flew down to dodge them. However, the armour was cumbersome, and he couldn't get down in time to save his racks of missiles from the energy blasts. They detonated, but Bob materialised an extra-thick layer of armour around him to avoid any real damage.

Bob flew up again, firing his two cannons at various ships and blowing them up. The flagship's cannons weren't opening fire yet, but he was besieged from all areas as ships began to dive-bomb him. Trading his cannons in for a pair of massive blades, he began to slice a path to the flagship, decimating all ships that came too close. He was nearly there, with only a short distance to go. For some reason, the flagship had not fired a single blast of energy. He put on an extra burst of speed, ignoring the energy blasts firing all around him; surely if he went fast enough, he could avoid most of them. When at the flagship finally, he noticed a DNA-lock door reading, "Human DNA only." He de-materialised one blade, pulled his hand out of his turbine suit and placed his finger on the reader. The door slid open and he stepped in.

"What?" exclaimed Morehk. *"No badass cut-a-hole-in-the-ship-and-jump-in manoeuvre?"*

I forgot about that, sorry, apologised Bob.

Alarms blared all across the ship, and a voice rang out with it. "Intruder alert!" it announced. "Another one has joined the first on the ground floor. Abort all current work and stop them!"

Security guards approached Bob from all areas and

opened fire. Immediately, Bob materialised cages around them and ran.

"That's the same as summoning a creature, Bob!" Morehk exclaimed. *"Well done! Why didn't you just kill them?"*

"I can't kill another human face to face. I just can't," Bob told him as his armour and weapons crumbled away.

"Tell Lance that and stop making excuses!" Soon, his strength began to suffer the same fate as his armour. Bob collapsed to the floor as more guards' footsteps could be heard crashing down the corridor.

*

In the background in his unconscious state, Bob could hear the clamour of voices, excited yet busy with something. He woke up and found himself without his turbine suit and chained with shackles to the floor of an extremely small prison cell, which he didn't have room to stand up in. Ten humans wearing elegant, gilded suits and gaudy badges of office strolled down the corridors, chatting with swathes of white-coated scientists. A man wearing a white turbine suit stood in the corner, motionless. In the centre of the scene lay something vast and undeniably deadly. It resembled a prototype of the modern spacecraft, which was like a spire with fins, but it was clear that its purpose was not transport.

"I don't want to be here; I have businesses to run!" complained one of the government members, a young man with a heavily styled hairdo. "That new croquet course has to be completed, but the inferior races are stopping its release!"

"Glen Murton, you're rich enough already," snapped a wizened woman. "I believe we should remove Primium from Atlas completely. We can become our own, pure solar system! Do you agree, Larry Egraf?"

"Indeed I do, Astra Yak," a bald, grinning man stated. "Where's that oaf Bert Jackson?"

"He accidentally went on one of the escort ships," Yak sighed.

At this point, a portly, bespectacled man with a devilish look on his face strode into the room. Bob recognised him from the news channel on Primium. At his entrance, everyone stopped what they were doing, fell silent and saluted him. All but Murton.

"Well," the croquet mogul announced in an overbearing voice, "that idiot Bert has let us down again. That old man Leif Trilt, despite a damaging assault on Ferraheim, died at the hands of the wretched elf and dwarf leaders. You should have me as the overall leader! I shall have a blockade of ships separate us and the inferiors—"

The man in charge slapped him suddenly across the face. "Pay respect to your betters, Murton!" the man snapped. "We all know you're only here because your fellow seat in the government, Victor Xena, bribed me with a large sum of money."

"THAT'S NOT TRUE!" hollered Murton, then he gazed accusingly at a man with a heavily receding hairline, presumably Xena. "Vic, he's lying right?"

"Yes," Xena replied. "And my views are that we should rename the upstarts' planets Primium 2 and Primium 3, and annex them to us as colonies—"

"Nobody cares about any of you!" whined the man. "I'm the head of this government! And we don't want to exit the solar system, waste ships or have those hated worlds in our sights. We want to destroy them and wipe them off the face of Atlas! And, by Heavenspire, we shall, with a new weapon I shall take credit for. Science department, what is it again?"

"Members of the government, I assure you this nuclear bomb is unlike anything used in warfare before," a scientist told the raucous group excitedly. "It can cause massive amounts of damage, wiping out everything over an absolutely massive radius—"

"So you tell me," the man replied, "but when will it be able to wipe out an entire planet in one strike?"

"The way it works is by splitting the nucleus of an atom. Around ten would make a continent uninhabitable—"

"That would be good, but I want the midgets and pointy-ears to see their new worlds totally gone, and those two mistakes erased from history completely! How will you make the bomb better?"

"I need an atom of stygigen, the gas that makes up stygir. But scans show that intruder number two has a stygir inside him for some reason! I'll try to extract it and use it in a bomb. The test for the Francium bomb will proceed in an hour."

"I must commend you on your discovery, Dr Shell. Mass produce them whilst you're at it. If they launch any attacks from space, they'll receive a smaller version of what their planet will get eventually."

"It's not really wise to use nukes like that—"

"Are you in charge, doctor? No! I, Mick Nugnodge, am! The leader amongst the leaders of the superior race in Atlas! Don't reply or I'll launch this bomb at you right now!"

"Yes, Leader Mick," came the meek reply.

Mick Nugnodge then began ordering Dr Shell to make more bombs and other explosives to use on everything non-human in the system. "You will be a hero of humanity, Shell! My subordinate! Also, on second thoughts, let's launch a few lesser bombs at the enemy worlds to spread terror before the planet-destroying blow. Hurry the test, and then head for Arcanast and Ferraheim."

"No…" Bob breathed. "These can't be the leaders of my race…"

"TECHNOLOGY IS THE BEST!" Mick roared. "WE'LL ELIMINATE THEM ALL!"

His followers let out a huge cheer at this. Whilst Bob and the rest of those trying to rescue the deities had not been affected much by the war, it occurred to him then that this was no longer a matter he could put to the side for his quest. A flimsy promise by this devious government about negotiating the end of the war was no argument against that.

"But why aren't I a god yet?" snapped Mick. He turned to Shell with an angry look. "I asked you to get me some divinite from the Heavenspire! I want to be Mick, the god of great leadership, the winner of the interspecies war! If it's too dangerous for a human to go so close to the sun, send a robot or something!"

"I've tried countless times," Shell told the furious politician. "I'm pretty sure every party in this war has. But every time something, be it flesh or metal, gets close to

Heavenspire, a massive solar flare erupts and incinerates it! It's almost like the divinite is defending itself."

Morehk, are you there? Bob thought.

"Of course I am! My strength's back too. Let's get out and kill that Mick guy whilst we're at it; he reminds me too much of Catarehk!" declared Morehk.

A thought later and Bob was holding twin blades, slicing his way out of his cell. His turbine suit was lying on the floor around ten metres away from him, and he materialised a shadowy tendril to grab it and put it on. Alarms blared anew, and soldiers swarmed in, wearing jetpacks and wielding energy blasters. They opened fire, but Bob switched his blades to large, domed shields, deflecting all their shots. Despite the barriers shielding him, the ongoing attack of the soldiers began chipping away at the dark structures.

"Well?" exclaimed Morehk. *"Is there any chance of you going on the offensive? Or any chance of you wanting to stay alive?"*

Part of Bob knew Morehk was right; part of him knew he could and had to wipe out the troops in front of him. But one thought, a shard of guilty conscience, lodged in his heart and, unknown to Morehk since the fight with Lance, prevented him from doing that. *I could not kill another human. Doing so would make me as bad as Mick. Half the soldiers had probably been forced to be in the army and didn't know what they were doing—*

"Yes, Bob, but you do. Materialise blades and slice 'em up!"

I can't, Morehk. I can't!

"I can sense your thoughts, Bob. A part of you knows

you should do it. I know you should do it or you will surely die. What would you rather be: a warrior who killed a few expendables or a corpse?"

Bob's shields were crumbling away like sandcastles. *No, Morehk, there has to be another way. We could negotiate—*

"Showing weakness? This is war, Bob! A few lives will be lost along the way. A few lives must *be lost along the way! Besides, don't you enjoy it, the feeling of the kill, the rush of adrenaline, the hunter's joy—"*

NO! I feel none of that!

"Of course you don't. You won't feel anything shortly. Do you remember the price of failing your side of the contract?"

Now that Morehk mentioned it, Bob could hear the echo of another voice. It reverberated in the back of his head, drowning out all other thoughts, all other parts of Bob's existence, and soon it would erase his being completely: *"Save yourself or become Catarehk's plaything. Your choice, Bob."*

The shields were fully down. All the soldiers fired at Bob simultaneously, but he flew up on wings of stygir black. Like an angel of death, he descended on the hapless soldiers, regretting the newly formed blades in his hands that cut the soldiers in half. Or did he? Maybe it was the feeling of power or Morehk's words? He hated to admit it, but it felt, well, kind of good. Spurred on by this alien feeling, he decimated the rest of the army. Soldiers, once filled with triumph, ran away shrieking only to be impaled on ebon swords. With every strike, every spurt of blood and every death, the voice of Catarehk faded to a dull hum, then disappeared completely.

"*They were running away,*" Morehk commented. Then, in a poor imitation of Bob's voice, he began to whine about how bad it was to kill others.

Be quiet, Morehk, Bob thought. *I can't believe I did it. That one part of me that had enjoyed it was not part of me, it couldn't be...*

"That's the spirit. Now, let's get on to the government and scientists!"

"*Not so fast, Morehk!*" a voice filled with fury roared in Bob's head, making him jump.

The man in the turbine suit walked towards him, with every step a loud stomp.

"Like I said, he has a stygir in him, so maybe he can use its powers—" began Dr Shell, before being cut off by a government member.

"FEND HIM OFF, NAPTHON!" the member yelled at the man, pointing a trembling finger at Bob.

"I shall, Leader Rupert Smithson," Napthon replied, his eyes ablaze with a crackling, flame-like energy. "The host of Morehk shall burn."

"*Asmodeus!*" Morehk called out to the man. "*If it isn't my favourite pyromaniac from my favourite husk of pyromaniacs! How's your host?*"

"*Go up in flames, Morehk,*" a voice like logs crackling on the fire spat back. "*Your desire to end life is a ridiculous and impure form of destruction. Thaumir may be the first husk, but its motives are mere embers compared to the bonfire Golachir, the fifth husk, wants to make!*"

"*As you can see, Bob, he's the most normal and friendly stygir out there,*" Morehk sighed.

"Just because you're in charge of communications

with your unnatural telepathy doesn't mean you're paid to chat!" Rupert whined. "You're my bodyguard, so get him already, oaf!"

Napthon flicked his wrist, and Rupert erupted in a burst of dark fire. In a few moments, he had become a pile of ash with a few black sparks dancing on it.

"Must I remind you to not kill members of the government?" Mick sighed. "And remind me again why we have to be here rather than using our mobile holoceivers?"

"If you wish to stop me, you can try," Napthon replied callously. "But I have saved each member of your ruling body at least three times each during this war, and you would fail without me. And I melted all the moving bots you control and cower behind."

"Did you have to hire the most deranged mercenary you could find near the borders of the Void?" another member whispered to Mick.

Napthon's ears pricked up and a moment later another pile of ash had been formed.

"His only price was to see things burn. I can see you were desperate to pay him." Mick smirked at the black dust by his feet. "Now let's eliminate the threat!"

More dark fire appeared, encircling Napthon's hands, then spreading to engulf his whole body. But he didn't burn from it; if anything, he was more invigorated. The turbines on his suit activated, and he shot towards Bob like a meteor. There was no time to react and, if two large pieces of rock hadn't crushed Napthon's turbine suit, he would have been fried.

"*Imryth?*" Bob exclaimed.

The elf in question was flying above them, along with Jeff.

"Jeff? Aren't you two meant to be stopping Longinus?" queried Bob.

"The others are doing that," Imryth replied. "We've come to aid you in stopping the bomb."

"No way!" gasped Jeff, with a horrified look on his face as he gazed at the massacred bodies littering the floor. "Bob, who did this?"

"There's no time to explain," Bob replied, ignoring the growing abyss in his stomach, "but the human government has all its plans and research on the bomb here!"

Gouts of fire shot out of Napthon's hands; he didn't seem to care where they landed, and even Mick and the other government members had to evade them. Some were immediately reduced to ash, but others escaped with singed suits. Bob, Imryth and Jeff only survived due to Imryth making a shield of earth to stop the fire in its wake.

"*Use my husk power,*" Morehk told Bob. "*Combine the strengths of our minds, and we'll easily take over Asmodeus!*"

Is there any way of doing that discreetly? questioned Bob.

"*We don't need discreetly, we need victoriously! Even if they find out about me, they'll be grateful I saved them!*"

Jeff and Bob combined the power of their energy blasters by firing on Napthon together, and scorched a massive hole through his chest. Imryth summoned a lightning bolt and flung it at him, and he fell to the floor, with only his head intact.

"DETONATE THE BOMB!" Mick screamed. "DETONATE IT OR WE'RE ALL GONE!"

"No, we're not," Napthon hissed, and his head lifted itself off the floor, supported by a body of fire. "The husk power of Golachir has more uses than just offence!"

"STYGIR?" shrieked Mick. He began to tremble, and then sprinted away, followed by any survivors from amongst the human government and scientists.

Suddenly, a wall of fire rose up, barring the way.

"No. You shall not leave until Arcanast and Ferraheim are no more. It was an elf and a dwarf who imprisoned me and it will be elves and dwarves who will pay," declared Napthon.

Bob, Imryth and Jeff launched more attacks at him, then Bob used his husk power. Parts of Asmodeus fell under his control, and Napthon's body began to fall apart.

"BY HEAVENSPIRE, YOU SHALL PAY FOR THIS!" Napthon yelled as his own flames began attacking him. "I might not have a full body now, but my flames will not consume me!"

"YOU HAVE NO RIGHT TO SWEAR AN OATH, PSYCHO!" Jeff bellowed, and he blasted him again. "NATHAN PAXTON!"

Napthon gasped at the mention of his old name and lost control of his flame body. Blood flowed everywhere like a lake as the injuries sustained by the fire became fatal again.

"How did you know?" Napthon wheezed, his control over Asmodeus' husk power returning. His burning body returned, just about stopping his demise, and he got up, with balls of fire at the ready. *How did you know?* he repeated, and he threw the fireballs at Jeff.

"We were literally learning about you a few days ago," Jeff replied as Imryth blew away the fireballs with a gust of wind and Bob began to shoot at Napthon. "I knew you were alive!"

"Well, boy, I should be dead," admitted Napthon. "But, with the help of some good old wind and air-scales, I went out of the system and, eventually, found the Void, when it was still a small patch of space. In there, you don't age; I was taken in by husk Golachir." He materialised a shield to deflect Bob's energy blasts and readied a massive ball of fire. "They too like to cause havoc with man's best invention, and, after they returned from some war, I contracted with the best warrior out of them, Asmodeus!"

"We must find a use for that stygir or we'll die… We can use him in our bomb!" Mick's feelings of horror ceased, and he began jumping up and down in glee. "Plus the intruder, so we can have two bombs. Or one big one!"

"But even the inferiors hate them; they're scum!" sniffed Yak.

"Leave it alive, annex the Void to Primium, and then kill it!" Xena commanded.

"Relax, Yak. When dealing with inferiors, the ones who pay us money can be superior!" Murton stated.

"Shut up, you idiots!" Imryth warned them.

"YOU'RE GOING TO DIE!" Napthon roared, and he hurled his fire at the government leaders.

The leaders would have all perished if it weren't for the intervention of a platoon of human soldiers. They jumped in front of the fire, taking the killing blow meant for their leaders. It appeared that, when Napthon had lost control of his flame body, he'd lost control of the fire wall as well.

The government members and their scientists dashed away from the fight, whilst Bob, Imryth and Jeff fought Napthon.

Out of the corner of his eye, Bob saw a fleet of escape pods soar away from the ship. He then used his husk power again; he had been charging it up for a long time. Instantly, nearly all of Asmodeus was under his control. The remnants of Napthon's human body fell to the floor, with a few trails of smoke materialising off it as he tried to use his husk power.

"It appears your power's run out," Jeff told the struggling Napthon. "This has been your last fire."

"What should we do with him?" asked Bob.

"*He's not really dying!*" Morehk told Bob in between munching sounds as he devoured Asmodeus. "*We have to finish him off fully or else—*"

Nice try, Morehk, Bob thought. *Catarehk isn't coming back in a long time.*

A few seconds later, Nathan Paxton had breathed his last breath.

"It sickens me to think that there are so many psychopaths like that," Imryth muttered. "Anyway, let's get on to tracking down the human government."

"*Do you really think that was successful?*" a voice sounded inside Bob, but not Morehk's or even Catarehk's – this one crackled and boiled with rage. "*The human government are far from your host's worries, Morehk.*"

"*Asmodeus?*" Morehk gasped. "*But I ate you! You shouldn't be—*"

"*Alive? Well, Morehk, have you heard of... a Stygir Covenant?*"

"No way! That was said to be almost impossible."

"Everything can be burned. Everything, no matter how resistant it may seem at first, will be evaporated or razed to the ground. You, as the second-strongest stygir, are one of those seemingly resistant things. But fire consumes all, and a gust of wind can start it up again as long as there are embers."

All of a sudden, Bob felt like something was suffocating him slowly; it was the same feeling when Lance, Pollux and Castor had invaded his lungs. Morehk controlled Napthon and Asmodeus, and, whilst Bob expected him to either try to eat them again or crumble their form apart, he forced them out of Bob's system instead. A mass of black gas came out of Bob's mouth and coalesced into the psychopath's grinning form.

"I hate to let someone else start my fires for me, but it appears I have to use the full terms of the covenant," Napthon told them.

An aura that was the shimmering gold of divinite surrounded Napthon, its brightness increasing by the second. Imryth summoned globes of water and sent them flying at him, where they sizzled harmlessly against his flames.

"It's pointless!" Napthon cackled. "Only your sea god's water can—" He stopped in his tracks as the vapour coming off him became a gust of wind, blowing most of the flames away.

"It was pointless, but by combining the after-effects of it with other magic, it will defeat you," Imryth told him. More flames appeared, but she noticed that, as they appeared, his aura dimmed. What that aura meant she had no idea, but it was definitely related to his ulterior motives. "Everyone! Attack now!" she commanded, and she followed up the wind with a blast of ice. When it melted, she added more water magic to the current water, combining their strengths to extinguish the flames on his shoulder.

Napthon didn't seem to attack now; he just basked in the eldritch light surrounding him. Had he given up? Bob and Jeff launched a combined attack with their blasters, firing at his shoulder and blowing his arm off. The aura's brightness reached a blinding level.

"COVENANT PHASE!" yelled Napthon, and the glow enveloped him fully, then seemed to brighten again, if that were possible.

The world behind Bob, Imryth and Jeff seemed to be replaced by a glowing, pink background, and they were drawn into it.

"The government still haven't paid me enough," they heard Napthon mutter. "It seems I shall be off to help them more, and they'll need my help, especially Bert Jackson."

THIRTY-THREE

"YOU THREE! THE ELF AND THE TWO HUMANS! WAKE UP! IT'LL AWAKEN SOON!" a voice screamed in Bob's ear, as someone shook him vigorously.

Opening his eyes, Bob saw a purple liskous – he could tell this was a female, due to the lack of whiskers – shaking him, Imryth and Jeff. For some reason, around her neck was a series of amulets used for magic. He seemed to be on a level landscape of jagged rock, surrounded by a wall of conflagration.

As soon as the other two were awake, she introduced herself as Novis. "Were you guys nominees?" she asked.

"Yes, we were," replied Jeff. "We've managed to find and rescue some deities, and also get the shifter core. Where's the rest of your group?"

"Dead, except for one: Dodsfald. He's an elf, has a grey beard and acts a bit odd. Have you seen him?"

"N-no," stammered Jeff, knowing he had made a mistake. "I'm sorry."

"How did they die?" asked Imryth. "Did they achieve anything?"

Bob and Jeff stared at her in shock.

"We did," Novis told her calmly. "We managed to rescue Galvok before Nugnodge found us and wanted us dead. I'm not sure what happened to Galvok, but Dodsfald fled, and the rest of us were trapped in this reality by Napthon. I failed completely in saving them."

"You didn't fail in anything, Novis." Imryth put a reassuring hand on the liskous' shoulder. "Your group might not become deities, but they'll be immortalised as the heroes who rescued Galvok and stood up to... What killed them here?"

"*Damn covenant!*" Morehk cursed.

What's that, Morehk? Bob asked it.

"*Theoretically, it's when a stygir and its host have minds so similar that they're almost identical. Over time, a bond stronger than an ordinary contract will form. They could be able to invent their own types of stygir creatures, something even Catarehk can't do, as well as charge up powerful moves, like making this realm and trapping us in it.*"

But then how did they survive being eaten?

"*When one dies, they slowly regenerate in the other's body. But all this was just one of Catarehk's crazy theories; it wasn't actually meant to happen!*"

I see, mused Bob. *I wonder if we can actually defeat the pyromaniac duo.*

"... and then, in about a few minutes from now, a part of the fire wall will disappear to reveal a staircase and then the One of Brimstone appears," Novis continued.

"Why would Napthon give us an escape route?" Imryth asked, puzzled. "It could be a trap."

"I remember reading up on him when I was younger,"

stated Jeff. "Every time he burned down a large structure, such as a village, he would give its inhabitants a very difficult way to escape, to watch them try to solve it. Of course, any survivors were finished off by him, but I think we can take him on now our group's bigger." He then noticed the amulets around Novis' neck. "You do magic? That's the first time I've seen a liskous practise the mystic arts. Are you a seculous?"

"Yes, I am," confirmed Novis.

"Good. Then, with two of us, we shall definitely escape," Imryth declared.

Jeff was no longer taking part in the conversation, but he was tinkering with his blaster using a pocket screwdriver and wire clippers he had kept on him before the quest started. Suddenly, a sound like a fire alarm but of a much greater volume sounded, reverberating around the entire reality.

"It's happening!" exclaimed Novis, and she made a complex, twirling hand gesture. Four pieces of slate-scale – which were grey but with a pattern of stygir-black, X-shaped markings – appeared in her hands in a flash of white sparks.

"*Magigade?*" Imryth spluttered in what seemed like a mixture of surprise and disgust.

"Yes, my magic is geoscalic; I can generate slate-scales and make new types of them based on my surroundings," Novis explained, ignoring Imryth's bewildered expression. "Take these stygirbane-scales; they're the best defence we have against Napthon's minions!"

Reluctantly, Bob took one and almost dropped it from the sheer pain it exerted on him.

"*I get that you're trying to fit in and keep me a secret,*

but don't hold that toxic crap!" Morehk cried, with pain behind his voice. *"It feels like I'm being shredded from the inside out!"*

I feel the pain too, Bob thought, tossing the strange rock from one shaking hand to the other. *But so will whatever creatures Napthon and Asmodeus have made.*

"Look over there!" said Jeff, and he pointed to a section of the flame wall that was dwindling away to reveal an obsidian staircase. They sprinted, or flew in Novis' case, towards it, before a behemoth fell from the sky, blocking their way.

Its craggy features, despite being hewn from the same material that formed the other stygir creatures, gave it the texture of a large piece of volcanic rock. Humanoid in shape, though with a pyramid for a head, the creature was not completely silent like its lesser kin; in fact, it said with a rasping voice, "I am the One of Brimstone, and Asmodeus has tasked me with defending this staircase."

Novis made another hand gesture, and stygirbane-scales flew at the One of Brimstone, like darts.

The creature breathed a stream of fire and incinerated the projectiles. "I HATE THOSE ROCKS!" it roared. "They crumble me away, so I shall crumble you!"

More scales appeared by the One of Brimstone's feet, and it recoiled in pain as the soles of its feet began to disintegrate, like some form of erosion.

"I'M STRONGER THAN THAT, SO I'M MORE RESISTANT, BUT YOU CAN SEE WHAT IT DOES TO US!" Morehk roared at Bob. *"DROP IT!"*

As the One of Brimstone crashed onto the floor, it formed a massive crater, and rock shards flew everywhere, with a shard catching Jeff in the leg. He cried out in pain, which drew the One of Brimstone like a moth to a flame. The creature rose up and did an ungainly jump towards Jeff, breathing fire whilst it did so. Bob dropped the stygirbane-scale and fired a volley of energy blasts at the creature, but it did nothing. Imryth summoned a gust of wind, pushing the creature away from Jeff and extinguishing the fire, but another series of shards soared through the air as it fell. This time, one left a large gash on Imryth's arm, and Bob would have died from the amount that hit him were it not for Morehk's powers.

"You're still alive!" Novis gasped as the human in front of her stood there after rock went through his head, chest and legs, unfazed. "What the—"

Her enemy took advantage of her surprise and threw a punch with one of its rocky fists.

"THERE'S NO TIME FOR WONDERING; LOOK OUT!" shouted Imryth, and she raised a pillar of steel to block the fist.

It proved no obstacle at all to the One of Brimstone, but it gave Novis a brief period of time in which to fly away. "Don't worry, it's powerful but it's slow!" she told Imryth.

"I'LL MAKE SURE YOUR DEATHS WILL BE!" bellowed the One of Brimstone, and it brought both fists down on the ground, sending a rocky spray at its opponents.

Imryth tried to incinerate them all with a lightning bolt, then fire, and then she raised a barrier, but – whatever stone the projectiles were made of – they seemed to be extremely robust and impervious to all Imryth had used. Novis made a new scale – this time it was grey with crosses the colour of the stone – and the projectiles all began to crumble away.

The One of Brimstone let out an ear-splitting howl of rage.

"I've been here long enough to invent a scale that's bane to whatever stone this place is made out of," Novis told her foe.

She lined the floor at the One of Brimstone's feet with stygirbane-scales, making its feet crumble away. Everyone thought this would be the end of the beast, which was now unable to move whilst stranded on a heavily harmful material, but they were proven wrong. Lowering its head to the floor, it let out a long, continuous belch of a yellow-tinged gas, which it used to propel itself upwards and then out of the stygirbane-scales. Bob, Imryth and Jeff combined their firepower at the airborne behemoth, but their attacks didn't even leave a dent on its rocky hide. Novis prepared more scales that countered the stone that made up the floor, and the shower of rock made by the One of Brimstone's landing was rendered harmless. In response, it let out an eruction of gas at them, but Imryth blew the gas away with a wind spell.

"Poison gas is cowardly," she told the creature, and she threw globes of water at it, which had no effect.

The One of Brimstone retched a stream of oil, splattering her in the inky-black substance. It then breathed fire, igniting the oil. Imryth let out a scream of pain as her flesh was set alight. Using every water-based spell in her arsenal, she managed to douse the flames and escape covered in first-degree burns. Whilst she was doing so, Bob, Jeff and Novis kept the creature busy by bombarding it from all angles with attacks. Whilst only Novis did any real damage, they all managed to distract it to the point of farce. Retching oil in all directions like a split tanker, the One of Brimstone was unsure whom to hit and couldn't keep up with the speed of its attackers. However, it knew that it would win in the end; if it just focused on incinerating the scales, neither side would damage the other, and it would become a battle of attrition, in which it had the ultimate advantage. Creatures of flesh and blood would tire eventually, and require food and rest, but not those wrought of stygigen. In between blasts of oil, it chuckled at the thought.

"Nothing's happening, Bob. It'll just end with the others needing rest and us fighting that thing forever. You need to use my nameright," Morehk told its host as he shot another useless energy blast at the One of Brimstone.

No, I can't. Now that they know about stygir hosts, they'll figure out I'm one and— thought Bob in response.

"And what's wrong with being one?"

Nothing. It's just a bit of sworn enmity against your race because they nearly destroyed our system for no apparent reason.

"I have a plan!" Imryth announced, struggling to move, due to all her burns, but moving nonetheless. "That thing's composition seems to be somewhat like rock. I'll make it crumble away with an earth spell!"

"But only Lapideis has the mastery over earth to do so!" Jeff told her, ducking to avoid a shower of rock. The shard in his leg dug deeper as he did so and he fell to the ground in pain.

The One of Brimstone began to throw a punch at him, but then Jeff fired a blast of neon blue energy from his blaster in an act that made the weapon shudder and explode. The fist recoiled in shock and what apparently seemed to be pain.

"FREEZING!" the One of Brimstone yelled, as it coughed up crusty bits of solidified lava.

"I managed to change my blaster so that the energy was cold instead of hot, for fighting these fire-based guys," Jeff panted, still not recovered from the pain caused by the shard.

"A good effort. I'll make sure yours wasn't in vain," Novis commended him.

She summoned a hail of stygirbane-scales, which crashed down on the incapacitated One of Brimstone. It screeched in agony as the scales crumbled away its head and began to do the same to its body. Suddenly, the erosion stopped, and the remnants of the One of Brimstone's body soared upwards, as if they were attached to strings. A new, larger body began to materialise, along with two heads, two legs and four arms ending in bladed fingers.

"IDIOTS! *DON'T EVER TRY THAT AGAIN!*" both heads howled in unison. "You've caused me too much pain today, and I shall inflict double that on you. I must thank you, though, for if any rock touches my heart, I regenerate immediately and get stronger!"

Novis threw more stygirbane-scales at it, but it didn't even bother to dodge. It just laughed its overbearing laugh as the rocks bounced off its new skin.

"Fool! I'm now immune to that stuff!"

Whilst it was gloating, Bob heard a faint chanting noise in the background and saw Imryth preparing to cast an incantation; it appeared that even seculihad to use the traditional method when heavily injured. "DON'T DO IT!" he shouted. "You're hurt enough, and, even if you weren't, only Lapideis could do something like that!"

Imryth didn't reply with words, but she held up a strange, stone-like object that she'd possessed since the defeat of Ghogiehk: the shifter core.

Of course, Bob thought.

According to liskous legend, those things could amplify and power various things, such as runes, guns and *magic*. Both the incantation and the One of Brimstone's gloating had come to an end. Any second now, the effects of the spell would be clear.

Nothing happened.

The One of Brimstone spat oil, covering the bewildered four entirely. But, just when it seemed it was going to ignite them, it began to howl as if experiencing excruciating pain. There was no visible effect, but whatever was happening to it was an opportunity to turn the tables.

"Morehk; honoured destruction; kerphan of Thaumir, the first husk; witness to the defeat of Chaigidir, the second husk; enemy of deities and stygir alike; spawn of the Void; subordinate of Catarehk, honoured light, and no other stygir; and holder of Bob Solis' contract," Bob chanted, his voice unheard over the stygir creature's screams.

Despite being inaudible, the nameright had the same effect, and a massive, shadowy explosion hit the One of Brimstone, disintegrating it.

Strange, thought Bob, *How come it didn't kill Lance but it killed that thing this time?*

"Namerights are defined by the invoker's will," Morehk explained. *"You didn't want to kill Lance, but you wanted the One of Brimstone to die, and it only hit the One of Brimstone because it was the only target in mind. Act like this more often."*

"What was that?" asked a bewildered Novis.

Jeff simply gazed at where their foe once stood, unsure whether what just happened was real.

"It was this thing: the shifter core." Imryth outstretched her palm, revealing the odd stone that part of their quest had required the retrieval of. She then let out a gasp from pain and slumped to the floor, as the burns on her shoulders were like searing coals.

"I have a cure for that!" Novis exclaimed, and she produced some white scales with red crosses.

"I'm... not accepting... any other types of magic than the normal one!" Imryth protested.

Ignoring her, Novis placed the scales on her skin and, at their touch, the burns began to fade away, like pencil marks being erased by a rubber.

"Anything other than elemental is wrong! What's a liskous doing learning magic anyway?" demanded Imryth.

"Imryth, stop," Jeff said. "What's the big deal?"

"Magic comes from the mind's power. Those with non-elemental magic have a malformed mind and shouldn't be learning it. One in every seven of them is a psychopath!"

"That's true," Novis admitted calmly, "but I'm not one of them. I was taught magic by my father, Contranaturum, the leader of the Thinkers of Mordrev cult before it collapsed."

"EXACTLY! A PSYCHOPATH!" shrieked Imryth. "That cult sacrificed thousands to their stupid fictional ruler for 'enlightened knowledge' or some crap. After that scum escaped his prison with his unnatural magic, where did he go?"

"Imryth, Novis' dad might've been evil, but she isn't," Jeff told her, again trying to break up the fight. "She's proved to be a valuable team member."

"Nah, it's fine," Novis said. "I get that a lot. No one knows a thing about Contranaturum, though, he's basically the liskous version of Napthon. Anyway, the staircase will soon close, so let's hurry."

"Wait," said Jeff, and he pointed to the spot where the One of Brimstone had died. Scattered around the area were a few wires and flecks of a silvery metal. "How did those get there and survive the explosion?"

Bob stifled a gasp as they appeared to be the same grey that had been pestering him since his contract's start.

"I don't know," pondered Imryth. "Maybe one of the dead nominees was a human?"

"Hurry!" called Novis. "In thirty seconds, you'll be stuck here!"

THIRTY-FOUR

The staircase seemed to be an endless spiral, forming a never-ending optical illusion that made people question their whereabouts. Circling it was another wall of fire, adding sweltering heat to the already tough toil of walking up it.

"Novis, are you sure this is the only way out?" panted Jeff, wiping a lake of sweat from his forehead.

Earlier on, Imryth had used a mix of water and ice magic to keep them cool, but Novis advised against this since it would to would cause Imryth to waste all her magical power before the next battle. Their apparent progress in scaling the seemingly never-ending spiral was dwindling with every passing minute.

"*The heat's in your head, Bob!*" Morehk told its host. "*Fire will hurt a stygir, but heat doesn't affect one. Move faster!*"

"That's right." The voice that spoke was child-like, with no apparent sign of whomever it belonged to.

Everyone looked around frantically, but all that they could see were the same flames and stairs. Except for Bob. Behind the grey-green flames, his Void-vision picked up an unimaginably large, green mass that was edging closer and closer towards them.

"You'd better get to floor two," the voice stated with a cackle, "Or I'll get you!"

A tendril of fire swam lazily out of one of the stairs and wrapped itself around Jeff's leg. He cried out in pain, shaking it frantically, but to no avail. Imryth tried to douse it with water magic, and Novis began to apply the healing-scale, whilst Bob aimed his blaster at the tendril and pulled the trigger. Instead of passing through like normal fire, it blasted away the part holding Jeff and triggered a howl of pain. Without hesitation, they sprinted up the stairs, the barrier of tiredness seemingly having disappeared. Whilst running, they attacked the fire around them, but they struck nothing except empty flame.

"Slow, slow, slow, the lot of you!" This time the voice brimmed with malice, with its owner feeling vengeful for the injury Bob had caused it. Multiple tendrils shot out of the fire at lightning speed, wrapping round their limbs and rendering them immobile. "I expect I'll be seeing you in between every floor!"

For some reason, the tendrils weren't burning, but nobody would question their good luck.

"This isn't a normal reality," breathed Bob. "It's alive!"

"Indeed I am," the voice stated smugly. "I'm Asmodeus' greatest work, the Ember of Deceit, and this reality is just a suit of armour built to house me. I am watching your every move and will catch you when you're too slow climbing between floors. But who found it out, you or your buddy the Sty—"

"So, what've you trapped us in here for?" Bob asked loudly, his voice drowning out the deadly secret the Ember of Deceit was trying to spill.

"Who found it out?" it repeated. "You or your bud—"

"Instead of setting us on fire, like I know you can, you've just trapped us in here to ask us questions; won't Napthon and Asmodeus be pleased that their greatest creation isn't killing us in two seconds flat like I know it could!" Bob didn't know what he was spluttering on about, but anything that would stop the Ember of Deceit's blasted speaking seemed like a good idea.

"BOB, DID YOU JUST ASK THAT THING TO KILL US?" screeched Imryth.

"So, you think I'm not their greatest creation?" the Ember of Deceit asked, its voice dripping with malice. "A great hunter toys with inferior prey, especially when it seems that prey's been sent here to entertain them. To start off with, I'll challenge you to a match of my favourite board game."

"HIGH-LEVEL SACRILEGE!" Morehk roared so loud that Bob wouldn't have been surprised if the others heard it as well. "I'M THE SECOND-STRONGEST STYGIR, THAT THING'S JUST A LOWLY CREATION, AND I WON'T STAND FOR THIS, BUT I WILL TEACH IT THE MEANING OF TRUE PAIN! *BOB, USE THE HUSK POWER!"*

"Now that's a bit risky," the Ember of Deceit chided as it set up a complex and detailed board with four figures. "That power can only control a part of me, and I think charging it up too much might exhaust your weak human buddy."

"Oh, that," Morehk sighed. *"Why did I sign the contract with you in the first place?"*

WHY DO STYGIR SIGN CONTRACTS IN THE FIRST PLACE? Bob exploded. *IF YOU'RE SO STRONG ON YOUR OWN, WHY THE HELL DO YOU NEED A HUMAN TO MURDER FOR YOU, TO USE YOUR POWERS, TO—*

"*In case that death ray is activated, because a stygir won't feel it in a human host,*" replied Morehk calmly. "*Although I see that, in this case, I'm paying a heavy price for my protection and disguise.*"

"Who's that thing talking to?" wondered Novis.

"Enough arguing and talking already!" whined the Ember of Deceit as the fully set up board was levitated in the air towards them.

It was bizarrely coloured and adorned with myriad rows of different-hued circles, all leading up to a large, golden one. At the opposite edge to the golden circle, the four figures stood on a square of grey. Bob then noticed that, whilst each figure looked like a featureless grey lump from a distance, each one bore an aspect of one of the four captives: wings, an amulet, a shattered blaster and a cloud upon one's head, which was green to Bob but a black that drains away all colours to everyone else.

"The rules of this game are simple," the Ember of Deceit told them. "You must get to the end to win. If you win, I'll let you go. If you lose, I'll kill you."

"That can't just be it," Imryth stated. "How do we move the figures with our arms and legs tied? What do all the colours mean? And what's stopping us from doing... this?"

Jagged rock formed around Imryth's hands and legs. Swiftly, she cut through the tendrils holding her, then she freed Bob and Jeff, who were on either side of her, in the same way. The Ember of Deceit howled and ignited Novis' tendrils. Disregarding this, Imryth sliced through the burning strands, her earthen gauntlets blocking most of the heat. With everyone free, they sprinted up the staircase.

And then Imryth vanished.

"Nobody likes a cheat!" scoffed the Ember of Deceit in an overbearing, patronising voice, waving a tendril with swirling wormholes for suckers. "So now that's one player down and one more prize to get if you win."

"Fine. We'll play," spat Jeff as more tendrils came out of the flames to ensnare them again. "But, seriously, what do those colours mean and how do we move?"

"You move by saying which path your figure will move on and for how many spaces. As for the colours, each path provides different challenges along the way. You'll have to ask the games master as we play, and that's me! Normal human, you move first."

"Who's the normal one?" asked Jeff.

"You, of course! Now move!"

Jeff gazed at the convoluted board, with the different paths forming an almost incomprehensible network. After a few minutes of thought and the Ember of Deceit nagging him for time wasting, Jeff enquired, "What does the green path mean?"

"That's the path of the small ones," the Ember of Deceit replied with a chuckle. "Always an interesting one."

That sounds bad, thought Jeff, and he asked about the red one.

"Now that's the path of five."

"I'll move to the end of the path of five," Jeff announced.

"Interesting," murmured the Ember of Deceit as the

figure bearing the broken blaster slid across the red path.

As it did, several circles flipped over to reveal warning signs and a sound akin to a fire alarm filled the staircase.

"Whoopsie. It looks like you triggered some danger circles. Unlucky!" declared the Ember of Deceit.

The sound reached a deafening volume.

"What does that mean?" Jeff asked frantically, trying to be heard over the cacophony. "You never said anything about this!"

"You never asked," replied the Ember of Deceit callously. "A danger circle sends your piece back to the beginning and gives you a penalty. For each one activated, the penalty gets worse, and you miss a turn. Let's see... the path of five, like the number attributed to Golachir. What else is attributed to the husk of my creator, human?"

Jeff shrieked in pain as he was set alight.

Bob and Novis begged desperately for the Ember of Deceit to stop the burning.

"I will, for a price. You'd better hurry, though; he'll soon be charcoal!"

"I'LL PAY THE PRICE!" Bob yelled.

Jeff kept on burning.

"Good. Your figure shall now move across every path but not reach the finish, starting from a path of your choice." The Ember of Deceit stifled a giggle of glee as it spoke. But Bob paid it no attention. "The path of small ones." For Jeff's sake, there was no time to ask any more questions, so Bob went with what he knew.

Immediately, the flames tormenting Jeff ceased. Unfortunately, the flames generated by the path of five were far more ravaging than those made by the One of Brimstone, so, whilst Jeff had escaped alive, his flesh was heavily charred and drooping.

"Nice pick," commented the Ember of Deceit as the figure with the cloud on his head began to move along the verdant circles.

Ten danger circles activated.

"It's always fun seeing if you can work out what you'll get, so I'll riddle you the answer. What's on top of the food chain?" enquired the Ember of Deceit.

"Humans?" asked Bob.

"No. What's *really* on top of the food chain?"

Bob started to retch and cough. He could feel something burrowing in his skin. Small bite marks began to appear on his skin.

"The answer is parasites, microbes and pathogens!" chuckled the Ember of Deceit. "I have to warn you though, one of the ten kinds of critters in your body is the one that caused the Great Plague. I assume the angry people on Atham lectured you about it, right?"

"*Idiotic creation,*" Morehk muttered as he turned Bob into a gaseous state. "*Diseases can't harm a stygir!*"

"Cheat," replied the Ember of Deceit, as it raised its wormhole tendril, and Bob and Morehk vanished. "Now, only the liskous is left. Your species is known for its cleverness; I suppose you can demonstrate this?"

"The game's rigged," Novis told the Ember of Deceit. "Every path is full of danger circles!"

"True. I said a great hunter plays with its prey and does not let it escape. Your path?"

Novis wracked her brain. She recognised the colours

and their meanings: her father's cult believed there was a danger with every single hue outside of silver and grey.

"The path of the past," she told the Ember of Deceit. "All the way to the finish."

"You remember that crazy cult?" remarked the Ember of Deceit. "Come to think of it, it was primarily made up of liskous members… Asmodeus' human host has something to do with them, so he told it to base the colours on that."

"Where's their leader?"

"And there's another prize for victory!"

The figure with wings moved across the board, flipping up many circles. Immediately, the world around Novis began to fade away, and she could tell what was coming next.

"Let's see how long you last," were the last words she heard.

THIRTY-FIVE

Novis felt as if she was diving through water, but all around her was just empty space. Below her, she could see a few humans, seemingly crying and screaming but making no sound. On descending closer to them, she gasped in shock as she recognised who they were: some of the candidates for the human government, who had gone missing before the election. As if tortured by something unseen to others, they thrashed around, with their mouths locked in a silent screech of pain. One noticed her and, trying to withstand whatever was tormenting him, began to mouth some words.

"Don't... dwell... on... one... moment... for... too... long?" Novis spoke out the words she was being told, but, at that point, they didn't seem to tell her anything.

The man nodded briefly, then fell to the floor and returned to his unusual state of pain.

"Believe me, you need to take those words of advice if you want to get out," a voice sounded. "But you won't."

"EMBER!" shouted Novis, brimming with rage. "You rigged the human election! These people would be way better leaders than Nugnodge and Murton. You helped to cause the war!"

"Oh, please," the Ember of Deceit scoffed. "I did the least work, plus I got the least credit. Asmodeus' host got all of it! There were about twenty-five candidates, but there are only five trapped on this path forever. You may not get trapped… and you may free the others… and then I'll tell you about that cult… but, of course, that won't happen."

She was becoming tired of the Ember of Deceit's pointless conversations and wished that the penalty would start already.

Suddenly, she was not in that unusual mass of empty space, but on the terrain of a planet she knew only too well, although – with the old-fashioned dwellings, candles, campfires and long fields of grass – it was completely different to the metropolis it actually now was in reality.

It was Primium.

"We finally did it!" exclaimed a dwarf wearing thick, bronze armour with gold runes. He picked up a portrait of a masked, silver figure and smashed it against a rock. "The Thinkers of Mordrev are no more!"

"I hate to be a killjoy, Galvok," wheezed Lapideis, "But the guy in charge escaped. There's nothing he can do with no followers, but it pains me to know he escaped justice."

Novis noticed the god's scars were still bright crimson and dripped blood, likely having been cut by members of her father's cult.

"Well, let's go look for him after we finish helping here," said Aeterno as he scanned the surroundings for any escaping foes. "You fought well, Lapideis; your scars are proof of that."

"Everyone, you're soon going to be at war with a race of deity-like beings!" Novis told the band of warriors.

They did not seem to hear her and carried on talking about the aftermath of the battle.

"You're just reliving memories, not time travelling," she heard the Ember of Deceit whisper. "Idiot."

"Wait! Someone's in the cult's secret base!" Hydrax's telepathic voice alerted everyone.

Out of what seemed like an ordinary house stepped a timid, purple liskous who was trembling with each step. Behind her, an elf with a deranged look on his face toyed with a human skull in his hands.

"Where is my father?" the purple liskous asked Hydrax. "If he isn't here, how will we get enlightened knowledge?"

"Your father… has gone to look for a new faith. But there is no such thing as enlightened knowledge. If you want knowledge, go and read a book," Hydrax told her.

"But how can there be no such thing as enlightened knowledge if I can do this?" she told Hydrax, forming an air-scale in her hand.

"It's me!" Novis exclaimed. As she did so, she felt a sharp pain in her left wing, as if someone had stabbed it. Looking back at it, she saw part of the top of it had disappeared.

"You really don't say," goaded the Ember of Deceit. "If this shocks you, you'll definitely end up like the would-be government members. Now, moving on…"

"Wait! I've got to see what happens to me!" Instantly, her whole left wing disappeared, painfully severed off by some invisible force. She figured out what was happening straight away, and took her mind away from that fragment of her past.

"Oh, so you've realised," the Ember of Deceit mused. "The past can tear apart the future, as goes the old liskous saying. Pay attention to that guy's words, or your entire body and soul will be held in torment forever."

A new scene unfurled before her eyes. This time she was running away from a group of elves, along with a group of familiar faces: the magigades she had known for most of her life and, with the exception of Dodsfald, had seen die at the One of Brimstone's hands.

"IT'S BACK TO THE ASYLUM OR TO THE NEXT WORLD FOR YOUR KIND!" bawled one of the elves, and he hurled a fireball at the fleeing group, which was intercepted instantly by a corpse.

"NECROMANCY SHOULDN'T EVEN EXIST!" another roared. "Eldrit taught us magic to control the elements, not to mock the dead! And what's a liskous doing learning magic in the first place?"

The two groups were then separated as flaming feathers flew towards the elves, which had to combine their magic to create a barrier strong enough to block the missiles.

"Leave them alone!" ordered a commanding voice. Volundur, held aloft by wings of fire, descended from the air, taking a few small moments to swish his cloak or give a heroic look to the magigades.

"You again!" an elf spat. "Your ego is larger than the amount of times these pieces of trash have caused havoc. One in three of them is a psychopath! Don't you remember the Thinkers of Mordrev?"

"Yeah, all you did was put the fire human in prison before he escaped successfully!" another followed up. "Our feats far outclass yours, so who are you to boss us around?"

"Well, what of the other two in that set of three?" Volundur asked scornfully. "They only have simple mental disorders, which are nothing to be discriminated against. You fools are lucky that the deities are off to chart the solar system or you would fill Paxton's empty cell."

"Fine, protect them, *hero*," one of the elves sneered. He then turned to the magigades and said a few parting words: "Don't act like this is the end. You're not meant to exist; you're a flaw in nature! When a cancer forms on someone's skin, they try to eradicate it, not make peace with it."

A small feeling crept up on Novis' right wing, like a scratch. She said nothing to the Ember of Deceit or anyone else; she just watched as a new scene manifested.

She was in a care home, dodging rocks thrown through shattered windows.

"*How pitiful,*" the Ember drawled. "*The pain, the suffering...*"

She expected her other wing to disappear, but nothing happened. Except for the fact that the scene around her ground to a halt, as if it were a video that had just been paused. Suddenly, she was floating; it was an odd sensation that lifted her out of the care home, past the sky and back to the odd region where the tortured humans stared at her, baffled. With them was the wing she lost.

"Is this... all you can do?" Novis asked the Ember. She felt mortified, but tried not to let the Ember know that. After all, the tingling sensation on her remaining wing was getting greater by the second.

Novis descended again, arriving at a grisly scene. Dodsfald was dissecting something so mutilated that Novis couldn't tell what it was.

"Please," a voice cried from within the mass of blood and flesh. "We didn't mean to throw those stones. Magic mess-ups and normals are equal..."

"No," Dodsfald declared with a laugh. "For once, I'll be above you, commanding you as part of the crypt! How does that sound?"

"Dodsfald, you're going too far," Novis' past self told him. "Either add them to your horde or let them live. We must defeat our enemies, but not by becoming worse than them."

"Fine," Dodsfald whined like a spoiled kid, throwing his dissecting tools into the macabre being, killing it. "Necro harvest!"

Their former bully turned into a flicker of white light and soared to Dodsfald's hand.

"This has to be the last one you do this to," the past Novis continued. "In doing this, you're just carving out a worse name for the magigades."

"Well, then, maybe I'm happy with carving it out," Dodsfald spat.

"You're trying too hard, Ember of Deceit," Novis told her captor, each word taking all her strength to force out. "Your mind games... can't harm me. They can't! Fight me hand-to-hand!"

"WHAT?" screamed the Ember of Deceit in surprise.

Instantly, Novis was back on the staircase, with Bob, Caesium and Jeff. For some reason, Jeff's flesh was uncharred, and Bob wasn't diseased. The flaming tendrils surrounded them, but, this time, they just shook with what seemed to be fear, and they could see what was behind them: a small, maggot-like creature.

"*That's what the filthy liar really is!*" stated Morehk, laughing heartily. "*Who's really superior? A shape-shifting, explosion-causing gas being that can kill deities, or a worm? THIS IS JUST LAUGHABLE!*" It materialised a shotgun in Bob's hands, which he dropped immediately.

"Look guys, someone else must've been here!" Bob announced, pointing at the weapon.

"Good," Novis said, picking it up and firing at the Ember of Deceit, which died instantly. She acted like she did before the Ember of Deceit's game: unharmed both mentally and physically, and determined.

"I… we saw what happened in the penalty," Imryth said to Novis. "I'm sorry, I didn't realise that's what magigades had to go through."

"It doesn't matter; it was just a simple mistake," Novis replied. Yet the haunted look in her eyes suggested otherwise.

"I really am," Imryth repeated. "I just… anyway, onto the next challenge."

They walked up the staircase at a steady walking pace.

On the next section of the reality, there was no stygir creature to face or even a speck of fire. They looked around, wondering what to do and if there was any way of escaping.

"You escaped the Ember of Deceit! Are you OK?" someone said with a heavy tone of concern. An elf woman staggered towards them, panting with the effort. Her head was adorned with an emerald circlet and golden antlers, and her eyes were pools of featureless gold. She wore clothing made of silk, yet it was bark coloured and flecked with moss. "Is anyone hurt? I excel in healing—"

Imryth bowed and fell to the floor. "It is good to know you are safe, goddess of nature," she responded.

"Please, call me Sequia," the elf woman replied with a chuckle.

"How do we get out of here?" Novis asked. "And how are you here?"

"It was the government from the fool planet and their henchman," Shekina began, then she apologised to Bob and Jeff, saying frantically that she meant no offence.

"It's fine; carry on," Jeff assured her.

"I was looking for Mekanyon's shifter thingy and then I was ambushed by one of Primium's mercenaries. For some reason, there was a stygir inside him, which dumped me at the top of this reality. I figured out that the reality would be destroyed after the deaths of all the creatures and the Ember of Deceit, so I've been killing them off. I think the only ones left are the one on the floor below us and the Ember of Deceit, whom I can't figure out how to kill."

Bob couldn't fathom how the frail lady in front of him could defeat several of Napthon's creatures, when he'd been struggling to defeat one, but he didn't say anything.

"The Ember of Deceit and the last creature are dead," stated Imryth. "If what you've said is correct, then this world should collapse any second now."

"You killed the Ember of Deceit? Awesome job!" Sequia commended them as their surroundings crumbled away to become the military ship from which Nugnodge and the others had fled.

"They're here, aren't they?" Suddenly, Sequia seethed with rage. "The human government? *Where are they?*"

"Yes, but all their research is…" Bob trailed off as he saw that the ship they were on had no bombs on it but was flanked by a large fleet of bomber ships and a large, highly decorated ship that probably housed the government.

"Hello, human military!" Asmodeus' telepathic voice sounded across the fleet. *"Where Leif started, we will continue, but with the new nuclear bombs instead of boring, old shock troops. Arcanast, here we come!"*

"Really?" sighed Sequia. "We're at war? I've been waiting to get my revenge on the artificial creations of man for too long…"

"We can handle this—" Imryth began

But Sequia waved her away. "I must destroy this entire fleet!" the goddess spat. "Take the escape pods, please."

"HEY!" a human soldier hollered. "WHO THE HELL ARE—" He was cut off as a bladed vine curled round his neck and crushed it.

"See you! Bye!" Sequia waved absent-mindedly to Bob, Jeff, Imryth and Novis before running to the ship's exit.

THIRTY-SIX

Mick Nugnodge sat around a table with the other government members, laughing with joy at their latest success. Bert had got on the right ship, Astra and Larry had stopped going on about removing Primium from the solar system, and Glen wasn't trying to start a fight with everyone. This was perfect. Now he just had to get Dr Shell assassinated by Napthon, then he could say he had invented the nuclear bomb.

"And now..." He raised his glass of wine for a toast. "To the destruction of the inferior races!"

"To the destruction of the inferior races!" everyone else chorused.

"WE'LL ALL BE DESTROYED!" came a shriek. Victor Xena dashed down the corridor, his face colourless with utter shock.

"Were the ship's toilets really that bad?" Nugnodge asked, frowning. "I could always have the cleaners killed—"

"He'll kill everything! Everything! I was hacking—" stated Xena.

"What? Our popularity polls?" joked Nugnodge. "Is that why Murton and Jackson were top?"

"Yeah, that's true; you hack things all the time," interjected a snickering Larry Egraf.

"All our annexing plans—" continued Xena.

"Your annexing plans," said Nugnodge.

"Will be for nothing. Look at what I found when I was hacking." Xena went to hand Nugnodge his phone.

Mick Nugnodge slapped it away and it clattered across the floor. "Chill. It's fine. Just think of the bombs!"

"Hey! Let Vic show us what he found!" Glen Murton stood up from his seat. "Do you not want him to show it because it proves you're a terrible leader?"

"Yeah, I'm with Glen on this one," said Astra Yak.

"I'm with Astra," added Larry.

"Isn't Arcanast on the other side of the solar system?" asked Bert Jackson, studying a chart of space. "That reminds me, why are there only four species in this solar system? They can't've all died because it was too cold on the outer planets."

"They died from the opposite," Napthon stated with a laugh as he walked into the room. "I saw to that. And, Bert, that map's upside down."

"Napthon, kill Nugnodge!" ordered Murton.

"Well... if you do that..." Nugnodge pointed to a diagram of a nuclear bomb. "I'll shoot the next one of these at you!"

"Well..." Murton stammered. "I have money, and I can buy those!"

"Yeah, and we'll back him up," added Yak.

"This is not a threat; I'll chuck this bomb at you!" repeated Nugnodge.

"Well, I really do have money!" reiterated Murton.

"None of this matters! All we're doing is aiding him in his—" began Xena.

"A MASSIVE PERCENTAGE OF THE FLEET'S BEEN DESTROYED!" Dr Shell shouted, running into the room and cutting off Xena. "We need to launch the bombs at the goddess of nature or we'll face even more massive damage."

"Fool. Only I can harm her," Napthon announced, smirking proudly. "And so can Asmodeus, who you will not use in your bombs or you'll be joining the species on the edge of the system."

"Well, I really will fire that bomb!" huffed Nugnodge.

"And I really will show you my bank account!" sniffed Murton.

"It feels so good to be able to talk to you freely, partner," stated Napthon.

"Indeed it is," agreed Asmodeus. *"But let's first see how those fools who hired you fend off Sequia. I remember Catarehk thinking she'd die easily, like their god of farming, but it was terribly mistaken. The goddess of nature killed many armies we sent out alone. Watching them try to fight, whilst not being as pleasant as starting a blaze, will prove the uselessness of humanity's rulers."*

"That's a great idea. And then, after the comedy routine, we'll incinerate any surviving actors," confirmed Napthon. The duo cackled manically as they flew off the ship, whilst the government made ready for battle.

"My friends and Nugnodge," Larry announced to the group, "There is still a way we can harm them. Do you remember our old friend Galvok?"

"No," replied Bert.

"The dwarf god who decided to fight alongside the enemy instead of going on Mekanyon's quest, who always acted like a stubborn army veteran and wouldn't help us in any way, even resisting Nugnodge's torture—" Larry continued.

"Maybe, *just maybe*, it was because he was a god!" exclaimed Murton. "And a god of protection as well!"

"The bald guy on Atham with the pink stuff in his head gave me torture instruments made of blue stuff that could kill deities," Nugnodge explained. "Egraf wanted to try something new; what was it?"

"I requested a blender of the material," Larry spoke, a grin creeping over his face like a chasm opening up. "Dwarf-size."

"Couldn't you have just put something in his mead the next time he went into a tavern?" asked Xena. "That's a bit extreme, even for someone like him."

"No! After I sent some underlings to run tests, I found out that deity's flesh, when pulverised by this metal, will temporarily give anything in contact with the flesh the deity's power. The more liquid the flesh, the better."

"Prove it," said Nugnodge. "How do I know you're not trying to make me drink his blood and then tell the news about it?"

"Incoming attack!" Asmodeus' voice rang in their heads. *"Sequia has begun her attack!"*

Looking out from the ship's window, the government members saw their army struggle in vain against the goddess, who decimated it without mercy. With a mad, hunter's glint in her eyes, she crushed the hull of a spaceship with long, thick vines that protruded from her fingers, then she watched as the crew died from lack of oxygen. If sound could travel in space, they would have heard her roars of hatred at all things technological and man-made. A squadron of escort ships, knowing they couldn't defeat a goddess, tried to retreat, but the antlers on her head grew, and she charged at them, rending them to bits with the antlers' various points.

Out of all in the pantheon, none seemed to exemplify their attribute like Sequia. For the goddess was not just a wielder of nature, she was its personification. Bob, Imryth, Jeff and Novis, watching from their escape pod as it descended to Atham, couldn't fathom how the caring, motherly figure had become a callous killing machine in a matter of seconds.

Another fleet of ships, more devoted to their corrupt rulers, tried to shoot her down, even though they knew it was futile.

With Napthon and Asmodeus gone, Egraf was forced to pull out a radio. "SQUAD DELTA! USE THE GODSBREW!" he screamed into it.

Sequia's hands grew into claws, and she swiped at the ships with lightning speed and accuracy. Screams could be heard from the radio.

"DAMMIT, LARRY!" yelled Nugnodge. "You blended that dwarf for no good reason! How were the ships supposed to drink it anyway? We could've had a propaganda-filled public execution, but no—"

"Wait…" a surprised voice came from the radio. "I'm alive! WE'RE ALIVE!"

Unscathed, the ships were covered in a golden barrier that Sequia's claws shattered upon. They then opened fire;

Sequia, thinking that her being a deity would make her invulnerable, let the energy blasts hit her. Much to her surprise, they didn't bounce off or break, but opened up a large hole in her chest. With a cough of blood, the goddess lost consciousness.

"No, ships don't drink, but they have an engine and fuel can be poured into it easily," Egraf explained with a smirk. "See? The ships are now temporarily deities of protection. I remember one of the main defences against the stygir in the war was Galvok's almost indestructible shields, and now they're ours!"

"You don't say!" commented Nugnodge sarcastically and plucked the radio out of Egraf's hands. "All forces, shoot her down!"

"No..." breathed Yak in shock as she took a look at Xena's phone and the latest thing he had hacked. "This can't be true..." She turned to Nugnodge. "Get the forces to withdraw! We've been fighting each other when we have a common enemy!"

"Yeah, yeah, the stygir," Nugnodge muttered dismissively. "Now, it's time to launch the bombs on Arcanast and Ferraheim. Murton, you're an expert on the different races and their statuses, which one should we eliminate first?"

"Elves and their magic could prove a big threat to technology," Murton replied. "Yak, let me see that." Murton gasped. "Such foolery! Vic, are you sure you didn't just hack an elf and dwarf propaganda site? This is ridiculous. I'm not believing it!"

"What's all the fuss?" scoffed Nugnodge, taking a look at the phone. "Did Xena accidentally give you a score of

1,000,000% when hacking the popularity polls again—"
Nugnodge stopped in his tracks, unsure what to say. Even
elves and dwarves who hadn't been bombed did not seem
to be the main problem anymore.

"What's more important, inferiors or this?" he asked
uncertainly.

"We must stop this thing," Xena declared. "This New
World's Gear."

THIRTY-SEVEN

"NO!" howled Jonas in anguish, tears streaming down his face. One moment they were victorious, but *now* Gary was gone. "This cannot be!" He turned to the deities. "You have to be able to do something. *You're divine, right? Can't you bring him back?* There's got to be a way!"

From Belial's sightless eyes and from those of everyone else, tears also began to fall. They had all viewed Gary as nothing more than a petty hacker, a traitor and Jonas' pet – and yet he had saved them all. Now there was no way to express their gratitude to him.

"There is a way," said Aeterno, and he ran his claw across the wound on his chest, opening it up. Blood poured from it and mingled with the red pool that had been Gary. The god's breath became heavier and his vision blurred, but he stood there stoically. "Shekina, revive him!"

The goddess obeyed, and the beginnings of a brain began to coalesce out of the crimson.

"*I shall help,*" a telepathic voice sounded. Hydrax ran a clawed fingernail across the length of his arm and the brain grew at a faster rate. "*You deserve a rest, Aeterno.*"

The other deities followed suit, adding their own

divinite-containing blood to the pool. Now everyone was filled with hope that Gary would come back alive. After some time, the golden glow from Shekina's hands dimmed, flickered, then faded. At their feet, a heart throbbed feebly, connected to a fully formed brain by a few blood vessels.

"I'm sorry," Shekina apologised, stifling a sob. "That power can only be used on the same being once per century. I'm afraid this is the closest thing he'll get to being alive."

*

"Antony, have you got it yet?" Cognitio asked.

"Yes," replied his troll friend, who was carrying the core of Tabris. "I also used the phasecraft to nip to the vault and get you some tools from there."

They both knew the ridiculousness of Cognitio's idea and how slim the chances were of them actually succeeding, but it was the only option at this point.

"This isn't the end for Gary!" Antony told the melancholic crowd. "Cognitio's thought of something that could save him! I know he's blind now, but I'll be his eyes. Will you pass me Gary's organs?"

Gently, Jonas picked them up and placed them in the troll's hands. "I wish you the best of luck," he told Antony.

For the next two hours, Cognitio and Antony toiled over their project to revive Gary in the confines of one of Longinus' huts, whilst everyone else held a conference to sort out further diplomatic relations between the deities and Longinus.

"We will take you back to Primium, but maybe not just yet, since a war's going on," Aeterno told Belial.

"Very well. But I shall journey with y—" Belial was cut off by a spewing of blood and vomit from his mouth. Falling to the floor, he writhed in agony as his skin took on a greenish tone and growths began to form on it. "Hestrium!" he managed to splutter.

A Longinist rushed to a hut and returned with a phial of foul-smelling liquid that resembled dirty water. He poured it into Belial's mouth, and the effects of the Great Plague began to cease. Around half of the Longinists suffered the same symptoms, with the other half dashing to their huts for the same substance.

"I thought you said you didn't have medicine," stated Nimbus.

"Hestrium isn't a medicine; it's a deterrent," Belial told him. "It gets rid of the disease's effects for about a day and then they return, but worse. Unfortunately, only Hestrus knew how to make it, so now we have nothing to protect ourselves. Anyway, the rest can go to Primium, but most of the deaths on your side were caused by me. I must go with you on your quest to try to redeem myself. "

"If you wish to do so. Any help in locating the last four deities would be much appreciated," said Aeterno. "Also, were any Longinists taken from Atham by the Grey Triptych?"

Before Belial could reply, Nimbus opened the Kumosphere and the humans they had saved from Ghogiehk poured out.

After sniffing the air, Belial let out a cry of joy and began to greet the familiar faces he had once thought were dead.

"If you saved them from that filthy gas cloud, then Longinus and the deities really are allies," he told Aeterno. "But what do you suggest we do about the rest of the Grey Triptych?"

"Well, their three leaders – Aurik, Ghogiehk and Hestrus – are dead. From what I've gathered, they can't really function without their leaders, and so we can consider the organisation dissolved. But one of their underlings said something to me… New World's Gear. Do you recognise those words?" Aeterno queried.

Belial shook his head.

"It unsettles me. Even if knowledge of those words is useless, I still want to know what their original plans were," stated Aeterno.

"Aeterno, Belial, I need to ask you some questions," Shekina told them.

Immediately, they noticed she had used her power to regenerate the skin on her arms and all signs of weariness from the fight had vanished.

"I became a deity in the middle of the Stygir War, and I don't yet know what the vaults you mentioned are," she explained.

Both god and Longinist tensed at the mention of this.

"I'll explain later, in case a mortal hears. That knowledge is for deities only," Aeterno confirmed.

"Also, I've heard that Lapideis died, and then somehow came back to life. Do you know how that works?" questioned Shekina.

"I do," a raspy voice sounded behind them. The elf who had summoned the corpses during the fight against Tabris appeared behind them, his hands aglow with white energy. He closed his eyes and began to concentrate.

"Who is this?" asked Belial, his nose wrinkling as he sniffed the air. "He smells of rotting corpses."

"This is Dodsfald," explained Aeterno. "We found him at the headquarters of the Thinkers of Mordrev—"

"The ones who worshipped a god they called the Silver One? The 'we'll get knowledge through sacrifice' guys?" Belial interrupted him. "I recall Grey Triptych members saying they were once part of that cult! Deathswind—"

"But he's on our side now!" Aeterno exclaimed.

Belial cancelled his attack.

Aeterno continued, "His mind has been very warped from birth, and the cult he was with didn't do anything to help this, but Cognitio sees something in him and is trying to get him to fight for Heavenspire. He has a unique type of magic: necromancy, the ability to reanimate the dead."

"Here is your god," Dodsfald announced.

A burst of white-and-gold energy lit up the area, and then a familiar brown liskous appeared before them.

"Where am I?" he groaned. "Is the quest over?"

"Lapideis!" Aeterno and Shekina exclaimed, rushing to their fellow deity's side.

"What happened to you?" Shekina asked.

"I don't know," the god of earth replied. "I think I called a ceasefire between us and Longinus, but then it turned out they had a traitor and… I'm not sure after that."

"Dodsfald, I thought you said your magic couldn't revive deities," Aeterno stated.

"I revived him," the elf stated smugly. "Necromancy doesn't work on the *corpses* of deities, but then I saw this one had crumbled away into a pile of dust, and I tried it on that. Unfortunately, undead gods don't act like proper minions and act as if they were living!" He began to rant about the necessity of a fully subservient horde.

Aeterno ignored him and spoke to Lapideis. "You went deusnova, didn't you?"

Lapideis nodded.

"That was a very irresponsible move. If you had just fought your opponents normally, you wouldn't've crumbled away—" responded Aeterno.

"And the original peace offerings with Jonas wouldn't have happened and we would still be fighting Longinus," Lapideis interjected, cutting him off. "It's like you say, we're the system's immortal protectors. It's better the armour breaks than the being using it."

"It's true; you also managed to show me that an alliance was needed," stated Belial.

"And your barriers saved us against Tabris countless times," added Shekina. "This whole part of the quest owes a lot to you."

Lapideis disappeared with a flash of white.

"Oh, for crying out loud! We get it; he was helpful," moaned Dodsfald. "First crying over the death of a simple human and now this! How cheesy!"

Ignoring him, Aeterno remembered suddenly that Bob, and likely some others, had been sent to deal with a bomb the human government were going to drop on the planet, and they had not yet returned. He asked the others about this issue, and Shekina and Belial said they would go and check what had happened to them.

"IT'S FINE; I WILL GO," the robotic voice of Tabris sounded.

At this familiar tone, Belial plucked handfuls of knives from his belt, and Shekina held up her callstaff.

"Relax, he's not Hestrus' killing machine anymore," Cognitio told them. "He's Gary."

Everyone else gasped at this notion, that the brain and heart sent down the road of death were now the behemoth in front of them.

"It's true," said Antony, appearing from behind Gary's foot. "Cognitio somehow managed to rewire the core to act as a life-support system for Gary's heart and brain, and make Tabris' body his."

"IT'LL TAKE SOME GETTING USED TO," admitted Gary, trying to lift up an arm clumsily. "BUT I MUST GO TO TELL BOB AND ANYONE ELSE WHO IS WITH HIM THAT LONGINUS AND THE DEITIES ARE ALLIES NOW."

Antony let out a gasp. "Galvok is dead, and Sequia is critically injured, near Arcanast and Ferraheim!" he exclaimed, looking at his board. "We have to hurry!"

"I CAN GET THERE IN TIME!" Gary told them, and ion thrusters slid out of his ankles.

Before he could fly off, Shekina used her wind magic to fly onto Gary's shoulder, since she needed to go and heal the injured goddess. The ion thrusters activated, Gary's wings beat, and the two sped off at an incredible pace. Unfortunately, as they did so, a barrage of strong wind levelled the remaining Longinist huts.

"I can sense something has been destroyed," stated Belial. "But it doesn't matter, for we will be home soon! Home, at last, and cured of this horrid plague!"

At this, the other Longinists let out a loud cheer.

"I understand they're friends now, but remember this is the group that killed over half of our nominees," whispered Cognitio to Aeterno. "We must make sure that their families don't find out the truth and that Longinus definitely do redeem themselves, as Belial said."

"I'm sure they'll be valuable allies," Aeterno replied. "Their quest for vengeance is over."

THIRTY-EIGHT

"We have eleven bombs," Nugnodge confirmed through the radio, uncertain that humanity would benefit from their victory.

Due to the fact that they were unsure whether the document was a fake or a piece of enemy propaganda, the government had opted to focus on finishing the war, but the only thing they could think of was the New World's Gear. As if bound to their minds by chains, that fell plan was all they could think of.

"The document mentioned something about a shifter core, which is that power gem thingy from the neutral cowards' mythology," stated Murton. "We should set up a blockade around Drakon to make sure nobody can get their hands on one. Besides, the cowards deserve it for saying the war's unnecessary and all that. Oh, and I can't be bothered to pay for that, so have them do it."

"Since the goddess is going to die soon, we'll distribute ten of them across Arcanast and Ferraheim, and launch the remaining one on Primium as a display of my power," Nugnodge continued.

"Bombing our own planet is not really a good idea—" began Dr Shell.

But Nugnodge yelled at him for disrespecting his superiors, cutting him off mid-sentence.

"The stories state that shifter cores are found in the furthest reaches of the system, so the blockade's not a good idea," Bert told Glen, trying to keep his composure stoic. "Anyway, we all agreed that we'll fight that threat once we've finished defeating the inferiors."

Nugnodge murmured the command to launch the first bomb, and his ship's pilot flew them closer to Arcanast.

"The war's been won," announced Larry, his face wrenched into a grin; like a sculptor with clay, he was gathering all the scraps of positive news and moulding them into an appealing vision of the future. "We've defeated two whole species. And, remember, a bunch of people are out there looking for that core. They've probably been trained by the deities, so there's no way that the Grey Triptych group can get it before them!"

This speech allayed a portion of everyone's worries, and the whole ship began to celebrate the beginning of the end for elves and dwarves.

*

On Arcanast, elves gazed up in fear at the spacecraft blocking out the sun. The injured magicians sent back home during the war combined their crippled power to form a shield, but they knew it was in vain. Any elf fighting the humans on the numerous battlegrounds across the system wouldn't know of the fate that would befall their new planet until it was too late.

*

"FIRE!" bellowed Nugnodge triumphantly.

*

Just before this had happened, the goddess of nature, Sequia, had been shot down by a squadron of human ships, and she lay limp in space as the military crafts encircled her, drawing out the kill to their satisfaction. The human government had thought this battle won and had forgotten about it; had they looked for a bit longer, they would have seen a blur of blue, speeding through space faster than the most elite craft. The ships didn't notice until it was too late.

His hands changing shape, Gary trapped half the ships in a longinite dome as Shekina began to heal the fallen goddess of nature. Realising the mistake caused by their pride and the certainty of their victory, the remaining ships fired all of their weaponry at Sequia, but the goddess was covered by Gary's wings. The energy blasts tore holes in the vast, blue structures, but they were sealed up swiftly by the regeneration their body possessed. Clumsily trying to move his wings back, Gary destroyed the majority of the human fleet unintentionally and nearly hit Sequia and Shekina as well.

"SORRY!" he apologised in his new radio voice, as his arms and legs began to change rapidly into all of their different forms, and his body keeled over. "I'M STILL GETTING USED TO THIS."

"Well, get used to it, machine!" snapped Sequia, narrowly missing a longinite brazier.

She then noticed the remaining ships were fleeing, and vines shot out of her hands, snaring all of them and crushing any weaponry they possessed. She flung them at the jittering Gary, where they exploded on contact. The longinite dome fell apart, and the ships inside were added to Sequia's kill count.

"AND THAT'S WHY YOU DON'T KILL YOUR DEITIES AND LOSE ALL FAITH IN NATURE!" she roared triumphantly.

Gary, who had now regained control of his new body, directed his movements and used his ion thrusters to stop himself being flung through space.

"COULDN'T YOU HAVE GOT RID OF THEM ANOTHER WAY?" Gary asked. "MAYBE SPARED THEM TO GET INFORMATION? ANYWAY, SOME SOLDIERS DON'T CHOOSE TO FIGHT, THEY'RE FORCED TO—"

"Shut up machine!" Sequia snapped. "You and your silver trashcan of a fake god are next!"

"Sequia, he's right," Shekina told her fellow deity. "Even if they have killed deities and fought against our species, we – as the system's rulers – should always act better."

"I'll take that information from you, but not from that," the goddess of nature replied bluntly.

Suddenly, Gary let out a loud gasp. "LOOK THERE!" he exclaimed, pointing to a large ship hovering above a nearby planet. "WE MUST HURRY."

At this, Sequia let out a bellicose war cry. "*MICK NUGNODGE'S FLAGSHIP!*" she roared. "Stay back, I have to destroy it!" Massive golden wings sprouted from her back, and she zoomed towards her prey.

Gary readied his ion thrusters, but Shekina told him to hold back.

"It's fine, Gary. When Mother Nature herself is angry, no living thing can stop her," she explained.

*

"YES! THE BOMB WILL FIRE!" Nugnodge screeched, jumping up and down triumphantly. "It's so cool; I'll fire bombs at every possible place I can once this is over!"

"Nugnodge, the goddess of nature—" Dr Shell began.

He was cut off by his jovial dictator. "Is dead! With these bombs, not even the New World's Gear and the Grey Triptych can stop us. We'll even enslave the stygir! And, any second now, the bomb will explode!"

Seconds passed, but nothing happened. Nugnodge peered out of a window. The bomb was there, yet it had stopped in the middle of empty space. A net of darkness suspended it just above the planet. The net was touching the bomb but nothing happened. Why the bomb was not exploding was a mystery. Everyone rushed over to Nugnodge's position and peered out of the window at the odd occurrence.

And then a familiar telepathic voice spoke. It was Asmodeus.

"*Enslave us, you sphere of flab?*" the stygir chided. "*Oh, please. Husk Golachir utilises combustion, and my covenant gives me control over it to the same level as your earth, sky and water gods."*

"What does that mean?" asked Bert.

"Any explosions and flames are mine to fully command. I can neutralise yours!" Asmodeus confirmed.

"Wow, I'm still confused," muttered Bert.

"He can take away the bomb's boom," Dr Shell told Bert.

"NAPTHON!" yelled Nugnodge. "YOU FILTHY TRAITOR! WHAT DO I PAY YOU FOR? RELEASE MY BOMB!"

"Sorry, but my host and I don't want to be slaves. However, I will warn you, a threat is approaching," responded Asmodeus on the pairing's behalf.

At this moment, they all noticed Sequia flying towards them.

"The godsbrew!" exclaimed Egraf. "Bert, to your left! Get it!"

Bert ran to the left. A thread of his trousers snagged on a chair. Bert stopped. "Can someone unsnag my trousers?" he asked.

There was barely time for everyone to express their frustration before Sequia tore the ship apart with her horns. The human government went with it, with every corrupt member dying in the wreck. So did any information on the New World's Gear. It all was destroyed.

And so humanity, leaderless and crippled, lost the war.

Everything grey on Napthon's vision disappeared. He grinned and congratulating Asmodeus on his plan. The pyromaniac duo had decided to return to their home now: the Void. Sure, Catarehk was against stygir leaving it for reasons other than his cause, but maybe he would let them off if they returned with a mighty weapon of war.

"The nuclear bomb," Napthon breathed. "So many things to do, right partner?"

Asmodeus chuckled and agreed.

However, just as they were about to begin their journey home, a colossal, blue figure noticed them and charged, his bladed fingers outstretched.

"Do you recognise this?" Napthon asked Asmodeus.

"No, I do not," his stygir replied.

"Well, let's burn it," suggested Napthon with a grin.

Ignoring them, Gary picked up the bomb and threw it as far as he could towards a cluster of uninhabited planetoids. It seemingly crashed into a region of empty space, and there it remained, as if frozen completely in time.

With a roar, Napthon threw balls of fire at Gary, but then the fire disappeared.

"Know not just the periodic elements, but the original four as well," someone said in Napthon's head. No, it was not Asmodeus. This voice did not belong to an ally. Was it the figure? No, Napthon realised, it was even worse...

Hydrax snared Napthon with his rope and made a sphere of water around him. "I remember you, you psychopath. When the trolls and all species like them fled to the outer reaches of the system, did you kill them?"

"*YES!*" Napthon replied using Asmodeus' telepathy. "*WE TWO... WE BURNED THEM ALL! THOSE SAVAGES NEVER STOOD A CHANCE!*"

Whilst it is customary to laugh in your enemy's face before they defeat you, this taunting was but a decoy.

Another more discreet string of thoughts told Asmodeus to leave Napthon's body and retreat to the Void.

"No, I can't!" replied the stygir. *"You're my host and partner in crime, so I'm not abandoning you!"* This, too, was thought on the same plane of discreetness, whilst Hydrax's mind was distracted processing Napthon's taunts.

The covenant will bring me back. My body will be the decoy; you just get to the Void!

Reluctantly, Asmodeus slipped unnoticed out of Napthon's form, his particles travelling individually so as to not be noticed. To Gary and Hydrax, Napthon had just died, spluttering his final thought about his genocidal rampages.

"Nuclear bombs and species-killers... it's a good thing we removed them both from our system. Gary, you'll make a fine god if the rescue goes as planned," declared Hydrax.

"THANKS, HYDRAX," Gary said. "BUT HOW DID YOU GET HERE?"

"I spoke and triggered my... never mind. I decided to help you because, as the ultimate controller of water, I stand the greatest chance of stopping Paxton."

The two then flew to where Sequia and Shekina were, and they all exchanged information on what had happened. Although with some reluctance from Sequia, it was decided that the elf goddesses – due to their influence on the dwarf and elf fighters – should halt all the battles between races across the system, as well as make sure the humans were spared. With new, less-corrupt rulers, humanity wouldn't start interspecies wars, and the four species of Atlas would be united once more. Hydrax gave Sequia and Shekina the spare phasecrafts he had, and words of farewell were exchanged.

"*Peace has been restored!*" exclaimed Hydrax jubilantly. "*I can see the system just as it was before any of the stygir and interspecies wars happened, can you?*"

"I HAVEN'T SEEN MUCH OF THE SYSTEM, JUST PRIMIUM AND ATHAM," replied Gary. "BUT I CAN DEFINITELY GET USED TO HAVING NO MORE WARS AND NO MORE DISEASES."

With that, both god and Longinist soared towards Atham, to spread the news of the peace.

THIRTY-NINE

His eyes opened. He was in a plain, white room. He couldn't remember much. Groggily, Caesium got to his feet and picked up his weapons. He remembered that he had been fighting someone – a Longinist called Hestrus – but not much after that. A glowing, golden light flickered in the centre of the room, getting slowly brighter and more prominent. Was this another of Hestrus' powers? Caesium began to dig with his wormhole-rune pickaxe, and he tunnelled to the top of the room, readying himself for a surprise attack. Now the light filled the whole room, gilding it, and Caesium had to close his eyes to avoid being blinded. The light disappeared, and, in its place, someone stood in the centre of the room. In a swift manoeuvre, Caesium jumped out of the wormhole, used his attraction-rune hammer to grab their weapons and strike them with his pickaxe.

"You should know that mortals can't harm deities," Kosma told him. "Anyway, aren't we on the same side?"

Caesium gasped and began to apologise.

However, Kosma cut him off. "Now, Longinus and the deities are allies. Hestrus was in fact a traitor, working for an organisation called the Grey Triptych, but I can't fill you in on everything. Let's go through that rift to Atham." The goddess pointed to a gaping tear in reality in the corner of the room, leading out to the barren planet.

They both jumped into it, where they were greeted by a scene of celebration. It seemed that the war was over; Tabris now housed the soul of Gary; and a purple, one-winged liskous had killed the Great Plague once and for all.

"So you can produce these," breathed Jonas in awe, holding a glowing white slate-scale, "and they can kill all diseases? Even the Great Plague? *Forever?*"

"Yes, it should work like that," Novis told the ecstatic old man.

"Then you are the saviour of Longinus," Belial commended her.

The other Longinists let out a loud cheer.

Elsewhere, Jeff and Gary were making up after their fight, and Aeterno was telling the tale of the fight against Tabris and the Grey Triptych for anyone who wasn't there when it happened.

Caesium noticed a group of elf magicians scolding another elf for his cowardice, at which he laughed and gave them feeble excuses.

"Necromancy isn't shooting cheesy death bolts at the enemy, it's summoning corpses to do the work for you. Everyone knows that!" the elf declared. To demonstrate, he summoned fallen human soldiers, a few elf magicians and even Caesium's dad.

Aghast, Caesium ran over to ask the elf what was going on.

"That's easy," he smirked. "I revived him to fight again.

Don't dwarves believe the spirits of their ancestors help them? Why can't the bodies too?"

"That's not right!" Caesium exclaimed, tears welling up in his eyes. "He was a noble warrior and a great father, and he doesn't deserve to be a zombie! Please, let me give him the proper dwarf burial rites to honour him."

"Dodsfald, do as he asks," a magician told the grinning elf sternly.

"If it's honour you're after…" Dodsfald muttered and paused, as if thinking. After some time he brought back another corpse, one that would infuriate the magicians: Volundur.

Dodsfald gestured, and Volundur gave Aesik a pat on the back.

"You are honoured by me," Volundur said in an unnatural, creaky voice that wasn't his.

"Thank you. I don't want to have burial rites now," Aesik replied in the same voice.

Caesium swung a punch at the elf, knocking him to the floor, and Caesium began kicking him as hard as he could. At first, the elf magicians cheered, then they joined in, adding their own blows to the onslaught. Eventually, Cognitio had to swoop in to save Dodsfald.

"WHAT ARE YOU DOING?" Caesium and the elves screamed in concert.

"He deserves everything he's getting!" Caesium clarified.

"Indeed he does, but there's still time for him to change, and only he can free the corpses in his horde," Cognitio replied calmly.

"It's only those two they care about," Dodsfald protested, spitting out a decaying tooth. "What about all the others? There's no difference, other than the fact that those fools don't know them, is there? I don't support discrimination!"

"Then release all of them," Cognitio told him. "Dodsfald, why did you run away? You were meant to stick by me for the entire quest! See me—"

"Settle your disputes later. Now we must search for Eitri and Eldrit," Aeterno interrupted, passing Jonas a phasecraft. "Belial has decided to come with us. With no war, it is safe for you and the other Longinists to return to Primium. There is something I would ask of you when you get there."

"What is it?" asked Jonas.

"Take charge of the new human government. We need a non-corrupt ruler, and you've already had some experience at that. Will you do it?" asked Aeterno.

Jonas hesitated for a moment, deep in thought.

"I BELIEVE IN YOU, JONAS," Gary told him. "I KNOW YOU CAN CHANGE OUR PLANET FOR THE BETTER WHEN WE COME BACK FROM THE QUEST."

"I'll do it," confirmed Jonas. "Bye, deities! See you after the quest!" He activated the phasecraft and disappeared, along with the other Longinists.

"*Well, that was a long-fought battle,*" stated Morehk. "Got in touch with your killing side a bit Bob, right?"

Shut up, Morehk, replied Bob.

"*Come on, that's no way to talk to the guy who is literally your arms and legs. So, the Grey Triptych, or whatever they were called, was a secret group trying to create a superior master race, or something like that. But now they're gone. So, the quest is over.*"

No, there's still two more deities—

"Pfft. Who cares?"

"My communication-scale says something," Cognitio said, putting the rock to his ear. "Eldrit and Eitri fell into a trap... but they've been rescued! I knew the nominees were competent. Let's give Mekanyon his shifter core now. The quest is over!"

"See? The quest's over!" Morehk told Bob in a superior tone.

Bob sighed as the glowing, metal plinth of the phasecraft appeared underneath his feet. Somehow, this vehicle had expanded to fit everyone and still have room.

"What is this?" asked Belial in disbelief.

"Just think of Primium, and this'll take us there," Cognitio told him.

Everyone thought of the technology-filled world, full of hope at the end of their journey.

Or was it the end?

Suddenly, the phasecraft began to emit a high-pitched whining noise and cracks began to appear in the white space around it.

"*What's happening?*" exclaimed Nimbus. "Cognitio, Aeterno, you made this thing; is this meant to happen?"

"Phasing material can't malfunction... there must be a bug with the technology part of it!" realised Aeterno.

Eventually, their vehicle shattered, and the dense, green canopy of a rainforest surrounded them. Like bars of a cage, the trees were packed close together, restricting their movements and they had the abundance of grass on a field.

"Are we on Gaia?" asked Bob.

"No, plants like this didn't grow on Primium," Nimbus muttered. "We must be on Manco."

"Manco?" Jeff gasped. "*The cursed planet?*"

"Silly boy," scoffed a smirking Nimbus. "It was only called that because some humans tried to set up a colony on it but were never heard from again. We found out their air- and wind-scale wasn't attached properly, so if they died of a curse it would be stupidity."

They heard a thud.

"Ouch!" cried Belial. "What did I trip over?"

A tablet akin to a gravestone stood next to the fallen Longinist, smothered in gold and various gemstones.

"Someone definitely came here before us," stated Aeterno.

"Maybe this is part of the trap Eldrit and Eitri fell into?" suggested Imryth. "There seems to be some sort of writing on it, but I can't understand it. Caesium, are these runes?"

"No," replied the dwarf, scrutinising the odd glyphs that were carved deep into the surface of the tablet. "I've never seen anything like this."

"Perhaps I can decipher them," Cognitio offered, running his hand over the tablet until he felt the glyphs.

Everyone else formed a protective circle around the tablet, in case danger struck.

After a few peaceful minutes, Cognitio had translated the entire tablet. "The title reads 'Wall of Truth, Fragment 1: Orders of the Sun'," he told them. "'The great god who watches over his followers from the sky, the Sun itself, has created the world, and will bring life and death in equal measures. Here is the Sun's holy planet, and anyone who desecrates this holy ground shall be sacrificed or we will feel the Sun's wrath.'"

"For Heavenspire's sake, it's the cults all over again," muttered Nimbus. "A crazy group of idiots fanboying over a sacrifice-demanding oaf. Anyone who believed in this must've been dropped as an egg."

"'Every day the Sun rewards his followers,'" Cognitio continued. "'And every night he goes through the white hole in the sky, which he covers up by day to attack other realms. For he is drawn to strength and power, and, to make sure this remains his holy ground, the greatest champions must fight to the death in the arena of the Sun.'" He ran his hand down the back of the tablet. "Wait, there's something more, called 'Wall of Truth, Fragment Two: Transitions in Life and Death': 'The pool of the Sun, next to the arena, either kills or rewards those who step into it. If it deems them a great warrior of the Sun, they will be transformed into a Huitzilon, which is a superior being of metal that can only die in battle. If they aren't deemed worthy, they will be burned to death by the molten gold filling the pool.'"

"It called itself a wall," Novis noted. "Where are the other bricks? All I can see are trees."

"They were probably destroyed when whoever lived here grew a brain," responded Nimbus with a snicker. "Anyway, with my wind and air powers, I can safely get us all back to Primium."

Everyone cheered, but then stopped after about a minute when nothing happened.

"*What?*" exclaimed Nimbus in disbelief. "Nothing's working!"

Thick, grey fog appeared all around them, blocking their view. Even Gary couldn't see anything or fly above it. They felt like they were being moved forward by some unknown force, yet they couldn't be certain for sure.

With his Void-vision, Bob could see grey shapes approaching them.

Or was it the other way around?

FORTY

Alex, Mekanyon's assistant, was jubilant. He kicked a mound of rubble, laughing with glee as it fell apart and flew in random directions.

The rubble had come from a once-great structure, which had gleamed like a star when it was whole; however, it was now a pitiful, half-dead mixture of debris, with the pulverised gold and gems strewn across the floor giving off feeble flickers in the moonlight. The remnants of its stone walls stood defiantly, stripped of their intricate detail but somehow not of their will to keep standing. Alex gave one a poke, then watched as it collapsed and broke on the ground.

"The arena of the Sun, huh?" mused a towering figure behind him. His head resembled a ziggurat, and his body was like an anthropomorphic extension of that ancient structure. Besides the yellow glow of his one eye, all of him was silver. "It's pitiful that I was once part of that awful religion."

"It doesn't matter anymore, Zecta," Alex told him. "Now you have joined the Silver One, and you were the first to convert from the Sun. The Moon highly commends you!"

"YOU TRAITOROUS FILTH! I'LL SACRIFICE YOU IN THE MOST PAINFUL WAY POSSIBLE!" came a roar from above them.

Trapped in a sphere of grey, a being of gold hurled insults at the two defiling his arena. He was at least four times the size of Alex and twice that of Zecta, with his head in the shape of a majestic bird's. Wings sprouted from his back, and cuboid-shaped structures with holes at the front were mounted on his shoulders. Thrashing around in a vain attempt to break the sphere was his tail, which ended in a long blade. "The might of the Sun knows no bounds, and, even if the false prophet has this rotten technology or whatever you call it, he will not be victorious! Silver tarnishes, but gold doesn't!" the figure declared.

"Capac, you are delusional," stated Alex with a laugh. "If the Sun is better than the Moon, then why is the Sun's priest trapped in the Moon's curse? Why have all the Sun's followers switched sides, and destroyed his arena and Wall of Truth?"

"Yes, why have you, Zecta?" spat Capac. "This scrawny fiend comes along with his metal trinkets—"

"Which make life much better," interrupted Alex. "It's wonderful technology."

"And his crappy new religion," continued Capac, "and you run to him like a greedy child! Then you destroy the Wall of Truth, which has shown us the ways of life for thousands of years—"

"No," Zecta told him. "No, it showed the Huitzilons the ways of life for thousands of years. I know some people who jumped into your pool of molten gold. They were the most fervent Sun-worshippers you'd ever meet."

"So you betrayed them!" exclaimed Capac. "And jumped into a pool of silver!"

"THEY DIED!" yelled Zecta. "They did everything to become a Huitzilon, and they were punished by your accursed Sun. Then Alex told me why. It's not who has the most faith in the Sun. It's who held one of the soulforger shifter cores you hid from us in this planet's vault! I chose the right side, and now I am a Coyolon, a superior being of the Moon. We all get one of those cores."

"It's the Sun's orders!" protested Capac. "I have the wings to fly to him and interpret his words; arguing with me would be like arguing with the Sun!"

Zecta raised his hand up and let moonlight shimmer on his palm. In a flash of argent light, a crescent coalesced in his hand. With a powerful leap, Zecta raised it above his head. "And this is what I think," he grunted, "of the Sun and his orders!"

The crescent descended, cleaving off both of Capac's wings. Alex laughed as they clattered to the floor. Capac howled; Huitzilons didn't feel pain, but that crescent blade had decimated his pride.

"I am the first of the superior beings, both Sun and Moon! You have just betrayed all of our kind!" Capac scolded Zecta.

"Really?" Alex enquired. "Stal told me otherwise."

"NO!" cried Capac in disbelief. "False prophet, you lie!"

Someone floated onto the scene, who was equal parts ethereal and physical: he had a tribal mask for a head and a tablet for a body, with the rest of him being an electric blue light. He had changed since the last time Capac had seen him: now his gold was silver, his mask had a quarter-moon motif, and his arms ended in lumps of lunar rock.

"That's a honogram or whatever the blue light thingy's called. He's gone!" declared Capac.

"Am I gone?" Stal asked no one in particular in a soft, hurried voice. "The flesh I once had counts as being gone; I was gone from your memories, or was I? Our meeting could burn brightly in your memory as I speak. The Sun-believing me has vanished, yet I am here, in a new form."

More bubbles of grey appeared, this time they were where the seats would have been in the arena.

"They have come, I see," Stal mused. "Those the Silver One has brought here for us to execute."

"Indeed the Moon did, Stal," Alex stated. "That's the power of our god."

Inside each bubble, a being stared out at their surroundings, confused as to where they were. Unexpectedly, one of their number was a gargantuan robot, but it too couldn't break free of its prison.

It must be the thing Hestrus was building, thought Alex, his teeth gritted together behind his armour. *What's it doing helping the deities?*

"*What superior being is that?*" asked Capac incredulously. "It doesn't seem to be one of your Coyolons; maybe it's another Huitzilon? You see that?" he jeered at the Moon worshippers. "The odds are stacked against the Silver One!"

"We'll see about that," spat Alex, and he summoned the rest of the Moon worshippers with a tribal cry.

From the midst of the trees they came, brandishing energy blasters along with their scimitars. They were unrecognisable from how they were the last time Capac had seen them – every one was a Coyolon, but none were individual. Unlike the elites of the Sun Cult – which were heavily stylised and bearing unique weapons of their mind's forging, and shining, gold elites towering over their flesh-and-blood human peers – these were featureless, silver humanoids with a yellow glow for an eye.

"It's time," Alex addressed his forces, "for the Moon to have his new supper."

*

Bob pounded on the sphere surrounding him, but to no avail. Even Gary, with his wide arsenal and tremendous girth, couldn't break out. In another bubble, Aeterno tried to alter space in order to free everyone, but when he tried, he received a painful electric shock. Nevertheless, he kept on trying, albeit to no avail.

"*Did you hear the Moon priest's thoughts?*" gasped Morehk.

Bob shook his head; he was too busy trying to free himself from his odd prison to gaze into the minds of others.

"*The New World's Gear! Thinkers of Mordrev, the Grey Triptych and the Moon Cult, they're all linked. Bob, don't give the shifter core to Mekanyon. Whatever you do, just don't!*"

For Morehk to show emotions outside his usual sadistic persona, especially fear and worry was something new for Bob. Part of him was uneasy, but a much larger part was suspicious. His stygir was now telling him it could not share its telepathic vision because shielding on the Moon priest's mind had activated.

So, something bad linked with every single evil group we've encountered so far is somehow going to happen when we fix the weapon stopping your kind from killing mine? Nice try, Morehk, responded Bob.

"It's not that! I couldn't care less about the other stygir! But this time it's serious, and it's not just our system that's screwed when you do that. It could be the whole universe!"

And why would someone whose main pleasure is killing care about the well-being of other universes?

Morehk fell silent.

Exactly, thought Bob. Then he felt pain course through his body along with a buzzing noise. He fell to the floor jittering.

"Sorry, no deity and stygir powers are allowed in my curse!" stated a grinning figure, who was unidentifiable behind gleaming, silver armour. "As those who've been shocked can tell."

"That voice… curse magic…" Novis muttered with a sense of fear in her voice.

"How about we sacrifice them to the Silver One now?" the figure asked his followers.

In response to this, they let out a loud cheer, and the identical ones readied their blasters; one of the two taller ones summoned a crescent blade and the other stood motionless.

"The Silver One… it's another name for Mordrev!" Novis exclaimed. "Contranaturum, it's you!"

Alex raised his hand, and she received a shock.

"No, I am Alex," he told her sternly. "My new name is human to show more respect to technology."

"What happened to your wings? And how did you create such a powerful curse?" Novis asked him.

"I cut them off along with my skin. I replaced both with this new technological dermis," he announced proudly. "It's much better. As for the curse, it took me around an hour to cover the whole planet with the technology of spacecraft, but three months to perfect it to the point where any intruders are detected, and I can trap them and send them to wherever I want."

Imryth and Novis were taken aback, for most mages would lose all their energy by sustaining a simple spell for a week.

"Now send them to the Moon!" Alex ordered.

Blasters rose to face them directly. Fingers tugged at triggers.

"WAIT!" Cognitio shouted. "You say the Moon's better than the Sun, right?"

"Lies!" spat Capac. "It's all lies!"

"I suppose we could educate them a bit before their death," said Zecta. "The Moon brings about a new age and enlightened knowledge, with technology. Everyone can be superior; plus the power the Moon brings is greater than anything the Sun or you unbelievers could possess—"

"Really?" interrupted Cognitio. "Then how about we prove it by having our greatest champions fight in the arena? The Sun did this, and many unbelievers were sacrificed this way, right? If the Moon is greater, show me, Alex."

This caused a tumultuous stir in the Moon Cult; the battles in the arena had been legendary spectacles, which they had massively enjoyed watching. Soon, they were cheering in agreement.

"No!" snapped Alex. "You're trapped in the Moon's curse, and that's enough proof. Troops, finish them!"

None of his followers obeyed him, and, since he had used up all his energy creating the curse, he could not fight them. With an irritable sigh, he agreed eventually.

"If we win, you lower the curse and give us the spacecraft you mentioned earlier!" demanded Cognitio.

"Fine," hissed Alex. "And if we win, you all die. I've altered the curse a bit so that any fighters who leave the arena will receive countless shocks. The Sun Cult and unbelievers, pick four champions each, and no deities are allowed."

"Who stands with me?" Capac asked the silver-clad crowd.

There was no response.

"Don't try, Alpac's not the only one who's left you now," taunted Alex.

"DON'T SAY THAT NAME!" roared Capac.

"Whoops! After calling your cult barbaric and escaping with those two stygir he found, he now calls himself Lance."

Capac let out a howl of anger and bloodlust. "AFTER I DEFEAT YOUR CHAMPIONS," he bellowed, "I WILL RIP YOUR SILVER HEAD FROM YOUR FRAIL BODY!"

"Anyway," said Alex "The Moon Cult shall enter its three greatest warriors: the ones chosen directly by the

Silver One, who form the elite unit that carries out Moon's very will... the Lunar Phases!"

At this, Zecta leaped into the arena with a swiftness that defied his bulky frame, cracking the ground as he landed.

Stal waved to those trapped in the curse. "The first one to enter shall be Zecta the Crescent!"

"Very theatrical, but I can only see two," scoffed Nimbus. "Then again, I wouldn't expect any more from a braindead cult."

At this, the Moon Cult threw insults angrily at the god, vowing to kill him first when his side lost.

"There are three in the ranks of the Lunar Phases," Alex told him. "And the fourth shall be our god himself."

"*The Moon?*" Nimbus exclaimed, before having a fit of hysterics. "What's it going to do, orbit us to death?"

Whilst the heated insults match continued, Cognitio and Aeterno began to work on a battle strategy. Judging by Zecta's title of "Crescent", the lunar phase where only a sliver of moon is visible, he was probably the weakest of their champions. They would have Gary as their fourth, since he was not a deity but possessed the most physical strength and weapons out of all of them. Antony, with his troll arms that could crush stone and metals as if they were dried-up clay, was an obvious choice. Capac was an unknown factor in this fight, although his hatred of the Moon would likely mean he would focus on Zecta.

"I will fight," confirmed Belial. "I must begin my atonement now."

"But your knives are only damaging to flesh and blood, and the enemy is metal—" Cognitio began.

However, Belial cut him off mid-sentence. "I will find a way."

"Gary, Antony, are you fine with fighting?" Aeterno asked.

Both said they were.

Bob was about to ask if he could fight, but the curse shocked him as soon as he thought of doing so.

"No deities allowed, silly boy," Alex told him.

"There must be some mistake," Bob replied. "I'm just an ordinary human!"

"Stygir have much in common with deities," Morehk stated. *"Enough to be affected by things like longinite or the rules of his curse."*

Jeff and Novis were about to ask the same, but then Caesium blurted out quickly, "I shall fight too! I was useless on Atham; I have to be useful to this quest in some way!"

"And there we have our four fighters," Cognitio told Alex. "Antony the troll, shall fight first, then Belial, the human—"

"I don't need their names!" snapped Alex.

"Then Caesium the dwarf, and then Gary the robot," Cognitio finished.

The bubbles around Antony and Capac disappeared, and the two landed in the arena.

Everyone bristled with anticipation as the three champions met each other's gazes. Antony introduced himself politely, Capac vowed to sacrifice them both, and Zecta recoiled at the sight of Antony.

"Filthy creature," Zecta spat. "Your kind shouldn't exist!"

"It seems we have a common foe," said Antony to Capac. "How about we temporarily ally?"

"Fine, unbeliever," Capac huffed. "May you convert after the battle's been won."

On Alex's signal, the battle began.

FORTY-ONE

Outstretching his palm, Zecta raised his arm to the sky, bathing it in the moon's light. Another crescent formed, which he grasped before adopting a defensive stance. Antony charged at Zecta, ready to throw a punch. Suddenly, a steady stream of pain coursed through Antony's hand. With a cry, he clutched his maimed arm, where the wound Gary had given him burned with an intense pain. Capac threw back his shoulders, and the structures mounted on them fired out a torrential rain of darts tipped with a sickly green fluid.

"Poison darts were your favoured weapon for keeping your human underlings in control," scoffed Zecta as the projectiles bounced off him. "Now I'm more than human, much more, and they have no effect!"

In a swift swishing motion, he swung his crescent at Antony, who grabbed his foe's wrist before the blade could cut him. Tightening his grip, he could feel his foe's hand cracking and being ground to silver dust. Zecta kicked Antony in the chest, knocking him to the ground. The Coyolon had always been an agile warrior, but his new, metal body added massive strength to the lethal strike. Antony's chest was bleeding heavily, and his breath came in wheezes. However, before Zecta could finish him off, the sound of sizzling filled the air. Although Zecta could no longer feel pain, he was sure he was being maimed somehow.

"I replaced the poison with a silver-destroying acid!" gloated a grinning Capac, who then leaped at his former devotee and punched him in the chest. "Just for you and the other traitors!"

Zecta's already melting form was cleaved apart by the blow, and the dissolving remnants were scattered across the arena.

But then, in a flash of silver light, he reappeared. Somehow, he was there again, unharmed and next to Antony, his crescent raised above his head.

It was only Capac's bladed tail that saved the wounded troll, parrying the blow just before it hit.

"Attacking the most wounded foe is for cowards," Capac spat.

"That thing is vermin," Zecta retorted, throwing his crescent like a boomerang.

The blade lopped off both of Capac's dart launchers and made deep gashes in his neck.

"Trolls, amongst other species, shouldn't be allowed to live," Zecta expounded. A new crescent formed in his hand just in time to parry Capac's tail.

"He chose to ally with Sun," Capac stated, jumping in front of Antony's wounded body and adding his fists to the fight. "Whilst still an unbeliever, the troll is more worthy of life than you."

His crescent still blocking Capac's tail, Zecta swatted away his foe's punches deftly with his free hand before landing a kick to Capac's head. The ornate, beaked lump of gleaming metal flew through the air, as the bitter remnant of a forgotten faith.

"And with that," Zecta exclaimed proudly. "The Sun has been eclipse—"

A pair of burly arms tightened around one of Zecta's arms, twisting it until it came apart in a shower of silver rubble. Startled, the Coyolon spun around, only to be greeted by another punch, cratering his chest this time. Antony, his wounds all gone, picked up a large piece of the broken arena and flung it at his foe, knocking him to the floor.

"*How are you still standing?*" spluttered Zecta, punching his way through the rubble.

"Don't insult a species you know nothing about," Antony told him, ducking out of the way of Zecta's deadly blade. "We trolls regenerate over time! It seems that longinite slows it down, but, other than that, it's fine!" He lifted up another large piece of debris to act as a shield. "Anyway, you regenerate as well!"

"THE MOON'S LIGHT GIVES ME STRENGTH!" shouted Zecta, slicing up the shield. "IT EMPOWERS ME!" Suddenly, he burst into flames. A familiar blade stuck out of his arm.

"Well, let's see what the Sun's light does to you!" taunted Capac, whose body had picked up his head and fixed it back on. "My blade, Sunswill, causes anything on contact to burn—"

There was a flash of silver light, and the pyre was no more.

By this time, Antony had gathered a large amount of rubble, and he chucked his rain of debris at Zecta, burying him. However, the Coyolon just burst out like he was getting out of bed; Sunswill was severed by his crescent.

"Capac," Antony said, "Do Huitzilons power up in any way?"

"This is no time for talking!" Capac snapped back, trying to hold Zecta off.

Unfortunately, Capac was no match with his weaponry severed from his body and soon found himself prey to the devilish crescent blade. In a matter of seconds, only a small portion of his torso, one of his arms and his head were intact. Before Zecta could finish Capac off, Antony had tackled Zecta and pinned him to the floor.

"FILTHY TROLL SCUM!" Zecta roared.

He tried to decapitate Antony, but Antony crushed his hand, and the crescent clattered to the floor. Capac managed to punch the Coyolon's leg, which shattered it. Antony threw another punch, but another crescent formed in Zecta's hand and sliced off the troll's arm.

"Death to your wretched kind!" Zecta spat.

"What do you have against trolls?" asked Antony, ducking out of the way of the crescent. "Why do you want to kill us?"

"Every reason!" exclaimed Zecta. "Before I ended up here, you *things* disrupted the natural order of life. You're malformed, hulking brutes, who were ruining society! Thugs and brigands!"

Antony let down his guard in shock.

"But, no, we must pity them, for they are discriminated against by everyone!" Zecta continued. The crescent descended. "The day they left the planet was the best day of my life!"

There was a spray of blood, a warrior falling to the ground, and another who was barely a head with an arm. Many more, watching the scene above, were unable to help.

"It is simply in your nature to act antagonistically!" explained Zecta, staring down at his bloody opponent and savouring his victory. "You are unable to add anything to life! But I fixed that."

Capac tried to hop on his hand to join the fight, but fell.

"Do you want to know why there are no trolls, orcs, ogres and the like anymore? The reason isn't the stygir. Well, partially," Zecta declared.

Antony could only see blackness. His breath came in shallow rasps.

Zecta went on, "A mercenary came along. Napthon was his name, and flames were his payment. So I tasked him with the extinction of those races!"

A closing eye reopened. A numb leg twitched. Surroundings reappeared. "And... *why?*" The voice was barely audible, but it caught Zecta's attention. "All I see... is forced, petty discrimination; that's why you want us to be gone?"

His wounds re-healed at a rate that exceeded normal regeneration. A new emotion blazed in his fully open eyes: not politeness, not surprise, not helpfulness, but anger. With a bellicose roar, Antony hit Zecta rapidly, with a speed and strength his opponent could not match. Quickly, the Coyolon was being reduced to dust.

"So, your pesky regeneration gets increased when you're angry," mused Zecta as his body was pulverised. There was a burst of light, and he was fully formed again.

"Well, so does mine! There's no way I can let one of you defeat me!"

"YOU'RE ONLY WINNING BECAUSE THE MOON'S IN THE SKY!" roared Capac, dragging himself towards the fight scene. He was now carrying the Sunswill in his beak, being careful not to cut himself with it.

In the midst of his blind rage, an idea that had brushed Antony's mind earlier came into focus. Leaping back from Zecta's crescent, he picked up Capac and then told him the plan. Before they knew it, Zecta was upon them, and Antony had to act the fastest in his life to throw Capac at their rampaging foe. In an instant, Zecta had shattered the Sunswill, but then Antony punched him. He regenerated, but the light that came out of him was very different. It was a warm, yellow-orange glow, for the Sunswill contained a substance that induced the very essence of a star. With that covering Zecta, the light given off by his regeneration would be that of a sun.

The effect on Capac was remarkable. Like Zecta, he regenerated his entire body immediately, but one of his arms was now glowing with a blazing, golden light blinding to look at.

"I don't know what you did, troll, but I commend you for it!" stated Capac, drawing back his glowing arm as if pulling a bowstring.

Out of shock, the crescent blade dropped from Zecta's hand.

"What? You thought you could keep my ultimate weapon uncharged by taking away sunlight?" Capac thrust his arm forwards yelling, "JUDGEMENT SOL!" An almighty stream of fire, almost the size of Gary, was shot out of his hand.

Zecta was incinerated so quickly that he barely had time for more than a scream. It took the remainder of Alex's deprived magical energy to move the audience away before they were hit. The flames kept on burning, showing no sign of going out; only Coyolons picking up large pieces of rock and forming a barrier stopped a full-scale wildfire.

"I heard Zecta wanted to tag out," Stal told Alex. "Alas, it doesn't matter, since his views on lunar supremacy have been disproven."

"Watch what you say," hissed Alex. "You're one of us now."

Stal continued, "Indeed, I have joined the Moon Cult to become reacquainted with my betrayer Capac, but not for revenge as such, just to see how the new society you're making will affect others and how it will expand – maybe into an empire or maybe something more. But will it expand? I feel that, whilst you're as technologically advanced as Primium, the tribal aspect will put people off—"

"JUST GET IN THE ARENA!" screamed Alex.

Antony fell to the floor, exhausted from his fight, for the extra regeneration he had experienced whilst angry had taken up nearly all of his energy and even the slightest movements were like deadlifts.

"Tag out," he breathed. "If Zecta could attempt it, I can do it!"

"*Why did you say that, Stal?*" exclaimed Alex.

There was no more magic Alex could expend to change the curse, so all he could do was glare furiously at Stal as a silver bubble formed around Antony and took him out of the arena, and Belial entered, casually spinning a knife in his hand.

"Win, to prove you're a useful Lunar Phase!" Alex told Stal. "Although that should be easy, as they've given you a crippled, blind opponent!" He laughed at the idea.

"After I get out of this arena," growled Belial, "you'll be in a similar condition."

FORTY-TWO

Belial could hear frantic muttering accompanied by the clanking of metal. One of the two others, Capac or the Moon one was frightened beyond belief. Unlike longinite, which gave off a faint odour he could track, silver and gold were undetectable to his senses. The sole thing he knew was that this would be the most hard-fought battle of his life.

"Capac," came a voice, sounding astute and deep in thought. "What was it that made you act that way? Shifter cores? Power? It could be saving your people, but I presume that, if you thought of that, it was merely a footnote to the first two I mentioned. Great tomes formed in your mind..."

"You're not alive!" shrieked another voice. "Your body is broken beyond repair in a cave!"

Following the direction of the first voice, Capac threw a handful of knives, anticipating the telltale sound of them hitting their targets. He heard a large number of thuds, but accompanied by a laugh instead of a scream.

"So, so interesting," the first voice declared with a chuckle. "You seem to be attached to these miniature swords a lot. Is that a knife-leg? Since when did your planet possesses the technology for robotic limbs? Intriguing indeed…"

"Stal, attack!" a chorus of voices sounded.

"You showed us your power before, now show it to them!" Alex added.

"Human!" the second voice exclaimed.

Belial turned his head to face it.

The voice went on, "Whilst he's musing, attack as one!"

Dashing towards the first voice, Belial activated his phase suit's power, sending knives flying in all directions. Again, there were thuds, but no additional sounds this time. Did the second voice really intend to attack as one?

*

Capac couldn't wait any longer. The human flailing around and shooting those useless knives that clattered off metal was of no help at all. Yet Capac couldn't stand the thought of losing allies for no reason, and he wouldn't fire his judgement sol for fear of the human, who was constantly leaping into his line of fire every few seconds and being incinerated. Stal just stood in one spot, contemplating the universe in his idiosyncratic way, either toying with them or not caring about the fight.

He shouldn't be there, thought Capac, and, eventually, he could no longer stand the stalemate they were in. Raising up his glowing arm, Capac yelled, "JUDGEMENT SOL!" and a formidable stream of fire spewed out.

To be hit by that fire meant eternal burning, which

neither water nor wind could put out, but there was no other effective way to hit Stal.

At least the human won't die for nothing, Capac thought as the conflagration engulfed the arena.

"Oh, you want to start a conflict?" Stal enquired, and part of his chest-tablet began to glow. "Well, that must be balanced with defence. Lunar dome." A shield of white energy, ethereal yet solid, protected him from the judgement sol, but it began to flicker away after a few seconds of being exposed to the all-consuming flames. Yet Stal was prepared. He brought his arms together in front of him, and the two pieces of moon rock that were his hands connected. They began to emit a blinding light as he shouted, "PRESENT ECLIPSE!"

Instantly, the judgement sol vanished; all traces of it had gone without warning.

Cursing himself for his stupidity, Capac charged towards Stal, firing acid darts rapidly. He thought, *Now that the human has died, it is up to me to face Stal again and—*

"I smelled fire. Lots of it," came a familiar voice.

Capac turned his head and saw the human, alive and unscathed.

"Keep on with that shooting attack!" Belial commanded. "I have a plan—"

"It's out of charge," stated Capac, hammering down mighty blows on the stationary Stal.

His opponent had summoned another lunar dome, though, and not even a single acid dart had touched him.

"How are you alive, human? Try to help!" stated Capac.

"I sense an item of much power," revealed Stal, "underneath the knife-leg's cloak, though said cloak has been burned away. Why do you choose to throw your knives instead of use it? Could it be the hunter's instinct, and the sheer excitement and thrill of stabbing and killing that you must feel?"

"To rely on fancy weapons leads to a terrible warrior," replied Belial as his phase suit thrummed and pulsated. "Also, even though I can't see, a bright-pink suit must look pretty ridiculous."

Stal began a speech offering his opinion, but Belial had more important things on his mind. "Capac!" he said. "What was that fire you hit me with?"

"It's an eternal flame," replied his ally, who had almost shattered the lunar dome. "A flesh-and-blood being like you should've been dead!"

"Perfect," replied Belial, and he leaped upwards. His phase suit now felt like a thick, woollen coat, with the sheer heat of the flames seemingly breaching the pocket dimension. Spreading his arms wide, he prepared to unleash a new attack.

"JUDGEMENT SOL: HELLION SHREDDER!" he roared as knives wreathed in fire shot out of the suit.

They crushed the lunar dome immediately and would have killed Stal if he hadn't used present eclipse again. The surreal move erased the fire straight away, but the knives remained, albeit that they were useless against Stal's metal-and-spirit body.

"Incredible! You wield the Sun's light!" exclaimed Capac as he melted away Stal's rock hands with his acid darts, then seized Stal's tablet.

It seemed the spirit part of Stal couldn't leave it and thrashed frantically, trying in vain to escape.

"Will you join the Sun Cult after this?" Capac asked as he tightened his grip, making the tablet crumble.

"Sorry, but no," replied Belial, trying to track down the smell of burning longinite. "Can you tell me where he is—" Suddenly, pain seared through Belial's stomach as he felt something sharp pierce it, then faintness overtook him.

"How dare you, scum!" Capac exclaimed. "To think I saw you as an ally! Luckily, I still have some poison darts to sacrifice traitorous filth like you to the Sun!" He turned his head to face Stal. "It was easy to defeat you once, and it'll be easy to kill you again!"

"WHAT ARE YOU DOING?" bellowed Aeterno from above. "WHAT HAPPENED TO OUR ALLIANCE?"

"Although he's helped us, keep in mind he's the angry ex-chief of a tribe that did sacrifices," stated Cognitio, who was next to Aeterno. "An ally by proximity, not design."

"Past ECLIPSE!" The voice sounded in everybody's head, faint at first but reaching a deafening crescendo.

The ruins of the arena began to melt away, and a new setting began to take form.

"Did you really kill me?" queried Stal, floating high above the arena. "Let's look at what really happened, Capac."

FORTY-THREE

"It's similar to that Ember of Deceit thing's powers from Napthon's realm, isn't it?" murmured Morehk. *"I don't want Capac to crumble away, though; he was hilarious."*

Whose side are you on? thought Bob.

"Ah! Two minds in a single body!" exclaimed Stal. "In disagreement, yet contracted by a bond to help each other... Your group carries some strange ones indeed."

"SAY THAT AGAIN, YOU TRIBAL SCUM!" snapped Morehk.

"Ah! Two minds in a single body..." Stal then stopped talking as a figure walked onto the scene. Stal looked down at Capac, who gazed at the figure with surprise playing all over his face.

Standing in front of him was a muscular human with long, black hair and a well-kempt beard that came down to his chest. He grasped a liskous staff tipped with an air-scale and wind-scale, which he used to bat his way through the thick foliage.

"Zecta!" he called out. "Alpac!"

There were no replies.

Shaking his head, he strode onwards, muttering about making a colony quick.

"Don't let the past swallow your future," said Stal. "That's the basis of past eclipse. I remember teaching Zecta's mercenary friend the sign for it, such was his liking for it… Any opinions yet, Capac?"

"*Me?*" the Huitzilon spluttered. "The human there was me!" Unbeknownst to him, shards of his golden body were flying everywhere.

The human that Capac once was carried on, before reaching a cave. He entered it and found his way around the obscure chasm by touch.

"Oh dear!" exclaimed Stal. "You went on some journey to get there! Let's skip ahead."

The horizons blurred as the world went out of focus again. When the surroundings reformed, Capac's past self had just entered the middle of a chamber that gleamed with light. All around him were markings of such an intricate design it would have taken a generation of artists to envisage, and at his feet was a pool of hissing, molten gold. His footsteps sounded like seashells being crushed, and, at his feet, he saw there were countless hand-sized rocks that glowed with a mixture of gold and silver light.

"Slate-scales?" he mused, kicking one into the pool of gold, where it landed with a satisfying sizzle.

Suddenly, a minute figure leaped out, startling him. He batted it to the floor with his staff, and declared, "Ferum or Stronto, whichever one of you two midgets this is, there is no time for your childish antics!"

At his feet lay a gold figure, featureless beyond its anthropomorphic shape.

"That's not one of your dwarf companions," an aloof voice declared. "That's what you just kicked carelessly into the molten gold."

"*Who said that?*" he shrieked, lashing out in all directions with his staff. "*What did I just kick in? Are you a ghost? Or just a very lonely native?*"

"I sense a boisterous soul, yet one so full of fear of the supernatural underneath the alpha-male façade," the voice noted.

"Not anymore!" spat the present Capac, who was still not realising he was withering away. However, as soon as he heard the arm that bore judgement sol fall to the ground with a clunk, he noticed and realised what the past eclipse was doing. "I see… the past's behind me, Stal!"

"What… were you thinking, Capac?" spluttered a voice from the ground.

Capac gazed in astonishment as the man he'd hit with a poison that killed in mere minutes stood up, breathing shallowly yet otherwise unscathed.

"The only thing you've sacrificed with your actions is yourself," growled Belial.

"Traitor, you should've been dead!" exclaimed Capac.

"Dead? By that?" Belial scoffed, laughing. "Whatever you hit me with, it was no Great Plague!"

"And the knife-leg yet lives!" announced Stal, with either admiration or surprise. "It is creatures like you who bewilder me. It would be a shame to kill you off, but I can prolong your life if we all cease our fight to watch the past eclipse."

Belial and Capac continued with their battle, but the latter was transfixed by the events he wished to forget. In the eldritch vision, Capac was talking to a towering figure of gold and iron, who was almost unrecognisable except for the tribal mask and tablet on his chest.

"Are you a guardian spirit?" shrieked the past Capac, throwing some of the stones at Stal, which bounced off with no effect.

"And are you really the head of a fearless force?" asked a chuckling past Stal. "You probably still sacrifice to your idols and cower at things you don't understand. No, I am Stal, and I was the only life form on this planet until now. You must be wondering what you kicked into the pool?" He gestured towards the reservoir of molten gold. "That was a soulforger shifter core; I suppose you've heard of them? It's fascinating how much of legend is rooted in reality."

Capac began to bombard Stal with questions: "Is there other sentient life on Manco? Why are shifter cores here? And what is this part of the cavern?"

"We're standing in a vault underneath the surface of the planet," Stal replied. "It stores artefacts from those whom this world belonged to originally. Those shifter cores, when in contact with certain metals, take your soul and forge it anew, with a superior body made from said metals. But from that point on, you must consume these cores in order to keep your soul in the body. A bit like nourishment; am I not right?"

Capac had lost interest and was busy examining a vast wall smothered in gold and gemstones. "Magnificent…" he mused. "With this god, we don't need the ones of Heavenspire anymore. We can have the perfect world order, one where might makes right!"

"It seems that you can read those," Stal noted. "An intellectual, I see."

Capac spun around, with an invigorated look on his face. "Stal, give me the shifter cores, and we will carry out Sun's will," he offered.

"I need those to sustain my soul. I decline," Stal replied curtly. "Besides, that Sun Cult was likely written as a—"

"It was written by the original inhabitants of this world," Capac interrupted him, clenching his fists. "You said so yourself. This race precedes even the knowledge of the liskous, and I intend to make sure it sees the light of day again."

"A primitive belief system like that?" asked Stal with a chuckle. "No."

Grabbing one of the shifter cores and clasping it close to his chest, Capac dove into the pool of molten gold, screaming as his flesh hit the sizzling liquid metal. A short time later, he emerged as a Huitzilon; he then lunged at Stal.

*

Belial ducked out of the way as Capac lunged, then threw a series of knives, which were dealt with quickly by acid darts. Ever since he had heard Stal activate past eclipse, his new-found Huitzilon foe had become much easier to battle: with his constant screaming at Stal, attacks flung in a blind rage and half his attention on the eclipse, it was as if Belial could now see Capac and predict his movements. However, it did not mean the fight had been won. Even in his weakened state, Capac was still a force to be reckoned with and was attacking Belial relentlessly at close quarters, a range the knife-thrower was unaccustomed to. To make matters worse, it turned out that Belial couldn't fire the hellion shredder an infinite number of times. Just like the judgement sol it was derived from, it needed something akin to sunlight to function, and that was lacking in the eerie setting of past eclipse.

Capac swung a fist, catching Belial on the side of his torso. Even such a glancing blow was like a sledgehammer, and he was bowled over and crashed onto the ground in a sprawling heap.

"You should've joined the Sun when you had the chance," Capac gloated, picking up Belial by the head. His grip tightened slowly but gradually. "Now experience the fate of those who betray the creator!"

"A creator you tricked yourself into believing in!" exclaimed Stal, as the past eclipse showed Capac breaking Stal's body apart.

At the sound of those words, the former priest of the Sun Cult was motionless with shock, giving Belial a chance to escape. Capac's past self went on to destroy the cavern and bring the Wall of Truth to the planet's surface, all whilst stuffing the shifter cores into a nearby chest.

"Sacrificing your civilised world for a life of bloodshed and sacrifices!" spat Stal. "I know for a fact that this new idea of the moon being divine came from another wall in the same chamber. You do too, or the fists that broke that wall should."

The eldritch powers of past eclipse were now taking their toll on Capac, his form eroding once more like a seaside cliff.

"And now, one more question," added Stal. "You sacrifice those who disobey you, right? But if all your allies disobey you, what will happen? None will be left to support you! The system has changed gears, Capac, and your world as well. Change with it, or crumble with the past!"

Screaming madly, Capac looked down and saw that his body was no more. A split second later, the head followed suit. The Moon worshippers let out a raucous cheer as their former ruler disintegrated and the past eclipse faded away.

"Physically adept, but psychologically fragile," commented Stal before fixing his gaze on Belial. "For the sake of the society I am interested in seeing the growth of, you will join him, knife-leg."

"And the Sun Cult is out of the battle!" exclaimed Alex victoriously.

*

Bob now knew that Morehk was right. Everything was linked, but he didn't know how exactly.

Use of the stygir powers would result in a shock, but he decided to use his Void-vision for a split second.

And, for a split second, the Moon Cult flickered an eerie grey.

FORTY-FOUR

"SEALED DEVASTATION!" yelled Stal, placing both arms across his chest.

Belial couldn't tell where his foe was, but he was ready to absorb the attack that would be flung at him. Stal spread his arms out and a beam of white energy fired at Belial. As usual, it was absorbed by his phase suit.

"Thanks for that," said Belial with a grin, and he too placed both arms across his chest; since Stal's arms ended in moon rock and his chest was a metal tablet, Belial had heard his action and had a vague idea of how to use it. "Sealed devastation!"

Nothing happened.

He tried again, whilst Stal laughed at him and his growing frustration.

"Enough laughing, attack!" snapped Alex.

"I understand it now!" gasped Cognitio. "How Belial's opponent activates past eclipse, and how all those techniques are made possible. BELIAL!" he called out. "SCRATCH OUT THE—" An electric shock racked Cognitio's body, and he dropped to his knees.

"No hints," stated Alex, "and no more gloating either. Attack already!"

"Very well," said Stal before soaring over to where Belial was and landing a series of punches.

Combined with the attacks from Capac he had taken earlier, Belial crumpled under the weight of them and fell to the floor.

Stal placed his arms across his chest once again. "Sealed devast—"

As swiftly as the wind, the knife-leg came up. It hit Stal at such a close range that it carved a groove in his tablet and became stuck there. The energy blast never came.

"Don't worry, Cognitio," Belial stated with a grin. "I figured it out, too. Dwarven runes!"

"Not as such, although the two are closely linked," explained Stal as he landed another blow on Belial's back, causing him to cough up blood. "The hieratics for all my eclipses and sealed devastation are gone now. A tactical move, I see." He punched Belial repeatedly, daubing his moonrock hands in crimson.

"Tag out," Belial managed to say, although nothing happened. He then fired a deathswind shredder directly down at the ground, evading Stal by creating a tall mound of knives. "Tag out!" he repeated, and he was carried away from the fight in a dome of silver.

"Interesting," commented Stal. "So the tag-out mechanism doesn't work if the situation is close combat. A double-edged blade, don't you think, Contranaturum?"

"Alex is my name!" snapped Alex. "The ways of technology are greater than the ways of the liskous! You should know the Silver One's true intentions. But there's something else that's interesting..." He pointed at Belial. "He does not have the regeneration of a troll, and his death is imminent if you do not wrap things up quickly! Good job, Stal, all doubts I had about you are dispelled."

*

Although he hated to admit it, Caesium was terrified.

He'd seen Zecta and Stal fight, with their metal-hewn bodies and devastating powers a potent force to be reckoned with. No matter how much he reassured himself and no matter how much he told himself that Cognitio thought he was a likely candidate for a god, his heart was still clasped by fear. Not even the thought of exploring a new planet could suppress his feeling of terror. Nevertheless, he gripped his pickaxe and hammer tightly, made sure his rune-carver was in its sheath, and, though he had to battle with every gram of his reasoning, told everyone he was ready to fight. He descended into the arena to fight against Stal, and took one final glance at the maimed form of Belial. It was for more than just his own life he had to win.

"STAL!" he bawled, making sure he did not stammer. "I CHALLENGE YOU!"

"Well, what else are you going to do?" his opponent questioned. "I suppose we could discuss the links between the runes of your species and the hieratics of mine, but I have a contract to fulfil with the Moon Cult."

Caesium activated the attraction rune on his hammer and pulled Stal towards him, then struck him with the pickaxe, wiping out many more hieratics. Stal swiped at him, but he dug a wormhole and escaped before he could be hit.

"Troublesome indeed," muttered Stal. "Yet I know those tunnels are temporary and disappear after a while. The cowardice you portrayed will still remain, however."

Provoked by that last remark, Caesium burst out of the wormhole and used his hammer to strike Stal across his mask, making a large dent and deep cracks. Caesium followed that up with his pickaxe, yet Stal hit him in the chest with such force that he was knocked back by a few metres. Luckily, his sturdy dwarven armour took the brunt of the blast, and he got to his feet, hurting but mainly unharmed. However, for some reason, he could not lift up his weapons. Looking down he saw that Stal, whose spirit arms had extended, had pinned both to the floor. One of the few remaining hieratics lit up.

"SUPERIORITY OF GLYPHS!" Stal yelled.

All of a sudden, the runes on Caesium's weapons disappeared. Swiftly, Stal then tried to punch the dwarf but was blocked by the pickaxe and hammer. Caesium saw that his rune-carver had been knocked to the floor, where it had scratched a line. A plan began to form in his head. He threw his weapons at the eyeholes in Stal's mask, then turned and ran.

"Running away is futile!" stated Stal, whose arms shot after Caesium. "It seems that, despite the stereotype of dwarven strength, all you can do is escape like a coward!"

Ducking down to avoid an arm, Caesium then began to dash in the opposite direction. Changing course constantly, the sheer randomness of his path made it difficult for Stal to hit him, let alone follow him. And then he stopped, looking at the floor and panting.

"Your stamina has sealed your demise," announced Stal.

He was about to strike Caesium, but then he felt pain – a feeling he hadn't experienced for a long time – course through his entire body. The sheer oddity of it made him scream excruciatingly and thrash around, shrieking to tag out. Beneath him was an intricate and complex rune of massive size. Amidst the complex network of lines it was made up of, the faint icon of an armoured warrior crushing a ghost in his fist was visible.

Caesium clutched his aching, unarmoured foot, which had held his rune-carver as he ran around. "Your spirit being sealed to another body has caused your demise," he panted as his foe was removed from the arena. "I never thought the rune of exorcism would be needed in the present day."

"What... WAS THAT?" shrieked Alex, as Stal drifted out of the arena. "A TINY BIT OF PAIN AND YOU CONCEDE?"

"Regardless, we have two champions left," Stal told him. "I've studied this society; it has a high chance of expanding—"

"You're not really on our side," Alex stated, cutting him off. "You're just a wandering ancient spirit who wants to analyse modern life. I let you join us for your hieratic power. Now there's no use for you!" Spreading his arms wide, he let out a cry, bellicose yet sophisticated – a sound from long ago.

Something swooped down from the skies at a speed too fast to see and a powerful energy blast blinded everyone momentarily. When Caesium could see again, where Stal once stood, an imposing figure had taken his place. They had the same draconic body shape as a liskous, yet were composed of shimmering, silver steel. Crosshairs swivelled around in their eyes and each digit on each of their claws ended in a drill and a miniature ray cannon. Adding to their arsenal, a titanic cannon crowned their head, bearing a resemblance to the crest of a prehistoric creature. Centred on their chest was something glowing red and pulsating, like a heart.

"THE TARGET IS COMPLETELY OBLITERATED," they told Alex in a deep, robotic voice. "NOT A SINGLE PARTICLE REMAINS."

"Good, good," Alex replied with a chuckle, clapping his claws. "Well done, Huaco! The Silver One's enlightened knowledge be with you!" He looked up at the Heavenspirians encased in his curse. "A few of you remember defeating my old cult," he explained, staring at each deity in turn, then diverting his gaze to Novis. "And one of you was a mistake that rejected its ways, despite your sole purpose being to carry on Mordrev's teachings!"

His daughter flinched at those words.

"The co-creator of the aforementioned mistake did end up being useful though and is now the second-strongest Lunar Phase," Alex confirmed.

"I AM HUACO THE GIBBOUS," announced the monstrosity that had incinerated Stal. "I ONLY OBEY THE SILVER ONE, BE IT MORDREV OR THE MOON." Jets ignited on her wings, and she soared into the arena.

Seeing the way she had dispatched Stal, Caesium had already burrowed into a wormhole to avoid the destructive blast she was sure to fire.

"WHERE IS THE UNBELIEVER?" roared Huaco, and she ran around the arena, firing rays in all directions. Descending from the sky above her, Caesium struck her head cannon with both his weapons, which he had inscribed with runes whilst in the wormhole.

Both weapons snapped.

"TAG OUT!" yelled Gary from above. "LET ME TAKE CARE OF HER, CAESIUM!"

"There's nothing you can do against that thing with no weapons!" added Nimbus. "Listen to the large, blue guy!"

But Caesium's mouth wouldn't move. Whether it was due to fear or bravery he couldn't tell, but he held his ground and began to carve a rune of destruction on his foe. Huaco shook him off and carved into his chest with both drills. Caesium screamed in pain, thrashing around and trying to avoid the gore around him.

Then a tendril of shadow grabbed Huaco around the waist and pulled her away from him.

Close to passing out, Caesium looked above him and saw his fellow Heavenspirians descend onto the battlefield. "I know her weakness..." was all he could muster before his eyes closed over.

"You've done more than enough," a voice sounded in his ear.

Although he had never met its owner in person, their presence reassured him that they would complete their quest in no time.

FORTY-FIVE

Imryth knew what she was doing was risky, to the point where her life was on the line.

Seculi have the power to store and gather magic, although the more they hold at once the less control they have over it. At that current point in time, the slightest mental slip could cause her to be electrocuted to death by the curse barrier. Straining her mind, she generated more of the mystical energy. A bead of sweat trickled down her forehead.

Down below, Caesium was fighting in the arena. She couldn't pay any attention to the fight, but she knew if her plan came to fruition, he – or, rather, they – would definitely win. The reason seculi are the greatest mages is because they hold the greatest power over magic: the ability to dispel it, if equal power is provided. Whether or not all the magic she held at that point was enough to shatter Alex's curse she did not know, so she continued her conservation of power.

"Dispel it!" she heard a voice, grand and imposing, command her. Whilst she had never met its owner in person, she knew enough about them to know they were right.

"DISPEL!" she shouted.

All her amulets and charms thrummed with the force of an earthquake as the anti-magic surged through them. Somehow, new magic energy flowed into her body, like a steady stream pouring into the sea, and she expended that as well. The curse evaporated in an instant, freeing the Heavenspirians.

"We've established peaceful relations all over the system and then we decided to check if any battles were being fought here," Shekina, goddess of empowerment, informed her.

Sequia stood behind her, held aloft by a moving dais of plants. A group of nominees formed around them, along with two gods.

One was clad in a robe that heavily resembled a nebula and wore a pendant that seemed to have a roiling vortex of energy instead of a stone. His shoulder-length hair was the colour of starlight, and his head was perked constantly upwards, carrying a feeling of superiority. "A brilliant plan, seculous mortal," he commended Imryth. "Although, without my presence it surely would've failed."

The other god had a beard the colour of obsidian, which trailed down to his feet in a series of gold-decorated braids, and he was clad in thick, silver armour. How he stayed aloft without any visible runes was a mystery to Imryth, and more so was the fact he wielded a hammer at least three times his size.

Throughout the Heavenspirians, joyous cries of "Eldrit and Eitri!" could be heard.

The hammer-bearing god, Eitri, flew down next to Caesium, and, immediately, a potent rune of healing that would have taken a regular dwarf a month to carve appeared, regenerating the dying dwarf's flesh. He then floated over to Belial and began doing the same.

"Inferior," scoffed Eldrit, the other god. "You saw my protégé Shekina and how she could heal people."

"NOW IS NOT THE TIME FOR YOUR FIGHTS!" snapped Aeterno before Eitri could respond. "Huaco and Bob have disappeared; we need to save him!"

Already, Alex was screeching in fury and giving the Moon Cult the order to attack.

"Hydrax, Jeff, Gary, Dodsfald and Novis – go deal with them!" commanded Aeterno. "The rest of us search the planet!"

*

From a hidden enclave in the thick canopy, Bob scrapped against Huaco. Somehow, he was freed from the curse just as Caesium was about to die. Seeing a hidden area, he opted to use the stygir power to pull his friend's opponent away and then battle her. Huaco tried to carve a hole in Bob's chest, but he just turned to gas. A fusillade of rays incinerated the gas, and Bob cried out in pain. The arm that didn't have Huaco ensnared transformed into a spiked club, and he brought it down on her head, albeit ineffectively. The ray cannons fired again, and Bob keeled over, losing control of his tendril arm. Huaco slipped easily out of its grasp and then flew upwards. The cannon on her head began to glow with the same energy that incinerated Stal.

"**Morehk; honoured destruction—**" Bob began. Before he could finish chanting, the blast fired. Somehow, he still felt conscious yet couldn't move a muscle. Looking around, he saw he was in the middle of a crater and his limbless body was riddled with holes.

"I HAVE LOWERED THE BLAST'S INTENSITY TO LET YOU LIVE," Huaco explained, lifting Bob up by the head, "FOR YOU WILL HELP ME CLAIM EVEN MORE ENLIGHTENMENT FROM MORDREV. **MOREHK; HONOURED DESTRUCTION; KERPHAN OF THAUMIR, THE FIRST HUSK; WITNESS TO THE DEFEAT OF CHAIGIDIR, THE SECOND HUSK; ENEMY OF DEITIES AND STYGIR ALIKE; SPAWN OF THE VOID; SUBORDINATE OF CATAREHK, HONOURED LIGHT, AND NO OTHER STYGIR; AND HOLDER OF BOB SOLIS' CONTRACT.**"

At these words, Bob felt a true lack of control over his body and soul. It was as if his very existence was a character in a video game, one he was spectating and someone else was controlling.

"ONE OF MY FUNCTIONS IS TO FORMULATE ENTIRE REN FROM FRAGMENTS. FINALLY, WE HAVE A TEST SUBJECT AND ONE WHO CONTAINS SOULS FROM TWO RACES. COME WITH ME; LET US SEE WHAT MY FORMER PARTNER WILL DO WITH YOU," commanded Huaco.

Against his will, Bob saw his body move. Morehk shouted in protest and spouted death threats at Huaco, yet – from Bob's perspective – its voice now sounded like it was speaking from very far away. His body followed Huaco, before the two were stopped by Cognitio. The emissary shot fiery chains from his staff, ensnaring his opponent, and flung her into the sky, where Shekina, clad in amulets summoned by her callstaff, blasted Huaco with a barrage of lightning. With a careless flick of his hand, Eldrit fired an electrical salvo at least three times larger, and Sequia added her own. Huaco cried out and her metal form began to smoulder, yet she still lived. She began to fire her ray guns, although the Heavenspirians seemed to be able to predict that move and dodge it.

"IT'S TEN SECONDS!" yelled Cognitio. "NOW!"

Bursting out of a wormhole, Eitri swung his hammer at Huaco's back, cracking through it. Raising his hammer to the sky, he bellowed a war cry, and runes of every shape and size began to form on it.

"MOREHK, PROTECT ME!" Huaco commanded.

Bob jumped involuntarily between the two.

"New rune construct: rune of the true path!" intoned Eitri. An unearthly, golden glow surrounded him, and a new rune appeared on his hammer. "ALLRUNE FORGESWING!" he shouted, bringing the hammer down on Huaco.

Bob's body jumped up to protect her, but the hammer swerved past him with uncanny speed and struck its quarry. The Lunar Phase was shattered in an instant.

Caesium had been right: he had found her weakness. When he was healed by Eitri, the dwarf had explained that the pulsating device on Huaco's chest was very much like a solar panel, only one that ran on the light of the moon. Despite the high power and quick firing of the ray cannons, there had to be a short period of time where she had to rely on melee only.

Overcome by what seemed like extreme tiredness, Eitri slumped to the floor. "The making of a new type of rune takes a lot of my energy," he explained, "but I'll still fight on."

Shekina cast her deity power on him, returning his stamina, and he jumped to his feet with vigour. Now free from Huaco's control, Bob slumped over. Cognitio knelt down at his side and gave him a canister of a deep-black gas.

"I still have this from the Stygir War. Take it, whilst no one's looking," he whispered.

Bob consumed the stygir remnants without question and felt his body regenerate. Everyone else stared at the phenomenon, baffled. A stray wisp of smoke came out of Bob's mouth, visible in all its draining blackness. It was at that point Bob noticed a small device, similar to a smartphone but thicker, lying next to him. Its hue was the same silver as Huaco and etched into the side of it were the words "PRR – Prototype Ren Reader. This can decipher a being's whole ren if a part of it is given." Knowing that this would be useful, he picked it up.

"So, Eldrit, do you now see why the plan involved Eitri getting the final blow?" asked Cognitio quickly. "I think that's five gold coins you owe me."

"I could've defeated it myself if I had done more than just give a flick of my wrist," replied Eldrit. "I just wanted to see that dwarf fail before doing it."

"*Really?*" cried Eitri. "*Then how come I defeated it in a single swing, you stuck-up, pointy-eared failure?*"

"And expended all your energy. I know not much can fit in your minute body, but it's still all gone," retorted Eldrit.

"Master, now is not the time for starting fights!" exclaimed Shekina. "We still have a shifter core to deliver."

"Bob, get up!" commanded Cognitio. "You've had one of those new cigarettes, or whatever you humans call them, haven't you? They need to put an age restriction on those."

"Y-yes," Bob replied awkwardly, before getting onto his feet and running after them.

*

"Useless!" spat Alex. "I gave that wench all my strongest weaponry, and she still failed! Plus she lost the prototype ren reader. Now I sense she's dead, without making any kills. She couldn't even give me a worthy successor."

Knowing not to annoy him when he was in a temperamental mood, the Moon Cultists agreed in unison, hurrying with the task he set them.

"We're being attacked!" reported one of them. "By two liskous, a giant being, a human and an elf."

"I'll take care of them! You all just keep on setting up the system," confirmed Alex. Now that he had a built-in speaker array and generated nourishment through lunar energy, there was no need for a mouth, but if he had one, it would be grinning broadly.

Devised by another Grey Triptych member – the double agent Hestrus – the Trisoul Power System could power war machines of immense girth, as long as three non-deity souls were given to it. The sight of Tabris, which was supposed to be the pinnacle of this revolutionary tech, fighting for them disturbed him greatly. What had happened to Hestrus?

But, in a few minutes, Tabris would not be the ultimate war machine. Their minds clouded by the propaganda he had stirred amongst the Moon Cult, three of their number were bound to 'offer themselves to the Moon', which they would, in a way. He thought back to when the Thinkers of Mordrev had experimented on sentient beings to achieve a greater knowledge of them, then sacrifice them to their god; they had wanted enlightened minds, and it seemed they had now achieved their goal. Back when everyone lived in huts and rode on horses, who would have thought such a grand construct was possible?

In the vacuum of space above them, Manco's moon, Occlon, stirred, sending strong winds racing about the planet it orbited. An aura of blue energy swirled around it, and glowing, yellow eyes cast their vindictive glare down below them.

"The last and strongest Lunar Phase," Alex breathed, before flying off to combat the invaders. "Occlon the Whole!"

FORTY-SIX

With a single flick of his wrist, Gary let loose a powerful wind, decimating the Moon Cult's ranks. Jeff, whose blaster had been repaired by Novis, launched cold energy blasts into the dwindling enemies, finishing them off.

"It doesn't even break when reversed," he breathed. "Thanks, Novis."

"No problem," the liskous replied. A strong wind knocked her off her feet. "Gary, will you try to only aim at them?"

"THAT WASN'T ME," Gary replied. "IT CAME FROM ABOVE."

The other Heavenspirians had just arrived, reporting Huaco's defeat. Suddenly, a discharge of energy bullets thundered through their ranks, though Dodsfald summoned Lapideis, who created barriers to block the majority of them. The ones that didn't, glanced harmlessly off the deities.

"Perish, enemies of the Moon!" screeched Alex, whose right hand had transformed into the end of an energy blaster, albeit one that looked infinitely more potent than any ever seen before. "Especially you!" he aimed at Novis and fired a volley so quick that not even Lapideis could block it. "Disgracing your bloodline!"

Just before the shots could hit her, she flew upwards, then summoned a volley of reddish-brown slate-scales to throw at Alex. Her father dodged them all.

Everyone else began to attack, but Novis commanded them to stop. "I know a deity should fight him, but I have to win for myself!" she exclaimed. "Focus on what's in the sky!"

"There's no moon!" exclaimed Eldrit. "Preposterous!"

From behind them, a chill voice rang in all of their heads, *"You are wrong, unbeliever. You and your allies will be the things there will be none of. What position are you in to challenge the will of the Moon?"*

A familiar, temple-like figure jumped out from behind them, bearing a crescent blade. Its only difference from the Lunar Phase that fought Antony was its ethereal form, which resembled a silhouette cast in grey. Gary crushed it underfoot, but soon more and more arrived.

"This is ridiculous!" spluttered Antony. "Capac and I killed Zecta!"

"No matter how many times the same foe challenges us, we will always take up the fight, as many times as it takes to reach an absolute victory," declared Aeterno. "Attack, for Heavenspire!"

*

Forming speed-scales, Novis just about managed to dodge the blasts from Alex's upgraded blaster. She tried to get closer, but it seemed that her father's weapon had unlimited ammunition.

"Accept your fate, mistake!" spat Alex. "I want to watch a creation I'm happy with at the moment!" Novis halted for just a split second, and that was all it took for him to blast off one of her arms.

"IF YOU'RE TALKING ABOUT THE FOURTH LUNAR PHASE, I ASSURE YOU THAT IT WILL SOON BE DEAD!" Novis hollered. Spreading her remaining arm, she generated an abundance of reddish-brown slate-scales and sent them flying at Alex.

However, her father just incinerated them all with his weapon. Then Alex cried out, clutching his back. A single scale, which Novis had made soar high above the rest, had circled back and struck him from behind. Growths the same colour as the slate-scale began to sprout all over him, slowing his movements and slurring his speech.

"Whasshh going on?" he managed to splutter before falling to the ground.

"Rust-scales," Novis replied bluntly. "Even your wonderful technology has its flaws."

Alex was silent, likely because his speaker array had rusted over.

"Before you say any more, I was never born to be anything," his daughter told him, giving him a sharp kick across the head. "I'm not just made up of my heritage; what I want to do, what I'm like and whom I fight for are values I decide, not based on the genes I carry. If I was a mistake in your ideals, I was a correction to myself."

A blast of energy struck Novis in the shoulder.

"N-not all metalshh rusht," Alex slurred, with the gleaming shape of his energy blaster poking out from his rusty form.

Clutching the hole in her shoulder, Novis soared upwards, building up magical energy for a devastating attack. Suddenly, Alex's blaster rusted and snapped into tiny fragments, much to the surprise of both.

"Unless someone has ultimate control over all things earthen," Lapideis stated through gritted teeth, with one hand raised and the other trying to fend off what looked like Zecta's ghost. "He's out of the fight, Novis; we need your help fighting Occlon!"

"STOP TALKING, CORPSE!" yelled Dodsfald, and the god disappeared in a flicker of white energy.

Rushing over to her allies, Novis saw they were besieged on all angles by millions of the spectral beings. Each one took on the visage of a Lunar Phase and, judging from the way the others struggled against them, had the same strength. Even Gary was struggling – not from their power but from their sheer numbers; as he crushed a swarm of them underfoot and blasted another, thrice the amount were hacking away at his legs from behind.

"Dodsfald, bring back Lapideis!" commanded Cognitio, destroying one of Huaco's power generators with his staff.

Unfazed, the Lunar Phase and twenty others charged the emissary, only to be blown back by a gale-force wind from Nimbus.

"We need him!" Cognitio declared.

"It's numbers we need!" replied the elf, and he thrust both hands forwards.

Countless undead, including Volundur and Aesik, sprang from them and leaped on the Lunar Phases. Whilst nowhere near as strong as their opponents, they distracted them long enough for the Heavenspirians to make a comeback. Slowly but surely, the number of the enemy was decreasing. Just as it seemed they were rid of the Lunar Phases, the dead began to flicker and fade away.

"I'm running out of magical energy!" exclaimed Dodsfald. "Any seculi, lend me some!"

Imryth and Shekina transferred their power to the necromancer, but they had used most of it in the battle and it was barely enough to keep the undead fighting for a few more minutes.

"Eldrit, you are an infinite source of magic!" Dodsfald shrieked. "Pool yours in too!"

"You dare speak to your god like that?" remarked Eldrit. "No, I'm gathering every ounce of my infinite power together for my own attack."

"Mortals, evacuate the planet!" commanded Aeterno. "We deities can't get hurt by them; we'll keep them busy. Deliver the core!"

"We aren't leaving you behind!" replied Bob. "The quest was also to rescue you, so that the system will still have its protectors."

Suddenly, a burst of blue energy from above struck Hydrax, incinerating his undamaged wing.

"I smell longinite, and it's not from my blades!" Belial declared. "Look above. What's there?"

Whilst holding off their attackers, everyone managed to glance up quickly and catch a glimpse of a terrifying sight. Occlon, the moon of Capac had come to life and gazed down at them spitefully. The blast that hit Aeterno had likely come from the longinite-blue aura around it, whilst, the ghostlike

Lunar Phases coalesced in its eerie, yellow gaze and were beamed down onto the planet's surface.

"How do you like the Moon Spectres?" it taunted. *"They are dead warriors of the Silver One, brought back to life; it is no miracle, and just one of the many powers of Occlon the Whole."*

"STAND BACK!" bawled Aeterno, and then he began to alter space. Trying to freeze time over an area the size of a moon would definitely freeze them all as well, making the quest fail. Instead, he compressed pieces of space around him; this was not enough to create black holes but enough to slow many of the Moon Spectres around him to a halt.

Immediately, everyone decimated the unmoving targets, whilst Aeterno focused on capturing more of their foes. However, a constant stream seemed to come from Occlon's eyes, and, even though the tide had been turned, the Moon Spectres only seemed to grow in number.

"KEEP THEM BUSY!" said Gary, taking to the skies. He only used his ion thrusters to fly, so as not to knock anyone into Aeterno's compressed space. "I'LL DESTROY THAT MOON!"

"I am more than a simple moon," remarked Occlon, turning its gaze to face Gary. Blasts of energy shot from its aura, clipping Gary's wings and destroying his feet. *"Now plummet and watch as your foolery has crushed your allies."*

One of Gary's hands changed into a harpoon attached to a chain. He fired the weapon, which soared at such a speed that Occlon couldn't react before it was impaled. Gary retracted the chain, pulling himself towards the final Lunar Phase, and punched its cratered surface, his second hand now a powerful drill. The drill bore into Occlon's eyes, cutting the constant stream of Moon Spectres being made and beamed down. Suddenly, Gary's vision went black. Luckily, his thrusters had regenerated, and he activated them; however, he was not sure what was going on, and his eyes were yet to regenerate.

"*You saw Stal use hieratics,*" explained Occlon. "*There is one that only a being of my power can control: the future eclipse! All the pain you cause will come back to you... I'd be careful what you do, robot.*"

"CAN YOU SEE A SYMBOL ON THAT MOON?" Gary called down to his allies on the ground.

Either they couldn't hear him or were too busy trying to stay alive. He felt his wings and thrusters disappear again, and the rush of air as he plummeted. Suddenly, he felt something wrap around him and crack beneath him, but nothing too reminiscent of falling on the ground.

"Try not to kill us, you metal buffoon!" someone snapped.

Gary's vision regenerated, and he saw thick vines wrapped around him, acting like a brace, and a trunk below him, which had survived his fall for the most part.

Sequia stood beside Occlon, killing a legion of trapped Moon Spectres with a blast of fire magic. "That moon's still alive. Kill it!" she ordered.

"DON'T WORRY, I WILL," Gary replied, and he took to the sky again.

Occlon rained down its blue fire, but the projectiles were all blown away by many winds. Imryth, Eldrit, Nimbus and Shekina had followed Gary upwards, defending him with their potent magic.

"I've finally focused all of my power together," spoke Eldrit. "You four distract it!"

"*I can hear you, proud elf,*" hissed Occlon, and it unleashed another barrage.

Gary's hands transformed into shields, and he bore the brunt of the blast, whilst Imryth, Nimbus and Shekina flew around him, peppering the Moon with their attacks. When Alex had implanted technology into the Moon and when Stal had carved the hieratic symbol discreetly in a deep crater, they had not thought of implanting anything to help it deal with multiple foes. Both had thought that the Moon Spectres, warriors forged from fragments of the Lunar Phases' souls and Longinus' printing technology, would be enough to take most of them out.

They were about to be proven wrong.

Trying to hit three fast targets was a struggle for Occlon, and when it tried to hit one, they would dodge, and the other two would strike it. It activated future eclipse, yet the power did not seem to work.

"There's a symbol inside one of the craters!" Imryth informed the others, as she shot a constant stream of fire. "I've destroyed it, but it keeps on trying to regenerate!"

"IT MUST HAVE A CORE LIKE ME!" said Gary as the moon's deadly eyes came back into being.

One of his shields became a net, and he ensnared Occlon whilst it was distracted. Imryth, Nimbus and Shekina flew away as this happened, and Eldrit's eyes began to thrum and glow with a light that changed colour every second.

"WAIT! DON'T ATTACK NOW! WE NEED TO EXPOSE ITS CORE FIRST—" began Gary.

However, Eldrit ignored him. "Who are you to think yourself better than me?" the god of magic scoffed. "I've waited enough!" He gazed directly at Occlon, with a smug grin playing across his face. "Magic, the ability to control the elements with your mind," he began with a superior tone, "is something you don't have to carve into rock; it is something that comes at a thought. And now you will face the infinite potential it possesses."

"TIME ISN'T INFINITE, THOUGH!" shouted Nimbus as Occlon summoned Moon Spectres to hack away at the net. "HURRY UP AND DESTROY THAT THING!"

The swirling magical energy in Eldrit's eyes glowed even brighter, to the extent that it seemed an aurora had formed in the sky. "Meticulous allmagic!" he cried. "Ocular phoenix!" From his eyes shot out a gargantuan blast of magic, at least four times Occlon's size. It bore the visage of the bird from elven myth, screeching as it soared towards its ensnared prey. All the aspects of regular magic – flame, water, ice and every other force of nature – crackled and coalesced across its plumage. With an agility seemingly impossible for something its size, it deftly avoided hitting the other Heavenspirians, and dive-bombed the ensnared moon.

Occlon struggled but could not escape Gary's longinite net. The final Lunar Phase was destroyed in an instant. Not a single fragment remained. After its prey had been destroyed, the phoenix lost its form, much like an ice sculpture melting, and the flow of magic poured back into Eldrit's eyes and disappeared.

Down below, the Moon Spectres had been defeated,

albeit with the help of altering the space around them; countless rifts marred the planet like unhealable scars.

"At least the idea of a curse will stop civilians flying here," remarked Kosma. "I sense the Mordrev cult leader is immobilised here, but I foresee he'll not give anyone information, no matter how hard we interrogate him."

"Let me," offered Bob. "But I would like to do it alone."

"If you wish," Shekina said. "Anyway, the rest of us will have to try to repair the phasecrafts – even the other nominee group's one doesn't work!"

Bob rushed off to where their curse-wielding enemy lay on the floor, encased in thick clumps of rust. *Morehk, when you read his mind earlier, what did you see?* he thought.

"I can't explain it," his stygir told him. *"It was only flickers of images, thanks to that curse he put up. But from what I saw, I now know what the grey means… and even Catarehk is the Heavenspire's ally now. Someone's threatening life's existence, and there will be nothing to kill ever again."*

"That's what you're concerned about?" sighed Bob. "If you want to kill so badly, kill this being that's the enemy of all. Who is it?"

When Morehk told him, he let out a yell of surprise, "No, you have to be mistaken! You made a mistake in reading Alex's mind! You have!" Using his Joule 1.0, Bob shot Alex's mouth area, revealing his speaker array.

"OCCLON!" Alex screamed in anguish. "My greatest creation… destroyed by an old-fashioned fool who disvalues technology! I'll fry his chicken alive! I'll add him to my organ collection! But not after I do the same to my mistake of an offspring—"

"Alex," Bob interrupted him. "The Grey Triptych."

"Is none of your concern!" the incandescent former liskous spat at him. "All you need to know is that our research on upgrading life is complete. You have killed Aurik, you have killed Hestrus and you have killed Ghogiehk, but our final leader will not die!"

"Is it you?" asked Bob, materialising a large cannon on his shoulder. "Because the last thing you said might be wrong in a few seconds."

"*That's the spirit!*" exclaimed Morehk.

"Sometimes, the minion looks like the leader and sometimes the leader looks like a minion," Alex replied. "Which is it, human boy?"

"If you're going to call yourself the Grey Triptych, don't have more than three leaders! Are you the final leader of the Grey Triptych?" asked Bob, charging up his cannon.

"And if I was?" questioned a smirking Alex. "Or maybe I'm not? Either way, the final leader won't die, and I know it. You don't have the heart to kill or the means to end the one behind this all. The final leader will not—" His speech was cut off by a cannon blast.

Bob materialised blades on the end of tendrils, and hacked and slashed at the mad former liskous until he was no more.

"*Ha!*" Morehk declared with a laugh. "*That was so good!*"

Crap, what have I done? thought Bob. *How we will interrogate him now?*

"*I'll tell you what you've done – you've grown,*" replied Morehk. "*You finally understand the thrill of murder. I have an idea: how about we ask the other Heavenspirians and see if their experiences add up with what I saw?"*

What you saw was false— Bob began

However, he was cut off by Morehk. *"Come on, who else could trap a deity? And I assure you that the stygir have no part in this!"*

Not believing Morehk's last sentence, Bob walked back to where the other Heavenspirians were fixing their crafts.

*

Following Cognitio's instructions, Jeff did some rewiring inside the phasecraft, dextrously fitting the wires back into their correct places. Now both groups' crafts worked perfectly, and they were on the cusp of completing their quest. But something didn't seem right to Jeff; something that made him question whether it really was an accident that they ended up on Manco surrounded by savage, metal people.

"The wires," he said, "it was like they were rigged to phase us here!" He showed everyone a complex mechanical device that he had found gripping the wires, with appendages built to misplace them.

"I remember showing them to all the ruling bodies of the warmblood races," Cognitio recalled. "The human government, with their access to all the most advanced technology, could've slipped them in easily."

"And then those fools would've killed off all the deities that oppose their filthy new ways," murmured Sequia. "But now they've failed."

"The quest isn't complete!" exclaimed Bob, as he ran towards them. "The Grey Triptych is behind all this, and they've been manipulating us from the start." As each fixed their gaze upon him, he felt unsure whether the information Morehk had given him was correct. After all, there is no way to truly understand a psychopath's mind. "Eldrit, Eitri, how were you captured?"

"It was another one of their silly fights," detailed Shekina. "The two of them were in some corner of Atlas having a full-on battle."

"He started it by being a self-conceited fool!" exclaimed Eitri, pointing at Eldrit. Before the god of magic could reply, Eitri kept on talking. "But there was something strange… Despite my usual need to ram this pumice-brain's head in, I would never do it on an actual mission. I can't remember why the fight started, but I remember smelling something foul before it happened."

"It was most likely yourself," smirked Eldrit. "Although the same thing happened to me."

"Gas!" gasped Caesium. "Just like in Ghogiehk's maze. Gas that controls behaviour!"

"And although I don't truly understand this Grey Triptych group, I know it had a focus on upgrading existence," added Jeff. "Maybe those horrid flesh-powered machines were an early attempt at that."

"Let's take Alex into account, too," stated Belial. "He was in charge of both the Thinkers of Mordrev and the Moon Cult. Both are the same as each other in that they focus on enlightened knowledge, which is a very similar goal."

"He was the last leader," spoke Bob. "And he died by

throwing himself in the midst of… four large space rifts and getting torn apart."

"Good one," chuckled Morehk.

"You'd better make sure you stay in control of those space rifts," warned Cognitio. "You don't know how they'll affect you if they influence you too much."

"Aeterno had to make them as a last resort," replied Bob as Morehk screamed his shock at Cognitio's deductive ability. "Cognitio, I think a member of the Grey Triptych is still alive, and they're the one behind all this." He then told everyone Morehk's information, and they were as flabbergasted as he was. "Kosma, you can look into the future a bit, right?" Bob asked the goddess of the future. "Can you check if my suspicions are true?"

"I'm sorry, boy, but after I use my checkpoint, it takes a while for that power to return to me," confirmed the goddess. "Anyway, I can only see the next few seconds. But your theory can't be true! It just can't!"

"It is a possibility," Aeterno conceded. "I have thought of a plan that will first see if your idea is correct, and if it is, stop him. Only you deities come with me. The rest of you, wait for us outside."

"No," replied Jeff. "We've been with you the whole time, and we'll stay for the final fight. I would especially like to see a battle of deities. I know I don't speak for everyone, but those who want to join you will come with you."

"Very well," stated Aeterno. "Let us go to Primium!"

FORTY-SEVEN

When they arrived at Primium, an unlikely sight awaited them. What they expected to be a war-torn dystopia verging on anarchy was an advanced, organised metropolis. Rows of skyscrapers stretched into the sky, and all the abodes were upgraded with surreal technology. In the town centre, amidst crowds of joyous humans, was a monument. It depicted a lance piercing a golden horizon that represented the future and was dedicated to the Longinus group, the rebuilders of the city.

"When we arrived to try to make peace, this place was verging on anarchy," breathed Shekina. "Jonas must've been hard at work."

Even Sequia was fractionally in awe at the utopic city. People began to notice the crowd of deities and other Heavenspirians, and gathered around them in awe, falling to their knees at the sight of the system's protectors and marvelling at the sight of a robot that rivalled their tallest skyscrapers in height. A few called out to some of the nominees, congratulating them on their quest's success.

"People of Primium!" Aeterno addressed the public.

"We come with the shifter core, the device that powers Industria!"

Raucous cheers erupted through the crowd like shockwaves.

"Now, let us go to Mekanyon!" concluded Aeterno.

"There is no need," a robotic voice declared.

The human crowd parted to make way for a familiar figure, which resembled a knight, albeit one covered in technological devices.

"Congratulations!" exclaimed Mekanyon, the green light behind his visor glowing brighter at the sight of the shifter core. "By Heavenspire, you have succeeded where I could not venture!"

"And you have recovered from the stygir attack," stated Kosma.

"I see Aurik, Lapideis and Galvok are not with you," the god of technology noted in a solemn tone. "Their bodies and souls are gone, but their deeds will always be with us."

"Not all," replied Dodsfald, and he summoned Lapideis.

"Mekanyon!" the god of earth exclaimed. "I am sorry. I went deusnova in a trivial fight."

"It doesn't matter," assured Mekanyon. "You are alive now, aren't you? Explain to me how you're alive like this later. Young elf, give me the shifter core."

Imryth didn't move.

A metal arm extended from Mekanyon's back and grabbed it from her hands. Immediately afterwards, the god shot into the sky, not knowing he was being followed by the other deities and their allies. Those who couldn't fly hitched a ride on Gary's back and those with no way of breathing in space were each given an air-scale and wind-scale by Novis.

"I wonder why he's in such a hurry," Imryth said. "Bob's theory could be correct."

"Gary, what have you found?" Jeff asked his giant blue friend. "What was Document 3+1?"

"BACK WHEN I WAS HACKING INTO THE BELOW-HEAVENSPIRE'S DATABASE, THERE WAS ONE DOCUMENT I COULD NEVER HACK INTO FOR SOME REASON," replied Gary. "LIKE IT WAS BEING PROTECTED. BUT THE TABRIS ROBOT'S MIND CAN MAKE AN ADVANCED LINK WITH ANY DATABASE IN THE SYSTEM, AND I'M MAKING A BREAKTHROUGH NOW. HEY, I THOUGHT MEKANYON WAS ABOVE US!"

"What do you mean?" asked Imryth.

Looking down, they saw they were being followed by the god of technology, his arms rippling with an array of energy blasters. Before he could open fire, another Mekanyon descended from the sky and destroyed the first one's blasters with his power.

"EVERYONE, GET BACK!" shouted the second one. "I'm the real one, but a stygir creature who could shape-shift has been our true foe all this time! I know how to defeat it, as I've seen it enough."

The fake regrew its blasters, but the real one was ready. Using his deity power, Mekanyon caused various pieces of technology, both junk and new machines, to orbit around him like electrons around an atom. The gears on his armour turned at an impossible speed, the dials thrummed and a silver aura formed around him.

"INDUSTRO-DOMINIUM!" yelled Mekanyon, thrusting his arms in the direction of the stygir creature.

A storm of metal and circuitry was flung at his foe, subjecting it to a quick-but-merciless demise. Like sand crumbling away, the stygir creature fell apart molecule by molecule, with the technology somehow absorbing its very being. A few seconds later, there was no trace of it.

"It was probably left here by its masters to create all those traps for you questing deities," remarked Mekanyon. "I see you have followed me. Well, of course you'd want to see our greatest weapon being rearmed."

With that, they all carried on towards Industria to restore the shifter core.

*

Eventually, they reached Industria. Although powerless and now little more than a lump of metal orbiting Primium, the giant turret looked majestic, with its formidable, silver form filling all who saw it with fear and awe. But something was different. Everyone remembered it as a single-barrelled defence weapon, yet in front of them was an extended, elongated attack system with cannon ends pointing in every direction and networks of equipment supporting each one.

Mekanyon gestured, and a compartment opened, where an empty shifter core-sized space waited to be reloaded. Not being technological, the core had to be inserted by hand, and Mekanyon had to attach individually all the various wires. Everyone else stood guard, in case

the stygir had sent another of their minions to get rid of
the turret.

See, Morehk, thought Bob, *you were just trying to
mislead me! There's no way your theory could be true. You
stygir were behind all this!*

"We really weren't!" protested Morehk. *"Wait, it could've
been that crazy Ghogiehk. But he's dead! Maybe he became
so powerful that his creations stay alive even after his death?"*

"MEKANYON'S BEHIND NEW WORLD'S GEAR!"
exclaimed Gary all of a sudden. "DOCUMENT 3+1
CONFIRMS BOB'S THEORY!" He brought down both
fists on Industria, shattering it. Pieces of Atlas' only hope
against the stygir floated in all directions; the remnants of
the mighty war machine were strewn like litter.

"Traitor!" spat Mekanyon, whose attention was now
focused on rebuilding Industria, his power reforming the
orbital weapon in an instant.

With one fist, Gary destroyed it again, and the end
of the other morphed into a holoceiver. Out came a
projection of a document. A document marked with the
grey-coloured emblem of a brain surrounded by three
gears. A document saved as Document 3+1. A document
with the header New World's Gear.

Immediately, Aeterno froze time around Mekanyon.
Or he would have, were it not for the clouds of black gas
that spewed from the god's armour.

"Unraveller gas!" exclaimed Belial, sniffing the air. "You
really are with them. Judgement sol: hellion shredder!"

Immediately, a tidal wave of fire and knives leaped at
Mekanyon, who would have dodged it were it not for a
wall of rock encircling him.

"You saved us," breathed Lapideis in shock, "and yet you've been conspiring against us all along?"

"I KNEW TECHNOLOGY WAS A MISTAKE!" screeched Eldrit, and he launched a volley of fireballs at Mekanyon.

"That's the one thing I agree with you on," added Eitri, as a spiked boulder formed in his hand from a rune on his armour. With uncanny strength, he threw it at Industria, shattering it.

Nimbus created a vacuum and sucked the shifter core towards his hand. Everyone, mortal and immortal alike, added their own attacks to the largest assault on a single being since the Stygir War, until not a trace of Mekanyon remained.

"Do you think he's dead?" asked Nimbus sarcastically.

"What you think is wrong," Mekanyon replied, forming from what appeared to be the empty blackness of space. He was still wreathed in unraveller gas, as if he had an infinite supply of the negating smog.

Novis summoned rust-scales and launched them at Mekanyon, yet it seemed that the god was immune to rusting.

"Cease your fire and listen! I'm trying to help you. This is all for Atlas; no, it's for all of the universe, for all existence, in every reality possible!" explained Mekanyon.

"What is?" asked Sequia, her words like razor blades. "Trying to destroy my home planet and forcing us to move, then joining a group with the half-arsed motives of a cult?"

"The goddess of nature," sighed the god of technology. "Immortal for the sake of lesser organisms our species overcame millennia ago. A creature of the past. No wonder you oppose me."

"Let us hear him out!" ordered Aeterno. "To truly understand him, we must know his motives. But first this..." He turned to Mekanyon. "How many leaders of the Grey Triptych are there, if there are not three like your name suggests? Answer falsely, and I vow to you that you'll be with Ghogiehk, Aurik, Hestrus and Alex very soon."

"Your race claims to be scholars," said Mekanyon, chuckling. "A Grey Triptych is three paintings that compose a single artwork. Art must have a painter who designed it to their will and ideals! Aurik must've told you he was the only god in the organisation. He was, at the time of its founding."

"And what are these ideals?" asked Cognitio.

"Simple," Mekanyon told him. "To upgrade life. This goal started shortly after I realised that the current state of living beings was insufficient and full of problems. The constant need to consume food will lead to famine should that food source go. Our bodies are susceptible to disease, and some kill us faster than our minds can come up with a way to cure them."

"True," muttered Belial, "just ask my people."

Mekanyon ignored him and continued, "Dangerous personalities, psychopaths and warmongers just add to the problem, causing pointless death and destruction to forced motives. And what of death itself? What of the fact that every being is doomed to end, sooner or later, maybe before they could achieve anything? Divinite isn't enough, for that requires the beliefs of mortals to sustain the body, and some of those worthy to have contact with it might go undiscovered or refuse to preserve their existence." He cast a glance at Cognitio. "All these are problems. I founded the Grey Triptych to solve these problems. Aurik was easily convinced, and his influence as a deity allowed the organisation to progress. But there was another individual with goals similar to me: a liskous on the search for enlightened knowledge given to him by a god he worshipped, one clad in silver armour. Alex offered to become my assistant and my representative in the world of hidden affairs. He was no true leader by any means but an excellent minion to the end.

"The fourth member was found when I was exploring deep space for answers, when the system wasn't destroyed and encircled by the Void, which was yet another reason we need an upgraded existence! Ghogiehk wanted the same, with his delusions of omnipotence leading him to want better 'creations' to rule over."

"GET TO THE POINT, YOU OVER-SHINY WASTE OF METAL!" yelled Caesium. Although he hadn't seen it, a member of the Grey Triptych had killed his dad indirectly by activating Tabris and giving it the orders to do so. This was the closest he'd get to avenging him, and anger rose inside him like geyser water. "What's this upgraded life? What the hell is it?"

"Definitely of no resemblance to you," taunted Mekanyon. "To begin with, it'll be a bit taller."

Cognitio had to restrain Caesium to stop him from attacking Mekanyon.

"Jokes aside, it is technology," Mekanyon confirmed.

"*What?*" questioned Hydrax telepathically. "*That's not life. At most, that's artificial intelligence!*"

"No," replied Mekanyon. "It is the upgrade from the biological. Look at Primium! It has advanced medicine, advanced communication, advanced everything – all thanks to technology! It has upgraded living, and now it shall upgrade life!"

"Tell me more," requested Aeterno, his staff in a battle position. "What are you planning?"

"The shift of media for our souls!" exclaimed Mekanyon. "Simply put, I will make all life mechanical organisms that are free from the troubles I mentioned earlier. First, communication troubles were behind us thanks to technology, and, soon, death will be behind us!"

"He's mad," muttered Nimbus.

"I am not!" snapped Mekanyon. "The Grey Triptych first tried to accomplish this using my first truly advanced technological creation: a strain of biomechanical nanobots that entered the bodies of Primium's population and tried to alter their genotype to a robotic one. It failed. I believe you call my faulty creations the Great Plague. Luckily, Aurik's powers of transference saved the planet."

Now it was Belial who attacked. At such speed he could not be restrained, he jumped off Gary's back and threw a stream of knives at Mekanyon. They were immolated by multiple energy blasters that sprang from the god's armour.

"DEATHSWIND SHREDDER!" shouted Belial, and flocks of knives erupted from his phase suit.

Mekanyon couldn't blast them all, so he formed two large, cubic structures above him. As if by some unseen force, half of the knives swerved from their course and hit those instead of their target.

"Longinite-attracting magnets," Mekanyon explained with an air of superiority. "And I see your strongest move either has a cool-down or a finite power supply." Raising his hand, the god of technology formed a cage with laser bars around Belial. "You will let me finish, mortal."

"YOU HEARTLESS FILTH!" snarled Belial in his confinement. "YOU'LL PAY FOR THIS!"

"Says an individual with the blood of many innocent beings, some of them children, on his hands," retorted Mekanyon.

Belial fell silent.

Mekanyon went on, "No life is perfect. No biological life, at least. Anyway, it was a worthwhile sacrifice. Three hundred or so individuals for the whole of existence? How much positive gain do you need to be satisfied? Furthermore, we even helped those who were worthy. Hestrus was a genius inventor and, although he declined at first, he was given a seat as our fourth leader. And we let him help the rest partially! The failed modification had to stay, to incapacitate the Longinists so the evidence wouldn't be found. Ghogiehk used some of the Longinists in his take on upgraded life, but his were macabre and bloody constructs that required flesh to move. But he couldn't take criticism, so one day he took them all and left, confining himself to a maze of his own creation."

"Enough pointless backstory!" snapped Eldrit. "What is New World's Gear? What is this quest we've been sent on? And what's the true point of the shifter core?"

"It's the finished product," Mekanyon calmly replied. "Thanks to me altering the archives of the past, shifter cores – an invention that precedes even the liskous – are now only known as objects from myth. But I invented one that will become legend.

"Soulforger shifter cores, as you saw, took the soul of a being and made a new body for it, using molten metal as a medium. The one you're holding now is similar. Using a blaster or some form of long-range weaponry, it will transmit waves that will upgrade all life forms in range to be mechanical!"

It was at that point that Bob remembered the One of Brimstone in Napthon's reality. How it screamed and howled when Imryth used the shifter core along with her magic, and how metal components were strewn across the spot it had died.

"But some life doesn't deserve to live," Mekanyon continued. "Microbes and gaseous beings such as the stygir will become metal dust, but I'm not just talking about them. I'm talking about those who oppose the wonders of technology: elves and dwarves! So, with the help of my stygir-like automatons, I faked a stygir attack and started the war, but not before getting Napthon to dispatch any government candidates who would want peace. The inferior races would've all died were it not for your interference. However, I had a feeling you would do something like that. So, from behind the scenes, Hestrus manipulated Longinus into culling your numbers; it was a shame about Aurik, but, then again, he was reaching the end of his usefulness. To spite me, that inconsolable fool Ghogiehk took the shifter core with him, so I needed you to get that back. And, should you succeed, the phasecrafts were all set to malfunction and take you to Manco, where Alex and his new cult were prepared to end you and return my core."

"But why not do it yourself in secret?" asked Cognitio. "That was the main flaw in your plan, Mekanyon."

"Because of time!" The mad god chuckled. "I needed to stall time and to have everyone distracted on this quest – this all-important quest – whilst I, the injured god, would secretly use my power to its full extent to upgrade my greatest creation to its greatest possible form! Such a feat would take a long time, and you have given me the hours to get away with it." He outstretched an arm and Industria reappeared. "A weapon with enough range to cover the whole of existence, including all realities, in a single blast!"

Shocked cries echoed throughout the crowd of Heavenspirians.

"This is the New World's Gear! The plan to save the multiverse!" crowed Mekanyon.

"So this is your true motive," muttered Aeterno. "But what of sentience? When the whole universe becomes immortal machines that don't need food and can't have malign motives, will they still think?"

"I will still think," confirmed Mekanyon, "and I will travel the better universe implanting the algorithms for basic sentience into all organisms. Don't worry, I'll keep your personalities fairly similar." He turned to Nimbus. "Give me that shifter core, Nimbus, or this vision of glory is just a vision."

"You're insane," breathed the god of sky. "You saved us from the stygir! You were our system's hero! And now you're just a delusional crackpot!"

"I have always been this 'delusional crackpot' of which you speak. Now pass me the core!" demanded Mekanyon.

"Never!" everyone else cried in unison.

Nimbus shattered the shifter core with a high-pressure gust of wind.

"So be it," sighed Mekanyon.

In the clouds of unraveller gas surrounding him, something bright pink began to glow.

"Let us take this battle somewhere else," he suggested.

The glow expanded and brightened, enveloping their surroundings.

"A nice and quiet place," the god of technology concluded, "where the cries of inferior life cannot be heard."

FORTY-EIGHT

Bob awoke in a vast, metal box. Somehow, it was like he was in broad daylight, but all he could see was an enclosed space with a ceiling thousands of metres above him and sturdy walls an equal distance from him.

There was nowhere to hide.

"Look around at Valkus, the arena reality," commented Mekanyon. "There are no phasing ladders, but, as in Inferd, one will appear when one side of a battle wins. What really makes this realm unique is the fact that its walls and space are unbreakable. Your moves, Lapideis and Aeterno; your moves."

Aeterno flew up into the air and swooped towards Mekanyon. The god of technology tried to gun him down, but his reflexes were too fast. Aeterno brought his staff down on Mekanyon's breastplate, cracking it in two.

"There's more to my worth on the battlefield than my power," Aeterno told him as he dodged a blast, then struck his foe's helmet. "Anyone mortal with no way of killing a god, retreat!"

The headgear cracked open to reveal only a whirring processor, but Aeterno was unfazed and shattered it. By this point, everyone had stood up, come to their senses and charged at Mekanyon. In an instant, the processor and armour had reformed, and Mekanyon soared out of Aeterno's reach. Gary aimed two longinite cannons at Mekanyon and fired, just as Kosma clipped his propellers with her beam. However, Mekanyon just grew new ones and jet boosters to dodge the dangerous, blue blasts. Hydrax's rope snagged Mekanyon's ankle and dragged him into the line of fire of Volundur, Sequia and Shekina. The god of sea doused Mekanyon in water as the elven deities fired lightning bolts at him. Eitri charged up his allrune forgeswing and hammered Mekanyon into the ground, with the rune of electric immunity shielding him from his allies' attacks. Yet the enemy god just reformed, stood back up and laughed.

"I hate this feeling of not being able to do anything!" exclaimed Caesium as he ran from the fight with Bob, Imryth, Jeff and Novis. "Is all we can do just watch the battle happen?"

"We all hate it," replied Imryth. "Yet we can't do anything against a god."

"There's only one of him," noted Jeff. "He'll go down in no time."

Bob tried to speak, but nothing came out. He was horrified to find out that the god who had saved his system and even flew him to Drakon was, in fact, the root of it all. This gnawed heavily at his mind, in addition to wondering whether or not he should risk revealing he was hosting a stygir to help fight Mekanyon. He fiddled with the PRR; the esoteric device told him to input audio or text for it to work.

"Yes, you can do something!" came a voice. Belial was still stuck in his laser-bar cage. "Free me. Now!"

Caesium tried to dig with his wormhole pickaxe, yet nothing happened. Jeff blasted the top of the cage off and the lasers deactivated. Sniffing out the deities, Belial then dashed toward them into the heat of battle.

"We're going back," Bob mustered eventually.

"*What?*" exclaimed Caesium. "But the deities clearly said to—"

"I know, but there's nowhere to run. This place is an indestructible box, for Heavenspire's sake! Shall we just cower in a corner to prolong the inevitable or shall we make a last stand?" questioned Bob.

"*Ooh, heroic,*" chided Morehk. "*Since when did you become such a noble paragon of virtue?*"

"I agree," responded Imryth. "Even if it's impossible, I'd rather try than lament in my weakness."

One by one, all the other mortals agreed.

"You put my honour to shame," muttered Caesium. "I might be the most likely to become a god, but you are the most likely to be a hero."

"*Or a limbless wimp who relies on me to get strong,*" teased Morehk.

One of Belial's knives clattered across the floor towards them. Bob picked it up and handed it to Caesium.

"Regain that honour then," Bob told his friend. "Everyone, try to find more knives. We attack, for Heavenspire!"

*

All around Mekanyon, the deities dropped to the floor, exhausted from their fight. Gary, whom Mekanyon saw as the biggest problem, was pinned into a corner by a swarm of drones armed with longinite-melting blasters.

"And biological life tires!" exclaimed Mekanyon with a laugh.

"What are you?" asked Lapideis, getting to his feet.

From behind a wall of rock, Dodsfald infused himself with the energies of the crypt and a ghostly, white light blazed in his eyes. He formed a javelin out of jagged rock and threw it at Mekanyon, who dodged it, but that was just a distraction. From behind the god of technology, another javelin ripped through Mekanyon's chest. Lapideis coated his claws in flint and raked them across the motors and batteries that seemed to be a substitute for Mekanyon's internal organs, and then he grabbed one. Mekanyon tried to reform, but began to appear around the grabbed motor and was shredded apart by rocks.

"You're not human anymore! What have you done?" asked Lapideis.

"I am the progenitor for upgraded life!" snarled Mekanyon. "I bear the prototype of my work!"

Unraveller gas clouded Lapideis' view, but he continued to chip away blindly at his enemy's reforming armour. "You're a machine!" the god of earth exclaimed.

"Therefore, I can fix myself with my powers," his foe retorted. "It has been fun playing with you all. I did not think you would push me this far."

A chainsaw on an extendable metal arm sprang from the forming Mekanyon, swooped past Lapideis and cut Dodsfald in half. The elf barely had time to scream before the two halves of his body fell apart into a crimson puddle. White light began to glow around Lapideis.

"A psychotic end for a psychotic soul," drawled Mekanyon. "I have no use for that soul."

"YOUR SOUL WILL BE OUT OF USE SOON!" hollered Lapideis in the final moments of his final life. "TECHNOLOGY IS OF METAL, AND METAL IS OF THE EARTH! DEUSNOVA!"

"Deusnova!" retorted Mekanyon. "It seems we are at stalemate, yet you are at the end of your life."

The two enhanced deity powers clashed and sparred, cancelling each other out at every turn.

"AND SO ARE YOU, YOU DELUSIONAL FOOL!" Cognitio roared, getting to his feet and panting from the effort. "NOW BE CRUMBLED AWAY BY YOUR OWN PRIDE!"

"You mistake my form for biological," spoke Mekanyon in a voice like grit. "Mechanical does not wear away!" he cried out, reforming fully. "And who is the delusional one now, you mortal fighting in a battle you cannot contribute to?"

A titanic foot descended onto Mekanyon, but motion sensors alerted him, and he flew away in time.

"FIGHT ME WITHOUT DRONES!" challenged Gary, grabbing Mekanyon with a fist.

The god struggled like a fly in a web.

Gary clenched his fist, crushing his opponent. "OR ARE YOU TOO WEAK?"

Everyone had regained their stamina and shot all their attacks at any fragments of Mekanyon remaining, making sure to destroy every last sliver of their foe. Minutes passed.

Nothing happened. Gary looked down at his hands, awed by the strength he now possessed. The strength he could truly say was his, now that the Tabris body seemed so natural to control. He could see Bob, Caesium, Imryth, Jeff and Novis running towards the fight scene. Just before he could tell them what happened, he felt a vibration inside his chest.

Mekanyon was still alive.

Drilling out of Gary's body with a pair of diamond-tipped drills, the god laughed in victory. An extendable arm on his shoulder held the remnants of the Tabris core.

"Never forget I was still deusnova!" commented Mekanyon with a cackle. "Nice technology you're made of."

The lights that were Gary's eyes flickered briefly, then went blank. The empty husk that once housed his soul clattered to the floor.

"I can't say the same for your soul. Again, it is unneeded by me," gloated Mekanyon.

"Although he didn't seem like it at first, Gary was a worthy ally who saved us all against Tabris," snapped Shekina. "With his life!"

"I bid you all come at me at once," ordered Mekanyon. "This is getting repetitive." From within his cloud of gas, battle technology of all forms – blasters, rockets, tank armour and so on – began to materialise around him. "Once more, I will not toy with you."

"Neither will I!" declared a voice.

Everyone turned around and looked in all directions to see where this voice was coming from.

"Drown in the waves, Mekanyon!" roared Hydrax, using his voice instead of his telepathy.

Even Aeterno and Nimbus had forgotten how it sounded.

"Is he doing it?" gasped Nimbus. "The sea deity's other persona?"

"Times are dire," replied Aeterno.

In front of their eyes, the god of sea began to morph into a completely different form. His azure hue began to darken to an obscure shade with flickers of navy blue and white froth beginning to form from between his scales. Growing in size, he threw his rope to the ground and let out a primal, formidable roar. Gone was the serene, placid being they knew; in his place stood a brutal and dangerous beast.

"Everyone," he bellowed, "like we did before, attack him all at once! But this time, leave not a molecule in our tide!"

Belial tossed knives to all the mortals, and the deities prepared their most devastating attacks.

"Interesting," mused Mekanyon. "Who knew the serene Hydrax had such a raging aspect? Unexpected... but face me! Attack me, you who oppose the New World's Gear!"

Needing no order, everyone charged at him. The altered Hydrax swung his fist and a wave travelling at immeasurable speed struck Mekanyon in the chest, ripping a massive hole in it. However, the attack was indiscriminate, and many deities had to dodge similar torrents that flew in all directions. Before Mekanyon could react, Aeterno and Eitri began to attack him, striking him with such force that his armour cracked like porcelain. At the same time, Sequia summoned a massive vine that crushed his helmet and the processor inside it. Kosma, Eldrit and Shekina used their beams and lightning to incinerate everything left.

Suddenly, the processor burst out of the vine, with two flamethrowers and a jetpack having sprouted from it.

"NEO-AERIAL BOMBARD: CAELUM PHAEDRA!" screamed Nimbus, and clouds enveloped his body, coalescing into the visage of a colossal dragon. As Nimbus opened his mouth, so did the visage, and a potent volley of lightning, cyclones and meteors rained down on the processor.

And then a barrage of lasers ripped through Nimbus' heart. The god collapsed to the floor. Behind him hovered half a processor and an advanced blaster.

"The teleporter was half-successful it seems," stated Mekanyon. "Soul download."

Shekina began her healing immediately, yet, before it could take effect, more blasters formed on Mekanyon's processor and they rained down a volley of fire on Nimbus, dicing his body into miniscule, unhealable, charred fragments.

"NIMBUS!" howled Hydrax, then he pounced at Mekanyon, his claws ready to swipe.

Mekanyon opened fire, yet each blast of energy was met with a miniature geyser that was potent enough to turn it to steam. Hydrax swiped, but Mekanyon avoided it deftly, then created a tesla gun. The god of sea roared and clamped his jaws down on Mekanyon, shaking him from side to side like a dog with a toy. Mekanyon's hand detached from his body and flew out of Hydrax's jaws, and the rest of his body regenerated from it, along with two tesla guns. Before he could shoot, an arm made of water erupted from Hydrax's back and crushed the weapons. Hydrax fired a stream of pressurised water, but Mekanyon dodged it as swiftly as an acrobat.

"He'll teleport now, to there!" announced Kosma, pointing to a spot in the air.

Belial threw a knife there, and the sound of metal being crushed filled the air as what was left of Mekanyon fell to the floor.

"Knives aren't technology," grinned Belial. "Goodbye, Grey Triptych."

Eldrit set the remnants aflame. And then Kosma cried out as she too was set aflame.

"Insolent fool!" spat Mekanyon, who had now regenerated back into a full set of armour. How he was alive after being hit with longinite was a mystery. The incandescent barrel of a flamethrower poked out of his gauntlet. "Always looking to the future, yet the future is now with technology!"

A stray jet of water from Hydrax doused Kosma's flames, whilst Cognitio, Caesium, Jeff, Imryth, Bob, Novis and the other nominees attacked the god of technology, their knives slashing at his armour. Mekanyon tried to create guns, but Cognitio severed them deftly before they could form fully. Hydrax roared and shot a massive wave out of his mouth. Immediately, it rusted Mekanyon, then crushed him into many metal fragments. Eitri brought down his hammer, grinding many to metal dust, and Eldrit followed it up with a stream of fire.

"THIS IS FOR MY FATHER!" yelled Caesium, bringing down the knife on a shard of helmet.

"And this for Volundur and Gary!" followed up Imryth, whilst laying waste to a clump of wiring.

"I said the teleporter was *half*-successful," elucidated Mekanyon, appearing behind them.

Jeff tried to stab him, but he flew into the air.

"Half of me was teleported somewhere else in this reality, and, as long as a single molecule of my form remains, I can grow a new body when the old one dies. You may be wondering how my deity power is so advanced," Mekanyon mocked, taking in the surprise on all his enemies' faces. "The answer is simple: you gave me the time I needed to upgrade it and master the upgrades. And I really must stop going easy on you. You've taken this to the point of no return."

"ENOUGH TALK!" shouted Eldrit. "METICULOUS ALLMAGIC: OCULAR PHOENIX!"

The visage of the mighty bird swooped at Mekanyon, but he didn't even flinch. Nor did he react when Sequia trapped him in place with a network of thick vines, and Belial threw longinite knives, which stuck in his armour.

"Magic absorbing field activate!" the god of technology declared just before the phoenix could tear him apart. As soon as the phoenix made contact with him, it began to disappear, as if it was going through a portal. Unscathed, Mekanyon laughed as Eldrit's most powerful spell began to vanish like steam.

Eldrit cried out, not in anguish but in pain, as he fell to his knees, clawing at his head.

"Bear in mind that my power is the creation and repair of technology; anyone can turn on a device. And this particular prototype absorbs not only the magic but the source of it as well," Mekanyon expounded. "Your mind."

"NO, IT WON'T!" shrieked Imryth, and she pointed a hand at Eldrit. "TAKE MY MAGIC ENERGY!" A sharp pain like a cold knife plunged into her mind, but she persevered for the fate of Atlas and countless other systems.

Shekina and Novis, the only two other seculi, added their power to the pool.

"*What are you doing?*" snapped Eldrit. "I'm more than enough to take out this shiny bastard and his parlour tricks! How the hell will I live down needing help from my apprentice and two mortals?"

"Because it means the universe won't get turned into that psychopath's toy box!" exclaimed Imryth. "The entire universe is on our shoulders, and maybe that's a burden not even a god can carry alone. Combined power is needed!"

Eldrit agreed reluctantly and took in everyone's magic. Immediately, the pain began to dull, yet it was still excruciating. Yet at the same time, he felt invigorated. The tail feathers of the phoenix, the only thing remaining of his greatest spell, began to give off a defiant glow.

"Observe as the great art of magic is bested by a simple voice command!" Mekanyon declared with a cackle. "Eldrit, if your mind is still intact, the war between humans, elves and dwarves is not yet over."

"Be silent for once, computer," replied Eldrit, getting to his feet. "Combined meticulous allmagic: phoenix of quintessence!"

The air thrummed with magical energy at such a rate that even the non-wizards felt a tingle run through their bodies. Behind the god, the phoenix re-materialised, yet it was not the same as it was before. A golden aura stemmed from it, and its feathers shone an otherworldly shade of brilliant silver.

Mekanyon had cut through the vines with a chainsaw and prepared his teleporter, yet, suddenly, a feeling unexperienced for many years rushed through his body. The god screamed in pain, emitting a mechanical screech that was horrifying to hear.

"MACHINES... DO NOT FEEL PAIN!" he howled, dropping to the floor in agony.

"Yet the soul does, and it seems yours is inside that suit somehow," Eitri retorted with a grin. He pointed to a complex symbol on the floor. "The rune of exorcism holds him. Attack at will, Eldrit!"

"As you can see, the prototype is not perfect," Mekanyon said through the pain. "Rune negating field, activate!"

Yet Sequia had prepared extra vines, which pinned him down once more. The phoenix swooped upon Mekanyon, with bolts of silver energy striking the god before it even reached him. Before its claws could rid the world of the god of technology once and for all, Mekanyon activated his teleporter and appeared in front of Eitri.

"YOU'LL PAY FOR THIS!" he yelled, and a battery of laser cannons emerged from his back. They fired at once, and their beams of incandescent light melted Eitri's armour and flesh.

Swooping into the fray, Aeterno demolished the cannons, causing them to explode catastrophically.

Shekina's healing and speed boost saved Aeterno and Eitri from being caught in the blasts.

"How am I still alive?" wondered Eitri. "Even though that new goddess healed me, I was hit by four deity-fired cannons! How..."

Behind Mekanyon, a dwarf lay slumped on the floor, his skin charred in places and a leg missing. A rune Eitri recognised as the rune of pain-sharing lay half-carved by his feet.

"Sorry, Eitri... I couldn't finish the rune in time..." Caesium wheezed, trying to get up but falling on his face. "Avenge... Aesik... Nimbus... Gary..."

"That's what I will do!" confirmed Eldrit.

The pain from Mekanyon's magic absorber was making it hard to control the phoenix, and its movements were slow and sluggish. Nevertheless, its rain of energy was proving more than effective, tearing apart Mekanyon's armour from afar, despite his magic negating field. With no arms and a crumbling torso, the god of technology was barely evading the attacks by Aeterno and Hydrax. Belial threw a wave of knives and Kosma fired her beam, destroying the processor. Before it could regenerate, Antony jumped up and cut Mekanyon across the breastplate with a knife. Powerless, Mekanyon fell to the floor. The phoenix descended upon his remains. With a bellicose screech, it spread its claws.

"Longinite-negating field, activate!" a crackling, robotic voice sounded. Mekanyon teleported out of the way and regenerated fully. However, he was not the same: the green light behind his visor flickered like a candle, and scratches of various sizes marred his usually shining armour.

"How much experimental technology must I test against you?" he asked in a heavily distorted voice. "Industro-dominium!"

From all around the reality, various particles that had once belonged to Mekanyon grew into larger pieces of metal and hovered above him. Eitri charged at him, with his hammer at the ready, but then Mekanyon teleported away, whilst sending the attack at the god of runecraft at the same time. Eitri barely had time to cry out before he was torn apart, molecule by molecule. A leg clattered to the floor – an armoured one. Mekanyon reappeared, one-legged and straining to stay aloft.

"NO!" Bob bawled.

"Magic… is… next!" Mekanyon mustered.

Sequia sent a thicket of vines at him, which he disintegrated with an energy blaster.

"Or you… guardian of natural life…" suggested Mekanyon. His propellers stopped spinning, and he fell to the floor. His armour cracked and shattered, leaving a wiry, metal skeleton.

The mortals threw their knives, cutting the wires like string, and the phoenix swooped upon its prey once more.

Then a strong gust of wind pushed Mekanyon up into the air, out of the reach of his attackers.

"NEO-AERIAL BOMBARD: CAELUM PHAEDRA!" roared Mekanyon, and Nimbus' most powerful attack obliterated Sequia, leaving not a trace of her.

"WE… WE CAN'T WIN!" yelled a nominee.

"Indeed!" mocked Mekanyon, with the little strength he had left. "For I have just finished downloading Nimbus' soul. Of course, I have yet to master what he has mastered, and I just have his last few actions… but prolong this fight and every mortal will die from lack of oxygen." He turned around to see a phoenix descending upon him.

"It's over," said Eldrit through gritted teeth.

Then, just before the phoenix could end Mekanyon, it stopped in mid-air. Eldrit, Imryth and Shekina fell to the floor, clutching their heads and crying in pain.

"Mekanyon's magic absorber has prevailed!" exclaimed Eldrit. "Disconnect your magic from mine." Before anyone could protest, he then shouted, "THERE'S NO POINT IN EVERYONE DYING WHEN ONLY ONE OF US CAN. OTHERS HAVE SACRIFICED THEMSELVES MANY TIMES… SO LET ME DO THE SAME FOR ONCE!"

Reluctantly, the other wizards withdrew their flows of magic. In his final moments, Eldrit didn't scream from the pain or mock anyone whilst he still had the chance. Struggling yet defiant, he turned to the other Heavenspirians and grinned. "I trust in you to defeat Mekanyon whilst he's weak. Magic and runecraft have failed, but not hope. Do it for Heavenspire!"

A lifeless body clattered to the floor and a phoenix disappeared.

FORTY-NINE

"And, of course, I don't want such a soul," said Mekanyon callously. "Magic... what rubbish."

"ELDRIT!" howled Shekina, and she began to charge up a colossal fireball

But Aeterno stopped her. "Wizards, I hate to say this, but there is nothing magic can do!" Aeterno said. "Take one of Belial's knives and attack as one. It seems that having too much experimental tech has damaged him beyond repair!"

Raging currents wreathed Hydrax's claws, and jets of water from the soles of his feet rocketed him up, where he met Mekanyon in aerial combat along with the other liskous.

Knowing there was nothing he could do, Mekanyon used Nimbus' power to plummet at incredible speed and dodge them. "Deusnova!" he exclaimed and his armour began to regenerate.

"DEATHSWIND SHREDDER!" howled Belial and countless knives struck Mekanyon.

It seemed that the anti-longinite field was failing, as Mekanyon's armour began to regenerate at a much slower rate. Mekanyon seemingly took no notice. He wasn't attacking, and there were no visible signs of him trying to do so.

Suddenly, Kosma jumped in front of Belial and cried out as multiple devastating explosions racked her body, seemingly coming from nowhere.

"I foresaw... microscopic explosives... emitted from his armour... killing you," she told Belial before falling to the floor.

"I hate using patents I haven't fully developed," spat Mekanyon. "There goes the beginnings of a new invention! Well, I foresee your timewarp checkpoint is somewhere in another reality."

At that moment, everyone noticed a vast swarm of large, neon-pink objects hovering above them all.

"Industro-dominium: plane ender!" cried Mekanyon.

With a glow, the swarm disappeared.

"Hestrus' reality is gone!" scoffed a laughing Mekanyon. "And with it your timewarp checkpoint and the future of organic life."

With his staff, Aeterno struck Mekanyon in the chest, and his body cracked and fell apart at the waist.

"Soul download!" Mekanyon cried out as his upper half flew upwards on a gust of wind.

Hydrax sent a wave of water at Mekanyon, but this was repelled by a gale. Cognitio and Novis tried to stab him in the back, but another strong wind slammed them to the floor.

"End the contract!" Morehk commanded Bob suddenly. *"END IT NOW!"*

WHAT? thought Bob.

"*I planned to contract with you to explore Atlas unseen and to combine our strengths, if you have any. But now my life and the lives of my prey are all on the line, and your weak body is holding me back. I give you complete authority for thirty seconds. Just command the end of the contract!*"

"I end the contract," Bob whispered as he was knocked to the floor by the winds.

An array of energy weaponry began to form on Mekanyon's arms.

"*But just one thought for you to keep,*" Morehk stated. "*You've only been able to come this far from using my strength. As far as I remember, your limbs are also sustained by me. Tell me, what will you do now?*"

Mekanyon was about to fire, but then a dark cloud struck him, ripping through his torso. Mekanyon teleported his head away quickly and then went deusnova, regenerating instantly into a full set of armour, albeit one more damaged and crippled than ever before.

"A stygir!" exclaimed Novis.

"At the moment, all life in the universe is allied," said Hydrax. "It fights with us!"

The god of sea then shot a pressurised stream of water at Mekanyon, only for a gale to blow it aside. That provided a distraction for Aeterno, Cognitio and Novis to charge at Mekanyon, supported by the knife throwing of all the living mortals. Shekina, unable to use magic, used her deity power to improve the strength of Hydrax and Aeterno.

Mekanyon's attention was on Morehk, and he tried to incinerate it, but it simply spread out its particles, dodging the myriad energy blasts effortlessly. Aeterno, strengthened by the power of Shekina, swung his staff at Mekanyon's head, yet the blow was dodged as if it was foreseen. Cognitio and Novis threw their knives, yet their stamina was failing, and the blades glided slowly through the air. Mekanyon incinerated them effortlessly.

"*KERPHAN, AVATAR OF DESTRUCTION!*" yelled Morehk, and he shifted into an ominous form. A ram-headed giant with eyes like burning embers stood in the midst of the reality. Towering over even the Tabris robot, its gargantuan arms ended in claws like jagged peaks. With the ease of a child picking up a toy, it grabbed Mekanyon swiftly and lifted him up to meet its smouldering gaze.

"You broke my teleporter!" cried Mekanyon, unable to escape Morehk's immensely strong grip. "And my winds don't affect you in the slightest! *What is this?*"

"*Your demise,*" replied Morehk. His hand closed slowly, shredding and crushing Mekanyon as slowly as possible. There was no fear of there being any remaining particles, for those parts of him that had been cracked even slightly by the stygir's umbral fist disintegrated immediately.

"*You have no right to rid me of my life or kills,*" rasped Morehk. "*Say your last words, so that you may amuse me in your final moments.*"

"OK!" replied Mekanyon, portraying something akin to fear. "My last words are..." The god of technology vanished.

"Soul download!" he stated, appearing behind Morehk.

The stygir barely had time to cry out "*Liar!*" before his form disappeared.

"Says the one who proclaimed me defeated!" Mekanyon laughed as his foe disappeared in front of him. "I developed and perfected this after the war against you... and it turns out a soul in an amorphous body can be downloaded instantly without destroying that body." Mekanyon's armour began to darken, taking on an ominous shade as the light behind his visor became a wispy mist. "Thank you for the power..." he rasped as Hydrax shot a blast of water at him. Without the slightest effort, his body split to avoid it, then he ripped through Hydrax's chest with a mechanical claw wreathed in shade.

Not even flinching, the god of sea crushed his opponent's claw with ease and brought the other down on his head. Mekanyon tried to fly away, but he was grabbed by Hydrax's other hand.

"ATTACK NOW!" bellowed Hydrax and everyone rushed forwards.

For some reason Mekanyon's armour began to crack apart and sparks flew from it like escapees from a sinking ship. "My... telepoRTER!" Mekanyon howled in a heavily warped voice. "It... doesn't... WORK! My stygir powers... AREN'T MASTERED YET!"

Hydrax tore apart Mekanyon's armour, watching as the once-regenerating shreds of metal clattered to the floor harmlessly. Aeterno, Cognitio and a horde of nominees approached the rogue god. With one final roar of effort, Mekanyon created an energy cannon and aimed it at Hydrax's head. Aeterno threw his staff with such strength that it broke the weapon's barrel.

"I can... FIX YOUR ONE-ARMED... body!" offered Mekanyon.

"Existence will never be perfect," Aeterno told him as the others began to launch their attacks. "But there will always be those who try to improve it as much as possible with their heroism, so others can live their lives in the closest thing to perfection as possible. You have failed to notice what the deities, what *you*, are meant to stand for."

"Why have THAT... when it can all be *perfect!*"

Raining down indiscriminately from a mortar-like structure that formed on Mekanyon's helmet, blasts of energy fire immolated many nominees as they charged. Belial sent out a deathswind shredder, destroying it.

And then Hydrax, drained by the hole in his chest, slumped to the floor. Shekina began to heal him, but Mekanyon had escaped.

In his hands a phasing ladder was starting to take form.

"New... World's Gear..." he rasped as a pink glow enveloped him. "I'm... COMING!"

*

As the attack raged on, all Bob could do was watch. He was powerless, truly powerless, to do anything. *Morehk was right,* he thought as he tried to master using his turbine suit with no arms or legs to manoeuvre him. Barely a centimetre off the ground, he advanced forwards at an almost non-existent pace. The colours he saw before the contract now hurt his eyes, which was a sting that added to the reality of his powerlessness. Now lasers of some sort were raining down from the sky. As he angled his head upwards, he saw one hurtling towards him. At the last minute, a large, grey hand blocked it. It would regenerate later, but it had been reduced to a stump for now.

"Let me carry you to the battle," offered Antony, picking up Bob in his arms. Due to his large hand, he could also pick up the PRR, which he scrutinised with interest.

"But I'm weak..." groaned Bob. "And weaponless..."

"Then what's this?" asked Antony, pointing to the Joule 1.0 strapped to Bob's waist. Without waiting for an answer, the troll lifted up Bob and ran into the heat of battle.

All around them, an army of what were once ordinary citizens charged their former saviour. Random thoughts crossed Bob's mind for no apparent reason; these were reflections on the quest: the fruitless effort that had culminated in the deaths of many deities. And then one of these subconscious flickers awakened something in his brain. It was an idea that could change everything, albeit one with a very small chance of success.

"The ren sums up a being's existence," Bob muttered to himself, remembering Morehk's explanation in the fight against Lance. "Words that sum up a being, said in a special way you need to hear to know... Antony, type this into the device!"

Putting Bob down gently, the troll then typed in what Bob said next. For a moment, nothing happened.

"REN FOUND," an automated voice suddenly rang from the PRR. It told them the secret name, but just uttering it caused the device to explode.

Looking back at the fight, Bob saw that Mekanyon had evaded Hydrax's grip and was producing something from his worn-out armour. Cracks littered the metal plating, revealing damaged wiring, broken gears... and the barest flicker of something else.

Bob knew what to do now. "THROW ME AT HIM!" shouted Bob. "DON'T ASK, JUST DO IT!"

With a grunt of effort, Antony launched Bob at Mekanyon. The god's motion sensors alerted him immediately. He readied his arsenal of long-ranging destruction, with the phasing ladder still forming.

"**New World's Gear**!" chanted Bob.

Maybe it was because the plan had dominated every aspect of the god's existence, maybe it was because he was the one to shift the world into this new age, or maybe it was because he really was the machine that would 'upgrade life' to his ideals. Whatever the reason, upon hearing those words, Mekanyon froze, if only for a second. In that second, any signs of stygir power disappeared from his armour.

Immediately, indescribable pain flooded Bob's body, which was the price of saying the ren of a being so much more powerful than himself. Whilst he suffered no external injuries, his very soul was set ablaze in an inferno of torture. Holding the stygirbane-scale was a pinprick compared to this.

But, a second later, it was gone.

"*DON'T CLAIM I'M DEFEATED WHEN I'M STILL ALIVE! I WILL BE THE ONE TO DEFEAT NEW WORLD'S GEAR!*" roared Morehk, before howling in pain.

The stygir had re-entered its host and had used the contract to take the side effects of saying the ren. Bob could sense it disappearing with every millisecond. Mekanyon's movements were drastically more sluggish, yet he was becoming faster quickly. The phasing ladder kept on forming as he held everyone back.

As Bob approached Mekanyon, the loss of his Void-vision signalled Morehk's demise. The unknown object became more visible: something glowing and pink. Being the most miniscule speck of bright colour amongst withered blacks and silvers, Bob could never figure out how he saw it. What he could fathom, though, was what it was and what to think as he made contact with it. *Take me to Mekanyon's power source.*

The phasing ladder was complete. Pink light enveloped Mekanyon. He yelled a cry of victory and a greeting to the New World's Gear. A complete phasing ladder was in his hands.

With the assistance of his turbine suit, Bob sent the Joule 1.0 flying from his holster. It was by sheer luck that he caught it in his mouth and fired off a shot with his tongue before phasing to a new reality. Whether the shot hit or not, he had no time to see; all around him a new reality came into being. It was a small, white room with a complex array of machinery at the end. Activating his turbine suit, he hovered towards it precariously to see what it was. Eventually, he reached it and was greeted by a silver cube with a thrumming purple aura.

A label on it read, "PIAJ – Primium's Inferior Arts Jammer."

"Of course," Bob muttered to himself. "There's no way simple gadgets could stop magic and runecraft." He angled his head, pulled the trigger and left a smouldering hole in the planet-dividing device.

The next thing in front of him was a large vat with incredibly complex control panels circling it. Yellow liquid bubbled inside it and kept a horrific sight afloat. Inside was a human, chained to the vat by his limbs. His lifeless, dark-grey eyes were wide open, yet there was no telling whether he was alive or not. A straggly black beard covered his mouth, and shrouding his torso and pelvis was a large, battery-shaped contraption.

"The limited human form, now part of something greater," a robotic voice rasped. Groaning and clunking, the damaged form of Mekanyon heaved his way towards Bob. "Currently, it is just a power source for one. How about we all become something greater? All of us, sharing an infinite power source? With infinite possibilities and endless horizons?"

"How are you here?" spluttered Bob, and the Joule 1.0 dropped from his mouth.

Mekanyon gestured and it exploded. One of the god's arms fell apart at the elbow immediately after. "Would I leave myself unguarded?" retorted Mekanyon. "You traitor to humanity! You destroyed the one way to keep the elves and dwarves out." At an extremely slow rate, an energy cannon began to grow on his shoulder.

"Aren't you the traitor?" replied Bob.

"HOW DARE YOU!" roared Mekanyon. "I AM HELPING LIFE BY UPGRADING IT! THOSE ELVES AND DWARVES CAN'T SEE IT, SO I WILL—"

"So you would try to encourage the killing of two races a deity was sworn to protect?" interrupted Bob.

His turbines whirred, and he soared towards the vat. Mekanyon fired. Bob crashed through the glass. The liquid splattered everywhere, and the man drooped. Spinning like a hurricane, Bob cut the battery-like contraption deftly in half with his turbines' blades. The energy blast hit him in the chest. Turning around, Bob saw the green light behind Mekanyon's visor was flickering more rapidly than ever before.

"I did not think I'd be defeated," the god whispered. "Especially not by a band of fighters containing wizards and rune users. I did not think the final blow would be caused by a boy whom I had to rescue from his parents. All of you have left life in this unideal state and stopped the final evolution... but I congratulate you for your victory."

Bob's vision grew faint.

"We shall go to the next world now, Bob Solis," Mekanyon stated. And then the light behind his visor finally switched off. A lifeless husk – the remains of what was once the god of technology – stood stoically, even in death, in a reality that was falling apart by the second.

It was the last thing Bob saw before his consciousness left him.

Two bodies hit the floor of Valkus.

FIFTY

"Deep down inside, he wanted to help. He thought he was doing good. And you killed him," a voice sounded. "You wished to join the deities' ranks after seeing them maintain the peace. Can you maintain peace or has your stygir friend plagued you with his psychotic nature?"

Bob was submerged in an ocean coloured like gold, yet more brilliant. Somehow, he could breathe, and he could hear a disembodied voice. It had a heavy accent, yet not one he could trace back to any race or region.

I had to, or the entire universe and all realities would be transformed into machines, thought Bob. He tried to speak, yet his mouth wouldn't open. *I wish I could've done something else, but he had already killed most of my friends and allies, and there was no other choice. I know contracting with Morehk was wrong, but I felt I had to at the time, or I wouldn't be of any use in rescuing the deities. But it doesn't matter. He's gone now.*

"So this is your view on morality," the voice mused. "You view yourself as weak; weak without Morehk, that is. What would you do without deity powers, should such a situation arise?"

I would fight the best I could and try to adapt as best as I could. And, after this quest, I believe I've grown stronger, along with everyone else.

"And if you knew that you would never defeat them, no matter what?"

Well, I'm not the only one who was on that quest, was I? There are others who want to protect the system and we can unite our strength against things we can't defeat alone. You seem to have seen the fight against Mekanyon – remember, I would still be stuck on the floor feeling sorry for myself if Antony hadn't been there!

"Bob Solis…" the voice seemed to grow louder gradually. "Though you be but an ordinary boy with an outdated firearm, you have the makings of a hero. One who could protect Atlas for millennia to come. But, remember, only the makings I see, the kindling – ignite the fire yourself."

What are you? Are you saying I could become a deity?

"This is merely a hallucination: a simple vision one gets when one comes into contact with divinite. I am merely part of the reaction that happens between mortal flesh and the metal of immortality. Bob, is technology inherently evil?"

Unable to come up with an answer, Bob struggled mentally for several minutes. Things like his easy life as a civilian and the twisted views of Mekanyon ran rampant in his head.

No, he thought eventually. *Mekanyon saw a bad use for it, but there are also good ones – it did defeat the stygir after all. It's a resource that can be used by anyone, for any purpose. We just need to make sure only good comes from it.*

"Then now comes the end of Bob Solis the mortal boy, giving rise to Bob Solis, the god of technology."

WHAT?

"Would you like to change your name upon godhood?"

N-no, I'm fine with my name. But I have one question: what is Aeterno's power? Something about it tells me it's not just an ordinary deity power.

"By no means is it merely a deity power. It is something more: something that has caused strife in the past and was sealed in the divinite. The one who sealed it ordered me to only give it to the most worthy soul in the system – one who wouldn't overuse and misuse it."

Somebody made *the divinite?*

The voice chuckled. "Look at the other metals, Bob! Iron, copper, zinc and so on – can any of these do anything as great as create immortal beings? It's the same with the vaults. They are the remnants of an— Alas, the reaction is complete. Farewell, Bob."

The golden liquid turned hazy before disappearing as a mist. When it cleared, Bob saw Aeterno and Cognitio looking at him. They were in an underground chamber of some sort, one heavily decorated, and laden with bizarre devices and long scrolls written in a script Bob had never seen before. Despite it being underground, they could see clearly. A flight of stairs in the corner seemed to go on forever, spiralling down into a wide chasm dotted by the flickering lights of many other rooms.

He gazed at one of the decorations, which was an etching into what appeared to be solid gold. Amidst the enigmatic sigils of the same kind the scrolls were written in, a gathering of humanoid figures with three eyes faced off to a swarm of anthropomorphic insects. Bob was surprised to see both species holding guns of some sort. The etching was so intricate that it appeared lifelike and drew Bob in, the desire to know the story it depicted filling him completely. He ran his finger over it, and the sounds of battle filled his ears. With a gasp, he withdrew his hand and fell back, with Aeterno catching him before he could hit the floor.

"Where am I?" Bob asked. "What is this?"

"You are under the surface of planet Submaer," Cognitio told him. "It's a world not many know about and is an ocean planet inhabited by large, single-celled organisms. We are in a hidden chamber, which is one of the vaults you might've heard Belial mention."

"These vaults hold vital information," Aeterno continued. "Magic and metalworking were both derived from a scroll Eldrit and Eitri found here. Their rivalry is said to have started from their different takes on the parchment. Similarly, Mekanyon invented technology after being inspired by the devices found here. It is the secret duty of the deities to delve into these vaults and try to make sense of what we find in them, as well as to keep away anyone who would use the information in here for wrong purposes."

"I can... I can stand!" Bob breathed. Looking down, he saw all his limbs had regenerated, which is an effect that happens when one first has contact with divinite. With a cry of happiness, he moved his right arm, gleeful at the feeling of having an appendage that wasn't generated by Morehk. A small bundle of wires formed randomly in his hand.

"The god of technology!" exclaimed Aeterno. "May you right the wrongs of Mekanyon. Try using your power a bit more."

Straining his mind, Bob thought of a simple gadget – a brick phone – and outstretched his palm. He then slumped to the floor with exhaustion, clutching a half-formed phone battery.

"Don't worry, it's natural," Aeterno told him. "Most deities needed to practise for weeks before they have mastery over their powers."

"Wait…" breathed Bob. "What happened to everyone else? Why am I here? And some divinite spoke to me, even though only the Heavenspire is divinite… How are relations between men, elves and—"

"After you delivered the finishing blow to Mekanyon, we saw you were on the brink of death," Aeterno told him. "Cognitio and I knew something had to be done, so we decided to start the deity ceremony on you quickly. There's a hidden network of phasing ladders linking all the vaults and the Heavenspire, so we made use of those. Don't worry, as long as one mortal knows of your existence and doesn't doubt you, you will not crumble away."

"What about everyone else?" asked Bob.

"Everyone else is busy mourning the dead," Cognitio explained, and a morose expression crossed his face.

Silence filled the vault.

He continued, "Too many have died: Volundur and Aesik, Gary, half the deities we were trying to rescue, half the citizens I sent to rescue them… *Ordinary citizens,* sent to their deaths by my foolish judgement, and all for what?" Tears began to well in his sightless eye sockets, followed suit by Bob's eyes. "And now Industria is destroyed. If the stygir find out, Atlas is gone."

"Indeed, it is tragic," stated Aeterno. "But they died protecting the system – no, the whole universe and all realities. Mourning their heroism wouldn't do them any good. They died so we can be alive and the common folk can enjoy the illusion of peace; let us live on for them and for the hope they've given us. Because they died so hope would not be extinguished."

"I guess you're right," murmured Cognitio. "But let us honour them by joining the funeral procession Antony organised on Primium. After that, I've heard the elves and dwarves want a conference with the deities over technology and the war."

"I have an idea for that!" Bob offered suddenly, drawing the other two's attention immediately. He then told them his plan to facilitate the three powers – technology, magic and runecraft – coexisting in harmony.

"An excellent idea," Cognitio commended him. "I have faith you'll soon become a great god."

"Is everyone else going to be a deity?" Bob asked.

"Belial feels he still has to redeem himself and declined, but the surviving nominees have more than earned their titles," Aeterno told him. "But enough idle talk, there are fallen heroes who need to be honoured and the aftermath of a war that needs addressing."

With these words, the god of space and time, the new god of technology and their noble emissary passed through a phasing ladder to right the remaining wrongs left by Mekanyon.

FIFTY-ONE

Four entire races wept as the sombre procession made its way across Primium.

A vast line of coffins and boxes housing scarce remains were pulled through the streets like a mortuary serpent, drawing the sorrowful eyes of countless crowds.

"The stygir killed many of the deities who were present here about an hour before, including Mekanyon," Cognitio told the citizens. "They played a large role in killing the menace, yet they paid the ultimate price for it. The brave nominees died trying to rescue the system's protectors in a feat deserving of more than godhood."

"THE BRAVE NOMINEES WERE SENT TO THEIR DEATHS BY YOUR STUPIDITY!" a man shouted as he threw a rock at Cognitio.

The emissary deflected it with his staff.

"I hope my daughter's death satisfied your lazy ass!" added the man.

"Hey! He was fighting too—" Antony began.

Cognitio cut him off. "Let them think what they want," he told his troll ally. "It's probably true."

"Ruddy great system's protectors you are!" a dwarf

called out. "The men need to pay reparations for the damage they caused, and you're not doing a single thing! I could do better if I touched that shiny rock!"

An old man with a beard wig pushed his way through the crowd, a look of horror on his face. "Where are you, Gary, my son?" Jonas asked with a look of excitement on his face.

Everyone was silent. The entire procession ground to a halt.

"There's no need for silence; it's me, Jonas! You know me; you sent me to rebuild Primium. How's Gary?"

"He d-d-died fighting the stygir," Antony strained himself to say.

Jonas let out a cry of anguish. "NO! MY SON!" he howled. "Tell me it's not true… after reviving him… after all that effort…" His eyes caught a series of gigantic coffins, one of which had cracked and exposed a chunk of blue metal. Jonas fell to the floor weeping.

Belial walked up to his fellow Longinist and placed a hand on his shoulder. "Gary died a hero. Ask anyone who was there. He fought like a god, and only trickery could make him fall. Yet he lives on, as a hero in the minds of all the Longinists and everyone else for that matter."

"Our family grows smaller, Belial," sniffed Jonas. "I tried to pick the safest jobs for Gary, yet still…"

"I feel your pain," Belial told him. "Let Gary's soul live on for eternity."

"Everyone!" a voice called. Aeterno flew to the front of the procession and gazed around at the melancholy swarm of Heavenspirians. "Honour the souls of these dead, because they died for the system. So we should live on! Revere these graves and engrave the names on them into your minds. They are the names of this decade's greatest heroes. The current pantheon of deities couldn't save them, but maybe these eight can. Step forwards Vakra, goddess of binding!"

A liskous with scales that changed hue across the black and white spectrum walked into view.

"Arise Jeff, god of tenacity!"

After rushing to the scene, the human boy waved to the crowd.

"I herald Amaphex, goddess of dreams!"

An elf with shimmering, black hair drifted into view to join Vakra and Jeff.

"Enter Baldaer, god of warriors!"

A heavily armoured dwarf had thundered into sight, hollering vows of protection to the crowd.

*

"Crap... I'm getting nervous..." mumbled Caesium, his now regenerated legs trembling. "Ummm... guys, why exactly did we decide to portray Mekanyon as a hero?"

"Don't you remember?" sighed Imryth. "We don't want to alarm the public too much. Say, do you know what happened to those under Dodsfald's control? They all deserve burials."

"I designed a rune to retrieve them, using my new powers. They're in the procession along with all the others, being mourned by everyone," explained Caesium.

Everyone looked at him with an agape expression.

"What?" Caesium asked.

"How could you use your deity power like that?" asked Bob. "I can barely create a lightbulb before passing out!"

"Yeah, and my magic is only a tiny bit better than before," added Novis.

"I don't know... but at least it worked," said Caesium.

"Unfortunately, Eitri died, but there is a worthy successor!" they heard Aeterno declare.

"Well, I'm up," Caesium said, and he ran off.

"Are you ready to tell them your plan, Bob?" asked Imryth.

"I don't know..." Bob muttered. "It seemed good in my head, but now..."

"You need to!" Imryth told him, "Or the conflict over technology could last way longer. You're the only one who has thought of something."

"And, for the first time ever, the mistake of having only one magic deity has been reversed!" Aeterno proclaimed. "For there are two types of magic, only one is rarer than the other. I present Imryth, goddess of elemental magic, and Novis, goddess of unconventional magic!"

The two new goddesses left, and Bob was left alone, trying to find the best way to express his ideas. He knew he was up next, and then Aeterno would beckon him to speak. *Maybe I could... No, that wouldn't sound good... or perhaps...* he thought.

"Now for the most controversial god to date!" Aeterno announced. "Yet one who hopes to end this controversy. Bob, god of technology, tell us how to fully end this conflict."

Trembling as he walked to join the new deities, Bob whispered his plan to himself. The crowd facing him was gargantuan, way larger than any group of beings he had ever seen. His parents and Dirk were probably somewhere amongst the swarms of clamouring faces, although he could not make them out. He tried to speak, but for some reason no words came out. His mind was whirring, but his jaws were clamped tightly shut.

"Who's paying who reparations?" asked an elf.

"Who killed our government?" asked a man.

Then suddenly, the reason he became a nominee shone brightly in his mind and broke his mental restraints. The men, elves, dwarves and liskous were in need of help. They were all looking to him. They were all looking to something.

"T-the government was corrupt," Bob stammered. "They were allied with the stygir and used their power to kill Galvok."

"SEE HOW CORRUPT HUMANITY IS!" someone yelled, and a cacophony of voices agreed.

"BUT THEY ARE NOT ALL OF HUMANITY!" Bob hollered. "They were definitely corrupt, but not their race. Why is it that three races that have coexisted for ages have started fighting?"

"TECHNOLOGY!" a large portion of the crowd roared.

"But now that can coexist with magic and runecraft!" Bob told the crowd. "Caesium, activate it! I think it's time they knew."

The new god of runecraft outstretched his palm and created a complex sigil on the floor. It lit up with a pink light, and an image flashed up.

"The rune of reality viewing!" Bob spoke. "If such a complex rune can work, why can't simple spells and markings work? There was a flaw in technology that nullified magic and runecraft, but I have fixed that."

Those roaring in discontent now cheered.

"There are more realities than just ours, and this is one of them. Look at the image!" requested Bob.

Projected by Caesium's rune, the Below-Heavenspire met the gaze of many fascinated citizens.

"This is where we were taught to be deities, but it can serve a different purpose. Let it be the birthing place of new knowledge, where men, dwarves, elves and liskous can combine their ideas for new ways to live and for the good of the system! But that is not all." Bob took a deep breath. "You ask me about reparations. Nobody is paying anyone anything." Not waiting for the crowd's reaction, he continued, "Instead, I shall find some way to link our four worlds together, so we can help rebuild each other's homes."

"Can you tell us anything on the Timeless Link?" an expectant elf asked.

"It's staying as it is," confirmed Bob, "but the meaning will change. Those two arrows can mean anything – the spiritual and the physical, or the past and the future – let each Heavenspirian citizen interpret them in their own ways. That way, it's like everyone's voice is being heard by the barrier protecting them."

These words coming from the mouth of a twelve-year-old boy sent frantic murmurs of surprise and admiration through the crowd. What had he, along with everyone in front of them and in the coffins, been through?

Bob continued, "Also, districts for users of magic, runecraft and slate-scales will be built on Primium, and each planet will have something similar. For we shouldn't be separate and different; we should be different and together, so that our combined differences brush away any weakness. Then we can shift gears to a new, infinitely better world. I call this the New World's Gear."

The crowd cheered their approval, yet not loudly, as there was still a funeral going on.

"The rest of Longinus and I can build these districts," offered Jonas, brushing away a tear.

"Then the system is saved!" announced Cognitio. Then, in a whisper to Bob he added, "For now. Industria is destroyed, and the stygir could attack again. That one who was with you got absorbed by Mekanyon, right?"

Bob nodded.

"You're a god of technology, right? I trust you to repair Industria, our best line of defence," stated Cognitio. "Or at least make a temporary decoy to avoid mass panic."

Bob paled at these words. "I will... don't worry," he replied, brushing away a drop of sweat.

"We were just deciding where these heroes should be buried," Cognitio told the crowd. "Their bodies shall be laid to rest in the Heroes' Endpoint, an honorary site in the alternate reality."

The crowd cheered again, more strongly this time. This was the future of the system; a spark in the darkness of the present, yet one that would soon glow brightly. Everyone cheered – the men, elves, dwarves, and liskous – and the most miniscule wisp of smoke, invisible to the naked eye, headed towards its host.

"Who would've thought you'd turn out this way?" a voice sounded in Bob's head. It was extremely faint and sickly, but it was there.

Everything turned red. The god of technology cried out in surprise, almost passing out from shock.

"*Remember, the stygir always gets the final say in the contract, Bob,*" Morehk whispered. "*I decide the end. Let's enjoy our godhood, god of technology...*"

New World's Gear: Transcendence

Industria, the orbital weapon that kept the Atlas system safe, has been destroyed and with it any hopes of stopping the mysterious stygir, should they plan to attack the system again. Its creator is gone, and not even Bob Solis, the new god of technology, knows how to rebuild it. The answers cannot possibly be found inside the universe, but, using the devices known as phasing ladders that allow the user to travel through alternate realities, maybe they can be found outside it…

Along with friends and enemies from his system, and beings from light years away, Bob embarks on a journey in a reality filled with extraordinary creatures, embarking on a quest set by a being known only as the Starfather. Multiple factions emerge, from lone swindlers to giant organisations with questionable motives. During this journey, the questions that have bewildered the deities and their allies remain unanswered but become more and more prominent:

Why did the stygir attack?

Who made the enigmatic underground vaults?

Who first controlled the fabric of the universe?

But, most importantly, what are they fighting for?

The beings of destruction known as the stygir came from husks, which are devices of unknown origin. Being factions as well as birthplaces, a stygir's husk denotes its power and status. Each husk is led by a kerphan, who is a stygir of utmost power with a unique form known as an avatar. Those who form a contract with one know about this, yet even they do not know everything about the shrouded past of these creatures.

Husk	Power	Key Member(s)	Status*
Thaumir (First)	Ability to control other stygir	Catarehk, ruler of all stygir (honoured light)	Alive
		Kerphan Morehk (honoured destruction)	Alive, but only a few particles remaining
Chaigidir (Second)	Can weaken deity powers to the point of uselessness	Kerphan Ghogiehk (honoured supremacy)	Frozen in time by Aeterno
Satharir (Third)	<Classified>	Kerphan Rofehk (honoured guile)	Frozen in time by Aeterno

Gamichir (Fourth)	<Classified>	Kerphan Storehk (honoured hunger)	Frozen in time by Aeterno
Golachir (Fifth)	Fire so powerful only Hydrax's waters can extinguish it	Kerphan Zamaehk (honoured blaze)	Killed by Hydrax
Thagirir (Sixth)	<Classified>	Kerphan Belphehk (honoured antithesis)	Alive
Harabir (Seventh)	<Classified>	Kerphan Tuvarehk (honoured hunter)	Alive
Maerir (Eighth)	<Classified>	Kerphan Aduramehk (honoured desolation)	Alive
Gamalir (Ninth)	<Classified>	Kerphan Lilehk (honoured corruption)	Frozen in time by Aeterno
Nehemir (Tenth)	Ability to override weak minds and use their powers against them	Kerphan Amehk (honoured spectre)	Frozen in time by Aeterno

* As at the end of *New World's Gear*

Introduction by the Author

So, here it is – my first book! I still remember when I thought up the story and characters in 2015; it all started when I was looking at a figurine of a knight I'd bought on a cycle ride from Poland to Slovakia. I began to reimagine him as something else, maybe a knight of machinery and immortality, and from that starting point came Mekanyon, the stygir, the deities and everything else. Then I thought up the story for the next seven books or so, and – along with someone I'll mention later – I came up with the rest. Two months later, I realised, "Hey, someone has to write this!" (It was just like realising you have to paint the unpainted Warhammer army you have used all your money to buy). And so began *New World's Gear* (*NWG*). I finished it just before the summer of 2018 and spent another two years preparing it for print. And here we are now…

Creating *NWG* has definitely been a worthwhile journey, and I heartily recommend writing your own book. Creating your own universe and story, and letting your imagination flow is such a gold experience. Anyway, it's time for some behind-the-scenes information on the Atlas system!

How the NWG universe came into being

A common start for books is to take something awesome, then shift it so it becomes your version of that awesome thing. There are so many pantheons in mythology with epic deities – Greek, Egyptian, Aztec, etc. – so I decided my book was going to have some myth-style deities in (but ones with no weird family issues or getting incredibly mad at mortals twenty-four-seven). My deities would be a bit different, though; instead of being immortal simply because they are, they would be heroes worthy of having such power. This idea of strength earned through heroism was inspired by the Toa from *Bionicle*. I also thought about how society has evolved over time and how a lot of people envisage a technology-based world in the future. Naturally, this would apply to all societies, including that of a Tolkien-style fantasy.

The divinite and phasing ladders came into being when I was thinking about how large the universe really is and wondering if there are alternate realities. And if all the elements in the universe aren't found in our system, what properties will the others have? There's so much to fuel the imagination; it just requires in-depth dreaming and thinking about every possibility, with brilliant music in the background. Have you heard 'Best Day, Best Way' by LiSA? It's amazing.

Story details

Usually, when a new resource is discovered, there's likely to be a conflict or at least some controversy over it. Since elves are usually caring for nature, and dwarves usually live underground and practise metalworking, they'd see no use for technology and that was where the war idea began; bear in mind that technology will be somewhat more advanced than metalworking and magic so a two-versus-one war would be more apt than a free-for-all. That's not to say that magic and metalworking are weak – all three systems have their different strengths, and I designed it like that on purpose. The liskous are my favourite race, and I designed them because I needed a dragon to go along with my fantasy theme, but why not have dragon people? And why not dragon people who have the strength and skill to break metal with a wooden staff? As you can see in the story, they generally behave like old, wise scholars (with a few exceptions, *ahem*, Nimbus, *ahem*), and are based on the revered, noble dragons of Oriental mythology rather than the dangerous, fire-breathing ones of European mythology.

As for planning the story, funnily enough, I created a character first, then the ending, and then developed a middle and beginning for that ending! Then, I thought of the basis of the rest of this series and the next ones. It was only then that I realised someone had to start writing this, and began the grind on Microsoft Word. Unorthodox, but that's what my mind came up with. It's also worth mentioning that the Ghogiehk arc and stygir contracts came from a series of dreams I had. Everything from Bob getting lost in the void up to Aeterno's nonchalant time-freezing and arm-cutting is just my subconscious put onto paper.

Characters

Mekanyon was the first character I created; his ulterior motives and design sparked the story for me. I began to think of the basics of his character, and the final fight against him was the first scene I thought of. The stygir were next, although it took me a long time to fully think up their name; I knew I wanted something that sounded like 'stygian' to fit with the myths and legends aspect, but I filled up both sides of an A4 sheet refining it!

The human government were caricatures of the negative qualities you wouldn't want in a ruling body, such as greed, warmongery and petty fighting. I know this ended up with them being simple, comical characters, but we already have serious villains such as Catarehk (who'll have more action next book) and Mekanyon to balance it out. Speaking of very simple characters, I realised really early on that Oakley wasn't adding anything to the story, but then I found a way he could. His untimely death serves as a reminder that the quest to rescue the deities was extremely dangerous, and that it took a combination of luck, knowledge and raw power to survive. Other, stronger characters also fall into this category; anyone could die at any moment.

After creating Mekanyon, I began designing the deities and Cognitio; I wanted them to seem like a new and interesting take on the mythical pantheon and have a stern mortal ally. I decided the main character would be called Bob as soon as I thought of designing him. Why Bob? There are two reasons. When I went to PGL in Year Six, the instructors taught us to sing a song about a forgetful goldfish called Bob, which we sang until every adult around us went mad. It became a class joke. The second was because of Lego *Star Wars*. The first Republic Gunship set came with an unnamed Jedi known as 'Jedi Bob'. Practically everyone who heard that the main character would be called Bob before the book was released advised me heavily against it, but he's meant to have an ordinary human name, because he's an ordinary human! Deal with it. Alex also has a human name because he idolises Mekanyon and human technology so much that he didn't like having the liskous name he was born with.

Speaking of Alex, his creation came about as a total accident. I was working at my desk on a storyboard when my elbow knocked over a large pile of unused character concepts. Around three or four landed on top of each other, and I realised that if I combined these ideas, I could have a decent character. But one I seemingly couldn't fit in anywhere! At first, I thought, *OK, I guess I just won't use him,* but then I found the perfect spot for him as a crazed follower of Mekanyon! To get his name I googled 'most popular male names' and clicked on a random year. A technology-obsessed being like him would want a classic human name after all.

I have to say thanks to Antony Lishak for giving me his really good character request; he gave it when Bob had just finished the fight on Primium so there was still time to add Antony the troll in.

Here are my top three characters:

3. Belial: When first I thought of him, I wanted a character who had been wronged in the past and had been led down a dangerous path of vengeance as a result. When I began designing him, I wanted to make him unique, and he quickly became one of my favourite characters. His shattered past gave rise to the angry, murderous knife-thrower he is, and his knife-leg and flayed face make for one of my favourite character designs, albeit a seriously edgy one.

2. Aeterno: The powerful guy with the big speeches. He is many things – a good and reliable leader, and a selfless fighter – but I think he mainly represents determination. It was he who travelled dangerously close to the sun to fulfil his dream and he who was ready to freeze himself in time to defeat Ghogiehk. And then he cut off his own arm! Without even a cry of pain! He's not just the leader of the deities because he was the first one or because he has shiny, golden armour. Of course, this led to him being a bit of a simple character at times, but, in my opinion, a mix of complex characters and simple ones is best.

1. Mekanyon: The character that sparked my story. Hee used to be my favourite character out of everything I'd planned and created, until certain events happened that made me dislike him somewhat. I wanted him to describe his motives in a way that would make him sound justified, and the point when you realise he was behind everything was meant to be the biggest plot twist. But I believe he's a

true and utter villain. People's emotions, imaginations and souls should never be sacrificed for a state of mechanical 'perfection.'

As with most modern works, some of my characters are based on existing characters. Mekanyon's motives were derived from the Stalker Fang's from *Mortal Engines* and Light Yagami's from *Death Note*, Aeterno's manipulation of space and time comes from Dialga and Palkia from *Pokemon*, and the stygir were partially based on the Makuta from *Bionicle* (Makuta are the best fictional species, don't @ me.) When I thought up the past eclipse, I knew I had subconsciously based it on something. I had no idea what it was until my English class began to study *A Christmas Carol* by Charles Dickens!

Changes from the original plans

Sometimes there were parts of the story that I had to change in order to make everything work. Here are all of them.

Named moves

"Seb, you've been watching too much anime again," was the feedback I was first given with this one. Yes, I was. I had been binge watching *One Piece*, and the fight scenes were awesome. One of the things that made them so great was how iconic each attack was. It wasn't just a punch spam, it was Gum-Gum Gatling. It wasn't just a sword slash, it was Onigiri. Adding named moves would spice up a high-action story like *NWG*. Whilst some people disagree with me, I think that, in order to give the special techniques more impact, they need names. There's just something about yelling the name of how you're going to defeat your enemy! Of course, only the most spectacular and powerful moves would need them though, or the signature ones.

Is this taken?

Every character needs a name that suits them. I spent ages jumbling random letters until I found something that sounded cool. However, it turned out when I was naming some of my characters, there were already other franchises using those names I thought were original! Back to the drawing board for me. In this day and age, where there are many fictional universes, it's a good idea to google the name you want and see if anything comes up.

Me being paranoid

I know how stupid this is, but I had two big fears when making *NWG*. Firstly, I was worried about people stealing my concepts. All my storyboards were hidden, and the ones I scrapped were shredded before being put in the bin. When people asked me what my book was about, I only said a tiny part of the story and not just because it would take too long to explain divinite, the Stygir War, the interspecies war, the Below-Heavenspire and so on. Secondly, I was concerned about my work being too similar to a story that had already been released and people thinking I'd copied it. For example, when I saw the movies *Venom* and *Fantastic Beasts and Where to Find Them* (great movies, don't listen to the critics) I couldn't help but think, *Crap! People are going to think the stygir are obscurus/symbiote rip-offs!* and I started to worry. It was pretty stupid looking back at it.

Longinus buff

Yep, I'm using video game terminology, because, at some times, I see it all like a video game: every character needs to be balanced in order to ensure longer and more gripping fights (and so the fights make sense.) Originally, Gary was the leader of Longinus, and it was a primitive society where they crafted their weapons out of the flint found all over Atham.

As you can understand, it would have been stupid to have them kill off a bunch of people armed with the latest weapons and then fight a group containing deities, some of whom could suck the air from their lungs and freeze them in time. It would be even more foolish to have deities be captured by them somehow! Ghogiehk could already negate deity powers with the power of husk Chaigidir, but these guys needed some way of countering immortals too. That's where longinite came from.

I then came up with the Ruling Trinity, Tabris and Lance, which was one of my top design moments. But they could still be frozen in time by the ridiculously overpowered (for a reason I might explain later) Aeterno. Come to think of it, so could all the villains! So I had Mekanyon manufacture unraveller gas. Finally, balance has been restored!

Human government

One of the problems I had to deal with was that if the system was racked with war, there would be more traces of it than just a few soldiers dotted here and there calling the nominees traitors. So, I decided to add an arc all about the human government, which was arguably the most corrupt of the factions. It would explore the problem of having the corrupt, the warmongering and the idiotic in charge.

Manco arc

As you can probably see from his superiority complex, cultism and tendency to sacrifice people to the Sun (and being overpowered), originally, Capac was meant to be the main villain of the tournament arc on planet Manco, but then Alex was created, and I altered my plans to involve Alex more – he was Mekanyon's main ally, after all! That started off the whole Moon Cult, Lunar Phases and the like.

What can I expect in upcoming books and series?

I like to plan ahead, so expect an expanded literary universe called Universal Scale. However, I'm not doing this alone. In parallel to the *NWG* series, I'm writing a series called the *Three Worlds Saga* with the legendary Ben Miles (the guy I said I'd mention). Currently, he's busy expanding the universe, adding to the lore and patching up plot holes carelessly left by me. Don't think I'm doing most of the work just because I created *NWG* and the next six myself. If anything, it's the other way around; we're like the Elric brothers, Johnny and Gyro, or Gon and Killua!

ACKNOWLEDGEMENTS

Thank you, Antony Lishak, for asking me to put a troll called Antony into my book (this was at the Polish Embassy in 2016, where I gave a speech on Harambe the gorilla, back when the meme was alive. If I remember correctly, I did another speech there on authors, dreams and *Fullmetal Alchemist*). I really enjoyed reading your book *Stars* and going to the embassy!

Thank you, Numair Tejani, for designing the symbol that became the Timeless Link. For free as well – you are a true hero of the Heavenspire!

Thank you, Dad, for your help with making the 3D timeless link for the front cover and getting *NWG* ship-shape.

And thank you to my team of loyal warriors at Matador: Fern Bushnell, Philippa Iliffe, Lauren Bailey and my amazing copy editor, for your help in making my dream become a reality.

Seb D Law is a seventeen year-old multifandom guy whose favourite works of fiction are *Bionicle* (the original 2001–2010 one) and *JoJo's Bizarre Adventure*. In addition to being a massive nerd, he loves listening to music; his favourite singer is LiSA and his favourite genres are J-Pop/J-Rock, Rock, Metal, Hardbass and Eurobeat. He started writing *New World's Gear* when he was twelve and finished it when he was fifteen. At the time of writing, he goes to Sutton Grammar School and lives in Wimbledon. His dreams are to become a great author, move to Japan and normalise non-oriental people being anime fans.

Follow him on Instagram @electrum._.sah and use the hashtags #newworldsgear and #universalscale for book-related posts!